Praise For

Extra Innings

"He's baaack! Ninety years after his death Teddy Ballgame
retakes center stage, swinging a bat for the Red Sox, flying
jets for the Marines and swearing up a blue streak. If you
like baseball, science fiction, or a good thriller, *Extra Innings*
is the book for you. It is Shoeless Joe Hardy meets Isaac
Asimov. No need to wait to see if the science of cryonics will
bring Ted Williams back to life. Bruce Spitzer already has."

——**Dick Flavin,** *Poet Laureate of the Boston Red Sox, featured with
Ted Williams in David Halberstam's best-selling book THE TEAMMATES*

"Over the years, many people have wondered just how much
greater Ted Williams would have been if he were not called
away to war, or if he had played in another era. Now, thanks to
Bruce Spitzer, we know."

——**Jim Lonborg,** *Cy Young Award-winning Red Sox
pitcher and member of the 1967 "Dream Team"*

"I knew Ted Williams, Ted Williams was a friend of mine—
this is Ted Williams."

—— **Bob Lobel,** *Boston sportscaster who once interviewed Ted Williams,
Larry Bird, and Bobby Orr together in the same studio*

"Bruce Spitzer has reverse-engineered the brain of Ted Williams, reanimated a great American, and created a novel with memories intact.

— *Ray Kurzweil,* *inventor / author / futurist*

"Ooh-rah! for *Extra Innings,* and boy what a ride. Ted Williams needed no more heroics to add to his service record flying in WWII and Korea, but Bruce Spitzer gives him a stunning new mission in *Extra Innings.* The novel and the author deserve a special salute for highlighting the leadership of the real man for a new generation, and brilliantly imagining his return to contribute once more to the proud tradition of the United States Marine Corps. Semper Fidelis, 'Caveman.' "

— *Col. Andrew J. Ley* *USMCR (ret.), F-4 and A-4 driver,* *and former CO of VMA 322*

Extra Innings

Extra Innings

He was the greatest hitter of all time. Cryonics brought him back to life in 2092. Would he use this second chance to win his first World Series or to become a better man?

Bruce E. Spitzer

Bear Hill Media

Published by Bear Hill Media

Copyright © 2012 Bruce E. Spitzer

Library of Congress Control Number: 2012900761
Extra Innings / Bruce E. Spitzer

ISBN: 978-0-9849569-0-6

Printed in the United States of America

Book cover design: Lisa Gambino/Patrick Feger. Photography: Glenn Bacci
Book layout: Cheryl Perez

For more information visit:
www.ExtraInningsTheNovel.com

For Pam and Grayson

Acknowledgments

This book is a work of fiction. However, its foundation is the very real fact that the remains of Ted Williams, one of the greatest ever to play the game of baseball, were cryonically preserved when he died in the year 2002. The 20th century life of Williams, from which I drew facts and information, was complicated, colossal and compelling. Imagining a second life in the distant future in this novel, I endeavored to be as accurate as possible with all references to his storied life and actual career.

I wish to thank numerous organizations, authors and individuals for their invaluable assistance and inspiration. The list includes the wonderful people of the Boston Athenaeum; the New England Sports Museum; the National Baseball Hall of Fame and Museum (who put up with my traipsing in on the morning after induction weekend); the MIT Media Lab and its Personal Robots Group; and the Smithsonian National Air and Space Museum, Steven F. Udvar-Hazy Center.

The authors who provided terrific background material included Leigh Montville *(Ted Williams: The Biography of an American Hero)*; Bill Nowlin *(Ted Williams at War)*; the late David Halberstam *(The Teammates)*; John Underwood *(It's Only Me: The Ted Williams We Hardly Knew)*; and, of course, Ted Williams the author *(The Science of Hitting* and *My Turn at Bat—The Story of My Life)*, both with John Underwood. The futurist writings of Ray Kurzweil and Robert Freitas Jr. were also enormously helpful.

In addition, I utilized many audio and video resources too numerous to mention. They were all instrumental in trying to find the voice and, particularly, the cadence of Williams' speech—colorful speech it was—while taking the requisite creative license.

Any errors, omissions or misinterpretations from my research and presentation in the novel are wholly my own.

The individuals earning many thanks for their guidance, advice, referrals, publicity, proofreading, marketing, creative work, counsel, support and all manner of encouragement include Skye Wentworth; Nan Fornal; Cheryl Rinzler; Joe Spitzer; Lt. Col. Bern Bradstreet, USMC (ret.); Major Josh Bradstreet, USMC; Bernie Willet; Dr. Neal Mackertich; Brian and Robin Furze; Bev Tilden; Jeanie Flynn; Geri Denterlein; Terence Burke; Che' Knight; Phil Gloudemans; Dick Flavin; Connie Hubbell; Jim Hirsch; Ray and Karel Simms; Carole and Dick Demaret; Stephen Dewey; Patrick Feger; Glenn Bacci; Cheryl Perez; Rick Rendon; Doug Wicks; Rich Eames; Diane McDermott; Jeffrey Cleven; Joel Shames; Bob Lobel; Suzanne McCarthy, Psy.D; David Ratner; Sally Funk; Gerry Pikl; Peter and Pierce Ridgley; Kelly Nowlin; Saralee Perel; Lisa Gambino; Capt. Lynne Burchell Heyer; Capt. Jeffrey Heyer; Holly DiMauro; and my eternal friend Frank DiMauro, whose encouragement knows no bounds.

I cannot provide enough thanks to my editor, Alan Rinzler, whose insight and thoughtful contributions were helpful beyond measure.

Of course, my special loved ones, to whom this book is dedicated, as always, deserve my deepest thanks for their support. Heaven hath no joy like family.

Finally, Ted himself is worthy of everlasting thanks for captivating so many of us in life and even death. Wherever your spirit is Ted, rest in peace. And if you do return one day, well, I hope you like the novel.

"By the time you know what to do you're too old to do it."

—Ted Williams

"It ain't over 'til it's over."

—Yogi Berra

One

(The Year 2092)

The headless body was wrapped in a sheath of translucent material, cooled in its refrigerated cocoon, and attached to numerous life-support systems. Skillfully cutting through the silken sheath at its apogee, Dr. Miles was splattered with blood. The cocoon instantly shrunk tight again, exposing only the neck. There was no more bleeding.

"The stricture and vacuum seal are working," she said.

The head-to-body transplant process had begun in earnest.

There were more than 30 people in the operating room in the nondescript gun-steel building toward the center of a six-acre Arizona industrial park. The room was an organized maelstrom of activity with a steady drumbeat of human voices and at least a dozen machines droning away, an equal number at the ready.

Doctors, computer technicians, biomedical device consultants, and experts in molecular nanotechnology, tissue regeneration, neuropreservation, vitrification and cryobiology applied their specialties. Nurses and orderlies moved quickly in and out. Everyone wore a surgical mask and scrubs with the

CryoCorp logo emblazoned on their chests, an icicle crowned by a pair of wings with a droplet of water falling off below. That antiseptic hospital smell was in the air. So, too, the malodorous result of defrosting human flesh.

"Let's reduce tension on the stitching to come," said Dr. Miles, and with a scalpel and a surgical saw she shortened the neck on the body to the appropriate length.

Dr. Miles glanced to her left at the now fully defrosted, disembodied head of Ted Williams sitting on its own smaller table. Three hours before, rivulets of rancid cryopreservation fluid had stopped oozing into the catch basin beneath the table that supported the head.

Thirty-eight years old, tall and brunette, strikingly attractive, commanding with her British accent, Dr. Elizabeth Miles was in charge. This was her destiny. Many cryonicists had come before her, but none had the tools or the technology to be ready as she was now. She would be the first person in the world to reanimate a human, a neuro-transplant process that involved placing the once-frozen head of Ted Williams onto the body of a donor. Conquering old age and achieving immortality was her mission.

A colleague leaned over and said softly into her ear, "They didn't teach you this at Stanford and Harvard Medical School; are you sure you're ready?"

"Why shouldn't I be ready?" she snapped. "This is not Nazi doctor Josef Mengele experimenting on unwilling patients 150 years ago. This is a patient who will be thrilled to be reanimated."

Dr. Miles called for the head of Ted Williams to be brought to the operating table. Its own cocoon of permeable-silken material was removed with careful attention to not jostle the brain. She glanced at the face and thought to herself, *he's going to need some work*. She began the transplant by counting vertebrae to be sure she had the right number and would make the right connection in the spine.

"Let's see . . . we've got the Atlas vertebra, the Axis . . . good, C1 to C7 . . . the proper number in the cervical column."

She began the delicate work of fusing the spinal cord, which required transplanting-in and grafting cord that was delivered by a company that grew it in weightless outer space.

In the microsurgical phase, Dr. Miles and a colleague identified matching veins, vessels, arteries, nerves and muscles on both necks and connected them with sutures and a laser.

Peering through an operating microscope she said, "More power to the laser, please."

Dr. Miles pulled away and squinted.

She hoped no one could see her knees knocking underneath the operating table.

"For God's sake, who wouldn't want to be reborn?" she said out loud, appearing calmer now, albeit engaged in a conversation in which she expected no answer.

For God's sake? Was it, literally or figuratively? she thought. She had for many years contemplated such bioethical questions related to cryonics. In her predominant view, and in the minds of many, it was God who gave man the ability to harness science and be implausibly creative in its application. Still, overarching questions raced through her mind. *Is this for everyone? What about quality of life? What will function, what won't? Will there be a propensity toward loneliness when loved ones and friends were part of another life, a life long ago?*

~ ~ ~

Dr. Miles looked at the clock on the wall of the operating room. She had been on her feet for 19 hours, with only a brief respite when her assistant surgeons and technicians were at work alone. She was concerned about the length of time since reverse-cryopreservation had begun on the head 36 hours before.

Working feverishly, she made the last pass with the laser on the outer skin of the neck. The head was now fully attached to the body. The sheath was removed. Fresh blood with synthetic anti-rejection properties was transfused into the new unit.

Dr. Miles scanned the naked body from head to toe and looked up. Appearing much like the headmistress taking the measure of her pupils before A-Level exams, she looked around the room. Peering into her colleagues' faces, she couldn't help but notice their heavy breathing, drenching perspiration and strained, furrowed brows above their surgical masks.

She said simply, "Right then, let's go."

A breathing tube connected to a ventilator was inserted into the mouth and passed through into the trachea.

"Let's do the checklist," she said. "Cardio?"

"Check," came the reply.

"Neuro?"

"Check."

"Vascular?"

"Check"

"Gastro?"

"Check."

And on it went. The team of surgeons and technicians each indicated that the many life-generation and monitoring systems attached by every conceivable tube and wire to the prostrate body before them were functioning properly.

"Good," said Dr. Miles. "Turn the ventilator on and give me mild stimulation to the heart."

The room fell silent.

Then, as if somewhere off in the distance . . . a faint ping.

And then another. And another. The heart monitor was recording heartbeats.

The staff looked at one another.

"We have cardio. What about the other functions?" said Dr. Miles.

One by one the doctors reported in. Each of the bodily functions was springing to life. Medication was administered intravenously to control blood pressure. As an extra precaution a pacemaker was turned on. Over the next half-hour all life-support systems other than pulmonary ventilation were removed.

Ted Williams was alive.

Removing her surgical mask, Dr. Miles said softly, "My God, we did it."

She kept her greatest fear to herself.

Two

At the conclusion of his first life, Theodore Samuel Williams died on July 5, 2002 at 83 years old. The headline writers and journalists had a field day and recalled his many famous nicknames with affection and respect. He had been known as The Kid. The Splendid Splinter. Teddy Ballgame. The Thumper. Funeral arrangements were not immediately announced. Not surprising, perhaps, when a celebrity passes. After the initial tributes and obits, a couple of days went by, and still no one had heard a word about funeral plans or his final destination.

Then the story broke: Ted Williams, the beloved favorite of every Boston Red Sox fan—hell, of anyone who loved baseball—had not been buried or laid to rest in the traditional manner. No. The breaking news was that he had been frozen. *Ted Williams was dead and frozen.* Ted the Frozen Phenom?

Many media, fans and friends of Williams were outraged when they learned that his son, John Henry Williams, had his father's remains shipped from Florida to Arizona, arriving at a cryonic preservation lab. His head and body were separated, suspended in liquid nitrogen in two separate containers, and cooled to minus 320 degrees. The hope was that one day in the distant future, when medical technology would allow it, he would be reanimated.

"A personal family decision," John Henry's lawyer and spokesman called it.

Later, in 2009, it was reported that the body and head may have been separated in error, and the head abused or damaged in the process.

Soon after the death, a family squabble over the remains ensued but John Henry prevailed in court. *Sports Illustrated* writer Tom Verducci reported that John Henry, who had tried to take advantage of his father's celebrity most of his adult life, hoped to sell his father's DNA someday to raise money.

The disconnected head of Ted Williams and his body remained in cryrosuspension until Dr. Miles intervened decades later in the year 2092.

~ ~ ~

At the time of the freezing the embryonic science of cryonics was viewed simply as *weird* science. It was steeped in mystery and possessed an aura of chicanery. The practitioners rarely gave interviews. At best cryonics was the last desperate attempt at immortality for very rich people.

In fact, very few people had even heard of cryonics, aside from a few who had listened to a rumor that Walt Disney was also frozen somewhere in the hope that one day science would be able to thaw him out and bring him back to life with as-yet-nonexistent restorative medicine and specialized tissue-regeneration techniques. Walt Disney may have desired reanimation (no pun intended), but he was no Ted Williams. Ted Williams was no Mickey Mouse. The furor over Williams went on.

~ ~ ~

Ted Williams was born in San Diego on August 30,1918. He was named after his father, Samuel Stuart Williams and Teddy Roosevelt, whom his father greatly admired. Samuel Williams was from New York and became a soldier, sheriff and photographer.

Ted Williams' mother May Venzor was a Salvation Army worker from El Paso, whose family was from Mexico but originally of Basque origin and rumored to be related to the Habsburg family of Europe.

"If I had had my mother's name, there is no doubt I would have run into problems in those days, [considering] the prejudices people had in Southern California," Williams once said.

Ted Williams was a tall, skinny kid, all arms and legs, even when he went to the major leagues at the age of 20. His primary goal in life was to become the greatest hitter who ever lived. Many said he was just that. He played 19 seasons for the Boston Red Sox, with nearly five full years off in the prime of his baseball career for service as a pilot during World War II and the Korean War. He was enshrined in the Baseball Hall of Fame on the first ballot.

He was a dichotomous man: magnanimous and moody, profound and profane. He could curse a blue streak and did so with regularity. The left fielder could dissect the hitting game like no other player. His eyesight was so good he claimed to be able to see the seams of a baseball as it neared his bat at over 90 miles per hour. His complete-season .406 batting average was held in awe.

Williams was considered by many to be the best pure hitter who ever played the game. A notorious pull hitter, many teams allayed a massive defensive on-field shift against the big lefty hitter. For most of his career he eschewed conventional wisdom and rarely tried to hit to the opposite field. He did once in a high profile way, during the 1946 World Series, and played poorly. He was also secretly injured. His Red Sox lost in the seventh game.

He went to the All-Star game 18 times. All of his 19 seasons in the middle of the 20th century were played with the Red Sox.

Williams could talk about hitting and give batting advice for hours on end. He was well known for delivering long lectures in a loud, booming voice about what he insisted was the "science of hitting." He said too many batters swung at bad pitches. His secret to success was to swing only at good ones.

Sometimes he let those go, too, waiting for the pitches that were best for him. His mantra: "Find a good pitch to hit." He was criticized for taking so many balls and quite a few strikes, giving up chances for runs batted in, or so the theory went.

The only thing in his life that inspired as much passion for Williams as hitting a baseball was fly-fishing. He worked as hard to perfect those skills as he did his ability to hit a baseball, and would lecture his friends intensely on the subject.

After being booed early in his baseball career, he appeared to be aloof and self centered, frustrating fans and, especially, the media, whom he mostly distained or ignored. He often appeared angry, especially at the press. They were relentless in alternately attacking him and idolizing him. Occasionally, after hitting a home run, he would spit in their direction.

Once, anger caused him to throw his bat and accidentally hit an old woman in the stands. Luckily, she was not injured but the memory of that awful incident haunted him for the rest of his life. He was also widely criticized by the press for being on a fishing trip when one of his children was born, even though he claimed the child was born prematurely. Even after hitting a home run on the last at-bat of his career, he refused to tip his cap to the adoring, cheering fans.

Always inquisitive, he would ask questions about any subject that interested him, study it, and become an expert. Never, in his mind, did he lose an argument.

After some initial hesitation, for which he caught flak, he entered the service in May of 1942 when the American war machine was still gearing up for World War II. Barely a high school graduate, he thrived in flight school and became a highly accomplished Marine pilot and instructor. In May of 1952 he was called back to active duty and into the Marines during the Korean War when the U.S. was in desperate need of pilots. He learned to fly jets and, this time, engaged in combat and was nearly killed.

Since he retired from baseball, astounding as his records were, fans and baseball analysts have wondered what his records might have been without those five missing years. Like the others in his generation who fought in either war, he regarded it simply as his duty. He didn't dwell on the lost time. He was proud of his military service, even though it came with great monetary and career sacrifice. Meaning no disrespect to the Red Sox, Williams often said the Marines were the greatest team he ever played on. Critics and commentators were surprised when he said this and never understood what it was in Ted Williams that appreciated and understood the discipline and chain of command in the Marines, but dismissed most other authority—especially people he called "the suits."

Despite all of his individual baseball achievements, the Red Sox never won a World Series while Williams wore their uniform.

In retirement he was elected to multiple fishing halls of fame and was a big game hunter. San Diego named a freeway after him, and Boston dedicated a massive highway tunnel under the harbor in his name. He mellowed somewhat and let people into his personal life just a bit. Gradually, baseball fans everywhere, even those who never saw him play, came to admire and revere the complicated legend that was the late Ted Williams.

Three

Six weeks after the reverse-cryopreservation Ted was still in a medically induced coma. For a man who had made history in his first life and now in a second, there was very little fanfare. As he lay still, machines and monitors tracked his every biologic function; a team of doctors and nurses monitored his progress and vital signs by the minute and the hour.

Dr. Miles had induced the coma to allow billions of nanotech devices to work inside the head and neck repairing tissue, particularly in the brain. Brain cell repair was necessary due to damage caused by the freezing and formation of ice crystals in the initial vitrification-preservation process that took place in 2002. Growth of nerve fibers was critical for survival and—dare she think it?—for cognitive abilities, memory, and quality of life.

There was also the matter of repairing a skull fracture, an injury that was partly due to freezing but also, she surmised, due to a rather disconcerting blunt force trauma. It seemed to be coming along nicely. A plastic surgeon, using old photos as a reference point, completed the first—if all went well—of many operations on the face of Ted.

The electrodes placed around the head, combined with an intracranial pressure monitor, provided a constant stream of data that was analyzed by computer and reported to Dr. Miles. As yet, all-important brainwaves were not detected. Otherwise, the head was working well with the body with no rejection complications, thanks in part to computer-designed artificial blood and a hyper-antibody-producing pump, a permanent fixture in the gut designed to destroy microbiological pathogens in the bloodstream utilizing specific mechanical phagocytosing nanobots in a digest-and-discharge protocol. Nutrients were introduced directly into the bloodstream by metabolic nanobots. A specialized belt worn around the abdomen transmitted the nanobots through the skin, nourishing the body, monitoring and adjusting caloric intake and nutrients.

~ ~ ~

Four more weeks went by and the CryoCorp medical crew had thinned. Dr. Miles checked frequently the computer monitoring all vital functions and inspected an electroencephalograph, but there were still no signs of brainwaves. Encouragingly, neurological scans confirmed that significant numbers of synaptic vesicles existed in the brain. It was enough, thought Dr. Miles, to stop the medically induced coma and see what happened. The work of the nanobots would continue regardless, even if the patient did not respond immediately.

The next morning the medical staff stood silently around the bed.

"Let's see what results," said Dr. Miles as she halted the anesthesia and removed the IV herself. Hours passed. And then . . . nothing.

Ted was still in a coma. Worse, there were no brainwaves.

~ ~ ~

After another six weeks, uncharacteristically, Dr. Miles had stopped bothering to put makeup on and barely combed her hair. Her once-beautiful eyes were glassy, her pupils dilated. At night, failing to sleep, she walked the widow's walk of her bedroom, staring off into a nonexistent sea, waiting for a ship she knew full well might never arrive.

At CryoCorp twice a day Dr. Miles came into Ted's room and checked the charts and medical monitoring devices, one of which was a handheld scanner that she moved over his body; it reported heart rate, blood pressure and other metabolic measurements. With a stethoscope she listened to his heart and then lifted his eyelids.

One of the nurses, Emily Shonefeld, walked into Ted's room. She was a middle-aged woman whose looks belied her age, as did her hairstyle. She wore her long, bright-red hair in a ponytail. Combined with her much-younger facial features, which included a small nose and freckles, she looked about 30 years old. The hair contrasted well with the snow-white hue of her nurse's uniform. Emily and Dr. Miles had known each other for years, and through this ordeal they had grown even closer.

"Oh, why should I be surprised?" said Dr. Miles. "We never had a guarantee this would work. We attempted to achieve something never before accomplished in the history of mankind. Why was I so confident that we were ready? And you know, Emily, I fear he never asked to be cryopreserved."

"Well, there's only one way you're going to find out. Don't give up hope yet," said Emily. "His vitals are still good. Even his face has some color to it. Although he looks a little hangdog."

She didn't say it, but Dr. Miles thought, *Even after plastic surgery, any face would look a little tired if it were frozen for the last 90 years.*

"Why don't you try talking to him?" said Emily.

"I have tried but, honestly, what am I supposed to say? 'Mr. Williams, please wake up. I don't mean to frighten you, but you've been reborn. Sorry if you didn't know anything about this. But you're alive again, so let's make the best of it ol' boy.' . . . I'd be afraid to open my eyes, too, if I were he."

At the door, Jed and Randall, two CryoCorp med techs in their mid-20s dressed in white jumpsuits overheard the conversation.

"You'd better be careful," said Randall. "He might wake up and if you're the first thing he sees, he'll imprint on you. You know, like baby geese. He'll be following you around the room everywhere you go."

"All right, that's enough out of you two," said Dr. Miles, waving her hand dismissively and suppressing a smile. "Make like geese and fly out of here."

Four

Another month passed and still no conscious response from Ted. *There is so much we've accomplished in medicine and science, but the depths of coma are still a mystery to us,* thought Dr. Miles. *The reality is I don't even know if we can call this a coma.*

Despite all of the difficulties, she didn't give up hope. She talked to Ted more every day. She taught herself to read box scores and follow the 2092 Boston Red Sox on her iMaster, a device that nearly every modern human wore on the lapel, shirt collar or hanging from the neck. In addition to projecting data, it was a personal digital assistant with its core function being e-memory, the recording of each person's daily interactions on video, in audio and in transcript to produce total recall. Each night the device was placed in a bedside cradle where it downloaded all of the day's information into a MyBox data storage appliance.

Before she left the campus of CryoCorp, six days a week Dr. Miles, and often her son, Johnnie, would read to Ted and go over scores, averages and the PanAmerican League pennant race with him. The Red Sox, once again, were trailing both the Yankees and the London Seafarers by 6½ games.

Widowed two years earlier, Dr. Miles thought it was important to spend as much time as possible with little, blond-haired Johnnie, and the only way she knew how was to integrate him into her time-consuming work life.

Besides, Johnnie had an infectious smile that spread a consistent note of happiness among the beleaguered medical professionals. His mother thought the staff could use the pleasant diversion. She was grateful to senior management for allowing Johnnie to be let in on the secret. She also knew they needed her exclusive expertise if they had any chance of succeeding in the reanimation—and ensuring the long-term success of the business.

She brought in sports history books, and they read to Ted the entire story of the Red Sox franchise. As if he could comprehend, she said how it was a shame he didn't live to see the victory in 2004 after a gap of 86 years, ending the Curse of the Bambino. There was another championship in 2007 followed by two more.

"Maybe if you wake up, Ted, you might be able to see the next one," she said.

And what a momentous occasion that would be. First a championship drought of 86 years that ended in '04. Then another, this one going on now for 60 years, and it too was called a curse—the Curse of the Samurai.

Dr. Miles was not a big baseball fan, but even she knew that the latest drought was called the Curse of the Samurai because a prior owner of the Red Sox, Christopher Galvano, had sold Sam "Samurai" Naguchi to the Yankees, just like Babe Ruth years before, to raise some quick, much-needed cash for his personal debts. Galvano, a former sportswriter turned eNovel hack, had purchased the Red Sox from the owners of his former eNewspaper. When his sports romance novels no longer sold so well and he wanted money for a stake in an offshore Internet gambling site, he traded away the team's young Japanese phenom Naguchi. Over the next 15 years for the Yankees, Naguchi proceeded to set the single season (five times) and all-time home run records, and led his new team to 13 world championships.

Yes, history repeated itself, or as Yogi Berra would've said, it was déjà vu all over again.

It was the fervent hope of Dr. Miles and Johnnie that reading some of the history to Ted might strike a chord. Nothing worked.

If there were any silver lining to be had from the situation Dr. Miles and the officers of CryoCorp considered themselves lucky that the media had not picked up on their attempt to be the first to reanimate a human being through cryonics. When she read or heard the news, she always feared a breaking story or rumor about Ted.

The gag order on the staff, Johnnie and even his nanny, seemed to be working. The nanny, Cecelia Gomez, brought Johnnie after school each day to CryoCorp. She was a small, 62-year-old unmarried woman of Mexican descent with a wrinkled, warm face and big expressive eyes. She had been with Dr. Miles almost from the day Johnnie was born. She and Johnnie had become particularly close since his father's death.

Each day she would ask Dr. Miles about Ted.

"Anything yet?"

"No, not yet," said Dr. Miles.

In the evenings Dr. Miles used her iMaster to project the latest *Sporting News* on the wall and she or Johnnie would read it to Ted. Finishing the baseball section for the umpteenth time, Dr. Miles and Johnnie bid goodnight and with an upbeat voice she said, "Better wake up, Ted. You don't know what you're missing."

Five

On a rare rainy day, a Saturday, Dr. Miles came in to see Ted at midday so that she could attend Johnnie's indoor Little League baseball game later in the afternoon. If it rained at all in the Arizona desert, it never lasted long this time of the year.

As usual, Ted lay motionless in his hospital-like room deep within the maze of production facilities, laboratories and containment rooms that comprised CryoCorp.

"How is he today?" Dr. Miles asked Emily.

"Oh, about the same," said Emily. "Although I did notice his blood pressure was a bit elevated."

"Hmmm," said Dr. Miles as she looked at the chart.

She raised Ted's eyelids to check his oculocephalic reflex and assess the integrity of his brain stem. Moving his head from left to right and monitoring his corneas, she witnessed the eyes moving in the direction opposite of the turning head. His pupils also reacted to light.

She wheeled around and looked at the electroencephalograph.

"Emily, did you see the monitor? He has activity!"

Through the many electrodes placed around the head the computer was recording activity at the synapses, small gaps between the ends of nerve fibers across which nerve impulses pass from one neuron to another.

Neurotransmitters were bridging the gaps in the brain and triggering more and more electrical impulses.

Ted had brainwaves.

"Let's try removing the ventilator," said Dr. Miles.

"Do you think it's too soon?" said Emily.

"Well, we can always put it back in."

Deftly, Dr. Miles removed the tube from Ted's mouth.

"He's breathing on his own!" said Emily.

A security guard appeared at the door and ushered Johnnie in wearing a Yankees uniform.

"Hi, Mom," he said.

Distracted, Dr. Miles at first didn't react.

"Johnnie? What are you doing here so early? Where's your nanny?" she said.

"Mom, I don't like it when you tell people I have a nanny. Cecelia doesn't like to be called that either. She said it would be all right to drop me off a half-hour early. I think she had to go shopping or somethin'."

Dr. Miles thanked the security guard and gave a warm smile to Johnnie.

"I need some more time, Johnnie," she said.

Trying to help, Emily said "Are you ready for the big game, Johnnie?"

"It's just another game," said Johnnie. "Besides, we don't win very much. I don't even know if I help the team at all."

Still distracted but forcing herself to focus on her young son, Dr. Miles said, "Of course you do honey. And you like baseball. Winning isn't the only reason you play. Remember? Have you been practicing the batting posture your coach showed you?"

"Hell, it's not a batting posture, it's a batting *stance*," came a deep voice from somewhere in the middle of the room.

Dr. Miles swung around and gasped. Ted Williams cocked his head, blinked, and stared her in the eyes.

"If you're gonna give the kid advice, make sure you know what you're talkin' about," he said.

"Ah . . ," was all Dr. Miles could manage.

She swallowed hard and, trying not to get overly excited, sat on the edge of the bed, and looked down at Ted.

"Good day, Mr. Williams, my name is Dr. Elizabeth Miles. Do you mind if I take a look at you?" she said slowly.

"Not at all, Lizzy. I'm Ted. But I guess you know that. Where am I?"

She began running a bio-scanner across his body.

He was conscious of strange sensations, including feeling the blood gushing through his body. He thought he detected the sound of pumping. The light coming through the window was annoying.

"So you know your name is Ted?" she said.

"'Course I do. And yours is Lizzy. We covered this already."

Smiling nervously now, she looked at her readings and said, "You are in a place called CryoCorp, in Arizona."

"Arizona? Never did much care for the place. Not much good fishing, 'cept along the Colorado and a little up north."

"So you remember fishing?" she said.

"Yes," said Ted with an agitated look on his face and his voice rising. "Say, what's this all about?"

"Well, your vocal cords are good," said Dr. Miles.

Word spread down the hall about the awakening and the limited number of medical personnel on duty, a couple of nurses and the two med techs, Jed and Randall, came running and dashed in the door.

"What am I doing here?" Ted demanded.

Taking a deep breath, Dr. Miles summoned up her most calm and self-assured bedside voice.

"Well, are you sitting down? . . . I mean . . . I know you're lying down. Well, anyway, I will just give it to you straight: Ted, have you ever heard of cryonics?"

"You mean that thing where they freeze people?" said Ted.

"Yes, that's basically it—when they are deceased, so that they might be brought back to life one day. Well, Ted, you have been brought back to life. The year is 2092."

"C'mon," said Ted, shaking his head. "This is another one of John Henry's practical jokes."

Immediately she realized he could not have asked to be cryonically preserved—her great fear.

"I'm afraid not," said Dr. Miles. "You've been dead since 2002—90 years ago—and we've brought you back to life through the science of cryonics. How do you feel?"

"Like a dumbass," said Ted. "Prove it to me."

Dr. Miles pulled out her driver's license and company ID badge, both indicating that she was born in 2054. For good measure, she reached across the bed, grabbed the iMaster and projected the Arizona Republic ePaper on the wall.

"See the date?" she said.

"Yeah, but—"

"Okay pick a newspaper, any newspaper," she said.

Ted threw out the names of all of the old newspapers in his memory, and city by city she projected the surviving papers on the wall in their modern e-incarnations, each with the day's date and some of the strangest headlines Ted had ever seen. She specifically avoided the sports pages.

"Well, whatever that device is, how am I to believe it? You got a TV in here?" said Ted.

"We have a compuTV on the wall," said Dr. Miles.

"A what?"

"Well, the computer and the television have merged. They are also in the mini-device we were just using to project images, but we have a large compuTV there on the wall. Just say 'compuTV—on,' out loud, and it goes on instantly," said Dr. Miles.

"You say it," said an incredulous Ted.

The others in the room tried to suppress giggles. Dr. Miles gave them a look to kill and turned back to Ted.

"Okay, compuTV on," she said.

It sprung to life. Ted chose not to talk to the compuTV and held the remote instead. He surfed through numerous newscasts, all with strange, unrecognizable news and a few dates confirming Dr. Miles' assertions.

"Well I'll be . . . ," he said.

He propped himself up to a sitting position.

"Can we see some baseball?" he asked.

"In due time," said Dr. Miles. "There is a lot to catch up on."

Still somewhat dazed, she was thinking, *How great to see him sitting up, and he is aware, fluent even.*

"You don't seem to be suffering from dysarthria or apraxia," she said.

"What's that?" said Ted

"Sorry—speech or motor function problems," she said.

Jed had wangled his way into Ted's line of sight.

"Hey, Mr. Williams, can I have your autograph?" he said.

Dr. Miles rolled her eyes. Before she could speak, Ted cut her off.

"How old are you?" he said to Jed.

"Twenty-four."

"Well, where are your manners, son? You nearly stepped on the little guy to come over here. I'll sign an autograph. But not for you—for him."

Ted pointed at Johnnie.

"C'mere kid," he said.

Johnnie approached the bed holding his baseball glove and ball.

"What's your name?" said Ted.

"Johnnie."

"Well, that's a fine name," said Ted, smiling. "You know I knew a Hall of Famer who wore that very same uniform you've got on. Have you ever heard of Joe DiMaggio?"

"Yes," said a timorous Johnnie, almost too afraid to utter any sound.

"Well, he was the greatest all-around ballplayer that I ever saw. And I saw a lot of them. I knew Joe's brother Vince, a fine athlete, and I played with his brother Dom DiMaggio, one of my best friends for life. Who's your favorite player?"

"Johan Johansson," said Johnnie.

"Never heard of him," said Ted. "Guess Lizzy is right, I've got a lot of catching up to do."

"My mom's name is Elizabeth," said a trembling Johnnie.

"The doctor is your mom?" said Ted gently. "Well, we'll just have to see if she minds me calling her Lizzy. She looks like a Lizzy to me. Can I sign your baseball? Anybody got a pen?"

Emily handed Ted a pen. He scripted what looked like a perfect signature on the sweet spot in between the seams of Johnnie's Little League baseball. He handed the ball back.

"There now, how's that?" said Ted.

Their eyes welling with tears, everyone in the room was silent. What she had to tell Ted next filled Dr. Miles with dread.

Six

Over the next week, Dr. Miles spent nearly every waking hour at the bedside of Ted. Johnnie came in for visits with his mom in the evenings. Ted slept a lot and, when he wasn't sleeping, they were running tests on him. He was not yet permitted to try to walk. He had lots of questions, as anyone would who had been dead for 90 years.

"So, Lizzy," he said, "I know I am me, but when I look down at my body, it looks and feels different. What's going on?"

The moment she had dreaded had arrived.

"Well, Ted," she said, swallowing hard, "you have a different body than the one you had the last time you were alive. We decided you needed a new body and we found a donor. Your head and brain are the same, though—with some modifications."

"So you sewed my head onto someone else's body? I'm fucking Frankenstein, is that it?"

"No, Ted, we're much more advanced than that," she said. "But you are the first to be brought back to life through cryonics. We used your original head and, yes, you have a new body. We gave you a body transplant. The most difficult part was the brain work and spinal cord fusion. The body was from a 25-year-old professional tennis player who died of severe trauma to the head, so the body was perfect."

"A tennis player? Huh."

"Did you ever play tennis?" she asked.

"Yeah, a little bit in retirement. But not that much. Never had time for much else other than fishin'," he said. "And I never liked the way those tennis guys looked in those sissy shorts."

"I see," said Dr. Miles. "Well, we decided that you had a much better chance at quality of life if your reanimation were done with a current and young body."

"Reanimation?" said Ted. "That's me, a fucking cartoon? You got a mirror?"

"Sure," Dr. Miles said. She reached into a bedside drawer and handed it to him.

Ted held up the mirror to his face and winced.

"I look like hell," he said. "Geezus, look at the scar around my neck."

"You are going to need a little more plastic surgery on your neck and your face, as well. We've done some already—when you were in a coma. We will take care of that soon," she said.

"I don't want to look like no baby-faced kid again," said Ted, "even if you can do that."

"We can do a lot today with face work. I would say we should give it a go for something that looks about 40. But we can talk about that later. Before the cosmetic work we're going to try to get you up and walking, and then you will undoubtedly need a good deal of physical therapy, but so far your reflexes look brilliant."

"Yeah, it'll be nice to get rid of the bedpan and the freakin' tube you've got goin' into . . . well, never mind. Tell me more about what it took for my brain to recover. Was that the hardest part?"

"Yes, it was. You see, near the end of your first life, you suffered several strokes. When your head was cryopreserved, it was as is. So during reverse cryopreservation and, in particular, while you were in a coma, we had to do some extraordinary medical procedures to facilitate your recovery."

"What kind of things?"

"Well, there are two kinds of strokes. There is hemorrhagic stroke, when a blood vessel bursts in the brain. Then there is ischemic stroke, when blood is blocked from getting to the brain. Both can cause severe damage and cause brain cells to die. We're not sure which you had in your former life. Of course, the result for both often is a loss of memory, speech and motor function as well. From our records and historic accounts, you experienced all of that. In addition, we were concerned about equilibrium and balance, because you had a history of inner-ear trouble early in your former life."

"So you know about my military service?"

"Yes, we knew that you stopped flying in Korea because of the ear trouble. Your ears even bled, if I'm not mistaken."

"That's horseshit. I was taken off the line 'cause I had already flown 38 combat missions and served in both WWII and Korea."

"Okay. Sorry about that. I stand corrected. Anyway, our technology today is much more advanced than what you may remember. Most of the brain work was performed through nanotechnology."

"What's that?"

"Basically, we injected tiny molecular machines into your bloodstream that targeted the damaged cells in your brain, repaired them and facilitated reconnections."

"Really? Boy, aren't you something? Gee, I wish I was as smart as you."

Dr. Miles couldn't tell if he was being sarcastic or was really impressed; she was leaning toward the latter.

"It wasn't a sure thing by any means. It doesn't always work in non-cryonic patients; thus we were concerned about what would result in your head. Like I said, this had never been tried before."

"Did I go through a body transplant or a head transplant? Which part of me is in control now?"

"Since the memory and personality of Ted Williams have survived, I think the consensus of the scientific and medical community would be that it was a body transplant and your original brain is still in charge. But you can decide for yourself what you want to call it."

"I'd prefer not to have to talk about it at all."

"Yes, I understand. But you've made remarkable progress. Ted, let me ask you, do you want to know about your family?"

"Well, yes," he said.

"I'm afraid I have some bad news on that front," she said. "You have no living descendants or heirs."

"Tell me about it," said Ted.

"Well, the entire extended family was on a family holiday and all were lost in an air crash. Some had made preparations to be cryonically preserved like you but the bodies were too mangled. I take it from your inferences since you awakened from the coma, Ted, that you were not aware that they made cryonic preparations for you?"

"That's correct," said Ted, scratching his torso through his hospital gown and subconsciously rubbing his neck.

"Unfortunately, your son John Henry died only a couple of years after you and long before the crash," she said. "Leukemia or something. He made arrangements and attempted to have himself cryonically preserved as well."

"What do you mean, '*attempted*'?'" said Ted.

"Well, I'm sorry to have to tell you, but in his will John Henry specified, with no exceptions, that when his body was cryopreserved—"

"Just say frozen," he said.

". . . that it should be *frozen*," she continued, "with a baseball cap on his head that said Hitter.net. Something went wrong during the freezing process and the hat shattered into a million pieces, causing the skull and brain to break in just as many."

"Just like him," said Ted. "Always workin' an angle, tryin' to sell something. Never had much luck."

"I'm sorry, Ted."

As Ted stared off into the distance, only the medical monitoring devices made any sound. After a long pause, he spoke.

"I've got another question for you," said Ted. "Why me? I mean, you must have had hundreds or thousands of frozen popsicles you coulda brought back to life. Why was I the first?"

"Well, the truth is complicated," said Dr. Miles. "Counterintuitively, you were a good candidate because you had some head damage, a cracked skull, although much less damage than John Henry. Management thought that if we could repair that and any brain damage, we could accomplish the next reanimation with aplomb. And if it failed, well, the damaged head was probably the reason."

"And an excuse," said Ted.

"Well, yes, but there would be lessons learned. Yours was the first with a frozen head, but keep in mind, transplant science, even full bodywork or head transplants, have been done for quite some time. Under the best ethical standards, of course."

"Of course," Ted intoned facetiously. "So, how did my skull get cracked?"

"We think some of it happened during the neuropreservation process—the freezing. Unfortunately, some of it may have occurred later when your head was being transferred to a new liquid nitrogen cylinder. I'm sorry to say your head may have been abused."

"Abused?"

"Yes, there was damage done that could have been avoided. Your head may have been hit with a wrench."

"A wrench?!"

"Yes. It's all a bit murky and unsubstantiated. It was so long ago. Anyway, the news of that reached the media and a big scandal broke out. It was one of the reasons why, years later, the assets and, well, *inventory*, of the original cryosuspension foundation were sold to CryoCorp. Investors believed that to make a go of this business it needed to be a for-profit corporation."

"Why was my head separated from my body?"

"That, too, may have been an error. But it turned out to be fortuitous because we now know you have a better chance with the new body."

"But surely, Lizzy, you must have had other guys or gals who could've been first—that filled the bill."

"That's true, but there was another factor. The board here at CryoCorp decided that you would be the best patient, given your past experience with, well, *managing* the media.

"So that's what they thought? That I—of all people—could handle the press?"

"Quite right."

"That's a laugh," he said.

"Well, perhaps you learned from your mistakes," she said.

"Do the news leeches know about this?" he said.

"No, they don't, we're keeping it a secret to give you time to adjust, but it's bound to happen sooner or later. We live in a world where news organizations gather and aggregate information at the speed of light. Everyone's a potential reporter and can make money by uploading news stories and videos and photos from their iMasters for immediate dissemination. You may find it a little unnerving that every social interaction is being recorded. Actually, it has reduced crime."

"Great," said Ted.

He then raised his eyebrows, lowered his head, and looked Dr. Miles straight in the eye.

"And the board gave no thought whatsoever," he said, "about the benefits that my celebrity would bring the company?"

She smiled. "Ted, I am impressed with your thinking. You are quite clever. I'll try not to take too much credit for facilitating your superior cognitive abilities and powers of deduction."

"You do that."

Dr. Miles was glad to have this difficult conversation behind her, knowing full well that the next step in the total reanimation of Ted would be the most grueling.

Seven

A week later, Ted was able to put weight on his legs, and three days after that he began to walk. To Dr. Miles, his first steps were like witnessing Johnnie's first steps all over again—only with a few more cuss words—and a walker.

He also received another facelift. There never was much of a scar on his neck, but now nothing. A nip and a tuck later, Ted grudgingly approved of his new 40-year-old facial aesthetic. Moreover, the tennis player's body was remarkably similar to his former self.

"I can't believe it," he said. "Just like my old, er, young self."

Taking him through the physical therapy under the guidance of Dr. Miles and the CryoCorp physical therapy team was either Jed or Randall, often both. He struggled at first with the walker but soon was picking up speed in the halls of CryoCorp.

Several hours a day he also sat in a small classroom at a workstation outfitted with a desk that faced a wall. On the wall was a tablet that he was required to touch periodically in response to commands and screen choices. The mental agility exercises were intended to test and extend his cognitive abilities.

Ted hated it all.

~ ~ ~

On a particularly ornery day, while using his walker with Jed and Randall riding shotgun on each side, Ted stopped.

"If you two longhaired freaks don't leave me alone, I'm gonna die," he said. "Oh, I forgot, I did that already. Tell you what. You two go over there, down the hall."

They walked about 10 feet away. He picked up the walker, flung it toward their heads and said, "duck."

They both squatted with their hands on their heads. The walker whistled overhead and took out a table lamp behind them with a tremendous crash. When they opened their eyes, they took in the carnage and turned back toward Ted. He laughed his head off, strolling with big, heavy-footed strides—on his own—back to his room.

"Wow!" said Randall. "I guess he's feeling stronger."

Thereafter, no walker.

Ted graduated to a gym where there would be endless days of grueling exercise. Jed and Randall no longer wore white jumpsuits. Now they carried clipboards, for some reason had whistles around their necks, and wore tight-fitting gym suits made out of some sort of strange, translucent material that showed off muscle definition.

"If either of you blows a goddamned whistle, it'll become a permanent part of your voice box," said Ted.

The gym was like nothing he had ever seen before. He utilized strength-training bands with the tension set by microcomputers. He walked on a treadmill that surrounded him in a virtual reality experience. Programmable scenes passed by with amazing sights, sound and even smell. It was absolutely real. One moment he was walking through ancient Rome, and then, at the push of a button, he was walking through an African savannah. A lion made a habit of stalking Ted, but soon Ted realized it would never catch up. If it chased him, he could pick up the pace.

"If I had my old rifle I'd shoot that bastard," he said.

To Jed and Randall he added, "Gee, this would be great if I didn't have to look at you two tour guides by my side every fuckin' minute. Let's switch back over to Rome so I can see what you two furballs look like in a toga."

The exercise regimen included playing catch with a medicine ball.

"Now this is high tech," said Ted.

By far he spent most of his time on a stationary bike. He was on the machine for hours and hours until finally he asked, "Why is this called a Gridcyle?"

"Because it's hooked up to the power grid," said Randall. "Every stationary bike in gyms all over America is on the grid. It is basically human-generated electricity. You're a mean green electrical power machine, Ted."

"Yeah, there's only one problem. I can't possibly be generating enough electricity to cover what it takes me to visit ancient Rome."

"Well, that's probably true," said Jed, "but every little bit helps."

~ ~ ~

Soon Ted was running on the treadmill, enough to perspire in his gray sweat clothes.

"Where's the 'Rocky' music?" he said.

No one knew what he was talking about.

Dr. Miles was pleased and impressed with Ted's progress. With weeks of physical and cognitive therapy, mind and body were merging into one cohesive unit.

Ted and Johnnie had switched roles. Now, when Johnnie came into CryoCorp, Ted was reading to Johnnie. The little guy loved it. Ted also began to regale Johnnie with stories of his playing days. Johnnie brought in a bat and Ted, after clearing some furniture, worked on the fine points of Johnnie's batting stance and swing.

"Remember, hold the bat with your fingers, not your hands," said Ted. "A looser grip will allow all of the muscles to work correctly."

"Like this?" said Johnnie as he swung at an imaginary ball.

"Yes, that's it. Now keep those hands up higher," said Ted.

Dr. Miles watched it all with astonishment and a quiet, content glow in her eyes.

"I'm fucking miserable," he said to Dr. Miles when alone in his room with her. "I'm itchin' to go outside, to see the new world—the real world."

"Yes, I thought that would be the case," she said.

Since he was not a prisoner, Dr. Miles knew that she couldn't confine him to CryoCorp much longer. She also wondered if all of his frustration was about being a captive in CryoCorp 24/7, or about something else.

"Let me see what I can do," she said.

Eight

It was eight o'clock at night, and Dr. Miles and Emily were sitting outdoors in the bleachers of a Little League baseball field under bright artificial lights. Desert insects swirled about in the incandescence, competing only with the sound of parents encouraging their youngsters on the ball field.

Johnnie's Yankees were beating the White Sox, and the little shortstop was smiling broadly after he just reached first base with a grounder up the middle.

Dr. Miles yelled, "Way to go, my little batsman!"

The cricket terminology coupled with the British accent produced a few swiveled heads, but she was oblivious in her enthusiasm for Johnnie.

Dr. Miles had noticed that she was one of the few single parents in the stands; the rest were couples.

Now in a hushed tone, Dr. Miles said, "Emily, did you notice that every parent here seems to be part of a couple?"

"No, not really," said Emily. "What's on your mind, Elizabeth?"

"I'm always confused. Am I a single parent? A widow? Both?"

"You're Elizabeth, and Johnnie's mom. That's all that matters."

"Well, not quite, but you have a point."

She shook off the momentary sadness she was feeling and refocused on the game only to let her mind wander off once again, this time to thoughts of Ted.

I've got to get someone to help me with him. I can't do it all. He needs more than his doctor. It's obvious he's not relating very well to the medical staff. He needs a friend.

At that moment her attention was drawn back to the field where Johnnie was receiving base-running instruction from his manager. The manager was bending over to look Johnnie in the eye at first base.

What a great guy he is, thought Dr. Miles. *The kids adore him; he just has a way with youngsters and his affection and cheering are infectious.*

In fact, Dr. Miles knew the manager, Marshall Cummings, from his visits to CryoCorp. He was a medical equipment salesman. She often wondered, given the equipment that CryoCorp had been purchasing, if he had an inkling of what had been going on.

Then it hit her. *He would be a perfect friend for Ted.* He was even a former professional baseball player, she remembered. Letting him in on the secret would be less risky, she reasoned, because he had a business relationship with the company. Moreover, he was more likely to be discreet because she knew him personally outside of the building.

She would do it. She would let Marshall Cummings in on the secret in the hope of helping Ted.

~ ~ ~

Johnnie's team was now on the field. He made a fine catch at short, and Dr. Miles shouted, "Nice gather, Johnnie!"

The Yankees won the game.

Dr. Miles said goodbye to Emily, moved down to the field, sought out Johnnie and gave him a big hug. Marshall was finishing picking up the equipment.

"Nice game coach," she said.

Johnnie interrupted, "Mom, it's *manager*."

"Right, sorry."

"No problem, Elizabeth," said Marshall. "Johnnie played a good game, didn't he?"

Marshall was a large African-American man about 6-foot-2, 45 years old with a big smile, and big hands that made him look as though he wore a catcher's mitt on each arm. He had a close-cropped, full head of hair that was graying slightly around the temples.

"Johnnie, there is something I need to speak to your *manager* about. Would you please wait for me in the car?" said Dr. Miles.

"Sure, Mom."

"Marshall, may I speak to you alone?" said Dr. Miles.

"Sure Elizabeth, let's go over to the bleachers," he said. They were now empty.

"Marshall, there is something important that I have to ask you. Have you been curious as to why CryoCorp has been purchasing so much life-support and physical therapy equipment from you?"

He was a little relieved that she didn't ask him why Johnnie wasn't playing more.

"Well, yes, it had crossed my mind," he said. "Because, well, your patients are not exactly ambulatory."

"Marshall, we've known each other for quite some time, both in and out of work. You're a good man, and there is no one else I can turn to for this. Can I trust that what I'm about to tell you, you will keep a secret?"

"Well sure, Elizabeth—as long as it's legal . . . and maybe if it's not," he said laughing.

She didn't laugh. He stopped smiling.

"Thank you, Marshall. Well, here it is . . . we have reanimated a patient in CryoCorp. We're keeping it a secret indefinitely to give him more time to adjust."

"Wow," said Marshall. "No kidding?"

"No kidding. Are you ready for the next part?"

"Ah . . . sure."

"The patient is Ted Williams."

Marshall's eyes grew wide, hyperfocused on the face of Dr. Miles, as if he hadn't heard her correctly. He opened his mouth to speak, but no words came out.

"I know it's a lot to absorb," said Dr. Miles, "but you should know this: He's gone through a lot of physical and mental challenges. He's making progress but . . . but . . . well, he needs a friend, a male friend, I think. Would you like to try and be a friend to Ted Williams?"

"Well . . . yes—hell, yes!" said Marshall.

Nine

With most of the medical equipment gone, the staff attempted to make Ted's room in CryoCorp look more like an ordinary bedroom, but the effect was something more akin to a cheap hotel room. Longing to catch up on recent history, he was in a chair reading *The History of the U.S. Marine Corps* when Dr. Miles walked in with a big smile on her face. She noticed the book.

"Semper fi," she said, sitting down next to him.

"Do you even know what that means?" he said.

"Actually, no. I just heard it once or twice. Some sort of greeting among you Marines, is it not?"

"It's Latin, short for *semper fidelis*—'always faithful.' It's all about the loyalty that we Marines have for Corps and country, even after we leave the service."

"Well, while we're on the subject of being faithful," she said, slightly awkwardly, "I think it's time we had another one of our long talks."

He looked at her blankly.

"You've been here, awake that is, for more than three months," she said, "and you've made tremendous progress, Ted. I'm proud of you."

"You sound like my mother," he said.

She ignored the dig. He was such a curmudgeon.

"Ted, I need to ask you something. I know you've been frustrated by the physical therapy and the mental agility exercises we've been putting you through, but I also know there must be more to your frustration than that. Are you happy about being reborn?"

"I ain't complaining," he said.

"But tell me more," she said. "I need to know more about what's going on inside your head. Please, tell me."

"Seems to me you know an awful lot about my head already, seeing as how you preserved it, sewed it on and all."

He looked out the window as the hot sun reflected off the many strange-looking cars he had been staring at for weeks now in the parking lot of CryoCorp. His focus returned to Dr. Miles.

"Well, it *is* nice to be able to get up each morning and feel again what it's like to be in a 25-year-old body," he said. "You did a good job and—"

"But what about your—"

"Let me finish," he said. "It's been difficult to get used to all of this, but I have always been a guy who makes the most out of life—or in this case a second life. I make the most of what I've got. I didn't choose a cryonic comeback, but I'm going forward. It is, in fact, a new opportunity."

"So you're okay about all of this?" she said.

"Yes," he said unconvincingly, "if you'll ever let me out of this goddamned place."

"Well . . . I . . . well, speaking of God, I have to ask you—"

"No," he said.

"'No,' meaning, don't ask or 'no,' meaning—"

"'No,' meaning there's nothing. I don't remember anything about dying or being dead for all those years," he said.

"So, no moving toward the light, no reuniting with loved ones?" she said.

"Nope, absolutely nothin'."

"Oh," she said, nodding her head as she processed the information. She looked him in the eye and saw that he had a strange look on his face.

"Ted, don't get upset by what I'm about to ask. Are you telling me the truth?"

He put the book down on a side table and turned back toward her with his face very close to hers. She thought he might explode, but his voice was calm, albeit stern.

"Look, Lizzy, I'm only gonna discuss this once—with you and you alone. What I tell you must remain a secret between you and me. Only you and me. Am I making myself clear?"

"Yes, of course," she said.

"Not only that, but I'm not gonna give you much detail, and I don't want you asking a lot of questions."

"Okay, what is it, Ted?"

"What I just said about an afterlife and God a few moments ago wasn't exactly true. There is life—at least a spiritual life—after death. And there is a God. I just don't want to talk about it and don't want anyone else finding that out from me."

"Can you tell me why?"

"Yeah, well, I just don't want people, when they eventually find out about me, to look at me as some sort of messiah. That's why I'm not gonna answer any questions about it. It'll just be between you and me, and no one else will ever get a thing outta me. Do you understand?"

"Yes, but tell me this," she said, "should I feel bad about pulling you away from that?"

"No. As I said, I've been given a second chance here, and I'm gonna try and make the most of it."

"That's good," she said, and paused for further contemplation.

"Can I ask just one more question?" she said, with her eyes bright and her mind whirring.

"Go ahead," he said, with mild irritation in his voice.

"When you were there, in Heaven—I assume it was Heaven."

"Yes."

"What happened when you came back here?"

"Well, I just disappeared, it all went black you might say, and then I slowly returned to consciousness here," he said.

"So you knew about John Henry and the other relatives . . . they were there?"

"Never mind, Lizzy," said Ted

"But let me ask you this . . ."

"Uh, uh uh, that's enough," said Ted.

"I see," she said, dying to ask more questions. *What does God think about what I did, bringing you back? What about the soul, did it come back, too? Is there a soul? Did you speak to God? Does God speak at all? What's in Heaven?*

It would all have to wait. Maybe someday he would tell her. The limited information was frustrating, but she recognized he was opening up just a little bit and that was good.

"Your secret is safe with me, Ted. You do know, like the Marines, I will always be faithful, be your friend? Do you know that?" she said softly.

"Oh, don't go gettin' all mushy on me, Lizzy," he said. "By the way, I assume by now you're okay with me calling you Lizzy?"

"Only you, Ted. Only you. Are you ready for your next big adventure?"

Ten

The next morning was another boring sunny day in the southwest desert. Dr. Miles came rushing in to see Ted.

"I have a surprise for you," she said. "This is Marshall Cummings."

The men shook hands.

"Glad to meet you," said Ted.

"The pleasure is all mine," said Marshall.

"Marshall is an ex-baseball player like you," said Dr. Miles. "He's also familiar with what we do here and about your situation. Today he is going to talk baseball with you and, well—you tell him Marshall."

"Ted, we're goin' on a road trip," said Marshall.

"I'm getting' outta here? Well, it's about time," said Ted.

"Ted, I brought a pair of khakis and a polo shirt," said Dr. Miles.

"How do you know they'll fit?" said Ted.

"I know a lot about you," said Dr. Miles, "at least your physical self. Make sure you wear sunblock; I wouldn't want anything to spoil your perfect complexion, Ted."

"You know," he said, "one of these days, you and I are gonna have to talk about your tendency to be a mother hen."

She nodded with a smile and said, "Well, I guess I'll leave you boys alone. Remember what we talked about, Marshall."

"Yep," he said.

She said, bye, and left.

"Guess you two have made some kind of babysitting pact," said Ted.

"No sir, not babysitting. I think you're going to have a good time, Ted."

"Well, anything is better than hanging out around here all day and every day. So, are you a doctor?"

"No, I'm a medical equipment salesman," said Marshall.

"Where'd you play ball?" said Ted.

"Rocky Mountain League. First baseman. Triple-A. Never got much further. Trouble hitting the curve ball."

"I'm an ol' Pacific Coast Leaguer myself. Didn't spend too much time there though," said Ted.

"Oh, I know a lot about your career," said Marshall. "I've got to tell you, I know you set all kinds of records, let's see . . . lifetime batting average of .344; 521 home runs with four home run titles; a record .483 career on-base percentage; and a slugging percentage of .634, eclipsed only by Babe Ruth; nine slugging crowns; and finishing in the top 10 in runs per game—"

"For crissakes, you're a statistical machine," said Ted.

"But as a black man," said Marshall, "the thing I've always been most impressed about was how during your Hall of Fame induction speech you advocated for the old Negro Leaguers to be inducted into the Hall. You were a man ahead of his time."

"Well, I lived to see it happen. Great athletes; they deserved to be in the Hall."

"Let me ask you somethin'," said Marshall. "I often think about my career—if I can call it that—after *you* retired, what did you miss the most?"

"Well, it wasn't setting records, or even the hitting itself, it was the close friendships with teammates. I didn't appreciate them as much as I should have while I was playing. But later, in retirement, you bet I did. I miss ol' Needle Nose—Johnny Pesky. And Bobby Doer, and especially Dommie—Dom

DiMaggio. They were some good friends. Maybe I can get in touch with their relatives, or descendants, whatever I should call them."

Marshall reached into a small bag he had been carrying with him and pulled out an old book with a faded cover and scratch marks and handed it to Ted.

"Well then, I think you'll appreciate this antique book—I bought it for you. It's David Halberstam's classic, *The Teammates*, about those very friendships—*your* friendships. It was written after you passed on."

"Ain't that something," said Ted, inspecting the book.

"Listen," said Marshall, "I hesitated bringing the book for you because I thought Elizabeth might not approve, in case it makes you melancholy. So do me a favor, and don't show it to her."

"Oh, the hell with her, I'm not the fragile big bastard that she makes me out to be. Thanks, Marshall."

"Well, I'd love to hear more about your career, but first, are you ready to go?" said Marshall.

"Hell, yes," said Ted.

"Then let's do it."

~ ~ ~

It was 11 in the morning when Marshall and Ted strode out the revolving doors of the main entrance of CryoCorp. Ted took four steps onto the sidewalk and, with the thought of relishing a breath of fresh air, stopped short and turned to Marshall.

"Geezus, how hot is it?" said Ted.

"About 120 degrees Fahrenheit," said Marshall.

"Is this normal for around here? I don't remember Arizona being *that* hot."

"I'm afraid it is," said Marshall. "A lot's happened since your first life, Ted."

"I wish people would stop saying that to me."

"Yes. I understand," said Marshall. "Sorry. Anyway, we've been going through the ravages of global warming, you know—the effects of too many greenhouse gases on the planet. It's had a profound impact all across the globe."

"Yeah, I kinda remember people talking about that," said Ted. "So it really happened?"

They walked briskly to the car.

"Yes, ice melt, rising tides and storms killed millions of people around the world. We were slow to respond, but there has been some good to come out of it, like this car," said Marshall. "Get in and I'll show you. We call it an FCV."

They climbed into what Ted thought a funny-looking vehicle, like nothing he had ever seen before. *A flying wedge.* Almost touching the ground, the rear hatchback rose up and inward toward an apex that made the car a scalene triangle. The edges of the rear hatch were highlighted with what looked like two tracks extending up from the pavement. The longer, windscreen-side of the triangle undoubtedly made it aerodynamic. The doors opened up like gull wings. It was a mystery as to where the engine was. Ted, a tall man at 6-foot-3, found that he had plenty of legroom; there was no backseat. The air conditioning felt good.

"Did you call this thing an SUV?" said Ted.

"No, no, no," said Marshall. "It's an FCV—a fuel cell vehicle. It's propelled by an electric motor, and it uses hydrogen fuel cells for propulsion. Fuel cells are stacked in the vehicle—that's one of the things that give it the odd shape—that, and the large hydrogen-gas and water tanks. The fuel cells create electricity through a chemical process using hydrogen fuel and oxygen from the air."

Marshall pulled the car out of the CryoCorp parking lot.

"Are the fuel cells like batteries?" said Ted.

"Well, not exactly. They'll never go dead as long as chemicals are moving through them."

"So where does the hydrogen come from?"

"We can pull in and fill up just like at the old gas stations," said Marshall. "The high-pressure hydrogen gas is created in various ways at chemical processing centers and delivered to the filling stations. One way is through the reforming of biomass and wastes; the others include electrolytic and photolytic processes. It's renewable stuff."

They were now on a freeway heading to an unknown destination.

"You lost me," said Ted, "but the bottom line is this doesn't pollute?"

"Right, in fact the only by-product is water vapor. This is one of the newer models; it turns the water vapor into water. When I fill up, my excess water is pumped out of the car at the filling station. The water is then recycled and helps us here in the desert to replenish the water supply."

"That's somethin'," said Ted, looking out the window. "So why is there a global warming problem?"

"Well, carbon fuels were the culprit, and it came on very fast. People never expected it would happen so quickly. Today, most of the old oil companies are virtually out of business. Those that are still around have diversified into hydrogen production. Carbon fuels have been reduced. But— and it's a big but—this happened too late. Global warming has advanced to the point where we don't know if or when it will reverse itself."

"Were there other kinds of cars developed?" said Ted.

"Someone, perhaps a whole county back east, I think, experimented for awhile with a mag-pull system. Drivers would hook up to the system at the bottom of their driveways and latch on. Think of it like the old San Francisco cable cars with the cables running underground pulling the cars. In this case magnets did the pulling.

"So what happened to it?"

"The experiment failed. In addition to being cost prohibitive—magnetic lines had to be run under every street—people absolutely hated the fact that after programming in their destinations at the bottom of their driveways, they had to queue up and poke along behind every other car heading for their destination. You didn't have to drive—your car was pulled along—which on the face of it was good, but you couldn't pass anyone or change your speed on your own."

"Yeah, I could see where that would be an issue," said Ted.

There was a pause in the conversation.

"So where are we goin'?" said Ted.

"Well, we're going to a major league baseball game."

"Great!" said Ted. He lit up and beamed, his smile reversing any remaining gravitational sag and making him look years younger again.

"Who's playing?"

"The Diamondbacks are playing the Tokyo Giants."

"Tokyo?"

"Yes, the major leagues have expanded, Ted; it's now a worldwide, unified game. The National League is now called the *Inter*national League and the American League is known as the Panamerican League. There are teams in Europe, South America and all over Asia," said Marshall.

"Huh," said Ted. "So tell me, how long ago did you play, Marsh?"

"I hung up the cleats about 23 years ago. Made it up to the show just once with Oakland in September. Next year, back down, and I never did make it again. Couldn't hit the curve consistently and I had a nagging back injury that wouldn't go away, especially at the plate."

"Musta been a big disappointment," said Ted.

"Yeah, afterward I earned a degree in biology. You know, you play the hand you're dealt."

"I, of all people, know what you're saying," said Ted. "Boy, oh boy, do I know."

Eleven

The hydrogen fuel cell motor propelled them silently through what was now an urban landscape. Ted was looking out the window and peppered Marshall with a question a second about what he was seeing.

Ted pointed. "These buildings, I assume they're buildings, why are they such odd shapes? Some of 'em look like baked beans."

"Well, you might call them stealth buildings, intended to hide from the harsh, hot rays of the sun. The curvilinear shapes and specialized materials reflect at lot of the sun's rays where flat surfaces would absorb them. It's more energy efficient."

Ted pointed again. "What's that over there?"

"You mean the vehicles on the rail? That's the pod system or PRT— Personal Rapid Transit—sort of a cross between a train and a car. People get on at stations, but they ride in small individual pods—they like the privacy. They punch in their destinations. It operates on a raised rail like a train, but it shuttles them off in multiple directions and bypasses the stations where they don't want to stop. That was an alternative to the mag-pull system."

They pulled into the stadium parking lot and, to Ted's amazement, an attendant directed Marshall to pull up and stack the front of his car up onto the rear of the car in front of them. Now Ted understood the purpose of the tracks on the rear of their own vehicle. When they opened their gull-wing doors their seats automatically swiveled to be sure they were perpendicular to the ground and could easily get out. Steps extended outward from the seats, bridging the gap to the ground.

Marshall handed Ted a baseball cap with no logo on it, and a pair of sunglasses.

"Here, put these on," said Marshall.

Ted thought the glasses looked like something from a space movie, with wraparound lenses refracting the rays of the sun in what looked like a multicolor prism, but since Marshal was wearing the same thing, he complied.

"Do us a favor," said Marshall. "Keep them on during the game. You may be recognizable to certain fans."

Ted nodded, exited the car, and looked at the massive building in front of them.

"This is the stadium?" he said.

It was shaped like a giant seashell, a clam to be exact. In fact, the stadium was nicknamed "The Clam." It was a rather incongruous moniker for a desert facility, although Ted imagined that a baseball field would fit quite well into a giant clamshell. Marshall explained that during night games, if it wasn't too warm, the top half of the scalloped shell opened via a retractable roof. For day games like today, the roof was closed for protection from the sun. Outside the stadium, people splashed in a group of pools surrounded by imported palm trees.

"Is this a beach or a ballpark?" grumbled Ted.

~ ~ ~

After making their way to the third base side, Marshall and Ted walked through a tunnel to get to their seats. As they moved toward the light, the stadium unfolded in front of them in all of its air-conditioned, retractable-roofed, resplendent glory. It wasn't Fenway or the Bronx, but Ted began to get that old thrill again. He took off his glasses. It was total sensory overload:

The green grass, the buzz of the crowd, the smell of peanuts. Strangely, though his olfactory memory searched for it, he smelled no cigars.

No matter, he was a kid again or, more precisely, *The* Kid. He could see and take in everything, thanks to Dr. Miles' restoration of his 20-10 vision. His lips quivered, his eyes became moist. The sudden rush of emotion surprised him.

The two made their way to their seats. Marshall was aware that Ted was a little taken aback, largely because he was silent. Ted, he already knew, was rarely silent.

"Are you okay, Ted?" said Marshall.

"Yes, 'course I am," said Ted, hiding his tears behind the sunglasses.

Marshall called over a hawker and asked for a Pepsi Pep.

"You want one?" he said to Ted. "It'll taste like what you remember, but it's much healthier."

They drank and watched pregame warmups silently.

The fences were all high, not like the green monster at Fenway that he remembered, but uniformly high. There were ads plastered, or actually, lighted, all over the ballpark.

"Don't the electronic ads shifting from one to the next distract the players?" said Ted.

"I don't think so," said Marshall. He leaned toward Ted's ear. "Ted, remember to try and keep your voice down so that only I can hear you."

"Okay, okay," said Ted. "I'm glad to see that area in dead center is kept seatless and dark—the batter's eye. During my playing days I asked for that. At the plate, too many white shirts were obstructing the view of the ball as it left the pitcher's hand."

"I never knew that you had something to do with the creation of the batter's eye," said Marshall.

Marshall pointed toward the roof.

"The lights are designed to mimic the movement of the sun, complete with moving shadows, to replicate the experience of a day game in the sunshine as closely as possible."

"You're kiddin'?" said Ted.

Ted looked at the players' uniforms and, except for some odd-looking logos, he was glad to see that the uniforms hadn't changed much. In fact, he thought they were positively retro, remembering the embarrassing pullover stretch uniforms players had to wear in the 1970s after he had retired.

A giant multisided scoreboard hung over the center of the field. Currently, it was playing what looked like a highlight reel made into a music video.

"Isn't that hangin' awful low," he said to Marshall.

"Well, batting practice is over," he said. "During the game it retracts in an instant just as the pitcher deals and then pops back down between pitches."

Ted said, "Be nice if they could let the sunshine in, but I guess it's kinda tough when it's over 130 degrees outside."

"Yes," said Marshall. "Occasionally, they'll open the roof during the day for spring or fall games, but it doesn't happen often, except at night. Besides, people like that scoreboard, which isn't available when the roof is open."

Ted watched strange-looking big players go through their pregame tosses in the familiar way: two groups playing catch, infield and outfield.

The crowd stood for the playing of the national anthem. Ted, always a patriotic man, was glad to see the American flag out in center field, although it lay motionless against the pole in the windless shell. He then was taken aback by the playing of the Japanese national anthem.

At the conclusion, he said, "Standing for that Japanese anthem is a little strange for me, being a Marine who was trained to—"

"I know Ted, I know," said Marshall.

Ted focused for the first time on the pitcher's mound, where the pitcher was taking final warm-up throws. Ted stood up fast, spilling his soda.

"For crissakes, the goddamned pitcher . . . it's a robot!"

Marshall looked around. People were staring, as if Ted had dropped down from outer space—or had been brought back from the dead.

Marshall put a hand on Ted's shoulder to sit him down, looked left and right, and hushed his voice.

"It's called a Botwinder," said Marshall.

Ted couldn't take his eyes off the contraption. To most people, the robot hurler was an engineering marvel. It was a machine with foreboding black, camera-lens eyes, in a steel-plated, gleaming blockhead. It had a glove on one arm, and the other arm was an absolute mechanical menace. There was a windup filled with metallic screeches, grinding metal on metal. The designers left the noise in for intimidating effect. There was an enormous leg kick. The delivery was overhand; the great screeching mechanical arm thrust the ball to the plate with steel fingers that Marshall explained were coated with soft, skin-like synthetic material. The kicking leg thundered as it hit the ground. The effect was daunting: A great machine with sensory and motor inputs, gears and oscillators, hydraulics, pneumatics and gyroscopes that propelled the ball to the plate at more than 120 miles an hour.

"Ted, we have a lot to catch up about," said Marshall. "Now you know why Dr. Miles programmed the media in your room to prohibit you from seeing any baseball. She didn't want to upset you early in your recovery. I should have prepared you, but we were so busy talking about other things, I got sidetracked."

"This is fuckin' ridiculous," said Ted. "People watch that thing?"

"Well, yes," said Marshall. He ordered two more Pepsi Peps but wished the stadium sold whiskey.

"You see . . . ," he stopped himself and lowered his voice yet again. "Early in the century, ballplayers were using performance-enhancing drugs. Some scandals occurred, but ultimately the leagues couldn't keep up with the innovative chemists who beat the drug tests. Year by year, both the drugs and the hitters became stronger. Strangely though, pitchers didn't seem to get any better when the drugs got stronger—made them too muscular maybe. It extended a few careers, but even the newer, stronger drugs didn't much improve major league pitching, perhaps because pitching involves so much more finesse."

"I would beg to differ. Batters are the ones who need finesse, among other things," said Ted. "So the hitters got better, but not the pitchers?"

"Yes."

"So the hitters were cheating?" said Ted.

"Well, that's one way to look at it, but it all became very confusing. They removed the asterisks from the record books, you know, BS and AS."

"What do you mean?" said Ted.

"Before steroids and after steroids. Anyway, the hitters became dominant. Records broke like glass. Everyone hit well over .400.

Ted caught his breath, but didn't say anything; he had heard a rumor.

"Yes, that's right," said Marshall, "your famous .406 batting record was surpassed, and by guys without any of your skill or hard work. And it got very dull, I can tell you. Despite the fact that at first people loved all of the long home runs, the games became predictable. The final scores looked like football games. You know, 28 to 20, 45 to 35? That's when the commissioner's office introduced the Botwinder—to compete against the better hitters. At first it was an experiment, but it soon caught on and became a permanent part of the game. The pitchers . . . the people . . . they were eliminated."

The game had begun.

"Is that radar gun correct?" said Ted, looking at the scoreboard that indicated the Botwinder was throwing at 122 miles an hour.

"Yes, it is. Yes it is," said Marshall.

"Geezus," said Ted.

They watched the game for three innings with hardly any hitting before Ted said he had had enough. He had a million questions and just as many comments. But before he made them, so as not to make another scene, he said "C'mon, let's get outta here."

Twelve

In the parking lot, Marshall's car, standing on its rear wheels, pivoted those wheels and slid out sideways from the stack of cars. When free, it gently returned to all four tires.

Ted gave Marshall a quizzical look.

"Gyroscopes," said Marshall.

They drove silently through the desert. Ted said, "Pull over. Let's go into this place."

Marshall veered off the road and into the parking lot of a roadhouse called the Cactus Club. A giant neon cactus attached to the end of the building climbed high into the sky, like a silo attached to a barn. The name of the place blinked on and off from the roof of the long, squat building shaped like a kidney bean with no visible corners.

"Ya think they got entertainment and regular folks in here?" said Ted.

"Yes, but Ted, I wouldn't advise you to drink—you know, alcohol," said Marshall.

"First of all, you ain't my mommy," said Ted. "Anyway, I never was much of a drinker. Never smoked either. I hated the smoke that hung inside every stadium."

"Well, you'll be happy to know then," said Marshall, "that all smoking is now illegal."

They went inside. Other than no smoke, the place seemed familiar to Ted. He liked these kinds of places. No big shots, just plain folks. The familiar smell of stale beer was in the air. It was dark, except for neon beer signs and the light over a pool table. In the center of the room was a huge rectangular bar with maybe eight people spread out sipping beers. Over in one corner a guy was fiddling with a retro jukebox that was playing strange music.

Ted and Marshall took seats at the bar. Marshall ordered two Pepsis from the bartender. The bartender was dressed like he came out of a John Ford movie. Upon further inspection Ted noticed the bartender's chaps were made out of something that looked like chrome and the music coming out of the jukebox sounded like synthesized animal noises. A sign on the jukebox said Top 40 EmoMamalia.

"Okay, tell me more about the goddamned robot," said Ted to Marshall.

"Well, first you have to know more about the performance-enhancing stuff."

"Just call 'em drugs," said Ted.

"Today, they probably aren't drugs as you know them. After you, ah, passed, and even before, the chemists were always a step ahead of the testing. It only got worse."

"Of course."

"The biggest manufacturers are companies called Getgo and RoidRealm. Anyway, the cocktail the players take includes steroids, human growth hormone, and a radioactive isotope called Anaradium-406—it was named as a homage to you and your .406 batting season."

"You're shitting me?"

"Nope. After taking it for a while, the uber-juicing guys regularly hit over .400—that's why your .406 record no longer stands—until they brought in the Botwinder, that is. Now they hit .325 to .350 tops, but need the radioactive 'roids to keep up with the pitch velocity. It's a vicious circle."

"It doesn't hurt them?"

"Well, yes and no. They manage, but there are side effects."

"Let me guess, guys glow in the dark—good at night games, I bet."

"No. But the guys are huge, and they all have tiny little balls, you know, testicles. Oh, and they're all bald—their heads that is, not their balls—though, I can't be sure of that."

"I did notice a lot of overly muscular guys, and the heads that I could see were bald."

"Yes, they take the stuff and overnight turn bald; bulking up takes just a few more days."

"Must be a lot of power hitters," said Ted, "but not very good at spreading the hits around the field."

He thought for a moment and then added, "For crissakes, the kids see all of this? What kind of lesson is it for them?"

Marshall made a remorseful nod and said, "At least the kids still pitch in Little League, but few of 'em want to."

They both drank their sodas.

"So this robot," said Ted, "what did you call it, a Botwinder? Doesn't a machine throw perfectly every time? You either can't beat it or, because you know where it's gonna pitch, you can."

"No, that's not it at all. First of all, it's pitching at 120-plus miles an hour. Secondly, it's got a repertoire of every pitch imaginable and it mixes it up—slider, curve, two-seamer, split-finger—you name it, even a knuckler, but that's a mystery to me, given that there are no real fingers. And—here's the kicker—it's onboard computer uses facial recognition and on top of that can be programmed, you know, information can be downloaded. It remembers each batter, his tendencies, and every prior at bat, and pitches accordingly. It's got artificial intelligence—tough to beat."

"For crissakes, it's taken the science out of the hitting," said Ted.

"Yup, the real science is in the design of the machine," said Marshall.

"But there is one thing I don't understand," said Ted. "No one walks any more because the pitches are machine-made perfect? Then why did I see an umpire calling balls and strikes?"

"Well, not every pitch is a strike, some are deliberate balls, and walks do occur, but there are very few. You see, because every swing in the past is stored in its database, occasionally the Botwinder will try to get guys out by making them chase bad pitches."

"I would try and decoy it, I think, but I can see why that could drive down the batting average. It's fuckin' bush league. They've ruined the game."

After a long pause, Ted said, "I've got another question: Geezus, you'd think with all of this advanced technology, they'd make the thing look more human, less like a robot. What gives?"

"Well, they did try that," said Marshall. "Originally, it was much more humanlike with skin and no shining metal. Ultimately, it became less anthropomorphic because people were too freaked out by it. And for marketing purposes the menacing-looking machine appealed to more aggressive fans."

The bartender came over and gave Ted another Pepsi.

"The woman across the bar has bought you a drink," he said to Ted.

Ted and Marshall looked across the bar.

"That woman?" said Ted to Marshall. "She looks like she's been hit with too many balls off the catcher's mask."

To be polite he nodded a thank you. The woman was dressed in jeans, a red shirt with a print on it that made it look more like a bandana, and a straw cowboy hat. It was obvious to Ted she was trying to project a younger image.

"Ted, look at her smilin' at you," said Marshall laughing. "She's got a thing for you."

"Yeah, well, I'm not interested."

"Ted, you've got to remember, above the shoulders you still look like an old leatherneck, but from there on down you've got the body of a 25-year-old. Chicks, ah, ladies, are gonna dig that."

"I was married three times," said Ted. "I know how to handle women."

"Yeah, sounds like it. Three strikes and you were out. I'm guessing your on-base percentage with other ladies was pretty good though."

"I had no trouble findin' 'em," said Ted. "Keepin' 'em was another story, I guess."

"How 'bout you? You married?" said Ted.

"Divorced. I've stopped countin' how many times I've struck out since then."

"Yeah, well, remember you can strike out seven out of 10 times and still make it to the hall of fame," said Ted. They both laughed loudly.

The woman across the way kept up a crooked smile. Sure enough, she rambled over and, sure enough, she was on the downhill side of inebriated. She approached from his back and touched Ted on the shoulder.

"Hey there, cowboy, what's your name?" she said. The "what's" was slurred, the contraction more like a long "z."

"My name is Ted. No offense, but I'm just talking to my buddy Marsh here, so I've got to tell you, you're barking up the wrong tree."

"Whaddya mean?" she said.

Ted leaned toward her ear. "To tell you the truth," he said, "I haven't had sex in 120 years."

She suppressed a burp and said, "Well, welcome to the club, honey."

"No, you don't understand," said Ted. "You see, I was reborn."

"Well, ain't that somethin'?" she said. "I'm born-again too!"

"Let's go, Bush," said Ted to Marshall.

~ ~ ~

They left the roadhouse and headed toward the car. In the parking lot Ted produced the keys.

"Hey, what are you doing?" said Marshall.

"You left the keys on the bar. Get in, I'm driving."

Before Marshall could stop him, Ted was in the car and it was beginning to move. Marshall flipped his door up and barely made it in.

"The freakin' car can walk on two wheels, and I didn't order keyless entry," said Marshall.

His head was thrown back as Ted hit the gas hard.

"Ted, it's been a long time since . . . Hey, you don't have a license!"

Dust flew behind the car as Ted spun out of the parking lot and onto the road. He quickly accelerated with little regard for the yellow line. A massive 24-wheeler went by too close for comfort, its air horn blowing all the way.

Ted let out a shout of delight that was something close to a whoopee. "Hot damn, this is fun!"

"Ted, you shouldn't be doing this," said Marshall.

Ted ignored him. On a bend in the road, they nearly clipped a couple of giant saguaros as the car fishtailed off the pavement kicking up more dust.

"Jesus, Ted. You're gonna get us killed!"

Ted accelerated down a straightaway. The desert landscape was a blur. Ted had a slightly evil grin on his face.

"Christ," said Marshall, "it's the soda! Ted, you don't realize, ordinary soda is much more powerful today. It's caffeine with oomph times 10. Your body's not used to it. Pull over."

Ted, still feeling giddy, looked at him and then accelerated some more.

"All right, you pine tar-soaked jackass, pull over this car right now!" said Marshall.

In a screech and a ball of dust, Ted pulled over, stopped the car and turned to Marshall with a big smile.

"Marsh, right off the bat I knew I liked you. Yes, sir. I take it you would like to drive the rest of the way this afternoon, my friend?"

They got out of the car and switched seats. In the waning desert sun Marshall drove the FCV back to CryoCorp at exactly the speed limit. Ted Williams kept up the questions and comments, the lessons and the lectures, on everything that was wrong with the first three innings of baseball he had witnessed in nearly a hundred years.

Thirteen

The road trip had the effect Dr. Miles had hoped for: Ted seemed to be in a much better mood. Marshall and Ted did not let on about all of the details from their little excursion.

Soon there were more road trips with Marshall. They went to the rodeo and even on a fishing trip to a mountain lake in northern Arizona. In addition to the trips, Ted's big enjoyment was spending time with Johnnie.

Despite Ted's pronouncement that the Botwinders had ruined the major leagues, now that Dr. Miles allowed him to watch baseball on compuTV, she and Marshall noticed that Ted was not just watching games but analyzing every move the Botwinders were making. He surprised himself with the amount of time he spent critiquing, reviewing in slow motion, and replaying the few successes that batters had against it.

~ ~ ~

It didn't take long for the reality to set in once again that Ted was still living in his depressing little room, still under observation, and still being treated like a guinea pig. Despite the trips, he was as ornery as ever, particularly about two CryoCorp corporate guys in suits whose names he could never remember. They would pop in frequently to ask how he was doing.

It was particularly annoying if he was watching baseball, as he was on a Saturday afternoon when the staff heard him scream, "What the fuck?!"

Dr. Miles and Emily ran down the hall and rushed into the room.

"What's the matter, Ted?" said a winded Dr. Miles.

"I'm watching the Red Sox game here and they called Fenway Park, Fenway Island. Then some guy hits a ball over the Green Monster and it lands in water. What the hell is going on?"

"Well, that area of Boston is flooded now because of global warming and rising tides."

"Holy shit," was all he could say, before he drifted back to the unfolding game.

"Perhaps we should talk about it later," said Dr. Miles.

~ ~ ~

Ted was adjusting well to his new body. In particular, he was delighted that his hand-eye coordination was dramatically improved.

Dr. Miles walked into his room to do what he thought would be one of her three-times-a-week exams. He immediately noticed a difference. She was not wearing her normal white lab coat. He took note of the fine definition of her breasts under a silk blouse. His eyes moved downward and he saw that she was wearing a short skirt that showed off shapely legs. She was slim, yet curvaceous, and really alluring. He quickly brought his attention back to her eyes so as not to be caught staring.

"All right, change of subject," he said. "We always talk about me. I want to know more about you."

"Okay," she said.

"How's my buddy Johnnie doing? I haven't seen him for a few days."

"He's doing great. He's got a big part in the school play, and the rehearsals aren't leaving him much time to do his homework. He wants to see you all the time."

"Well, bring him back in here as soon as you can. I love kids," said Ted.

"I know you do."

"Anyway, I know you're a single mom, divorced I take it?" he said.

"No, widowed. Johnnie's dad died in a car smash a little over two years ago."

"Oh, I'm sorry. Tough on the kid, I bet?"

"Yes, tough on him, and me as well."

"Of course, I didn't mean to—"

"Yes. Well, life goes on and Johnnie's such a good child. And then there's my work—"

"Yeah, my mom worked a lot when I was a kid. The Salvation Army. Geezus, she was never home. Hard to argue against a charitable organization or, in your case, scientific progress. Say, how about on our next road trip Marsh and I include you and Johnnie?"

"That would be nice, Ted. Very nice. He'll love it."

Fourteen

The promised outing was less of a road trip and more of a picnic. The group included Ted and Marshall, Dr. Miles and Johnnie, and Emily and her young son, Billy, about Johnnie's age. As was common in Arizona, they set off fairly early in the morning to avoid the full crush of the midday sun.

Scratched out of the craggy terrain of the North Mountains, their destination was Tapatio Cliffs, a picturesque park that included a manmade lake, overlooked a golf course, and even had a little ball field. The field wasn't much, really, just a backstop and a diamond, but it reminded Ted of the little places where he had learned to play as a kid in San Diego.

They settled in on a cliff-shaded hillside surrounded by small golden hedgehog cacti, lavender-colored western dayflowers and sporadic basketgrass. Emily spread out three blankets she had brought along. Ted pointed to the lake and said to Marshall, "Any fish in there?"

"Don't know. And we're not going to find out. I didn't bring any fishing gear along, just my duffle with baseball stuff for the boys."

"Well we wouldn't want to leave these two beautiful women anyway, 'cept for some baseball maybe," said Ted.

"C'mon boys," said Marshall, "let's go hit a few."

They jogged about 100 yards down the hill to the ball field, and Marshall pulled out a bat and several balls and began hitting to the two boys. The women unloaded the contents of a picnic basket and Ted volunteered to help. Emily excused herself to go find a restroom.

Ted took in the desert landscape—red, orange, and even purple hues, beautiful in the long shadows created by the morning sun. It was the first time he really appreciated the desert, probably because he wasn't being blasted by the full force of the sun.

He and Dr. Miles sat on a blanket looking off in the same direction toward the ball field. He took a deep breath, bordering on a sigh.

"Kinda nice, isn't it?" said Ted.

"Yes, it is," she said, relaxed and smiling and leaning back on her hands. "We really should do this more often."

He leaned over and placed his face two inches in front of hers.

"I'd like to know if I can kiss you," he said.

She blushed.

"Uh, Ted, I don't know. Yes, yes, I do know . . . that would be inappropriate. I am your doctor."

She slid sideways, pulling away.

"Ted, it's not right," she said, turning her head left and right to make sure neither the ballplayers nor Emily witnessed what had happened—or didn't happen.

"You know," he said, "there was a time when I would not have asked. I woulda just made a pass at you."

She straightened her hair and patted down the sides of her blouse as if they had been mussed.

"I understand, Ted. I really do. And I appreciate that."

"Well, with your help maybe I can do a lot of things differently this time around," he said.

"You're off to a good start," she said sincerely, wondering if her blushing and body language gave away conflicting emotions.

The conversation was interrupted by the approach of Emily who seemed not to have noticed what transpired. Seeking a little space, Elizabeth said, "Ted, why don't you go down and help Marshall play with the boys while Emily and I finish spreading out the food?"

"Yeah, that bush leaguer doesn't know what he's doin'," said Ted.

~ ~ ~

Down on the ball field Ted grabbed a glove and said to the boys, "Let me get on first and you two throw 'em to me."

Marshall stood at the plate and hit to the boys on the left side of the infield. With eagerness, sprinkled with laughter when they missed a few, the boys threw a number of balls to a smiling Ted who shouted encouraging words to both Johnnie and Billy. He caught several balls before it hit him.

He was playing baseball again.

Ted caught the next few in a sort of silent trance, staring at his glove each time he caught a ball. Marshall interrupted his stupor.

"Hey, you big stiff," he yelled from home plate, "come over here and take the bat."

Ted obliged. While the boys waited, Marshall moved to the mound taking several balls with him.

Ted picked up the bat and held it softly in his hands at home plate. He thought it felt odd or, more precisely, his fingers did. These were not the heavily callused hands he once had but something else entirely. He liked the fact that the soft hands made him feel every inch of the wood better, every grain, every knot. Moving his hand over the bat he could feel the wood grain flow—parting, rejoining, arrow-heading—in perfect layers. It was as if he were viewing a fine work of art, not unlike a blind person, appreciating it in full tactile meditation. He looked down at his hands as his fingers began to drum along the bat handle like the slowmotion playing of a flute.

"Okay, you ready, buddy?" said Marshall, not grasping at all the enormity of the situation from Ted's perspective.

Standing on the right side of the plate, Ted looked up. In an instant a ball flew by the big lefty, passing over the plate and crashing into the little backstop. Then again. And again.

From the hillside, Dr. Miles and Emily were now standing and viewing with full attention what was taking place on the ball field below.

"Hey, rookie, when you gonna take a cut?" said Marshall.

Somewhere in the deep recesses of Ted's neurologically preserved, nanobot-restored mind, the rookie comment touched a nerve. Except perhaps for the almost imperceptible gritting of his teeth, the kids at third and short, Marshall on the mound, and the women on the hill, were all unaware that he was now out of his self-imposed stupor.

Marshall pitched again, and the crack of the bat removed any doubt.

As if pulled by unseen strings, the two boys wheeled around in unison to try and catch the flight of the ball. One was silent in awe, the other, after a split second of wonderment, simply said, "Whoa."

On the mound, Marshall did his own spinning, 180-degree turn, and tried to spot the ball as it soared across the desert sky, so far out of sight that only a distant dust-buster of a landing gave any clue as to how far the ball had traveled. Nearby, a jackrabbit ran for cover.

Elizabeth gasped, her hand quickly covering her mouth.

Ted said nothing, dropped the bat, and proceeded up the hill to rejoin the ladies.

For the rest of the morning hardly anyone said much of anything at all. Even the boys were quiet. Everyone conspicuously avoided speaking about what they had witnessed.

Ted and Elizabeth had a few extra things to think about.

Fifteen

A week later Dr. Miles walked into Ted's room and said, "Ted, I've been told the board wants to meet with you."

"What board?"

"The board of directors here at CryoCorp."

"Okay, what do the big shots want to talk about?"

"Well, I'm not at liberty to say, but I'll be with you when we have the meeting. It's on Thursday of this week. Can you make it?"

"Seeing as how I don't have much of a set schedule, I think I can make it."

~ ~ ~

On the morning of the meeting, Dr. Miles walked into Ted's room. She was in a dark blue suit with funny-looking lapels, not her normal white medical coat, nor the silk blouse. He was dressed for the meeting in a light blue, button-down Oxford shirt and khaki pants, the attire he normally wore, all provided by CryoCorp.

"Well, since you'll be meeting the board I bought you this," said Dr. Miles. She held out a tie.

"No way. I can't stand ties," said Ted. "I'm not wearing a tie—not even one of those bolo numbers."

She didn't know what a bolo was and said, "Okay, I just thought I'd let you know that the board will be in business attire."

"I got it. I'm fine with this."

"Right then, let's go. We'll take the lift up to the third floor," she said.

They walked down the hall and took the elevator up, went down another corridor and into a sun-filled, wood-paneled boardroom. The room was overflowing with suits and ties.

"Any Marines in here?" said Ted.

No one raised a hand.

"I didn't think so."

"Ted, I know you know Dr. Bernard Cromwell, our CEO," said Dr. Miles. Ted remembered Cromwell from his brief visits to Ted's room.

Ted shook hands with him.

She followed Ted around the room and introduced him to all of the board members. There were 16 people in the room, including four women, and they all were similarly dressed. The common theme was dark suits. What stood out to Ted was the cut of each suit—even the women's attire. Each suit had strange pointy lapels that stretched all the way to the shoulder. The lapels were all fastened at the shoulder with gold buttons. To Ted, the effect was military-like, almost like wearing epaulets. The men's ties were narrow, all bright colors, in various pastel shades.

Ted turned to Cromwell who was seated at the head of the table and said, "Are these uniforms?"

"I'm sorry?" said Cromwell.

Dr. Miles leaned over and whispered to Ted, "This is standard business attire."

"So," said Cromwell, "how are you doing Ted?"

"I'm fine, but I'm curious as to why you brought me here today."

"Well, right to the point, I like that," said Cromwell. He smiled a rather false smile.

"Ted, we've all been monitoring your progress, and let me say we're all very proud of you. Elizabeth reports that you have demonstrated significant cognitive and physical improvement. As you are our first person to be reanimated, we are just thrilled, and we hope that you are, too."

"Yeah, I'm thrilled," said Ted in monotone.

With the exception of Dr. Miles, the rest of the room brandished plastic smiles.

"Yes, well, we're all very glad," said Cromwell. "Ted, we are here to discuss your future with you. I presume you have been wondering what the future will hold for you now?"

"Well, as a matter of fact, I *have* been wondering about that."

"Good. I hope you can appreciate what we're about to tell you. You see, patients at CryoCorp come to us with a patient suspension fund. That is a fund provided by the patient or family that, due to the accumulation of interest over time, is capable of supporting ongoing whole-body or neuro-cryonic suspension."

"I get it," said Ted. "It's the dough that keeps the lights on and the freezers chilled."

"Well, yes," said Cromwell. "But it's a little more complicated than that. Ninety years ago, your estate provided what was then thought to be sufficient funds that, with interest, would cover ongoing suspension. The investment even included a percentage calculated to cover the cost of revival and other unknown contingencies that could crop up over time."

"So, what did it cost my estate to *suspend* me?" said Ted.

"Oh, about $120,000 at the time," said Cromwell, "which was a bargain, given that it costs $8.5 million today."

"A bargain," said Ted.

"So, even though the corporation established an acceptable working capital base at a significant multiple beyond the projected suspension care and revival costs, it was only minimally acceptable," said Cromwell.

"Speak English and give it to me straight," said Ted.

"Yes, of course," said Cromwell. "The bottom line is, due to the high cost of your reanimation—the coma care, the post-revival therapy, etc.—we cannot continue to support your staying here at CryoCorp. The funds from your estate are gone. The money has run out. The good news is you are fit to leave."

"Trust me, as much as I have come to appreciate your lovely little hotel here, I want to leave as fast as I can. But what am I to do for money?"

"Well," said Cromwell, "the board has seen fit to give you six months of living expenses. The stipend is based on a cost of living standard carefully calculated from current economic indices, of course."

"Of course."

"Well, I'm glad you understand," said Cromwell.

"Isn't that just dandy?" said Ted. "So, where am I gonna live?"

"I'll let Dr. Miles tell you the good news on that front, Ted," said Cromwell. He had the smile again.

"Ted, we have done some research and, apparently the Williams Family Foundation, established after your death, owns a piece of real estate that houses university fellows in the biosciences from the Massachusetts Institute of Technology," she said. "The document that established the program contains a provision stipulating that any Williams descendant can live there."

"And how will you establish that I am a descendant without tipping off the—what are they, trustees?—and the public as to who I am?"

"I've been doing some research," said Dr. Miles, "Although we thought everyone was dead, I found a distant cousin of yours who can step up. He will allow you to move in clandestinely in his place with a little incentive: the CryoCorp scholarship at MIT for his child. He doesn't know who you are."

"And this house is where?" said Ted.

"It's a townhouse in Boston."

"You're jokin'?"

"No," she said.

"And for spending money, what will I do after the gracious stipend from CryoCorp is gone?"

"I will help you find a job," said Dr. Miles.

"Well, gentlemen and ladies, it's nice to know that you've got this entire circus all figured out," said Ted. *'Bring 'em back to life and show 'em the door with lunch in a brown paper bag.'* Wouldn't you say so, Bernie?"

"Well, Ted, I—"

"No need to explain any more," said Ted. "Now if you folks would excuse me, I'm going back to my room to pack."

He stood up to leave the boardroom, and Dr. Miles hurriedly followed after him.

". . . If only I had a bag to pack or anything to put in it," he muttered under his breath.

Watching him from the door, Cromwell turned back to another board member.

"This is going just as planned," he said. "This will work to our advantage, just as I said it would."

~ ~ ~

At Ted's room, Dr. Miles hurried in after him and shut the door. She was out of breath. He was grimacing.

"Gee, that went well," she said.

"Lizzy, this is exactly what I expected. Those big shot bastards don't give a damn about me. All they care about is the bottom line."

"Well, that's not entirely true. Give them some credit; they've pledged to keep your situation a secret for as long as possible to give you more time to adjust."

"Look, I want to get out of here as much as anybody, but I am concerned about what's going to happen to me after the money runs out. In my entire life—the last one that is—I was always able to support myself, even on a military salary."

"Ted, I meant what I said about helping you find employment. You rushed out of the room before I could tell you the rest."

"Which is?"

"I'm moving to Boston with you. Not to live with you; you'll have your own place. The company has a small operation in Cambridge, across the river from Boston. Bernard didn't want me to go but, unfortunately for him, I'm the only cryonicist in the world right now who has successfully reanimated a patient. He needs me. I'll go back east and help to expand the business—without divulging your secret. My contacts at Harvard Medical School should be able help me recruit new patients; that was the deciding factor for Bernard."

"I don't want you to do this for me," he said.

"It's not for you—or *just* for you. I grew up in Boston, the later years. I went to medical school there; I want to go home. I must warn you, however, that I think Bernard is up to something he's not telling me. I've been getting an odd vibe from his close confidants on the board—all the more reason for me to be close to you in Boston."

"I didn't know you were from Boston. And what about Johnnie?"

"Well, I want him to experience that part of the country, too. Growing up here you might think the whole world is a desert. Besides, maybe you can give him some more batting tips."

"Yeah, I don't suppose he's gonna get that from you."

"Anyway, you and I leave in two weeks," she said. "I'm going with you to get you settled. Cecelia will take care of Johnnie while I'm away. I'll come back; then we'll all move to Boston in a few weeks."

"Have you told him yet?" Ted said.

"No, not yet."

"Well, bring the kid in so that I can talk to him about it with you, too. Do you think he'll be upset?"

"He'll be leaving some friends behind, but he makes friends easily, and we have some relatives there that he already knows. Plus, I'm bringing part of my team with me, including Emily. So he'll have Billy to play with."

"Lots of changes," said Ted.

"Yes, but sometimes change is good."

Sixteen

Ted's departure day began with his reading the news on an eReader to which he was adjusting. He was astounded that there was very little international news.

"Are there no conflicts in the world?" he asked Dr. Miles.

"Well, a few, but not many," said Elizabeth. "Generally, there has been a good deal of peace because so many nations have been consumed with and bonding over the fight against global warming and so much flooding. The environmental problems have required that people work together globally to save the planet, minimizing local and regional conflicts."

"What about the Middle East?" said Ted.

"The oil demand disappeared, which was good for us, but that made the region even more fractious. The Arab and Muslim uneasiness with Israel has continued. We still have terrorist attacks, often emanating from the region, but security and police work, particularly the use of technology, have improved and helped to mitigate the problem."

Emily and a couple of other nurses, along with Jed and Randall, came by to wish Ted well. He didn't want a fuss made over him, but he was almost gracious about it. When they left, Marshall came into the room, and Ted's face brightened.

"Hey, Bush, ole buddy, good to see ya," said Ted.

"I wouldn't miss the chance to say goodbye to an old leatherneck fisherman," said Marshall.

"Speaking of which," said Ted, "you've got to promise me you'll come east and I'll show you my old salmon river in New Brunswick."

"It's a deal. Say, Ted, before you go. I have to ask you, why do you call me Bush?"

"'Cause you're a bush leaguer. Just a term of endearment, my friend. A term of endearment."

"Well, goodbye, good buddy," said Marshall. "I'm gonna miss ya."

"Oh, knock it off. I'll see you soon," said Ted.

They gave each other that manly hug, more back slapping than actual hugging. The eyes of Dr. Miles were misty.

Cecelia came to the door with Johnnie. He came running in and jumped into Ted's arms.

"Whoa there, tiger, we'll see each other again soon."

"Goodbye Mr. Ted," said Cecelia. "You have a good trip."

"Thanks, Cecelia. Now Johnnie," said Ted, "remember what we talked about. When we get to Boston I'm takin' you to a game at Fenway and we're gonna work some more on that swing of yours."

"Cool," said Johnnie.

"So are you ready?" Dr. Miles said to Ted.

"Ready as I'll ever be."

Marshall and Ted shook hands one more time. Ted grabbed a small gym bag that contained all of his possessions.

"Looks like we'll have to go shopping when we get to Boston," said Dr. Miles.

The comment went unanswered. They headed downstairs and out the front door of CryoCorp.

"It just occurred to me," said Dr. Miles, "Ted, you've resided in this building for 90 years."

"Being frozen like a fish stick, I wouldn't exactly call that *residing*," said Ted. "C'mon, let's go."

They hopped in a CryoCorp car in which Dr. Miles had already placed her luggage. On the way to the airport, they were largely silent. The driver did not know who Ted was, and Dr. Miles had warned Ted about it.

As they passed the entrance to the airport, Ted noticed two signs. One said "SkyHarbor, next left," and the other "SpaceHarbor, next right."

The driver took a hard right and Ted, knowing that he was not free to ask too many questions, bit his tongue. After passing through a security gate, the car was given clearance to head out onto the tarmac. It stopped next to a strange plane with small wings and what looked like enormous fuel tanks. The driver placed the bags on the tarmac and sped away.

"Now that we're alone," said Ted, "what is this thing?"

"It's the CryoCorp private rocket plane," said Dr. Miles. "The company wanted you to head back east in style."

"Rocket plane?"

Seventeen

On the SpaceHarbor tarmac, Ted stared up at the rocket plane in awe.

"The pilot knows who you are, Ted," said Elizabeth. "He's a full-time employee of the company and the brother of one of our board members. He's excited about meeting you."

They walked up the mobile aircraft steps as the ground crew hustled to stow their luggage. At the top of the stairs a flight attendant and the pilot greeted them.

"Ted, this is Captain Rogers," said Dr. Miles. Ted shook hands.

"Let me guess, Buck is the first name," said Ted.

The pilot laughed. "No, it's Mike, Mike Rogers."

Rogers had removed his jacket and wore what looked like a very familiar pilot's uniform underneath.

"Well, good to meet you, Mike Rogers," said Ted. "Can you show me around?"

Ted looked to the right. The cabin looked like what he imagined a plush, private plane would look like. Dr. Miles and the flight attendant, Julie, a tall, svelte woman with bobbed brunette hair, headed toward the rear of the plane. Julie wore a pair of wings on a jacket that looked like the boardroom attire. But this suit was all red. Ted and Rogers headed to the cockpit.

"You being an ol' jet jockey, I thought you would appreciate this," said Rogers. "What did you fly, Ted?"

"I was an instructor in Corsairs in WWII. In Korea I moved up to the first jets, flew F-9s in combat," said Ted. "That was a thrill, 'cept I damn near bought the farm on a couple of missions."

"Wow, I've seen photos of those old beasts, tough to control, I guess?"

"Not so bad," said Ted, "until the day I took ground fire, lost all of my hydraulics and had to come in on the belly."

"Well, you've got to tell me more about that," said Rogers.

Another pilot moved into the cockpit area. "This is my right seat," said Rogers, "meet Bill Kreamer."

They shook hands. Julie came up and said they were all set in the cabin.

"Ted, how would you like to ride in our jump seat here up front?" said Rogers.

"Boy, that would be great."

Ted sat in a seat immediately behind Kreamer, perpendicular to the pilots, but he was able to see all that they were doing. Rogers and Kreamer completed their preflight checklist.

"Geez, this is a rocket? We're goin' into space?" said Ted

"Well, just barely, for your benefit," said Rogers. "We take off and land like an ordinary airplane. We've got an air turbo ramjet plus two rocket engines. At about 10,000 feet we'll fire the rockets and get nearly vertical, pulling three and a half Gs. Nothing you can't handle. We'll accelerate to nearly Mach 4 and then hit our apogee at about 350,000 feet—over 100,000 kilometers above the earth, just into the edge of space. We're still suborbital though, about 63 miles up."

"What do you use for fuel?" said Ted.

"The engines burn a mixture of isopropyl alcohol and liquid oxygen and then alternate with liquid vessileum. After we hit our apogee, mostly we glide in, but I can use the air turbo ramjet if we need it."

"How long does it take?" said Ted.

"We'll be in Massachusetts in about 45 minutes."

"Holy shit."

Ted let it sink in and then said, "I knew guys in the big war that saw the Germans fly rocket planes. They said they were death traps."

"Well, we've come a long way since then. It's safe, though not very economical," said Rogers.

"You mean not commercial?"

The engine noise was louder now, and Rogers raised his voice as Kreamer taxied out to the runway.

"Yes, precisely. I have a job because of the good graces of CryoCorp. The only rocket planes in the sky today are private, and government passenger transportation. We just haven't figured out a way to make it commercially viable for the public. There were some attempts, but it's too expensive to operate on a commercial level."

"I guess so," said Ted. "We're travelling 63 miles up to move less than 3,000 miles across the country."

"Well, we're doing it a little differently today to give you a bit of a thrill," said Rogers.

"So I am about to become one of the privileged few."

"Yes, you are," said Rogers.

The captain instructed everyone to secure their oxygen masks and reminded them about seatbelts.

Rogers said into his radio, "This is November-three-four-seven-five, are we cleared for take off?"

Ted was transfixed by the activity in the cockpit but knew enough not to disturb the pilots.

The tower acknowledged, "Roger that, November-three-four-seven-five, you are cleared for take off on runway 27 Right. Have a nice flight, CryoCorp."

Captain Rogers made a turn, and the great expanse of empty runway unfolded ahead of the rocket plane. "We're cleared for takeoff," he told the passengers and crew. The rocket plane careened down the runway at normal jet speed and roared into the air.

"We'll be climbing gradually," he said to Ted, "until we're well out of the valley, and then we'll ignite the rockets."

At 11,000 feet he did just that. The rocket plane pulled up nearly vertical. Ted was amazed at how relatively quiet it seemed. *We're outrunning our ability to hear our own aircraft*, he thought.

The G forces were significant but not entirely uncomfortable—at least for Ted. He pulled four or five Gs in his combat jet when making hard turns. And that was in the days before fully pressurized flight suits. Dr. Miles was another story. She had always been a white-knuckle flyer and this was no exception. She held onto the arms of her seat with a death grip.

"Prepare for a little weightlessness," announced Rogers.

In what seemed as though it was no time at all, the rocket plane reached its apogee. As if hurling over the top of an imaginary mountain peak, Rogers flipped the jet and pointed the nose of the plane downward.

The weightlessness lasted just a short time. A pen floated out of Ted's shirt pocket to his delight. The fun was way too short. Dr. Miles would not have described the flight as fun under any circumstance.

They glided into Worcester International Airport and landed at 45 minutes right on the button. Kreamer deployed a parachute, and the rocket plane decelerated.

"Boy, I tell ya, that was more fun than hookin' a tarpon," said Ted.

"Glad you liked it," said Rogers. "Welcome back to Massachusetts."

Eighteen

D r. Miles and Ted piled into another car and their driver headed east. Worcester was nothing like Ted had remembered it. It was, however, green, and a refreshing counterpoint to the desert. The air was a comfortable 85 degrees, but warm thought Ted, for early spring.

"Hey, how come we didn't fly directly into Boston?" said Ted.

Dr. Miles pressed the button to close the window and partition them off from the driver.

"This is the closest major airport to Boston now," she said.

"What do you mean? What happened to Logan?"

"It's gone, underwater," she said.

"That too?" he said.

"As you know, global warming has taken a toll on many coastal cities. The flooding happened quite fast. Much faster than many scientists had predicted. Eustasy, or the rise in sea level, was the direct result of changes in the world's climate. Basically, it was ice melt that caused major problems."

"You mean sea ice melted and caused flooding?"

"Yes, but the sea ice was not really the problem. Think of a glass full of ice water: When the ice melts, the water stays at the same level. The real problem was the melting of land-based ice and snow in both of the Polar

Regions. That water drained into the earth's oceans and caused major flooding worldwide; quite accurately, a sea change.

"So tell me more about what happened to Boston."

"Well, it's mostly below sea level. The hills are still there—Beacon Hill, Dorchester Heights, Charlestown, but they are islands now. The rest is a lot like Venice. In fact, it was amazing how the city responded to the rising tide, or didn't respond at first. The flooding was devastating in every way, and for a long period bureaucratic infighting and bungling prevented any kind of action. When the city finally responded, it was already mostly flooded after several large storms. It imported millions of tons of impermeable marble from newly discovered quarries across the Adriatic near where the old Venice foundations came from—Trieste and Croatia are the locations, I believe. Anyway, with government grants, the buildings that could be saved in Boston were jacked up and supported with the new marble foundations—Venice was saved in the same way. In Boston, many of the new foundations were laid on top of submersed wooden pilings."

"I think I remember—weren't a lot of the buildings in the Back Bay already on pilings?" said Ted.

"Yes. As you know, the area was once a tidal basin that was filled in— hence the name Back Bay. Today the Back Bay streets are canals with water traffic."

"I can't believe it."

"It's all true," she said.

"I can understand fixing brownstones and brick buildings, but what happened to the skyscrapers?" said Ted.

"Some were torn down. Others were retrofitted and waterproofed, giving up the first floors to the water. It turns out that retrofitting so many buildings eventually dragged the economy out of the mud, and the city is prospering again."

The car zipped along the highway. Ted stared out his window. "What about other cities?" he said.

"Well, New York took an entirely different approach. After several large storms killed thousands, it built sea gates and, since Manhattan was already an island, it built high levees and sea walls. Manhattan and the other boroughs are now walled in way below sea level. A lot like New Orleans used to be."

"And New Orleans?"

"It's gone, I'm afraid."

"What about San Diego?"

"The Navy base is bigger than ever; the bay extends all the way up to the mountains in the east. A lot of land was lost."

"Florida?"

"Just a smattering of islands," she said.

There was so much to comprehend. Ted's mind was racing.

"So, how did they save Fenway Park, or Fenway Island—I can't get used to that."

"Basically, the place was waterproofed, jacked up with the special marble, and made into a kind of fortress with a moat around it."

"Geezus."

"Oh, and one other thing: I'm sorry to have to tell you this, but the tunnel they named after you is long gone, like the airport it led to," she said. "However, the ferry terminal we're headed to has been named in your honor."

He just shook his head.

"I know it's hard to contemplate but, actually Ted, you may just find that you like Boston now. It's quite pretty in a Venetian sort of way."

The car had traveled about 15 miles since leaving Worcester when Dr. Miles said, "We're almost in Hopkinton where we'll catch a ferry at the head of the Charles River and travel into Boston on the boat. Please wear sunglasses. Most people wouldn't recognize you because they're not expecting you. But this is Boston; old photos of you are everywhere. And so I'm afraid sunglasses should become a fixture. I've brought you a new pair."

She handed the sunglasses to Ted.

"They're aviators—you've worn them before I'm sure," she said. "Classic. Never out of style."

"Yeah, I'm worried about being stylish," he said, with obvious sarcasm. "Hopkinton is navigable?"

"Yes. Back in your day the Charles was just a trickle there. Now it's a mighty river."

"Didn't the Boston Marathon begin there?"

"Yes," she said, "but now it's an annual boat race."

Nineteen

At the Ted Williams Ferry Terminal, their high-speed hovercraft, carrying 500 passengers, departed for Boston. It covered the 30 or so miles from Hopkinton, past the Newton and Brookline islands, and into Boston in the astonishing, sprint-like time of 30 minutes.

Remembering his days living in South Florida, Ted said, "Faster than a Florida fan boat."

Approaching the city from the west was surreal. Boston Harbor was now a four-sided affair. At a distance the city was more striking than ever: a huge metropolitan archipelago, with gleaming, water-borne towers rising Oz-like out of the sea, the modern incarnation of the lost city of Atlantis. Ted thought *Venice never looked like this.* Close in, one could recognize the red patina of so many brick buildings. The water traffic was death defying and unremitting, wave upon wave of marine activity.

Ted and Dr. Miles exited the ferry at the Kenmore Marine Station, a granite Italianate terminal on stilts, attached to a sea of floating docks filled with commuters. Ted was astonished by all of the watercraft. There were ferries, tugboats, barges, water taxis, and modern amphibious duck boats that looked like the ones he recognized from his war years. They were moving people by the busload, or was it *duckload*, he wondered? Adding to the traffic, personal watercraft were darting in and out everywhere. The scene was utter madness. He even spotted a couple of gondolas.

Then, a spark of recognition: The familiar layout of Kenmore Square— sans streets. The confluence of Beacon Street and Commonwealth and Brookline avenues was now underwater. The sea was lapping up against the buildings of Kenmore. Ted scanned the foundations and strained to see the Istrian marble that made it all work.

Looking skyward, he saw a sign, literally—a sign. It was familiar yet very different. On top of one of Kenmore's buildings an enormous neon sign featuring a giant red triangle was shining brightly even in the midday sun. The triangle was made of what looked like hypodermic needles. At the bottom was the word GETGO. He remembered Marshall's description of the company as a producer of the infamous steroid cocktail that all of the baseball players were using.

The sight of it all, combined with his memories, was bittersweet. Ted longed for the city of his past but marveled at the spectacle he now witnessed. As he had done so many times since his reanimation, he choked back his emotions. He was not an emotional guy he told himself over and over again.

He snapped out of it after surveying the scene in more detail. Kenmore was as commercial as ever with souvenir shops, floating pushcart vendors, and a float-thru McDonald's. Pizza palaces dominated the waterscape. Several food vendors advertised seaweed.

He and Dr. Miles hurried across a dock to a waiting water taxi. Ted turned to the driver and said, "Take us to Fenway." Dodging other vessels, the driver hit the throttle of the small, center-console boat and began cruising up the Brookline Canal next to the Bridge of Sighs that connected the Kenmore Marine Station and Fenway for pedestrians traversing the MassCanal. They stopped at a red waterlight. On the other side they could see the great green and brick edifice of Fenway.

The place, to most Bostonians, remained a shrine. It was entirely surrounded by a dock. To the left down the Lansdowne Canal, rising out of the water like the Pharos in the ancient city of Alexandria, was the ever-present and eternal landmark wall known as the Green Monster. Only now the "land" in *land*mark took on more meaning.

"Geezus," said Ted. "The joint was always old and moldy, but now it's got barnacles on it."

He soaked it all in as the boat chugged along slowly.

"How do people get here?" said Ted. "They can't all come by boat."

"I think they have an underground train station that lets them up into the island—look, there's a sign for it," said Dr. Miles.

"You mean you're not sure?" said Ted.

"Well, ah, I've never actually been in Fenway," she said sheepishly.

"You grew up here and you never went to a game?"

"Well, I didn't move here from England until I was 12. And I had other things I was interested in, like books and medicine. Are you the one to lecture me on single-minded pursuits?" she said.

"That's a helluva good point, doctor."

"Now, if you ask me about cricket . . . ," she said.

"Cricket," Ted said dismissively, in the way that people do when they exhale and speak at the same time.

The boat continued up the Brookline Canal and turned left onto the Yawkey Waterway. Ted made note of the white marble foundation now supporting the brick walls of Fenway and thought it looked strange, especially in contrast with the red brick. But it was unmistakably Fenway. And unmistakably an island.

They made another left and entered the Van Ness Canal on the south side of Fenway. Where the canal met the Ipswich Waterway. There, near the dock, was Ted in bronze with "The Teammates." He didn't know this existed. He nodded at the statues to get the attention of Dr. Miles and they remained silent behind the driver. Larger than life, the bronze figures rose out of the water.

"I've seen all I want to see," said Ted, and Dr. Miles instructed the driver to take them into the Back Bay.

~ ~ ~

Back Bay and Beacon Hill had always been where the city's elite lived, and that was still the case. The one big difference now: Back Bay was water-filled, with the magnificent brick, brownstone and marble homes all facing their own canals.

The water taxi floated into the neighborhood from the west and cruised down the Grand Commonwealth Canal past the old red-roof-tiled Somerset Hotel, now private residences. Out of earshot from the driver Ted whispered, "I used to live there, during the season. Walked to Fenway from there every day."

Originally modeled after the Champs Elysées, the Grand Commonwealth Canal was still a main thoroughfare and passage into the city, but it offered no trees; only a great assortment of boats. Venice meets Paris. In fact, the wide canal and glimmering water made the stately homes somehow more captivating.

The taxi turned left at the intersection of the Exeter Canal and then right onto the Marlborough Canal. The new home Elizabeth had found for Ted was on the upper end of Marlborough, not far from land that rose out of the water on what was once the hill on Boston Common, now forming the leading edge of Beacon Hill Island.

The water in this end of Back Bay was filled almost exclusively with gondolas and a few water taxis moving people to and from their homes. At the upper end of Marlborough Dr. Miles said, "This is it," and the water taxi pulled underneath a boat porch.

The neighborhood was replete with 19th century townhouses that were either brownstones or in the academic brick style. Most featured bow fronts. Every other house had a boat porch or porte-bateau that was added later— utilitarian and architecturally consistent.

Ted's home was magnificent. Under the grand entryway designed to cover visitors disembarking from watercraft, marble steps rose out of the water. The brick façade was simple yet elegant, like so many of the homes preserved in the Back Bay. The red brick was offset with elegant cornices and bay windows on every floor.

"Welcome home," said Dr. Miles, as she and Ted entered the double doors of the stately, fully furnished, three-floored building.

"Seems too fancy for the likes of me, but I suppose it'll do for a while until I get my bearings," said Ted.

"Take a look around, choose any bedroom—there are a lot of them," said Dr. Miles. "I think you'll like the media room. I'm going to my hotel, but I'll send a boat for you in two hours and we'll go get a bite to eat."

She hailed another water taxi and left, leaving Ted to wonder how the hell he went from the desert to waterworld in one fell swoop.

Twenty

Ted rambled through the house exploring. He chose a bedroom on the second floor in the front of the house that had a nice view of the canal. He spied another room on the top floor facing south with good light coming from the windows and a skylight. *Good place for tying flies*, he thought.

There was also a fully equipped gym with microcomputer-driven, strength-training bands coming out of a wall. Another virtual reality treadmill was up there. There was also a strange device that looked like a chrome revolving door with pads to push, to make it go around—for resistance leg training, Ted surmised.

The kitchen was filled with appliances he didn't recognize. No matter, he wouldn't spend much time there. Also on the first floor were a billiards room with a big table that he thought was nice, and the media room that Dr. Miles had mentioned. There was no basement, only water.

The media room was dark. The centerpiece was a giant screen centered on one wall with eight cushy chairs facing it. In the center of the room was a small table with what looked like a controller or a remote with a touch screen. It was labeled compuTV. Ted picked it up and it sprang to life, lighting up.

He nearly dropped it when a disembodied, digital voice said, "What is your name? What would you like to watch?"

He put the remote down, but the voice didn't go away, emanating from somewhere up near the screen.

"What is your name?"

Ted didn't answer.

"What is your name?"

Finally, out of frustration, he said, "Mr. Big Wood."

"Hello, Mr. Big Wood. What would you like to watch?" said the voice in cloying digital monotone.

"How about naked women with cocker spaniels?" said Ted.

"Searching," said the voice.

After a moment it returned. "Sorry, I cannot find programs about naked women with cocker spaniels. Please make another selection."

"What's *your* name?" said Ted.

"VR," said the voice.

"VR?" said Ted. "What's that stand for?"

"Voice Recognition," said VR.

Unnerved, Ted said, "Well VR, you got any baseball, maybe old-time games?"

"Searching," said VR.

In about 30 seconds hundred of choices came up on the big screen and VR said, "Please make a selection. Talk to me or use the remote."

"This might not be so bad," said Ted.

"I'm sorry, I did not get that," said VR.

"Oh shit," said Ted.

"Is 'Oh, shit' a baseball game?" said VR.

Ted said, "Geezus," picked up the remote and hit the off button.

"Goodbye, Mr. Big Wood," said the voice.

A short time later Ted heard a knock on his door. When he answered, a man said, "Are you Ted? I'm here to take you to the Hotel Dongkou."

"The Hotel Donkey?" said Ted.

"No, the Dongkou International. It's 'round the corner and named after a place in China, but whada I know?"

As they walked out the front door the man said, "Name's Danny. This is my gondola."

The word gondola sounded like 'gon-doe-ler.' They shook hands and Ted said, "Good to meet ya."

As the boat moved around the corner Ted could see that the Grand Commonwealth Canal now emptied into a bay that was once the Boston Public Garden. *A lot of nice greenery was lost*, he said to himself. Straining on his gondolier's pole, Danny maneuvered the boat toward the front of the hotel at the end of the Commonwealth Canal.

"Geezus, this hotel, it's the old Ritz," said Ted.

"You, my friend, are a good historian," said Danny. "Not many people know that."

Ted remembered that Mr. Yawkey—the former owner of the team and his boss when he played for the Red Sox—used to live here.

He realized he had nothing with which to pay Danny.

"Not a problem," said Danny. "It's all been taken care of."

Ted entered the hotel and made his way to the café where Dr. Miles was already seated at a table with a view of the Newbury Canal.

"Hello, Ted, did you get settled in okay? I forgot to tell you that the fridge was fully stocked and there is tinned food in the cupboards."

"Yeah, I saw that, thanks."

The waiter came over, took their order and left. Ted ordered a steak and Elizabeth, a salad.

"So what do you think of all this, Boston that is?"

"Well, I was looking forward to being able to take long walks. It looks like that's out of the question."

"I suggest you take a water taxi and go over to Beacon Hill. You can almost see it from your place it's so close. When you get off there, you can walk up and down the neighborhood to your heart's content."

"I've got a question for you," said Ted. "Is there any good fishing around here? My guess is the water's gotten too warm."

"I'm sorry, I wouldn't know, Ted. Warmer water would impact fish populations, wouldn't it?"

"Yes, it would," he said. "Geezus, it's bad enough I'm a fish out of water, but I'm also in a world with water out of fish."

"Well, perhaps not. The impact of global warming was different in each area."

"I'm wondering about the current salmon population, although there never were any close to here. Only up north in Maine and in New Brunswick where I used to have a fishin' lodge. The fish need colder water."

The waiter came with their dishes and Elizabeth said, "Bon appétit."

"You see," said Ted, "a salmon begins life in freshwater with the hatching of the egg. The salmon then changes in size and grows from fry to parr to smolt. After a few years the seaward migration of the smolt begins. The fish is anadromous, moving from freshwater to saltwater as hormonal changes take place. Still, there are many phenomena in the physiology of the salmon not well understood, like osmoregulation—adjusting the osmotic concentration of solutes in body fluids to environmental conditions. As the fish moves from freshwater to seawater it must adapt to the salinity transfer. Of course, later on, when the salmon spawn and return to freshwater from the ocean, the reverse occurs. The upper end of the thermal range for coldwater fish like salmon would be about 65 degrees Fahrenheit—unless the fish have somehow adapted."

Elizabeth, fork in midrange, sat with her mouth open staring at Ted. She shook her head vigorously to snap out of it.

"*Now,* who is the clever one?" she said.

"Well, my good doctor, there are four things I know really well: hitting, flying, and fishing."

"That's only three," she said.

"I can't tell you what the fourth one is in polite company," he said with a wry smile.

He hoped his flirting would produce a response but there didn't seem to be any.

"Oh," she said flatly.

After a pause, Elizabeth added, "I have something else to give you," and handed him a phone. "This will allow you to pay for anything you need."

"A phone? How do I pay with a phone?" said Ted.

"Actually, it works like a credit card. You just push this button and wave it to pay for something," she said. "Cash, as you knew it doesn't exist anymore. We're a cashless society."

"Guess I shouldn't go looking for coins in the cushions back at the house," said Ted. Then he noticed the name on the phone: Ted Wilson.

"Hell, you coulda consulted me about the name."

"Well it's close," she said. "Easy enough to remember but not so close as to draw attention, I think."

After the meal they grabbed a water taxi and floated down Newbury to go shopping. Hard as it was, they found the plaid shirts and khaki pants that Ted was looking for, plus some warm weather golf shirts.

Ted said he'd like to go browse through a bookstore and they parted ways. Ignoring the eReader back at the house, he bought several old-fashioned books on history, fishing and global warming before he retired to the serene shores of what used to be Marlborough Street.

Twenty-one

Dr. Miles returned to Arizona to tie up loose ends as Ted settled into his new life in Boston. He took those long walks up and down Beacon Hill and for the first time, literally and figuratively, began to feel comfortable in his own skin.

The independence was nice, but he also longed to talk to people. He made friends with Bev, the mail carrier. Danny the gondolier stopped by frequently, and Ted called him often to take him to Beacon Hill. Each morning Ted went over to Copley Square where he talked to the guy who ran the newspaper stand—at least that's what Ted called it. In fact, there were no newspapers, and the locals called it the media stand. There were racks filled with magazine covers but no magazines. What looked like magazines were actually ads for downloads. Ted decided it was a bad idea to ask him how he made money.

Dry and resplendent, Copley Square was, more than ever, the central landmark and gathering place in a city surrounded by water. The comparison to St. Mark's Square in Venice was inescapable. The grand, Romanesque Trinity Church occupied the position of St. Mark's Basilica. To the right of Trinity Church rose the ancient, reflective Hancock Tower in nearly the identical position as the Piazza San Marco's exquisite Campanile Bell Tower. All the way across the square, directly opposite Trinity, the red-roofed Boston

Public Library took the place of the Napoleonic Wing of the Procuratie. It was no small irony that most of the lobby and other interior architectural details of the BPL were in fact Venetian by design.

Such details were lost on Ted, although he became a frequent visitor to the library and admired its comfortable environs and helpful staff. It was there that he learned about modern fish populations and that his beloved Miramichi River salmon still existed in New Brunswick, Canada, albeit, at the upper range of their water-temperature tolerance.

At home, after many tries, he finally was able to get VR to work to his satisfaction. He was particularly unnerved, however, by the hologram news and sports on the compuTV. Whenever what used to be known as a talking head spoke up, the person popped out of the screen and was standing in the room in a full-body hologram display, giving new meaning to the reporter's phrase "stand up."

"The first time it happened," he told Dr. Miles, "it damned near scared the shit out of me."

He also taught himself to use the Internet. Online, he ordered bamboo and saltwater fly rods and a voluminous amount of material and equipment to tie flies. In the room upstairs with the good light, he set up his fly-tying operation. In short order, the mail boat delivered on a daily basis all manner of gear and fly-making supplies intended to fool a fish into hitting ingeniously disguised hooks. In addition to rods, reels, line and leaders, the deliveries included a rotary vice; a bright light and magnifier; a light head magnifier; wet, dry fly and nymph hooks; thread; beads and coneheads; and feathers, hackles and fur, including speckled hen backs, goose biots, quarter saddles, calf tails, elk hair, crosscut rabbit fur, and buck tails. A tool kit included hackle clamps, a dubbing needle, hackle pliers, twister and scissors.

Over days and days of such deliveries, with Ted opening each package in excitement at the door, Bev, the mail lady, took to calling Ted the evil scientist. It was more or less confirmed when he appeared at the door wearing a lighted wrap-around magnifier over his eyes after tying flies.

"So whaddya creatin' in there, freakin' FrankenBambi?" she said. "I don't know if I should report ya to Customs, Fish & Game or the ASPCA."

~ ~ ~

In Arizona Dr. Miles and Johnnie were preparing for their big move east. She had purchased a condo while in Boston and was trying to decide how much stuff they could take and fit into the new place. Johnnie was anxious about the move, but it helped that Cecelia, a widow with grown kids, would move with them.

Dr. Miles was also focused on her CryoCorp duties. The company had a small information and induction center in Cambridge, but her new job would entail expanding it to a full-scale containment facility with cryopreserved patients. On top of everything else, she was worried about Ted and still concerned about what he wanted to do to support himself.

She talked to Ted almost daily on the phone.

"Nice of you to call and not forget about little ol' me," said Ted.

"Ted," she said, "I'm coming to Boston in a few days to get the condo in shape for Johnnie and Cecelia, and I'll return to get them and supervise the move a week or two later."

"Sounds like you got your hands full," said Ted.

"Yes, indeed," she said. "You don't know the half of it. Are you feeling okay, Ted?"

"I'm fine," he said. And trying to change the subject: "Wait 'til you see what I've done with the place."

"Well, you sound great. So, I'll see you soon then. Bye."

Ted hung up, never telling Dr. Miles just how much he missed her and how much he was looking forward to seeing Johnnie again.

Twenty-two

Elizabeth arrived on Ted's canal in a water taxi. Several very proper Boston ladies were cruising by in their personal watercraft driven by their personal boatmen. The boats were discreetly motorized, with billowing canopies and banana shapes, looking rather like ancient Egyptian vessels, perhaps something Cleopatra or King Cheops would have used, a papyriform boat, but on a smaller scale and in teakwood.

In addition to their gaudy boats, the ladies had one other thing in common: They were all staring at Ted Williams. Ted had obviously walked out of his second floor window and was fly-fishing with his saltwater fly rod atop of the boat porch of his stately townhome. The women were aghast.

"Ahoy there, landlubber," shouted Elizabeth from the taxi.

Ted did not immediately answer. He continued making a series of fine arcs with his fly rod. Caught in the light of the sun, Elizabeth admired the elegant and precise movement of the line, like a metronome, but decidedly more graceful in the hands of a skilled artist.

"Danny the gondolier says there are some striped bass in here," said Ted, attired in his plaid fishing shirt.

"I see," said Elizabeth from her boat. "Well, there are an awful lot of very elegant Boston ladies tsk-tsking you for fishing in their refined neighborhood on top of the porte-bateau."

"The what?" said Ted. "Speak English, will ya?"

"Porte-bateau. It's French. It means the boat door or boat porch."

"Well, pardon *my* French, but I don't give a shit."

"Do you mind if I come in?" she asked.

Ted climbed back in the window and came downstairs. He greeted Elizabeth with a big hug.

"It's nice to see you again, Ted."

"Well, I'm damn glad to see you too, Lizzy," said Ted. "A fella could get lonely in a big place like this with no visitors."

She was surprised by his candor. After a tour of the fly-tying operation and over several cups of coffee, they got caught up on recent history. Dr. Miles also told him that she wanted him to come over to Cambridge in a few days for a complete physical. Before he could reply, there was a ring of the doorbell.

Elizabeth looked at her watch. "Oh, I almost forgot, that would be Amanda."

"Amanda? Who's Amanda?" said Ted.

"She's an old friend. She lives around the corner on Beacon. I thought you might become friends. She doesn't know about you," said Elizabeth, as they both headed to the door. Ted knew what she meant.

He opened the door and the two women greeted each other with squeally voices and big hugs.

"Ted, this is one of my oldest friends, meet Amanda LeMond," said Elizabeth. "Amanda, this is my friend Ted, ah, Wilson."

Amanda and Ted locked eyes. To say they shared a moment would be an understatement. After a long look that ended in smiles, the tension ended when Ted stammered, "Hello, nice to meet you. Come in."

A former model, Amanda was 36 years old, six feet tall, blond, blue-eyed, and what Ted would characterize as statuesque.

They moved to the kitchen. Ted poured a cup of coffee for Amanda and refilled the other two.

"So, how do you two know each other?" said Ted.

"Amanda and I are the oldest of friends," said Elizabeth, "ever since I moved to America. When I went off to university, we took different paths. I have missed her terribly and now I'm looking forward to spending more time with her. Right, Amanda?"

"Oh, it's going to be great," said Amanda. "Ted, I understand you knew Elizabeth in Arizona?"

"Yes, that's right. She's known me for a long time—not as long as you, though."

"And now you've moved to Boston too," said Amanda. "What did you do in Arizona?"

"Ah, I was in freezers," said Ted.

"Oh, my father was in the appliance business!"

"And what do you do?" said Ted.

"I run a boutique on Newbury," said Amanda. "It's called 'Amanda.'"

"What goes on in a ladies' *boutique?*" said Ted. He pronounced the word parts and syllables hard—"boo-teak."

"All kinds of strange and mysterious things," she said. "We even have a secret handshake, only performed after an exquisite manicure, of course."

"Yes, I can see that," said Ted.

"Amanda is a talented businesswoman," said Elizabeth. "She is very modest. What she has not mentioned is that she has started her own, very successful clothing line with accessories."

"Ted, this is a great place you have here," said Amanda. "Can you show me around?"

"Sure," said Ted. They proceeded upstairs and started at the top with the fly-tying room. After moving through the big house, they were down again on the first floor. Ted walked Amanda and Elizabeth into the media room.

"So, this must be where you spend a lot of time," said Amanda.

"Well, I'm still getting used to the new system," said Ted. "It's been . . ."

He was interrupted by VR.

"Hello, Mr. Big Wood. Would you like me to search again for naked ladies with cocker spaniels?"

The women looked at each other; one bit her lower lip, the other the knuckles on her perfectly manicured index finger; they both giggled under their breath. Ted huffed a "goddamn it," and pounded his fist on the controller. The machine went silent.

"Still working out the kinks—I mean, trying to get the thing to work right," he said.

"Yes, indeed," said Elizabeth.

Twenty-three

A week later Ted called Amanda at her boutique and asked her out. She accepted the invitation with delight. During the call he asked her not to mention the date to Elizabeth, telling Amanda that he would explain later.

That afternoon he went across the Charles to meet Dr. Miles in her office at CryoCorp for his physical. A water taxi made the trip in just over 15 minutes. Apparently, Cambridge had adopted the New York City approach to flood management. The city was below sea level, enclosed on the river side by a seawall.

The CryoCorp offices were near the campus of MIT among a cluster of companies working in the bio and computer sciences. The buildings were not the odd-shaped rounded edifices Ted had noticed in Arizona, but the exact opposite. Many had odd rooflines, some with corrugated steel and other materials of unknown origin, supported by columns at gravity-defying angles, and tilted walls—architecturally avant garde to be sure. *But what do I know about modern architecture?* thought Ted.

Surveying the interior of Dr. Miles' office he said, "So this is the new place? I like how you've decorated."

"Yes, maybe by sometime next year I'll have opened all of the boxes," she said. "Follow me next door and I'll examine you."

Ted was slid into a machine that was more like a tunnel. After sliding him out she checked his vital functions by hand.

"So, Ted, any problems? No headaches, earaches, dizziness, lack of coordination? How are you sleeping?"

"Like a baby."

"And you're on your exercise regimen? Any problems to report?"

"No."

"Well, you're doing amazingly well. You'd tell me if you were experiencing any problems, right?"

"Right," said Ted. "So when is Johnnie coming?"

"He arrives tomorrow with Cecelia."

"That's great. When he gets settled in, I'll come over to see him."

"He'll like that," she said. "Ted, have you thought at all about how you're going to make a living when the CryoCorp money runs out?"

"No. I'll find something."

"Well, I was thinking, we need to hire some orderlies here. Would you be interested?"

"Orderlies? You mean people who clean up crap? No thanks."

"Well, it'll be a slightly different function here, but it could lead to other things."

"No offense, but I think I want to stay as far away as I can from your cryonic cronies. Someone could mistake me for a fish stick and toss me back in."

"Well, I'll let you know if I think of anything else," she said.

~ ~ ~

Two nights later Ted rehearsed the many details he would have to make up about his past for Amanda, so as not to tip her off about his situation and who he was. *I don't have to tell her right away. This might not even work out.*

He picked her up at her place on the Beacon Canal and they went over to Locke-Ober for dinner. The restaurant was one of the most formidable culinary institutions in Boston. In existence since about 1875, it featured a grand L-shaped bar made of mahogany from Santo Domingo and carved by French artisans. There were chandeliers that dimly illuminated the club-like dining room with a painted ceiling of leaves, flowers and mythical animals in the deep greens, yellows and browns reminiscent of an Etruscan spring. There was stained glass in the style of Tiffany and French mirrors. Located incongruously down a small alley, the city literally grew up around the place, and the flood stopped just short of it. Normally, less-fancy places like diners were preferable to Ted, but this was Boston. There weren't many diners here, and he wanted to make a good impression.

They were seated in the formidable main dining room with its wood paneling and ancient silver. They looked at menus. Amanda was wearing a plunging neckline and a radiant smile.

"This seems so wonderfully clandestine," she said. "Why didn't you want Elizabeth to know?"

"I just didn't know how she would take it, you know, my meeting her friend and the next minute asking you for a date."

"Well, I'll be the cloak to your dagger anytime," she said.

"A normal guy might blush at a comment like that."

"Are you blushing?"

"No, I don't blush. In fact, there's not much that gets me flustered."

"Except, maybe, your voice recognition system in the house."

"Yeah, let me explain—"

"There's no need. I'm a dog lover, too."

Their cocktails made it easier to laugh. Amanda ordered steak tartare and Ted ordered the lobster thermidor that he purposely called lobster Theodore, telling the waiter they should rename it. Amanda laughed. Things were going well for Ted.

"So, you're retired," she said. "And so young."

"Yeah, well, you know how it is. Life is too short."

They ate their meals and enjoyed more cocktails, delivered with regularity from the formally dressed waitstaff.

"What made you choose to live in Boston?" she said.

"Well, I grew tired of the desert. Wanted a change of scene."

"You're a successful entrepreneur who could live anywhere. I would have guessed you would go to Hollywood," she said, "because you wear sunglasses indoors—and the good looks."

"I, ah, have sensitive eyes." He took off the aviators. "So, you think I'm good looking?"

"And a sparkling conversationalist," she said.

After a few more bites, Amanda lifted her glass and said, "Here's to you. I'm so glad you decided to live in Boston."

After dinner they went for a long stroll, arm in arm, up and down cobblestoned streets under the gas lamps of Beacon Hill. Ted hailed a gondola and they enjoyed an all-too-short ride to the steps of Amanda's condo on the Beacon Canal. Ted paid the gondolier with his phone, and the fellow poled off.

In the dim gaslight, Ted and Amanda embraced and kissed for a long time. In the silence of the night, as the water lapped rhythmically against the marble steps, Amanda tenderly held the side of Ted's face with one hand.

"Thanks for a nice night," she said. "I had a great time."

Ever the sparkling conversationalist, Ted said, "Me, too."

He didn't need a boat to get home; he was walking on water.

Twenty-four

At 8 the next morning, a Saturday, Ted was knocking on the door of Elizabeth's condo. Other than the knocking, the high-rise building was silent. Elizabeth answered the door in her bathrobe, yawning. Ted was holding a baseball bat.

"Ted, how nice to see you—so bright and early."

"I hope you don't mind, I made friends with the doorman and he let me in."

"No, not at all, he's always free to let a strange man with a baseball bat come up to my apartment."

"Is that Ted?" yelled Johnnie from another room.

"Hey, Johnnie boy, come out here," said Ted.

Johnnie came running out, still in his PJs. Ted crouched down to greet him. Johnnie was glad to see a familiar face in his new environment.

"I've got a surprise for you kiddo," said Ted, and handed him the bat.

"Wow. Thanks!" said Johnnie.

"Get dressed, we're going somewhere to use it right away," said Ted, and Johnnie dashed off.

"I hope you don't mind," Ted said to Elizabeth, "Marty, the media stand guy, told me where I could find some batting cages."

"Don't mind?" she said, "I think it's great. Thank you, Ted."

Johnnie reappeared wearing a Red Sox cap.

"I see you've adapted to the local customs already," said Ted. He and Johnnie headed downstairs. Outside, the doorman hailed a water taxi, and they climbed aboard.

"Where are we going?" said Johnnie.

"Over to Dorchester Heights. They have some batting cages there."

"Fun," said Johnnie. "What's a batting cage?"

"It's a fenced-in place where you can take swings and work on your hitting."

It dawned on Ted he didn't know what would be doing the pitching. *A Botwinder?*

It was a beautiful warm day, and the waters around Boston shimmered as the boat sped over to Dorchester.

"You know, I was glad to see that you kids still use wooden bats," said Ted.

"Well, what else would we use?"

"I think at one time the Little Leaguers started to use aluminum bats, but the pros never did. In my mind, wood is the only way to go. There's nothing like a wooden bat. Finely tuned, grain just right. Makin' one is an art form; using it is a science. All good wood bats are made from Northern white ash. Hardest wood around. Usually cut in Pennsylvania and upstate New York. You still gotta check for quality. Straight grain is the most important thing, but I like knots on the barrel, too—the wood is harder. Your bat there is a genuine Louisville Slugger, made by the Hillerich & Bradsby Company in Kentucky."

He leaned over and whispered into Johnnie's ear. "They used to make bats personally for me."

The boat pulled into a bustling dock, and Ted and Johnnie hiked up a steep hill to get to the batting cages. Looking out over Boston Harbor, the site was very near the location where Revolutionary War patriots placed cannon after frantically moving them all the way from Fort Ticonderoga in New

York, forcing the British to abandon Boston for good in the opening rounds of the American Revolution.

At the batting cages, sure enough, Ted spotted Botwinders doing the pitching, albeit, not the high-quality machines that pitched in the major leagues. While they looked less menacing, Ted still thought they looked ridiculous. Coaches and players, fathers and sons lined up at each of the four batting cages waiting their turns. Ted and Johnnie entered a queue.

"I know you don't use these machines in Little League," said Ted, "but remember they're pretty sophisticated. They will throw you strikes and balls. Swing only at strikes. So many players, even major leaguers, never learn this lesson. They swing at bad stuff. Instead, let the pitcher do the work."

Ted and Johnnie reached the front of the line, and Johnnie entered the cage. At the door, Ted looked at an electronic control panel, waved his phone, and punched in what he considered a good pitch velocity for an eight-year-old. How the Botwinder got the message he had no clue. Ted had his arms up on the outside of the chain-link screen and was peering in at Johnnie. After about 10 cuts Johnnie had hit nothing.

"C'mon kid, just keep your eyes on the ball and relax. Try shortening up your swing a bit 'til you get used to the pitch velocity."

"I'm a little scared," said Johnnie.

"What for?" said Ted.

Johnnie put down his bat and walked over to Ted to talk to him through the screen so no one else could hear.

"Ted, I've never faced a screeching metal pitcher. Plus a seven-foot guy with big sunglasses is telling me what to do, and he just happens to be the greatest hitter who ever lived."

"You are your mother's son, my boy. Are you sure you're only eight years old? I'll tell you what, I'll lay off if you get back to the plate."

Johnnie soon began to connect with the ball. There were many more instructions but Ted delivered them in a less intimidating way, mostly by offering up compliments first. Johnnie finished with a couple of crushing line drives.

"How's that, Ted?" he said with great pride.

"Awesome, my boy, just awesome," said Ted.

Johnnie walked over to Ted.

"You wanna take a few swings?" he said.

Both the mind and the heart of Ted raced. There were a lot of people around, he thought. *Best not to draw attention to myself.* But he had all he could do to resist.

"No, son, we came here to focus on *your* hitting today."

The enjoyable morning was completed with a lunch of burgers and fries. Johnnie was all smiles. Over ice cream, Johnnie said to Ted, "Don't eat so fast, you'll get a brain freeze."

"You bein' a wiseguy?" said Ted.

"Yup."

And so it went for the Greatest Hitter Who Ever Lived and his young protégé.

"Next time we'll go fishin'," said Ted.

Twenty-five

The next couple of weeks were busy for Ted, although he did not look for a job. Instead, he was spending money like a drunken Marine. He bought a Boston Whaler and outfitted it with a powerful outboard for fishing excursions. It still had the familiar center console, but the entire unsinkable hull seemed to be made out of some kind of composite that felt like a hard rubber material, not the fiberglass that he remembered.

Next, he visited a personal watercraft dealer and purchased a two-person Jet Ski. He promptly took to roaring around his neighborhood, making waves. The society ladies were not amused. He tied up both of the craft in the water alley behind his house.

He took Johnnie fishing. Ted taught him how to cast with a fly rod, and they had a full day catching blues off Boston Light.

A day later, on her way to the boutique, Amanda surprised Ted, who was grilling a steak on top of the porte-bateau and once again drawing stares.

Remembering his lobster Theodore reference, she called, "Hey, Crustacean Man, may I come in?"

"You bet, come on up," he said, "I'll throw another steak on the grill."

"Sorry, I can't stay, Ted, but I'll come in for a bit."

He showed her the new toys out in back of the house, with particular attention to the Jet Ski.

"It has 300 porpoise power. It'll do zero to 50 knots in seven seconds. C'mon, hop on," he said.

"No, I can't," she said half-heartedly.

"Yes, you can."

"No, look at me. I have high heels on, a designer dress—and fabulous accessories, I might add."

"I noticed. Nothing like a little salt spray to bring a glow to your cheeks."

"Don't I have a perfect complexion already?"

"And modesty, too," he said.

He jumped on the Jet Ski and grabbed her by the arm. Amanda made a minor screech, more out of delight than anything else. She fit snugly behind him on the long seat and grabbed him around the waist. The two sped off for a wave-making, thunderous tour of the grand waterways and back canals of the Back Bay. Out in front of the townhouse Ted's steak burned to a crisp.

~ ~ ~

During a two-week stretch, Ted and Amanda went on eight dates. For Ted, each day was spent planning each evening's events, except on the weekends when they spent every hour together. There were candlelight dinners, moonlight strolls, and midnight dalliances that didn't include sex yet. She seemed to be willing and certainly he was, but he wanted to be sure the timing was right. He suggested that they drive up to Vermont for a long weekend.

Ted rented an FCV for the trip. As they approached their destination in Manchester, Ted said, "There used to be good fishin' here on the Battenkill River. Now I understand the trout are gone due to the warm water."

They checked into the historic Equinox Hotel. After a sumptuous dinner, of which each of them hardly ate a bite, they went dancing in a small ballroom with a big band. Slow dances were all that interested Ted and Amanda. While the band played classic Sinatra, Cole, Bennett and Tormé, they melted into each other's arms.

In the moonlit shadows of the majestic Green Mountains, they danced off to their room. A roaring fire, a couple of glasses of champagne and the do-not-disturb sign on the door were mere props.

Feeling the soft skin and wonderful curves of Amanda in the nude were enough for Ted to thank God that he was alive again.

"I am rock hard," he said with as much relief as enthusiasm as they rested their foreheads on each other.

"Yes, you are. Let's put it to good use," she said

In a passionate embrace under a soft comforter, Amanda called out Ted's name.

"How am I doing?" he said.

"You're batting a thousand."

"Well, my little lady, you couldn't possibly know what that means to me."

It happened right then and there: Ted fell for the mistress of the moonlight metaphor. She may have been *Vogue* to his *Field & Stream*, but quite the catch.

Twenty-six

Back in Boston, Ted was tying a purple Egg Sucking Leech, a Jock Scott and a Black Bear when the doorbell rang. Slightly irritated, he hurried downstairs, his annoyance assuaged by the thought that it might be Amanda.

"Oh, it's you," he said.

"Nice to see you, *too*, Ted," said Elizabeth. "Can I come in?"

She took off her sweater and placed it on the back of one of the living room chairs.

"I was worried about you," she said. "I haven't heard from you lately."

"I'm fine, as you can see."

"So, what have you been up to?"

"Not much, just knocking around the house."

Thinking that she might want to fill in the blanks for the time he was spending with Amanda, he hurriedly added, "Hey, I bought two new boats. One's a Jet Ski, actually."

"That's, ah, nice," she said. After a pause, she added, "Ted, those are expensive items. I know you live rent free, but shouldn't you be more concerned about your money running out?"

"Look, I've said this before and I'll say it again, *you* are not my mommy. Lay off, Dr. Frankenstein."

Elizabeth said nothing. He could tell by the look on her face that she was hurt.

"Hey, I know you are worried about me, and that you care about me," he said, "but I've got to live my own life."

"I do care about you," she said. "You may think that you are just some clinical experiment to me, but that's not it at all. I *want* to see you live your own life. But I am also very practical. In your former life you made a living that's not open to you now. I know you didn't ask for it but you were reanimated with no way to support yourself. Yes, I'm a little worried."

"Don't worry," he said. "I'll have a job soon. In fact, I've been looking—"

The phone rang.

"I'm not going to get it," he said.

"Well, who could be calling you?"

"Who knows? Probably another mailorder company."

While they were talking, Ted's automated voice answered the phone, and then a sensuous voice was broadcast into the room.

"Hi, Crusty, I just want you to know that I had a fabulous time last night. And your breakfast was sensational. Bye."

"Oh my God," said Elizabeth. "That was Amanda. The two of you are . . . are—"

"Yeah, let me explain the Crusty thing—"

"I don't want to know."

"Yeah, but—"

"Have you told her? Does she know about you, Ted?"

"No, not yet. In the beginning I figured, why tell her right away? It might not work out. Now I'm probably going to have to tell her."

"How serious is this? When are you going to tell her?"

"When the time is right, that's when I'll tell her."

"How will you know? What will you say? What if she reacts badly? Have you thought about any of this?"

"Yeah, some."

"'Some?' That's it?"

"Hey, Lizzy, you are pretty damn self righteous for the person that got me into this. I'll take care of it. Just butt out."

And she did, slamming the door behind her.

~ ~ ~

The next day she butted back in.

Elizabeth and Amanda met for lunch at the Top of the Hub. Boston from 52 floors in the air was breathtaking, and it never became less so with repeated visits to the Prudential Tower. They ordered soup and salads and sipped San Pellegrino.

"So, you sounded like getting together for lunch was urgent," said Amanda.

"Well, yes," said Elizabeth.

"So what is it?"

"I know that you have been seeing Ted."

Amanda bit her lower lip and said, "Yes, I have. In fact, I adore the big lug. Never in my wildest dreams did I think I would be dating a fisherman."

"He is a *fly* fisherman. You're not dating Captain Ahab."

"Well, he floats my boat, for sure. He *is* a little Gregory Peck-ish. John Wayne, certainly."

"Well, you're going to have to break it off," said Elizabeth.

Amanda gave Elizabeth a sideways look and said, "Elizabeth, you never told me you had a thing for Ted."

"I don't have a *thing*; we're just good friends."

"He was concerned about your finding out about us," said Amanda. "What is it then, a friends-with-privileges situation?"

"No. Nothing like that; there isn't anything between us."

"You're lusting after him from afar? Is that it?" said Amanda.

"No, I am not!"

"Well, tell me then. Why do you object? Does he have some criminal past?"

"No. It's just that . . . he . . . he . . . has some health issues."

"You mean an STD?" said Amanda.

"No, no, no."

"Oh my God, he's got something terminal?" said Amanda.

"No, that's not it. But that's all that I can tell you because I am his doctor."

"Gee, thanks for all of the frank talk. What's a little specificity amongst girlfriends?"

"You just don't understand."

"And you're not telling me."

The lunch ended as cold as the gazpacho soup.

~ ~ ~

Ted began searching earnestly for a job. He searched online classified ads but most of the jobs involved office work. Even if he was qualified he couldn't see himself sitting in an office all day. The major problem was he had quite a hole in his work history. There was just no way to explain what he was doing for the last 90 years. The freezers gambit would only go so far. References were out of the question. His options were limited.

Amanda invited Ted over to her place for dinner. They drank his favorite wine, sparkling burgundy, and hung out in the kitchen while she cooked.

"You know," she said, "I had lunch with Elizabeth the other day, and she was acting very strange."

"Yeah, well, she can be that way."

"Did she act odd to you, Ted, when she found out about us?"

"Yeah, a little."

"She acted as if there are things that I don't know about you," said Amanda. "She even suggested we break up. Is there something that I should know?"

"No. She's just being an old mother hen."

"That's it? There's nothing you want to tell me—that you're the bastard child of Bigfoot and a farmer's daughter? Maybe you're a bank robber, and you give all of the money to the poor? Is your middle name Robin, you hood?"

They kissed in front of the stove.

~ ~ ~

The next day, Ted told Danny that he wanted to find a job, anything on the water. Half jokingly, Danny told him the Back Bay Water Taxi Company was hiring. Ted went over right away. In the job interview, they didn't care much about his background except the fact that he was an experienced boatman. They hired him on the spot.

Ted knew the job was beneath him, but he needed some income. Danny thought, *I've never seen a guy living in a neighborhood like this drivin' a taxi, but maybe it's like those railroad buffs who retire from executive careers to take a job as conductors because they like trains so much. Ted does love the water.*

Ted was on the job a week and decided he mostly liked it, not the surly customers that often appeared, but being out on the water in the fresh air, albeit in a city. The drawback was the time away from Amanda, fly tying and fishing. And, of course, it didn't pay much. One thing was perfectly clear: He did not want Amanda to know what he was doing.

She started to wonder why he wasn't available as much. He was evasive.

"Very busy," he said. "I'm working on a few projects here and there. Nothing that I should bore you with."

For Amanda, it would have been part of his allure: Ted the mystery man, entrepreneur, outdoorsman, bon vivant, if only she hadn't been worried about the health issue that he didn't want to talk about.

Ted's ruse was nearly shattered on a Wednesday afternoon on the Newbury Canal when he was picking up two ladies who lunch. As they stepped into the water taxi, Ted glanced up to see Amanda walking out of her boutique just across the canal. He sped off, escaping detection. The women held onto their enormous hats and then held on for dear life.

Twenty-seven

On his day off, Ted made a big wake behind his Jet Ski all the way over to Elizabeth's building. He tossed the keys with a little float on them to the valet, said hello to the doorman, Vick, and headed upstairs to the 24th floor. He knocked on the door and Cecelia answered.

"Hello, Mr. Ted, come in."

Hiya, Ceal," he said. "Boy, have you been cookin' again? The place smells great."

The condo had a much more lived-in feel or, more appropriately, moved-in, compared to his last couple of visits.

"I see you've been working your magic on the household," he said.

"That's me a regular magician," she said. "Are you hungry?"

"No, Ma'am. I'm just here to pick up Johnnie Boy."

Johnnie and Elizabeth appeared simultaneously, Johnnie with his bat. He gave Ted a hug.

"Johnnie, you promised me before you left you would pick up your room," said Elizabeth.

"Go ahead son," said Ted. "I'll wait for you and talk to your mom."

Cecelia went to help Johnnie, and Elizabeth and Ted sat at the kitchen table. She was not inclined to discuss the lunch with Amanda, or any other controversial subject, and simply said, "So, what's new?"

"Well, you'll be happy to know that I found a job."

"Ted, that's great! What are you doing?"

"Driving a water taxi."

"Well, do you like it?"

"It doesn't pay much, but, yes, I do."

"Well that's good," she said.

"Do me a favor," said Ted, "not a word to Amanda."

"Ted, you are keeping a lot of secrets and asking me to do the same. I don't want to see either of you get hurt."

"Is that it, that's all that you're concerned about?"

"Yes, of course," she said.

"Let's not get into it," he said. "I came here to take Johnnie out and have some fun. Okay?"

"Okay."

Johnnie ran out and yelled, "I'm ready."

~ ~ ~

They screamed over to Dorchester on the Jet Ski in no time at all, Johnnie holding on to Ted with one hand the other hand holding the bat on his shoulder. The batting cages were not crowded, and soon Johnnie was inside whacking away against the Botwinder.

"Choke up some more," said Ted. "Don't try to pull it. Swing through the ball and try to hit it straight through the box."

Johnnie was making progress. Ted was pleased. "Good man. Try to quicken your swing now. Batspeed is the key."

After about a half an hour of batting, Johnnie was fatiguing. He walked over to Ted at the screen and said he needed a rest.

"Hey, why don't you give it a try?" said Johnnie.

"No son, we came here to work on *your* swing."

"C'mon, Ted, you can show me how."

He didn't say it to Johnnie, but Ted was more than a little afraid to pick up a bat. *Was the last time a freak occurrence? How will I perform?* On the other hand, there weren't many people around.

"No son, you swing away," he said.

"But Ted, I want you to show me how to hit to the opposite field, and the hip and wrist-action stuff you've been talking about."

"I don't want to hit against the . . . the robot. I can't stand the thing."

"Why not? I didn't like it either at first, remember?"

"Okay," Ted said, "but I never hit to the opposite field."

He picked up one of the rental bats and walked into the cage.

On the outside of the cage, Johnnie looked at the control panel and didn't know what to do.

"Just push 90 on the MPH key pad," said Ted.

Ted moved to the right side of the plate. He held the bat above his left shoulder. He drummed his fingers on the handle. It felt good. *The bat feels right, maybe 32 ounces. Just make contact. Swing with a slight uppercut . . .* Calmness took over. Something in him said this is the natural order of things. This is where I am supposed to be. His response was instinctual—a practice swing.

Not unlike a single action revolver, his hammer was cocked and ready. Before he could pull the trigger, sweat began pouring down the sides of his face and beading up under his aviators. The Botwinder began to move and Ted flinched.

As if unleashing the pent-up energy of a great volcano, Ted's right foot moved forward. The ball sped toward the plate. The hips began to rotate, the shoulders moved, followed by biceps, forearms, and then sweat-covered wrists. The body uncoiled with a massive outward breath. And then, a great crack of the bat. The ball, as if shot out of some secret weapon, barely missed the armor-plated Botwinder and then settled into the net at the end of a truncated, velocity-filled line drive.

All of the adrenaline in the world seemed to be coursing through his body. He breathed a sigh of relief.

"Ninety-five," he said, and Johnnie complied. Again, a wicked line drive.

"One hundred," Ted yelled—and another great shot. It happened again at 105 mph.

A crowd began to gather. He did it at 110, 115, 120, and then the crowd gasped when he hit a screeching liner off a 122-mph pitch.

The zone he was in, or the spell, whatever you want to call it, was broken with applause from the crowd as the Botwinder maxed out at 125-mph and Ted smacked the cover off of the ball. He didn't miss a single pitch.

What the hell, tennis players hit balls that fast, he thought. *But not with a cylindrical, tapered bat.*

Johnnie was in awe. As the crowd stared at the mph meter, they applauded again.

"C'mon," said Ted to Johnnie, "let's go home."

As they walked away, someone in the crowd said, "Who was that guy?"

Twenty-eight

Ted continued to drive his taxi and to see Amanda over the next
week, but she thought he was decidedly aloof.

Over dinner at Chez Pierre, she said, "Is something wrong?"

"No, nothing's wrong."

"You seem a thousand miles away," she said.

In fact, his mind was just a few miles away, in a batting cage on
Dorchester Heights. For a week, in every waking hour, he couldn't get away
from thoughts of it. He didn't want to. His mind was consumed with how
good it was to hit again. Every piece of it: The concentration, the swing,
making contact, the adrenaline rush. *And the body, the body,* he thought.

They finished dinner, and Ted took Amanda home. They kissed at the
door.

"Would you like to come in?" she said.

"No, I've got a busy day tomorrow."

"Okay. I'll miss you. Call me," and she closed the door.

As Ted reached the bottom of the stairs, he hadn't noticed a man lurking
in the shadows in a small boat.

"Hey, Ted," the man yelled. As Ted looked up, bright lights—obviously
photo flashes—pierced the darkness and illuminated the canal.

"What the . . . ?" said Ted.

"Bernard Cromwell says hello," said the man. He zoomed off in a hurry. Ted knew it. His world was about to change.

~ ~ ~

He spent a restless night. He finally fell asleep and in late morning was awakened by pounding on his door, over and over again. There was crowd noise. He peered out the window and he could see news crews crowded onto his doorsteps. A flotilla of boats surrounded his home. TV drones hovered overhead. It was media frenzy.

He went online and he could see that the *Boston Globe* had broken the story with his picture on the front page. "Ted Williams Lives," screamed the headline in end-of-the-world type.

Epapers all over the world had picked up the story and ran it with tremendous headlines: *The New York Times*: Greatest Hitter Reanimated; *Tokyo Shimbun*: Williams-san Awakens; Rome *Il Messagero*: He Knows About God; *London Times*: American Baseballer Returns From Dead; *The Wall Street Journal*: Williams to Lift Cryonics Business.

Ted picked up the mobile to dial CryoCorp in Arizona and hit the numbers so hard he nearly broke his index finger. He looked at his watch.

"Judas would be arriving at the office just about now," he said aloud to himself.

"Bernard Cromwell, please."

"Yes, who's calling?"

"Ted Williams."

"Yes, Mr. Williams, please hold."

Cromwell took a long time to get to the phone.

"Ted, hello, how are you?"

"Listen, you syphilitic son of a bitch, goddamned mother—"

"Ted, I know you're upset—"

"Upset? You stinkin' piece of horseshit. You coulda given me a heads up. And don't tell me you didn't know about it. Your stupid photographer was a dumbass, you money-grubbing bastard."

"Ted," said Cromwell, "you were observed hitting baseballs. How long did you think your anonymity was going to last?"

Ted repeated his assertions about Cromwell's lineage and threw the phone across the room. He turned around and was startled to see Elizabeth in his living room.

"How did you get in here?" he said.

"Through the back door; I have a key, remember?"

"Well, you shouldn't sneak around like that; I coulda taken your head off, thinkin' you was one of them slugs out on the doorstep. Just got off the phone with your boss, Bernie. We had a pleasant conversation."

"Oh, I wouldn't have known by the way you threw the phone against the wall."

"Well, what do you expect? That rat bastard set me up. He tipped off the *Globe*."

"How do you know this?"

"Ol' Bernie never thought that the photographer would be so stupid as to drop Bernie's name. And look at the story; the details could only come from CryoCorp sources. Anonymous pricks. Did you know about this?"

"No," she said, with a pained expression of both insult and hurt on her face. "If that's true, it's inexcusable. Reprehensible. I'm sorry Ted."

"Not only are they surrounding the house, but the phone's been ringing off the hook, too. The only call I took was from Marshall."

"Ted, we've talked about this many times. It was inevitable that the story would come out. Not like this, perhaps."

"You're goddamned right, not like this. Geezus, even little Johnnie was able to keep it a secret."

"That's my point. Growing lists of people were in on it. I think you should be thankful that you had a decent amount of time to prepare. Are you prepared?"

"I know how to handle those reporter bastards."

"Do you? Did you handle it well in your last life?"

"Mostly, I ignored the sons of bitches."

"Well, you might want to rethink that. They will be relentless. Perhaps you can get them off your back. If an alligator is going to live in your house, you'd better feed it occasionally."

"Screw them. I'm not going out of my way in the least for those bastards."

"One thing is for sure, if you *do* talk to them you'll have to clean up your language," Elizabeth said.

"And what about Amanda? Have you spoken to her?"

"No, I'm gonna—"

The phone rang. Ted found it on the couch and picked it up.

"Ted, how could you not tell me this?" said Amanda.

"Amanda, let me explain," he said, looking at Elizabeth.

"Oh, you mean little details," said Amanda, "like you're the first person on earth to be reborn? I'm the main squeeze of Boris Karloff—who knew?"

"I was gonna tell you, it's just that—"

"How could you keep this from me? Actually, you know what? I don't want to hear it. It's too creepy," she said, now crying. "I can't see you anymore."

She hung up.

"She doesn't want to see me anymore," he said to Elizabeth.

He plopped down in a chair. With a furrowed brow he stared off into the distance. Outside, the media crowd continued its relentless clamoring.

"I'm sorry, Ted," said Elizabeth.

"Oh, fuck," he said.

~ ~ ~

The next morning, the media vigil continued around the front and back entrances of Ted's house. He was a prisoner in his own home. Around one o'clock, the predetermined time, Ted heard a big engine roar from somewhere down the canal. He quickly looked out the window. It was his buddy Marshall.

The rescue was in full motion. Marshall ripped toward the porte-bateau in a massive speedboat. Ted grabbed a small bag filled with clothes and a box of flies and ran out the front door. Distracted by the oncoming boat and now scattering in the water and on the steps, half the reporters and photographers missed Ted as he ran down the steps through the media scrum. Marshall barely slowed. Ted hit the bottom step and in one fluid motion he jumped headfirst.

Marshall turned to see him land on the seats and then gunned the cigarette boat leaving all of the media people soaked in the wake.

"Hiya, Bush," yelled Ted.

Like Revere and Dawes, they rode out of town fast, and with the help of horsepower.

They raced all the way to Hopkinton, jumped in a waiting car, sped to the Worcester airport, and took off for New Brunswick, Canada, without a single reporter on their tail.

Twenty-nine

The next day, ePapers, websites and television stations all over the world went with a picture of Ted diving through the air into Marshall's fast-moving boat. Ted thought he looked like Bobby Orr scoring "The Goal" in game four to win the 1970 Stanley Cup.

They were Huck and Jim, escaping on the river. Not the Mississippi but the Miramichi. Not a journey of self-discovery, but a journey not to be discovered.

Safe in a small fishing lodge, all by themselves, they were surrounded by old black-and-white fishing photos and salmon mounts. Marshall was making breakfast. Ted was drinking coffee at a small table off the pine-paneled kitchen.

"So, how did you manage to leave Arizona?" said Ted.

"Well, my assistant coaches can run the Little League team for a while and my sales job, I can do that from anywhere."

"I appreciate it."

"Don't mention it. It was kind of exciting, actually. So how did you find this place?"

"On the Internet; I used to have my own place just downstream. I want to see if it's still there when we go out later to get rods."

"And there's still fish in here?"

Ted nodded with an enthusiastic look on his face. "I think so. I did a little research to be sure. The water is still cold enough up here. Maybe only by a little."

Marshall brought scrambled eggs and bacon to the table on two plates and sat down.

"So, you were surprised that Cromwell did this to you?"

"I shouldn't have been. All my life—I mean my former life—people tried to sponge off me. Made it particularly hard to know who was a real friend and who wasn't."

"Tough with the ladies, too, I bet," said Marshall. "Not meetin' 'em, just wondering what they were up to."

"Exactly. That's why this thing with Amanda—"

"Well, maybe you can explain it to her. You know, I can't claim to know a lot about women, being divorced and all, but I'm guessing she was more upset about the fact that you didn't tell her than by what she learned."

"I'm not so sure."

Marshall just nodded. He didn't say it, but he was thinking Amanda was the wrong kind of woman for him anyway.

"How old were you when you first turned pro?" said Marshall.

"Eighteen," said Ted. "Why are you asking me this?"

"Just curious. Just curious. So, what are you gonna do next, when you get back to Boston?"

"I don't know. The thing with Amanda is over. I can't go back to my job. Geezus, I'm not even sure I'm gonna be able to move around anymore."

"Well, the house is yours to use—it's not connected to CryoCorp."

"Yeah, that's a good thing, if I can get in and out of it."

"Maybe you can make peace with the reporters, you know, give 'em a little something in return for leaving you alone."

"I'm not sure that's gonna work, and boy, right now, I don't give a shit.

Ted shook his head from side to side and Marshall nodded silently.

"So, whaddaya say? Let's go fishin'," said Ted.

~ ~ ~

Ted needed to see his old lodge before they would hit the water. The men drove quite a distance and then hiked a considerable way through the woods until Ted spied his former home-away-from-home for 40 years, White Birch Lodge, located on the banks of the southwest branch of the Miramichi. The lodge looked mostly the same except for a new addition on one of its flanks. They kept their distance. Marshall could see more than a little bit of emotion in Ted's eyes. Ted was silent until finally he said, "C'mon Marsh, let's go."

Back at the car, Ted explained that most of the best fishing on the Miramichi was private water. There were actually several rivers in the area, branches of the Miramichi, tributaries and the like, all lined with a series of fishing lodges. The place they were renting was on the northwest Miramichi, much less developed now than the area around the southwest branch. The place was serene, beautiful and, to Ted's relief, still quite pristine, a riparian paradise. Anglers were challenged and rewarded by water that featured boulder-strewn streams, channels, gravel bars, eddies and pools, all viable candidates for containing big fish.

The singular quest of almost all of the local denizens and visitors was the great Atlantic salmon. The fish could reach 40 pounds here in the heart of New Brunswick. The salmon season lasted from April to October, much to Ted's frustration during his playing days, matching almost exactly the schedule of the old baseball season. He made up for lost time after his retirement. The rivers in the region were filled with water that runs down from the Historian and Christmas mountain ranges to the sea. For Ted, every day spent fishing here was Christmas morning.

On their way back to their own lodge and its riverbank they stopped at an Orvis outfitter and geared up with rods, reels, waders and nets. Ted had enough of his own hand-tied flies for the two of them. The time for talking was over.

On the river they separated but stayed in view of each other. Knee deep, Ted began an elegant series of graceful, rhythmic motions intended to land a small fly quietly atop the running water so as not to spook the fish into cutting and running. Marshall stopped his preparations just to study Ted some 100 yards upstream.

Ted was now a personal, good friend. But as Marshall studied the master at work, he could not separate his thoughts about the science that now would forever be associated with Ted Williams—the historic and now, not-so-secret, cryonic achievement. Marshall's transcendent moment came when he realized that not only was Ted a master fly caster, but he *remembered* how to fly-fish.

With rod and line still motionless in Marshall's hands, the spell was broken by a shout from Ted.

"Hey, Bush, you gonna get that thing wet?"

Momentarily flustered, he yelled back, "don't you worry about me."

Marshall started a clumsy dance with his own fly rod, but he still could not take his eyes off of Ted's pas de deux, a delicate ballet between man and rod with synchronized rhythms intended to land fly, leader and line upon the water in precisely the right order, and in precisely the right spot. Marshall had witnessed Ted's first swing of the bat with his new body back in Arizona, and Ted had told him about the recent batting cage experience. Now, Marshall wondered, *how could a man with such power also exhibit the finesse required for this?* How could *this* man do it?

Ted hooked a large salmon and laughed aloud at the sheer joy of it. Marshall laughed along with him.

After Ted released the fish, he was all smiles . . . until he glanced across the river and saw the photographer. The fishing trip was over.

Thirty

All the way back to Boston, on the plane and in the car, Ted let off a string of expletives that would have made even a fellow marine blush. For the first time, while traveling in the FCV out of the Worcester airport, he noticed all of the roadside signs. There were billboards for Getgo, Roid Realm and other steroid cocktails along the highway. Ted turned on the radio and there was a 30-second spot by Johan Johansson, shilling for Getgo. In broken English, the Swedish expat called himself, "The big left fielder for the Red Sox."

Since the fishing trip was cut short, Marshall decided to stay with Ted for a while in Boston. When they returned to the Back Bay, there seemed to be even more reporters staked out at the front and back of Ted's house. The fishing photo appeared online around the world that evening.

For the next five days and five nights, as the media herd grew outside, Ted and Marshall holed up at the lower end of Marlborough with the shades drawn. They ordered beer, pizza, Chinese, Thai, Italian—just about anything that could be delivered. Marshall always answered the door. Flashes would pop and then a collective groan would be heard as the mass of photographers realized Ted was not the person at the door. Since Ted disconnected the door chimes, deliverymen were given a special knock, a code really, indicating to Marshall that it was okay to answer the door. After such deliveries, the reporters interviewed the deliverymen. Out back, they picked through the Williams' garbage.

Inside, the place began to resemble a frat house during rush week. Clothes were strewn about. So, too, were pizza boxes and Chinese takeout cartons. The smell of beer, old food, popcorn and farts, all mixed to form a kind of testosterone-laden weapon of mass destruction. If any of the bastard reporters broke in, they might be driven back by the impenetrable force field.

Over in Cambridge, Dr. Miles had her hands full as well. The offices of CryoCorp were similarly besieged. She referred most of the media to the Arizona headquarters, but the local media still wanted a local story. Mostly, they wanted Dr. Miles. Out in the desert, Bernard Cromwell was getting more than his 15 minutes of fame. Business was booming as people came in to make arrangements for cryonic preservation.

Headquarters had sent more staff east to Boston to help Dr. Miles with the onslaught. A lot of the new business was reporters pretending to be customers just to get a story. Requests to meet with her, Ted Williams' doctor, were declined more often than not. There simply were not enough hours in the day.

She knew Ted had come home because she saw it on compuTV. She phoned and told him she was on her way over and said that she would have help. About a half hour later Ted and Marshall were momentarily perturbed when they heard what they perceived as a scuffle at the back door. It opened and in walked—pushed through, really—Elizabeth with Jed and Randall.

"Well, look at this, it's a CryoCorp convention," said Ted. "So this is your muscle, Lizzy? Freak and Frack?"

"Jed and Randall were sent out here to help with the, ah, business imperatives and to assist me in particular," she said.

"A lot of help these scruffy bastards are gonna be," said Ted.

Elizabeth surveyed the living room.

"Oh my God. Just look at this place," she said. "And the smell—"

"Yeah, I have to admit, we let things get a little out of hand," said Ted. "I don't like a messy house. My mother kept a messy place, and I hated it. We haven't been able to make too many trips outside with the garbage."

Oblivious, Jed and Randall began eating some stale popcorn.

"Well, we're going to clean it up," said Elizabeth.

Like a drill sergeant, she directed Ted, Marshall and the two assistants until the place reached a semblance of normalcy. The smell would linger for some time.

When they were through, Marshall, Jed and Randall settled into the media room and started watching an old movie. Ted and Elizabeth sat in the kitchen drinking coffee.

"I'm not sure if this media deluge is going to end," she said to Ted. "Have you thought about what we discussed—meeting with them?"

"Yes, I have, and I will not."

"But what kind of life is this for you?"

"Feeling guilty, doctor?"

"Well, yes, I am."

"I'll tell you what I need," he said. "I need a hotel where I can live. You know, a place with security, a place where the operator can screen my calls, where I can come and go and not be seen all the time. I used to have that over on Comm Ave."

"Commonwealth Avenue is now under water, and so are your finances, Ted. How could you afford such a place? You can't work. Not unless you get the media off your back. Even then, they're probably not going to go completely away."

"I just hate giving in to the sons of bitches."

"I know you do, but look at it this way, some opportunities could come out of it. Maybe someone will give you a job again."

He sought to change the subject. "Have you heard from Amanda?" he said.

"No. I've tried to reach her. I think she's upset with me, and I'm worried about her," said Elizabeth.

"Yeah. She won't return my calls either."

Thirty-one

A day later, Ted and Marshall were having a long talk about the miserable existence they were living, trapped in a mansion in Boston's most affluent neighborhood.

"Geezus, I don't know what to do, Marsh," said Ted. "Lizzy doesn't know how bad my money situation really is; it's just about out, and I can't go to work. I called, and the taxi people just laughed. It'll be like that at other places, too. You know, all my life I never worried much about money, probably because we never had much when I was growing up. Even when I started playing pro ball, my only concern was seeing that my mother was taken care of. I even reduced my contract myself one year with Mr. Yawkey after I didn't play well. Money just sorta always took care of itself."

"I would guess that your celebrity had something to do with that," said Marshall.

"Yeah, but I never squandered much. Didn't drink, go to fancy places, carouse much."

"Didn't have to, the women came to you, I bet," said Marshall.

"Yeah, that's true," chuckled Ted. "The wives spent their share of my dough. That's for sure. I spent my money mostly on travel, fishing and such. But even my places in Florida and Canada were not fancy-pants places. By most standards, anyway."

"So, what *are* you gonna do, Ted?"

"I guess I'm gonna have to meet with those bastards in the press. The problem with the press is they all feel like they have to out-do each other. They don't give a shit about who they smear in the process."

"Yeah, that's probably more true today," said Marshall.

"I know they screwed me last time. But I guess I coulda tried harder to be a little more accommodating. I think I know what I have to do. Hell, what's the use of a second life if you don't try and do things better?"

"Ted, my man, you are becoming a deep thinker. I have an old friend in the public relations business—in Boston. You know what he says about PR? Perception is reality. If people perceive you're a straight shooter, they'll give you a break."

"That's a load of horseshit," said Ted. "Then again, whada I know? Do you think you can call in a favor with this friend of yours to set something up with the press? I don't want anyone from CryoCorp there. I'll tell Lizzy to butt out, too. She and Little Lord Bernie Fauntleroy have been doing their own thing with the media anyway. He's a bigger prick than an Arizona cactus. He and the press deserve each other."

"I'll set it up."

Ted gave him a thankful nod. "I appreciate it."

"Be prepared, Ted. They are gonna need a lot of stuff from you. Why don't you work on some pithy quotes or statements like, 'I guess now we can say that Ben Franklin was only partially right.'"

"What do you mean," said Ted.

"'The only thing certain is death and taxes.' We can remove the death part, thanks to you—the medical marvel."

Ted huffed but smiled.

"You better stick to medical sales, Marsh. I'm not about to give the press any new names to call me."

Thirty-two

Marshall's friend put the pieces together and scheduled the press conference at the old Parker House hotel at the foot of Beacon Hill. Now, added to the list of great events that happened there—literary meetings of Ralph Waldo Emerson, Nathaniel Hawthorne, Henry Wadsworth Longfellow and Oliver Wendell Holmes; visits by Charles Dickens and Ulysses S. Grant; the announcement of his run for Congress by John F. Kennedy; the launching of her run for president by Dakota Fanning—would be the post-reanimation press conference of Theodore Samuel Williams.

Ted entered a mahogany-paneled room dressed in his standard blue button-down shirt with an open collar and khaki pants. He moved to the podium and stood in front of a bank of microphones larger than a cornfield. The room was filled with digi-lights and hundreds of reporters. Despite all of the enhanced lighting, the flashes were blinding.

"I'd like to make a statement, and then I'll take your questions, I guess."

He unfolded a piece of paper and began to read rather stiffly from the comments he had prepared the night before.

"I know there has been much interest in me by you 'Knights of the Keyboard' and 'Lancelots of the Lens.' It is my hope that in return for my addressing you today you will give me some peace and privacy."

The room was very tense; people were hanging on every word.

"I know you are all interested in the first human to be *reanimated, re-*vived, *re-*born, or *re-*gurgitated."

The room burst out in laughter.

"Whatever you want to call it . . . I don't know what to call it yet, but I certainly don't like all of the medical terms like cryopreserved."

"The news reports have been filled with speculation about my willingness to be preserved before I became deceased, I guess because it was controversial when I died. The answer is, I did not ask for the cryonics stuff. And that's all I'm going to say about it or my family. I will not answer questions along those lines.

"Having said that, I've never been one to look a gift horse in the mouth and I intend to make the most out of this life. Now I'll take your questions."

The room erupted with shouts of "Ted, Ted, Ted," in ear-splitting volume. After leaning back from the onslaught Ted said, "Okay, you in the red blouse," pointing toward a particularly attractive young reporter.

"Ted, you have been to the great beyond, you passed over, if you will. Is there a God? A heaven? A hell?"

The room grew instantly silent. After what seemed an eternity, Ted said, "I probably shoulda addressed this in my opening statement, that is another piece of information I'm gonna keep to myself."

The room, as if in a practiced Greek chorus, groaned in disillusion in unison.

"But Ted . . . , " shouted the young woman before she was shouted over. The room inflated again with screaming voices. The reporters could not resist the temptation to wave their arms like schoolchildren.

A lone male voice rose above the rest, in the odd space amid the cacophony and said, "You are refusing to answer the one question that has been in the mind of all humans since the beginning of recorded history."

Ted leaned forward into the mics and said, "Let's move on."

Another collective groan. And then hands and arms went flailing about again unabashedly.

"Ted, Ted, Ted . . ."

Ted pointed to another reporter who said, "What does it feel like?"

"It feels all right," said Ted. "It's taken some getting used to. Remember my last frame of reference was as an old man. Now I've been given a new body. It was strange at first, but boy it feels good now."

Another reporter shouted out, "Do you remember everything from your former life?"

"Yeah, except from the last bit of my life, you know, when I went downhill fast. That's the remarkable thing, you would think the damage then—strokes and all—would have made this impossible, but the damage was reversed—other than a lack of a few memories surrounding my decline."

"So, what do you think of this world in the late 21st century?"

"Well it's a little wet—obviously, you mean the climate change, I take it?" said Ted. "I suppose the only good part is that you all have adapted. A lot was lost though, and millions of people died, too, I understand, from the flooding and starvation and such. Millions more—what do you call it?—were *displaced*?

"But, my generation killed a lot more in the wars and all. Not that I consider Hitler or Tojo part of my own society. America was always, at least in my day, on the right side of things. But I guess we set the wheels in motion for the climate change. I'm not pleased about that."

"Do you miss friends and family, Ted?"

"Well, sure I do. But there's nothing I can do about it. I've made quite a lot of new friends already."

"Ted, will you play baseball again?"

"Absolutely not. I can't stand what they've done to the game. All of the drugs, and robots as pitchers. I always thought most pitchers were dumbasses, so maybe it was inevitable they would be replaced."

More laughter. Ted was on a roll.

"Ted, rumor has it you were seen working out in a batting cage."

"The only cage I'm in is the one you guys put me in."

And so it went.

There were questions about what he planned to do next, what he would do with the rest of his life, what he did for enjoyment and on and on.

"Fishing," was the reply to most of the questions.

There were more God questions, the reporters not-so-cleverly couching the same questions in different words, all of which he would not answer.

Then a reporter asked, "Ted, getting back to the family thing, is it true that you once elected to go fishing instead of being there for the birth of your child?"

"This is over," he said loudly and stormed away from the podium.

Thirty-three

A media flotilla followed Ted and Marshall all the way back to the house and surrounded the building again.

"You cannot expect 'em to bug off in a day," said Marshall.

"Yes, I can," said Ted in disgust.

Ted and Marshall were sitting in the living room drinking a couple bottles of Stella Artois. The shades were still drawn.

"Ted, you did a good job with those media hounds. It's not easy holding your ground and stickin' to your guns."

Marshall, too, was curious about the God question but knew better than to push Ted.

"It never ceases to amaze me," said Marshall, "when the press shows up on the doorstep of people, who maybe just lost a kid or something, and the reporter sticks a mic in the face of the parents. And the parents talk to them! 'What are you feeling right now?' the reporter asks. Me, I would tell 'em, 'I'm feeling my boot going up your ass.'"

"Just doin' their jobs," said Ted in a sarcastic voice.

Elizabeth called to compliment Ted just as he and Mashall settled into the media room to look at the headlines.

"I saw you on compuTV. Well done," she said.

"Yeah, the headlines are scintillating. The words 'God question' seem to dominate. It doesn't look like it helped much to get them off my back," said Ted.

"Well, maybe you have to give it some time," she said.

"A person who needs a job doesn't have time—you told me that," he said.

"Remember my offer still stands for you to work at CryoCorp."

"Yeah, right, over my dead body—oh, I forgot, you already did that."

She ignored the remark.

"Well, I just wanted to say that you handled yourself very well in a tough situation. And I totally understand why you did not want to discuss the God situation. You were spot on."

~ ~ ~

Three days later Marshall and Ted said their goodbyes and Marshall headed back to Arizona. Ted tied some flies and then took a break to open his mail. There were four separate letters from advertising agencies. All of them wanted Ted to do commercials for their local clients. Perhaps this was the break he had been waiting for.

He was an experienced spokesman. In his playing days he did ads for Moxie, a local soft drink company that also gave him his own brand of soda, Ted's Root Beer. He appeared in ads for Wilson brand baseball gloves. He did an ad for a General Electric skillet in which he was cooking. His relationship with the Sears, Roebuck Company began just as he left the game and lasted well into his retirement. They attached his name to everything from baseball bats to fishing boats.

His other choices were not so distinguished. His image appeared in ads with fellow baseball players Joe DiMaggio, Stan Musial, Bob Elliott, Ewell Blackwell, and Bucky Harris, all hawking Chesterfield cigarettes. For the privilege of using Ted's image, Chesterfield paid him 50 bucks. He, and quite a few players used in a long series of Chesterfield ads, never smoked.

In retirement, he did another cigarette ad, fishing and smoking, for Lucky Strike, particularly appropriate perhaps for a batting champion who would argue until the cows came home that any pitcher who notched a strike against him got away with a lucky strike. His image was plastered on poker chips. And the pièce de résistance: his unauthorized likeness appearing on the front of packages of Champ Prophylactics, three condoms to a package. (Three strikes and you're out?) In a mid-20th century act of advertising subtlety, on the cover of the condoms he was, of course, swinging.

Ted took a meeting to talk to the latest advertising guys who wanted a piece of him. He traveled up to the 84th floor of the 100-story Emirates Tower, Boston's tallest building, built after the flood. In the lobby of the advertising agency of Beswell & Company he announced who he was and then waited, staring out of the high windows at nothing. *What a waste*, he thought. *A building this high in Boston often is in the fog.*

After a few minutes he was escorted to a large conference room filled, as usual, with suits. These suits were more brightly colored than the Arizona species that he remembered. Ted was dressed formally in a shirt with a collar.

Introductions were made. Jackson Beswell, the head of the agency, got right to the point.

"Ted, we want to represent you. As I think you know, we are not just an ad agency, we're also a management firm. We want to represent you and the Ted Williams brand. Your story is certainly unique. We are the one firm that is uniquely qualified to facilitate brand equity transfer for the Ted Williams brand, that is, successfully carry over the Ted Williams of your former life to your new life, and do it in such a way that is unique and dignified, of course."

"Of course," said Ted.

"I am confident," said Beswell, "that we can make you once again into an iconic brand—fabulous and unique."

"You sound like a unique company," said Ted sarcastically.

"We are, Ted, we are."

"And there's money in it for me?" said Ted.

"Well, not much at first, but we'll put in escalators that trigger based on the performance of the ads."

~ ~ ~

Over the next four weeks Ted traveled all around greater Boston shooting a series of ads that Beswell promised were the jumping-off point to a "very unique" career. Back on Marlborough, Ted sat down and asked VR to play his new reel. Ted's image appeared on the screen.

"Are you in the market for a used car? Hi, I'm Ted Williams. Take it from a guy who's been around the block a couple of times . . ."

"Ted Williams here. Are you looking for new furniture, a comfortable lounger, a couch to lie on—a new mattress, maybe? Well, I'm an expert on reclining and deep sleep . . ."

"Hi, I'm Ted Williams. I've always appreciated a good beer, and there's nothing like a cold-brewed beer. Take it from a guy who knows cold . . ."

"This is Ted Williams. When I'm in New Hampshire, my favorite place to shop is the Second Time Around Antiques Marketplace . . ."

The money was good enough so that Ted, at least for the time being, did not have to sell off the only fishing boat tied up to the rear of a Back Bay mansion.

Thirty-four

Feeling rather lonely, though he would not admit it—even to himself—every other day Ted dialed Amanda, at home and work, to no avail. After a couple of weeks, and after contemplating just showing up at her doorstep, he gave up.

The number of media people staking out the house and trailing him around had diminished, but he was still hounded by reporters with requests for one-on-one interviews, all of which he declined.

His commercials hit the airwaves with less than satisfactory results. Research showed that people giggled, and didn't take him seriously, and maybe were a little put off by him.

Soon, the offers began drying up.

Ted met with Beswell again.

"It'll get better," explained Beswell. "We'll work on the unique selling proposition for each product and your brand will become more recognizable."

"Yeah, well, uniqueness is like that sometimes," said Ted.

Bernard Cromwell sensed an opportunity and offered Ted the chance to be a spokesman for CryoCorp. Ted refused.

"You're already using my goddamned name. I'll keep my image to myself," he said.

~ ~ ~

Over breakfast at the Four Seasons Hotel, Ted and Elizabeth endured stares from other guests but were largely left alone. Apparently, the paparazzi were less inclined to trample into a large establishment with a reputation for protecting guests and diners.

"So, I'm sorry to hear that the commercial work is slowing down," said Elizabeth.

"Yeah, I wasn't really happy with the quality of the stuff I was getting anyway," said Ted.

"Yes, I sort of noticed that. Well, would you like to help me get some new patients?"

"You mean shill for CryoCorp? Hell, no."

"No, I mean vouch for me. I've quit CryoCorp. I submitted my letter of resignation to Bernard yesterday, and I'm opening up a private practice here in Boston."

"To practice cryonics?"

"No, family medicine."

"Well, Dr. Miles, there is hope for you yet."

"Thank you, Ted," she said with derision.

"Tell me. Why did ya leave?" he said.

"Well, first of all, I was unhappy about the way Bernard and the board treated you and the way they handled the disclosure. It was rubbish. Secondly, Bernard and I disagreed on the timetable for reviving the next patient. He wants to do it now, but I put my foot down and said I would not do it until significantly more time passes and we see how you do. I've heard that other companies have tried reanimation but no one has succeeded."

"So, am I still an experiment to you?"

"Ted, don't be cynical, or sarcastic, or whatever it is you are doing. I just think that it's too early. We need to monitor your progress for quite some time, maybe years more, and see how it goes. But Bernard, I believe, wants to strike while the iron is hot. And he likes the attention and wants to focus more of it on him and CryoCorp. He's going to have trouble, though. Without me, I don't think they will be able to reanimate anyone for quite some time."

"So now you're hanging out a shingle? Is that what doctors say?"

"No. We say, come to us if you *have* shingles."

"Where will you practice?"

"I'm already looking at some space on Beacon Hill. Emily is coming to work with me."

"Good for you. If it wasn't 8 o'clock in the morning, I'd order cocktails for a toast."

"Well, there are always Bloody Marys and mimosas—in Britain, Mimosas are called Buck's Fizz."

"How do you know this? You left when you were 12."

"I am worldly—some might say sophisticated."

"Yes, indeed," he said.

Eating toast and drinking a toast, Ted and Elizabeth looked to the future.

"I'll try to scrounge up some of my buddies from the neighborhood to be your patients," said Ted.

"'Scrounging up' doesn't exactly sound like the most efficacious way to recruit new patients," she said. "In fact, I'm not sure, but there might even be AMA rules against it."

"I'll just tell 'em you're no longer doing the Frankenstein thing, just working on colds, hemorrhoids and ingrown toenails—that kinda stuff."

"Gee, maybe I should reconsider and call Bernard back," she said.

"You wouldn't. This is great. Let's drink another toast. To happiness and new endeavors," he said. They clinked again.

"You know, in my former life, I didn't drink at all until I retired from baseball," he said.

"Yes, I know. You've told me that a couple of times. I'm not sure you should be drinking now."

"I'm fine," he said.

"I would like to continue to be your personal physician. Is that all right with you?"

"You can be my doctor," he said.

He fiddled with the silverware, she with a few locks of her hair.

"Hey, how's Johnnie doin?" said Ted.

She drew in a breath and exhaled with contentment. "He's well. Very well."

"Tell him I'm coming over tomorrow, and we're gonna play some ball."

Thirty-five

Ted and Johnnie went over to Harvard to play catch. *Never too early to get the kid excited about going to college,* thought Ted. Indeed, they were playing catch right in the middle of Harvard Yard. He wore the aviators as students, professors and what looked like researchers in lab coats, walked by.

"Did you ever go to college?" said Johnnie.

"No, but I often wished I had," said Ted. "Learning can be a lot of fun. And I'll tell you something. It's one of the secrets to happiness—learning throughout your life. Makes you grow as a person."

"How come you didn't go to college?" said Johnnie.

"Well, I was a good ballplayer, and the offer to play professional ball came before college. Not sure I coulda afforded college anyway. That's why the offer of money for playing baseball was so attractive; my family didn't have a lot of money back in San Diego. Plus I loved playing baseball, was good at it."

They were only a few feet apart, but Johnnie was now winding up, throwing as if he were on a pitcher's mound. Ted began to crouch.

"I'll tell ya, when I went to flight school during World War II, that was a lot like college," said Ted. "Started out right here in Mass., at Amherst. I was proud that I was able to keep up with the college boys. I had to work real hard to do it, though."

"Do you have to be real smart to be a pilot?" said Johnnie.

"Well, yes. Today, I imagine, even more so," said Ted. "Math is particularly important. Science too; understanding the physics of flight and some mechanical engineering—knowing how your aircraft works, its limitations—is always important."

As the game of catch and the discussion went on, Ted began to notice an older man leaning against a tree, just watching him and Johnnie.

"Johnnie, my boy, you are throwing great," said Ted.

In his catcher's crouch, Ted turned his head, and the man's eyes met Ted's. The man smiled.

The man walked over to Ted who continued catching and throwing back to Johnnie. The man stopped a few feet away and said, "Ted, Ted, can I talk to you for a minute?"

Ted realized he could no longer ignore him and put his hand up to Johnnie in a signal to stop.

"Look mister," said Ted. "I'm just trying to play catch with my buddy Johnnie here, and I would appreciate being left alone."

In a hushed voiced, the man said, "Ted, do you know who I am?"

Just then, the recognition hit him and Ted said, "You're Mr. McBride, owner of the Red Sox. I've seen you interviewed on compuTV."

"Yes, I am," said McBride. He stuck out his hand and the two men shook.

"I see that you're still throwing righty—and batting lefty, too," said McBride. "Just like old times."

"How do you know how I'm batting?"

"Well, I know someone that saw you in the batting cage. He also said that you were hitting pitches up to 125 miles per hour."

"Those radar guns can be wrong."

"True, but my guess is that it wasn't that inaccurate. Ted, take my card. Give me a call. We'd like to know if you would consider trying out for us—playing baseball again."

"Well, I don't know Mr. McBride, it's just that—"

"No pressure. Just come in, and let's talk. Good to see you, Ted."

They shook hands again, and McBride walked away. Ted tucked the business card into his pocket and stared at McBride as he headed off. Johnnie came running up to Ted.

"Who was that?"

"Oh, just some guy," said Ted, still staring. "Just some guy."

~ ~ ~

Back on Marlborough, the idea of playing baseball again swirled around in Ted's head; he was like a June bride dreaming about her wedding dress. He tied several flies. It had always been this way; tie some flies, relax, and engage in some deep thought. He was particularly pleased when he completed a classic featherwing fly and then moved onto a few hairwing numbers.

As his thoughts focused on baseball, he told himself over and over again that playing again did not make sense. He hated the idea of playing against the Botwinder. He would be surrounded by drug-taking teammates, and he would never take the cocktail. *That would put me at a disadvantage, wouldn't it? What if I failed? Will the new me be able to put up with the grind of a baseball season that now lasted for nearly 200 games?*

On the other hand, he missed it. Every ex-player does from the moment he retires. *I love the competition; the camaraderie; the strategy; the science of hitting; the sights—even the smells.* Even the long, languid pace of the season in the hot summer sun had its appeal.

He was intrigued. *If the radar gun was correct, I was hitting the Botwinder at a higher rate of speed than all of the juice junkies across the major leagues. What gave me such power? Where did it come from? Is it sustainable across an entire season?*

He couldn't help asking himself, would he be accepted by the players, the press, the fans?

His mind wandered back to his playing days. Old players never die when thoughts turn to gripping the bat again. For Ted it was an existential experience. He took full responsibility for creating the meaning of his own life, and that meaning, at least in his former life, totally revolved around hitting.

His physical self had stopped tying flies and was staring at a wall, but his mind was in another place and time altogether.

He could feel a palpable adrenaline rush as once again he stood at the plate. What he was imagining, he could hear in echoes. The ball was careening toward the plate; there was a split second of decision-making, and then the release of limbs in all-out coordinated effort to connect with the baseball.

And the smell. He could smell the burn of the bat after it connected with the ball. Then the recoil, followed by the tracking of the ball.

Thirty thousand people stood up. Heads turned throughout the ballpark. They watched the white ball with 108 red stitches soar, as if in slow motion, in a great arc toward the wall. In no other sport is there such a pregnant pause, a pause filled with so much anticipation. After the ball cleared the wall—sheer pandemonium.

He had goose bumps even from the thought of it.

He pulled Mr. McBride's card from out of his shirt pocket and made the call. After all, he rationalized, *I need to make a living.*

~ ~ ~

Danny the gondolier, this time driving a water taxi, took Ted over to Kenmore and walked with him the last couple of hundred yards or so over to Fenway. Ted told him why he was going.

"So, you nervous?" said Danny.

"If I was, I wouldn't tell ya," said Ted.

They walked over the bridge that spanned the MassCanal.

"You know why they call this the Bridge of Sighs?" said Danny. "Not because it's like the one in Venice, but because of all the disappointment heard on it over the years from fans leaving the ballpark."

"Yeah, yeah," said Ted.

They walked across a pedestrian drawbridge that connected to the dock that ringed Fenway. Danny said, "Good luck buddy," and slapped Ted on the side of the shoulder.

Ted announced himself to security and a guard escorted him into the bowels of Fenway. The place had changed a lot. There were modern appointments everywhere but it still was a confined space. The guard led Ted to a conference room where McBride and three other people were waiting.

Geez, I hate boardrooms and suits.

McBride said, "Ted, good to see you. This is Mike Leonard, our GM; Carl Strongman, our director of player personnel; and, of course, our manager, Buck Pearson.

"No offense," said Pearson to Ted, "but this is a little like meetin' a ghost."

"None taken," said Ted as they shook hands.

"Ted, thanks for coming in to see us," said McBride. "We are very interested to know if you would be willing to play baseball again. We think it would be good for you and good for the Red Sox. We haven't been winning much lately, as you know, and having you on the team would help us bring more people into the ballpark. That's what it's all about, and compuTV income, of course."

"Of course," said Ted.

"But we have a lot of questions, as I'm sure do you," said McBride.

Pearson couldn't contain himself and rushed into the conversation.

"Is it true you were hitting a baseball at 125 miles an hour? That's above the legal limit of the Botwinder in the major leagues."

"Yes, it is true," said Ted, "providing the radar was accurate. I think it was. I've never seen pitching that fast and, honestly, I was goddamned surprised myself."

"Well, Ted," said Leonard, "how do you think you were able to do it? Are you taking the cocktail?"

"No!," said Ted in a booming voice. "I am never going to take any of that goddamned crap. I hate what it's done to the game. I hate that you let your guys hit against a robot. I'm not even sure why I'm here."

"We'll get back to that in a moment," said McBride. "First, can you tell us why you think you are able to hit against such ball speed?"

"Well, I have a theory. You know that I am now sporting the body of a deceased 25-year-old tennis player? From what I understand, tennis players are now hitting a goddamned tennis ball traveling at them at 170 miles an hour. I'm not saying it's as difficult as hitting a fastball from 60 feet, six inches away with a narrow bat. However, the tennis player's body combined with my former vision, coordination, memory, experience and such, may be makin' it possible."

The hosts all nodded their heads with wide eyes.

"You guys look like executive bobbleheads," said Ted.

"I ain't no executive," said Pearson.

"You do understand this is a business?" said Strongman. "As such, you do realize, Ted, if things work out and you are able to play ball again, we can offer you a multimillion dollar contract. Do you have an agent?"

"Hell, no. And I don't need one."

"Well, that's refreshing," said Leonard.

"Ted, you got somethin' against the Botwinder?" said Pearson.

"It's a goddamned mechanical contraption," said Ted. "I've seen a few games, and I hate it. I hate what it's done to the game. I hate the fact that all of the guys are taking the juice. I hate what a vicious goddamned circle it's created."

"That's a lot of hate, Ted," said McBride. "Are you sure you want to be here?"

"Geezus, I don't know. I'm just an old ballplayer and the thought of playin' again . . . Well, the only way to describe it, I guess, is that it's intriguing."

He didn't let on that he was also desperate for money.

"Do you think you can play with guys who are, ah, taking a different posture than you on the supplements?" said Leonard.

"Supplements? That's what you call 'em, eh? Well, as long as I don't have to participate in the taking of the goddamned things."

"If you don't need them, we don't care," said Strongman.

"Well, Ted, can you come back tomorrow?" said McBride. "We'll have the batting cage set up and give you a little tryout."

"That'll be fine, Mr. McBride, that'll be fine."

They all shook hands with Ted, and McBride asked one of the security guards to walk Ted to the exit.

Back in the conference room, Buck Pearson added a postscript to the meeting.

"This just might work," he said. "That hate, or anger, as long as it's manageable in the clubhouse, and directed more at the Botwinder, that'll be his motivator. People said anger was what fueled his success in the past—trying to destroy every pitcher he faced and knockin' the shit out of the ball."

The bobbleheads nodded in unison.

Thirty-six

The next day Ted showed up at Fenway with his own bats. In the clubhouse all by himself he dressed in a red sweatshirt and loose-fitting gray sweatpants, tied the laces on his cleats and made the walk through the tunnel out to the Red Sox dugout. *Geezus, glad to see they fixed the tunnel. In my day it was flooded every other week.* He shunted the emotions as he climbed the dugout steps and hit the morning sunlight.

Who said you can't go home again? Clichés and conflicting emotion were impossible for him to ignore. *I want to be here. I shouldn't be here. Damn, this is great.* That was the turning point; there was no thought of failure, only success. The competitive juices were flowing. For Ted, the only question was, did the Botwinder have any stuff that would surprise him? He already knew he had the bat speed. But could he hit all of the junk, anything it would throw at him?

Buck Pearson met him on the field. Mr. McBride and the other execs were up in the owner's box. It was a brilliant day, warm with no wind. Ted looked around. Fenway, viewed from the grass, no matter how many times you hit the field, was always a thrill. He could hear the echoes of all of the crowds, the cheers, and—in Ted's memory—the jeers as well. He had a thousand-yard stare.

"Ted, Ted, are you ready?" said Pearson.

"Yeah, I'm ready," said Ted. "Just let me do a few stretches and swings to warm up."

He grabbed two bats and began to swing, first slowly and then with more intensity. He then took a pine tar-soaked rag he had brought along from home and rubbed both bats. The Botwinder appeared out of the garage door in the triangle in deep center field. As Ted knelt rubbing his bats, he tried to pay no heed to the giant machine as it strode purposefully toward the mound. But it was impossible to ignore. Ted was full of contempt for it but still marveled at its agility. It held a glove on the right mechanical hand and would apparently pitch him as a lefty.

"Is this tin can goin' to throw to me only as a southpaw?" Ted asked Pearson.

"We'll have it switch midway through," he said. "We've programmed it to throw you all kinds of stuff. Be prepared for any pitch. Ted, just try to get over it being a robot, and think of him as the best pitcher you ever saw."

"Does he have a name?"

"Naw, none of 'em do. We just go by his number—forty two."

For the first time it dawned on Ted that Botwinders did not wear uniforms. Its number was painted or applied to a metal panel on its back.

"Can Botwinders hear?" said Ted

"Yeah, but not like you and me. It'll respond to voice commands from me or Joe Klein, my pitching coach, but it won't respond to the crowd, distractions, stuff like that."

"You need a pitching coach?"

"Well, he's sorta more like a tech repairman with a little baseball knowledge for good measure. He actually carries a little toolkit in his pocket out to the mound."

"You're shittin' me?"

"Nope. Mostly, though, he doesn't use many tools, just re-programs the thing from a key pad just above the Botwinder's left hip or installs computer discs."

"The science of pitching, eh, Buck?"

"Are you ready?" said Pearson.

"Yeah, let's go."

A young Red Sox catcher jogged out from the dugout and stood behind home plate as Ted entered the right side of the batter's box. Pearson stood behind the batting cage.

"Does he need to warm up?" asked Ted.

"Usually not," said the catcher. "During games he does it to warm up us catchers."

Ted gripped the bat loosely and took a couple of practice swings. He stood ready. His fingers tapped on the bat handle. The Botwinder pitched with a conventional windup—if you call metal-on-metal and considerable grinding and screeching conventional—and delivered, of all things, a first-pitch change-up to the plate. At least to Ted it looked like a changeup. He let it pass, although it looked like a strike. He stepped out of the batter's box and glanced up at the radar board; it registered 89 miles an hour.

The next pitch, a fastball, came flying in on the inside corner and Ted ripped it for a single to right. One hundred and five miles per hour registered on the gun. The Botwinder was obviously programmed to increase the speed because over the next eight pitches the velocity increased to 120 miles an hour. Ted hit them all with varying degrees of success, spraying the ball around the right side of the ballpark.

"How's it feel?" said Pearson.

"Feels good," said Ted, staring at the Botwinder.

The next pitch, a curve, Ted swung on and missed. "Goddamn it," he said.

Once again, the Botwinder wound up and delivered a fastball, this one inside and low. Ted exhaled a heavy breath and swung. The ball, as if launched out of a cannon, headed toward the right field fence. As the screaming liner flew toward the wall, Ted yelled out, "That'll be in the bullpen."

"We ain't got a bullpen," said the catcher. "No need with Botwinders."

As the homer bounced around in the bleachers, Ted felt momentarily foolish until he looked up at the radar board and it read 122 miles an hour.

He stepped out of the batter's box and turned toward Pearson.

"Is that the max speed?" asked Ted.

"That's it—by rule," said Pearson. "Take some more cuts."

Ted continued to rip the ball—all to right field, but ripping nonetheless. And he did it when the Botwinder switched arms, grabbing another glove that was behind the mound.

"Can he do that in a game?" said Ted.

"He can switch in midinning but there are limitations," said Pearson. "Can't switch in the same at-bat."

"Gee, throwing the hitters a break, aren't ya?"

The next ball produced another home run, this one a towering shot to deep center field. And then another to right. And then another. The most impressive thing was not only the high speed of the fastballs, but the hits were coming off multiple pitches as well. Curves, sliders, forkballs—Ted was hitting them all.

"Okay," said Pearson. "I've seen enough."

Up in the owner's box the suits were ecstatic.

"Ted," said Pearson, "I ain't seen nobody hit like that who ain't on the juice."

"Yeah, well, you just did," said Ted.

"What if you did take it?" said Pearson. "How good would you be then?"

"Don't even think about it," said Ted. "I am never, repeat never, going to take that goddamned stuff."

Ted looked out at the Botwinder as it turned to head toward the garage door and thought it looked dejected. But it was probably just anthropomorphism.

"All right," said Pearson, "I hear you loud and clear. Let's see how you can catch and throw."

He put Ted in left field and watched as he played long toss with a batboy. After about 10 minutes, Pearson stepped up to the plate and yelled to Ted in left to catch and throw home. Pearson hit a series of flies and grounders. Ted's range was excellent and he played balls off the towering Green Monster like he'd been there before. Just as important, when he threw home, the throws were powerful and accurate. Most reached the catcher on a rope; a few were one-hoppers.

"Come on in," yelled Pearson.

Ted jogged in toward the batting cage.

"How'd I do?" said Ted, despite knowing the answer.

"Ted, good buddy," said Pearson, "I think you'll be just fine."

Mr. McBride, Leonard and Strongman were now on the field. They all shook Ted's hand and congratulated him on a fine display.

Strongman said, "Ted, do you have another hour or so to take a physical with our doctor? He's right here in the ballpark."

"Yes, that'll be fine."

"Also, we need to review your medical records and talk to your doctor. Is that okay?"

"Yes," he said, "but let me tell her first this afternoon."

Thirty-seven

Ted gave Elizabeth the heads up, and three days later Mr. McBride called Ted.

"Ted," he said, "we'd like you to join us, to become a Red Sox player again. We have a fine tradition. You were a part of our past and we want you to be a part of our future. Let me let Mike Leonard go over the details with you."

Leonard said, "Ted, do you have an agent yet?"

"No, I don't need one."

"Okay," said Leonard. "Then here is the offer: We're prepared to give you a one-year contract worth $50 million. We know it's not a lot of money, and it's only one year, but you are—that is, the new you—a bit of an unproven player. Before you say no—"

"Done."

"I'm sorry, I didn't catch that," said Leonard.

"Done deal," said Ted.

"Well, fine, Ted," said McBride, clearing his throat and jumping in again on the speakerphone. "Congratulations. We hope you are as excited about this as we are."

"Thanks, Mr. McBride. Yes, I am. I just want to make one thing perfectly clear: I will not be required to take any juice."

"We understand," said McBride. "Honestly, as astounding as it seems, it looks like you don't need it."

"Ted, come in tomorrow about noon and we'll have the papers drawn up for you to sign, and we'll go over plans for a press conference," said Leonard.

Ted knew the answer but he asked the question anyway: "Is a press conference really necessary?"

"Well, I think you know, Ted," said McBride, "it's a part of the game."

"And a game it is," said Ted. "See you tomorrow."

Ted switched off the phone and sat alone in his Back Bay mansion in stunned silence. *This is really happening. I am going to play baseball again.*

The phone rang. It was Dr. Miles. "Where can we meet? I'd like to catch up with you," she said.

"Let's go over to the Beantown Diner," said Ted.

~ ~ ~

When Ted walked in Elizabeth was already seated in a booth. The counter was busy. The place smelled like fried onions and half the patrons were eating pie.

"This is my kind of place," said Ted.

"I know it is," said Elizabeth.

They each ordered a cup of coffee.

"So, what's new?" said Elizabeth. The "so" was long and hard.

"It looks like I'm gonna be playing ball again—thanks to your recommendation."

"It really wasn't a recommendation, just a medical opinion," she said.

"Well, whatever it was, it worked. Thank you. What did you tell them?"

"First, they were very interested in what it is that made you so special, able to do what they told me you were doing. I told them I didn't have an answer for that, that it was a surprise to me, too. You know, the uncharted territory and all that. They also wanted to know if I thought you had the stamina to play baseball again. There was particular concern about the rigors of a full season. I told them that from a medical standpoint you have exceeded all expectations, and how well you have done ever since you were reanimated. I had, I have, no reason to believe that you cannot do it."

"Yeah, well, we'll just have to see, I guess."

"I also warned them that under absolutely no conditions should you take the cocktail."

"Yeah, I told them that, too, though not for medical reasons."

"Ted, are you excited about this? Is this what you really want?"

"Well, it will take me away from fishing. But, running out of money and all makes fishing trips a little bit difficult."

"Is that the only reason you're doing this, for the money, that is?"

"Geez, doc, I didn't know you were a psychologist, too."

"Ted, I'm serious. This is an important decision for you, and I care about you. I want to know that you've thought this through. For example, I know that you are conflicted about the whole Botwinder situation."

"Yes, that's true. But the way I see it, I've been given a second chance to achieve something that eluded me the last time. I never won a World Series. I've looked at the lineup of this team, and I think with my bat and a few good guys comin' up through the farm system we'll have a chance to do it. As for my other motivation, although I never complained about it, I—and a lot of other people—wondered what my career would have been like if I wasn't called into the service twice. I know it's under different circumstances, but now I get to see what happens—me in my prime. Besides, I am a ballplayer. It is who I am. There is no ballplayer on earth, and there never will be, who would give up a chance to play forever if he maintained the skills to keep playing."

"You gave it up for the Marines."

"That's true. But only temporarily, and there were more important, bigger considerations than just me. It was a matter of patriotism and love of this country—which gave me a lot. You know, I never regretted the military service, just the way they went about it, callin' me back the second time under shitty circumstances."

"So what happens next?"

"There's a press conference scheduled for next week, and spring training begins in one month. And, oh, I'm moving out of the house."

"You are?"

"I'm gonna need a place where I can come and go and not live in a fishbowl. A place with security, where they will screen my calls. I did this once before, you know."

"Yes, I remember your telling me about it. What place are you considering?"

"I've been talking to the doorman over at the Dongkou Hotel about a suite; he's kinda one of my buddies."

"Well, perhaps you should talk to management next."

"Yeah, I will."

It was settled. Easy as pie.

Thirty-eight

Ted made arrangements to move into a roomy suite at the Dongkou. It wouldn't be as spacious as the Marlborough address, but he did have three bedrooms, one of which would be a spare room to tie flies, and he would benefit from all of the amenities and services of a major hotel, not the least of which was more privacy and security on the residential floor.

The Red Sox were excited about introducing Ted at the press conference. Remarkably, word did not leak out about it until it was announced the day before the conference. The reaction in Boston was palpable.

"Ted's created more buzz than a bear in a beehive," said Buck Pearson.

Ted was not excited about meeting the press again.

He entered the media room at Fenway with Buck Pearson and Mr. McBride to flashes and a commotion unlike anything ever seen at Fenway. Reporters were literally fighting for position, the writers especially ticked off at the satcast and compuTV people, who were shoving them aside for the best camera angles and sightlines.

"Okay, okay," said Ted to the press as he stood beside Mr. McBride, but he was largely unheard because McBride was in front of the bank of microphones. McBride spoke up to begin the proceedings.

"It gives me great pleasure today to introduce the newest member of the Boston Red Sox, who just happens to be the oldest member as well. All of you know Ted's remarkable story. What you may not know is his desire to play baseball again, to become an active member of this team again."

He turned toward Ted and said, "Ted, I would venture to guess that in the history of sport no team has ever un-retired a uniform number. Well, number nine, we're un-retiring yours."

McBride produced a Red Sox jersey with the number 9 on it and handed it to Ted, who held it up across his chest. Cameras flashed away as Ted grinned and placed a Red Sox cap on his head.

"Ted, why don't you say a few words," said McBride.

"I'd like to thank Mr. McBride and the entire Red Sox organization," said Ted. "It's not often that anyone is given a second chance to relive a dream and that's what I am about to do. Being a member of the Red Sox and being a Marine were the greatest privileges in my former life, and now I am about to get a second chance to take care of some unfinished business. I enjoyed a great career, but while I was here, we never won a World Series. After I, ah, passed, it happened, but it's been a long time since the last one. And, so, Ted Williams is here to bring another World Series victory to Red Sox Nation. That is my goal."

More flashes and shouts in the room, "Ted . . . Ted . . . Ted."

"I know you have questions. Yeah go ahead," he said, pointing to a reporter.

"Ted, in your autobiography—I read your book—you said you had walked away from baseball, never to look back, no regrets, never wishing to do any of it over again. And now this."

"I did say that, didn't I? Well, I guess it all boils down to this: I believe I'm able to compete. I couldn't when I said that, but now I can. Also, I think I'm gonna enjoy this more—appreciate it more—though I'm not sure what it's gonna feel like battin' against a machine every day."

Ted pointed to another reporter.

"Ted, baseball has changed a lot since you last played. Are you going to be able to hit the Botwinder, will you take the juice?"

"Yes, I can hit the Botwinder. No I am not, and I will not, take the cocktail—not unless it's one with gin in it."

The reporters laughed.

"But, Ted, how can you compete with the Botwinder without the cocktail?"

He went on to explain his theory about the tennis player body combined with his baseball mind and added, "It's just a theory. I'm not sure why it's working but it is; I'm hitting faster pitches now than I ever could in my former career. Then again, nobody ever did throw that hard to me back then. Maybe I coulda."

The reporters nodded in unison and an audible "hmmm" could be heard.

Another reporter said, "Ted, this new body of yours, and the whole reanimation thing, are you tough enough for a long baseball season?"

"Well, we'll find out shortly. That's what spring training is for. We'll just take it one day at a time and see how it goes."

And another: "Ted, what position are you going to play?"

"Well, that'll be up to Buck. Right now I'm just focusing on making the team."

"Do you still throw righty and bat lefty?"

"Yes, that's correct. I don't know what that says about human physiology or neurology, but I guess my brain has driven my new body into that old habit. If you know anything at all about my history, I always believed I was a more natural righty—would have been a better hitter that way—but for some reason I started batting lefty, and it became habit. So it is now, too."

Another reporter: "Ted, how does it feel to be in Fenway again?"

"You know, all of us ballplayers always derided the place—it was old. It's even older now, but you cannot ignore the history, the quirkiness, the uneven dimensions. I'm glad the musty ol' goddamned place is still around—even if you do call it Fenway Island. Being a lefty batter, unfortunately, I won't get a chance to soak as many balls as my teammates who hit 'em over the Monster in left."

"Have you met any of your new teammates yet?"

"No, just seen them on compuTV. But I'm looking forward to it. Probably the thing that old ballplayers miss the most is the camaraderie between players. As you know, I can talk hitting for hours and hours."

"Do you think you'll be able to help your teammates with their hitting?"

"Absolutely not. I'm gonna be asking for *their* help adjusting to hitting the Botwinder. But I think I can lick it. Hell, I *know* I can. If a hitter doesn't have confidence, he doesn't have nothin'."

"One more question," said a Red Sox PR guy.

"Ted, do you have any message for Red Sox fans?"

"Well, I guess, if I have one it would be this: I'm gonna be a better, more fan-friendly player. You have my commitment on that. In my former life I was full of insecurities and couldn't stand the booing early in my career. I held a grudge with some fans—not all of 'em, I always liked the kids—but some, for most of my career. Well, I'm ramblin' here, but I think you'll see a difference. What's there to be upset about? I have a second chance to play the game I love. I'm gonna make the most if it. It's a pretty good opportunity. It's a *hell* of an opportunity."

"And the media? How will you treat us?"

"Well, you are a different matter altogether. Maybe if you scratch my back, I'll scratch yours. On second thought, I don't want to go near you mangy mutts. Although there are a few good lookin' women in the room."

The male reporters in the room laughed nervously; the women rolled their eyes.

With one answer too many, the PR guy ended the news conference.

Thirty-nine

Ted wanted to make the most of his month of free time before heading off to spring training. In reality, there wasn't much free time at all. He moved into his new digs around the corner; he made arrangements to dock his personal watercraft at a nearby marina; and he asked the Red Sox to supply a personal trainer. The personal trainer came to the hotel each morning at 6 to work out with Ted in the well-equipped gym on the residential floor of the Dongkou.

Ted soon discovered, to his pleasant surprise, that few neighbors on the residential floor ever used the gym. The workouts were a departure from his former life when baseball players smoked, drank heavily, and hardly ever worried about fitness. Nowadays, they were more disciplined, worked out more, and, as a group, focused resolutely on a regimen of heavy-duty drug use.

He knew that to try to compete with all of the 'roid ragers, he had to be in tiptop shape.

In between workouts, at least a couple of days a week, he took Johnnie after school to Fenway. Johnnie was in awe.

"You see that lone red seat way out there in the right field bleachers?" said Ted.

"Yeah," said Johnnie.

"Well, they're not really bleachers anymore, but they were when I played. Anyway, that red seat marks the distance of a home run I hit, the longest home run ever hit in Fenway, although I'm guessing it's been surpassed by the 'roid ragers."

His voice turned solemn. "Don't ever take the drugs, Johnnie. They're no good."

When no other ballplayers were around, Johnnie would sneak in a little hitting at Fenway with Ted pitching to him.

On two weekends he and Johnnie traveled up to Maine to get some fishing in. Ted was still teaching Johnnie to fly fish, and Johnnie was becoming quite good at it. Hitting and fly-fishing—a chip off the old bat.

On the way home from the last trip, Ted said to Johnnie, "You know, I'm leaving in two days for spring training."

"Yeah, I know," said Johnnie.

"You need to listen to your mom, do good in school and keep on practicing your swing. I've made arrangements for a personal coach to take you out to Dorchester once a week to get some swings in."

"Thanks, Ted. When will you come back?"

"Well, spring training lasts about four weeks, and then the season starts. Whenever we're home, you'll have tickets and can come to Fenway with your mom. I'll see you then and between home games. Won't have much time for fishin', though, least not 'til the season ends."

"Are you nervous about playin' again?"

"No, just a little excited is all. I'm hopin' it'll be fun, like the old days."

"Was it always fun?"

"Most of the time. Sometimes I was an angry guy, though. You see, I was young, and immature, and insecure. Do you know what that means? Well, it means not sure of myself. Oh, I knew I could hit all right, but being a young kid away from home, that's not always easy. And then it's hard to know who to trust sometimes. I just turned it around and acted out a lot. And of course I was a little spoiled—in my adult life that is. I don't expect you can understand that, but maybe someday you will."

"Did anger mess you up?"

"Well, some people said it *helped* my hitting. But I would disagree. What helped was my intelligence, the way that I could analyze pitchers. That's what helped."

"Will you be able to analyze the Botwinders?"

"That's a good question. I'm working on it. Been reading a lot and talkin' to Buck Pearson. Supposedly, the Botwinder gets better against you the more he plays you because he stores all of the information from former at-bats against you—which is what I used to do against pitchers. With the Botwinder, basically, you're playing against a computer. I figure I'm gonna be like those ol' Russian chess players who were able to play against and beat a supercomputer. That's me—Tedskarov."

"That's funny," said Johnnie.

They both raised their arms and clunked the bottoms of their fists together.

"Hammer 'n' nail," said Ted.

"Hammer 'n' nail," said Johnnie.

Forty

In two days, Ted got on a flight headed to Asheville, North Carolina. *This is strange*, he said to himself. *Spring training is supposed to be in Florida—Sarasota or Fort Myers.*

But those places didn't exist anymore, not to speak of, anyway. Spring training was now in the sunny mountains of western North Carolina. With Florida largely underwater, the Grapefruit League had been replaced with the Pine Tree League.

The Red Sox Mountain View Complex consisted of four ball fields, two just for practice and two that were stadiums. The bigger stadium was where the major leaguers played throughout spring training with a capacity of 25,000 fans; the other was where the Red Sox Single A team, the Asheville Tourists, played most of its games. There, the scoreboard was rather low-tech, forever reading "Tourists vs. Visitors." The complex also included a series of rectangular batting cages with pitcher's mounds and home plates. There was also a large field house with classrooms, and an enormous gym.

Ted settled into a large hotel that, during the rest of the year, was normally used by the tourists—tourists with a lowercase "t."

The first day of workouts was nothing like anything the team had seen before at spring training. The media gang was tremendous. In addition to the grizzled baseball reporters for whom this was an annual pilgrimage, there were press from around the world. Many were young reporters or "faces" that had no background covering baseball.

They were all there to see Ted, of course, and the regular beat guys couldn't stand it. Ted, intending to not let it get to him, came off as amused by it all, especially the constant elbowing, figuratively and literally, for his attention. He complied with management's request and agreed to participate in daily press conferences.

Besides the media attention and the site, what struck Ted as odd was that spring training was now shorter. With no need for pitchers and catchers to report early, and no need for pitchers to build up their workouts—no need for pitchers at all—the major leagues elected to move faster into the regular season—just a month down the road. Another factor: It was no longer cold in places like Cleveland and Boston, and the season could start early with little threat of bad weather. It was, of course, all about the money.

The Appalachian spring training would be a trial in many ways. Ted found the whole thing offensive. Not the shortened length due to lack of pitchers, but the idea that hitters did not require a fair amount of time for working out the kinks, getting the timing down and, in his case, getting used to the Botwinder. He longed for the simple gifts in all of the spring seasons in his memory.

Ted did understand, however, that another major purpose of spring training was still the idea that you had to get to know your teammates, a new crop of them invariably coming in every year. Ted was among quite a few new additions. The Red Sox had once again finished in the middle of the pack the year before, and Mr. McBride, biting the bullet, was intent on bringing in a new bunch of talented players that would make the Bosox competitive again.

The competition would be tough. With no pitchers, the roster was now limited to 20 players. *Not so bad*, thought Ted. *That's actually a little more space for position players than when I played.* But there was plenty of competition from all of the young guys and the newly signed stars. Then, of course, there were the veterans. It was always a tricky dance when new players were added to a team. Many times, it's clear where people are going to play. But in some cases the players have to earn their positions and others must fight it out to keep their jobs. In sports, as in all of life, it has always been thus.

On the first day Buck Pearson took Ted around the clubhouse to introduce him to all of his teammates, many of whom were guys jockeying for positions.

Ted surveyed the room full of players in various states of undress. Though he had prepared himself, he was still a little shocked to see the results of the 'Roids-HGH-Anaradium-406 cocktail. Even the little guys were big. And every single one was bald. He refrained from calling them eggheads, but that was his first thought.

The room grew silent as Pearson made introductions. First was shortstop Lester Minster, a little guy from the South side of Chicago.

"Damn glad to meet ya," said Minster.

Ted liked that, a shortstop that sounded a lot like him.

Next was second baseman Jesús Calingo, from the Dominican Republic.

"Como tu ta," said Calingo.

"This is third baseman Ephram Moses," said Pearson, to which Ted said, "Holy shit, we've got Jesus and Moses on the same team."

The rest of the team erupted in laughter, but Calingo and Moses were not amused.

"Just having a little fun, boys," said Ted to the two infielders.

Moving on, "This is, ah, outfielder, Johan Johansson," said Pearson.

His pause before saying "outfielder" was awkward. Johansson had spent his entire career with the Sox playing left field, and now it was widely assumed he would be moving to center with Ted on the team. The big Swede gave a dispassionate nod.

Ted stuck out his hand. Before Johansson offered his own hand, he stood up. It seemed to take forever and when he finished standing Ted was staring up at all 6 feet, 7 inches of him. Ted guessed Johansson was probably blond had he not taken the cocktail and lost all of his hair. They shook hands.

Johansson never uttered a word, just nodded again. With his height and massive shoulders, Ted thought Johansson was better suited for football, but he could have said that about all of the over-infused specimens surrounding him.

And so it went around the room. Pearson showed Ted his locker next to that of catcher John Smith from Oakland California, whom Ted immediately called "Smitty." Ted had met guys from Wisconsin, Alabama and Oklahoma, as well as those from Japan, Cuba, Russia and Sweden.

"Geezus," he said to Pearson, "it's a goddamned United Nations in here."

"You've got to remember," said Pearson, "with global warming, baseball has spread around the world. There are a lot more temperate places now where the game can be played."

"Yeah, I guess so," said Ted. "I remember I started to see guys playin' from all over in my former life, but not like you have here. This'll be interestin'."

Forty-one

Pearson called Johansson into his office and made it official: He was trying out Johansson in center and putting Ted in left. He talked about Ted's experience with the Green Monster in Fenway and, in an effort to placate Johansson he talked about the Swede's better range and strong arm. Johansson, always a man of few words, said, "That's fooken great, Buck."

The press immediately jumped on the controversy, calling it the "Appalachian Complication." They tried to elicit negative comments from both men.

"Hey, I'm just followin' the instructions of the skipper," said Ted. "We're focused on getting in shape and winning."

Johansson said, "No fooken kom-entt."

Ted wasn't worried about Johansson. He felt more alive than ever. He had to pinch himself. *I'm playin' baseball again!* In addition to what a great feeling it was to be taking swings on a regular basis, in the mountains he was able to take long walks in the evenings. Smitty often accompanied him. The two naturally talked baseball. Smitty was thrilled to be able to pick Ted's brain about hitting, and Ted was thrilled to tell him about it. Smitty was an accomplished, veteran player but Ted, as he did with so many others, wasn't hesitant about telling him what to do at the plate.

Of course, the talk also came around to the cocktail. And Ted had lots of questions.

"When did you start takin' it?" he said during a walk.

"As soon as I turned 18," said Smitty. "That's when everyone starts if you're a good prospect."

"Geezus, you were just a kid. Couldn't you do without it?"

"No, not really. It improves performance. So it's a given that guys who are serious about playing are gonna take it. We need it to compete against the Botwinders."

"What are the side effects—besides the obvious ones? There's got to be side effects. What about the radioactivity?"

"Well, it's in a very small dose and the pills are coated or something. Not many of us understand it; we just know the combination works great. There is occasional nausea, big bald heads, and the small gonad thing. Some anger. We don't have kids because we don't want to pass on any problems. And people do die younger, but it's what we do for the game."

"Geezus, I thought I sacrificed a lot for the goddamned game—privacy and all—but nothing like this," said Ted. "I still don't know why you fucking do it."

"We're competitive."

"Good answer," said Ted. "Helluva an answer. I guess I can understand that much, but . . ." He shook his head.

"Look, let me ask you something," said Smitty. "In your former life, you did what conventional wisdom told you to do, right? Well, it's no different now."

"Well, I broke a lot of conventional wisdom, too," said Ted. "For example, players smoked, and I didn't. I always knew it couldn't be good for you. Hell, I didn't even drink 'til I retired—'cept malted milk shakes. And my batting was different—I was more focused."

"You were a Marine, right?" said Smitty. "So you know what it's like to be a part of a team—both on the playing field and the battlefield. You answered the call, man. There are some people that question the sacrifices made in war, but you took those chances. This is no different. This is war. This is about honor and dedication. We are baseball players. We're all trying to win the World Series—and beat the Botwinder."

"I can respect the World Series goal," said Ted, "but not the Botwinder ambition. Didn't the 'roids come first? It may have been before your time, but the Botwinders were added to compete against *you* guys."

"Doesn't matter now," said Smitty. "We have to do it now to compete."

"And another thing," said Ted. "You are a catcher. I noticed catchers don't give the pitcher signs anymore. Doesn't it bother you to be dictated to by a machine? And, how do you know how to set up for the pitch?"

"Well, you're right, the Botwinders know what to do and call their own games. As far as setting up behind the plate, I do it and the machine generally hits my mitt. It's true, sometimes I guess wrong about what it's gonna throw, so I've got to be ready to catch anything. It's a lot like catching a knuckleballer—you need to be ready to catch it wherever it goes. Also, I'm the field general. The skip is in charge, naturally, but I direct the defense. Of course, I throw runners out; I guard home plate. I try and schmooze the ump lookin' over my shoulder. I take pride in all of that."

"*You* are a goddamned specimen," said Ted. "I do admire your commitment."

They were walking on a footpath in a meadow surrounded by southern pine and dogwood trees.

"You know," said Smitty, "we have something in common."

"And what would that be?"

"I have had a body transplant like you."

"Really?" said Ted.

"Don't be so surprised; probably a million people have had the surgery—though yours was the first to include a head that had been frozen. I don't remember much at all about my operation, just what my mother and father told me. I was only three years old. My parents said I was a sickly baby.

Failure to thrive, I think they called it, some kind of growth-inhibiting organic disorder."

"Did they put in an order for a catcher?" said Ted.

Smitty laughed. "Nah, they were just happy to have a toddler who survived."

"And after your parents went through all of that you rewarded them and sacrificed the same body by taking the juice?"

Smitty pursed his lips and nodded without replying.

~ ~ ~

There were maybe 50 guys at spring training including an abundance of rookies that the Red Sox had invited to train with the veterans. Most knew they didn't have a chance in hell in making the big league team of 20 players, but they were glad for the opportunity to strut their stuff. The number of players made intra-squad games easier. And, of course, there were many games against other teams in the Pine Tree League who visited the Sox or whom the Sox visited, often playing two in a day—for which the Sox would use a split squad.

There's nothing like playing against another team to see how you stack up. Typical in spring training, the lineups were loosey-goosey as Pearson worked the rookies in and out to play with and against the veterans.

The press followed every single move and speculated on all of it. In daily press meetings, in the tradition of so many managers before him, and so many southerners, Pearson was a master of talking a lot and not really saying anything. But he knew that he was still giving them something, and that was helping them with their jobs.

Ted was another story. He gave them an earful, pontificating on hitting mostly, and wisely staying away from comments about other players. He also tried to keep his mouth shut about the Botwinders, not yet having fully figured them out. Privately, his analysis of the Botwinders was intense. With their artificial intelligence and data-storage capabilities, they also began to analyze him.

The press followed his every at-bat with tremendous intensity, even batting practice. They commented on every swing. They marveled and speculated about how a guy could be frozen for 85 years and have his severed head reattached to a tennis player, and then possess the muscle memory and new skill to hit a fastball at 122 miles an hour—without taking the cocktail. "The phrase 'new and improved' has never been more accurate," wrote one reporter.

Normally, the reporters were too numerous to gather around his locker, and so Ted mostly participated in organized press conferences in the media room, and he spoke just after Buck Pearson.

At odd times, if the reporters were few in number, the PR staff would let the reporters catch him at his locker. But they still asked the same questions over and over again, always about his body, cryonics and how he does it.

"I don't know how I do it physically, medically, whatever you want to call it," said Ted. "It's just there."

Then, out of the blue, came a more interesting question: "In your book, Ted, *The Science of Hitting*, you carved the strike zone into 77 different cells and tell readers that you only swing at pitches in the cells that are your sweet spots, or the fat pitches, and avoid the worst cells in the lower outside corner. Given your new body, are your best cells still the same?"

"Well, that's a damned good question. What's your name, kid?"

"Jack Paul, Boston eNews."

"Well, Jack, good job doing your homework, but, no offense, that's for me to know and the Botwinders to find out."

"But won't they eventually find out? And they have more control to hit the weak cells than the live pitchers you faced." said Paul.

"Yeah, but if they go there too often, I'm gonna adjust and hit 'em. These Botwinders may be smart, but they ain't smarter than ol' Teddy Ballgame."

"But isn't the most important thing for a batter to swing at good balls—balls in your cells?"

"Sometimes you gotta take what you can get. There's usually at least one pitch in every at-bat that's gonna be in your sweet spot. Don't forget, Botwinder or not, he's still gotta hit the zone to get strikes and strikeouts. It's about patience, is all."

Somebody else jumped in, "So, you're figuring out the Botwinders, Ted?"

"Well, I've got some work to do, but the way I see it, they've got to figure me out."

What he didn't say, and would never say, was his own personal theory that, machine or not, some of the Botwinders may have tendencies that he could capitalize on. He was working on it, talking to other players in private about it.

A young female reporter jumped into the fray. "Ted, some guys hit .350 in this league. Do you think you can match that against Botwinders throwing at 122 mph?"

"Geezus, when I played the last time there were no women in the locker room. Guess it's another thing I'm gonna have to get used to. Boys, if my towel slips, you let me know."

Nervous laughter filled the room from the men.

"Anyway, good question, darlin'. The only way I know how to answer it is to say that, so far, I'm doin' okay. Can't fully explain it, though."

Another reporter chimed in: "Ted, have you thought about how much better you *could* be? Are you gonna take the cocktail?"

"No, goddamn it, and quit asking me."

The strike zone questions were a surprise, but the others about the medical stuff or the cocktail were repeated every day until he would shout, "That's it," and turn around to his locker. The Red Sox PR staff would then quickly usher the press away.

Across the room, Johan Johansson was annoyed when the media attention switched to him and the predominant questions were about Ted.

"How are you adjusting to center?"

"Fine."

"Can you tell us how you're feeling now that Ted Williams has taken your old position?"

"Fook off."

Forty-two

The Yankees were in Asheville to duel against the Red Sox and the fan and media attention, already at a fever pitch with Ted in spring training, was off the charts. Pearson didn't like it at all. Spring training was supposed to be about working at a measured pace to get ready for the season, and this had all the trappings of a post-season series.

Added to the numerous storylines was the tension between Ted and Johansson. The Swede continued to be belligerent with the media, Ted and Pearson, which pissed the manager off no end. Before the game, Pearson called them both into his cramped little office.

"Look," he said, mostly looking at Johansson, "you two better work out your differences. There are enough distractions around here. Ya'all are gonna be teammates and playin' next to each other in the outfield. Now, I don't give a rat's ass how ya feel about each other personally, but when you're on that field and in front of the media you better act like teammates."

Ted said, "Hey, Skip, I don't mind playin' with the little Dutch boy."

"I am Sveedeesh! An you, a komp-pleet mor-oon-a."

"If I was you, ya Swedish meatball," said Ted, "before calling anybody a moron, I'd learn how to pronounce it."

Johansson began to move toward Ted when Pearson quickly jumped up to stand between them. He was way overmatched at 5-foot-8 standing between two hulking 6-plus-footers, but he stood his ground.

"I'm not gonna say this again. If you two don't cut out this shit, I'm gonna bench ya both. Knock it off! Now get out there and focus your goddamn energy against the fuckin' Yankees."

The game went off without a hitch, with no more visible animosity between the two. The Sox played well against the Yanks, winning 8 to 5. Ted went three for five against the pinstriped Botwinder, whom he thought was just as dumb as all of the other Yankee pitchers he'd ever known. Johansson went three for five with two home runs.

~ ~ ~

Midway through spring training the team was beginning to gel. Pearson had a good idea of the roles the rookies would play, if any, and the newer members of the team who weren't rookies, like Dimbrowski, Sakamoto and Ted, began to play well together. For his part, Ted was not happy with his progress against the Botwinders. He was batting .319, but the best batters in the Pine Tree League were doing better. Even on his own team, Johansson and Moses were batting .336 and .328, respectively.

Ted's frustration stemmed from the fact that he was not hitting enough for power. The Botwinders seemed to be giving him enough stuff to hit, but he wasn't in a groove in which he felt entirely comfortable. Pearson thought he was just trying too hard and encouraged him to "just lay off the gas pedal a little."

That kind of advice annoyed Ted. After all, he wrote the book on hitting. He didn't need Buck Pearson, batting coach Mac McCarthy or anyone else telling him how to hit. Never mind that he was hitting against a mechanical pitcher with artificial intelligence that was storing away every bit and byte of information about him and using it against him in subsequent at-bats. He refused to give in to the notion that the Botwinders were superior in any way, or to the thought that he should be using the cocktail to match the higher levels that many of his teammates and the competition were playing at.

To Pearson he simply said, "I am gonna lick those mechanical bastards."

McCarthy was an affable guy, a baseball lifer, who could have been a manager anywhere else had he not been so loyal to Pearson. He worked with Ted on his swing, but it was a little like Rembrandt taking Painting 101, except for the fact that the Botwinder was a totally new canvas for Ted.

~ ~ ~

With one week to go before the regular season began the Sox were in Louisville to play against the Cardinals. On the morning of the game Ted took advantage of some free time and visited the Hillerich & Bradsby Company for a meeting about an endorsement deal. The company, which made Ted's personal bats more than a century before, was thrilled to do a deal with Ted, even though he was an unproven commodity in his new incarnation. They just figured that they would make the most of it for one season and see if Ted— and the publicity—would take off from there. Ted didn't need the million-dollar offer but he liked the fact that he had a reliable source in which he could turn to make his bats.

He had learned from his recent advertising experiences in Boston, and he thought he was more adept at structuring a deal to put his name on bats. It was a deal that would improve over time as his performance improved and his value increased. Still, the legal language and clauses in the contract were more complicated than Jarndyce and Jarndyce, but Ted signed it anyway without showing it to a lawyer.

While he was at the Louisville Slugger factory he ordered a bunch of new bats made to his personal specifications. In his former career, he made a point of beginning each season with a heavier bat and then, as the season progressed, he would move to lighter ones. Contrary to many hitters who hit for power, he believed that a lighter bat produced greater bat speed and that was more important—even to hit for power—than a big piece of heavy lumber. Now that he was facing the Botwinders hurling at 122 miles per hour, he went with all light bats, ordering all of them at 31 ounces. He picked his own lumber while he was there, leaving instructions to choose only the wood with fine grain and as many pin knots as possible because the knots are harder than the rest of the wood.

~ ~ ~

That afternoon Red Bird Field was filled to spring capacity. During warmups, Ted, Johansson and the Sox right fielder, Sakamoto, were shagging flies and trying to get used to the field's notoriously short warning track. A native of Japan, Sakamoto was another new addition to the Red Sox, coming in a trade over the winter from the London Seafarers. As Ted was wont to do, he quickly nicknamed the new player, calling him "Shitty" or "Sake" or "Sock-It-To-Me." None of which, Sakamoto seemed to understand or care about.

It was a hot spring day, about 90 in the shade, and Ted was just as hot at the plate. By the top of the ninth inning when he came up to bat for the last time, he already had hit two monstrous homers, and a single through the gap in right center. In his attempt to go four for four, in the batter's box he stared at the Botwinder with what Pearson noted was "a shit-eatin' grin." It was as if he knew something the Botwinder didn't. Sure enough, the first pitch—a fastball low on the outside corner—he lifted like a golf shot over the center field fence. Two men were on and the Sox now led 8 to 6.

After high fives and congrats back in the dugout, Pearson thought Ted was in some kind of zone.

"Ted, what did you see out there?"

"Just seeing the ball good, Buck."

Pearson turned to McCarthy and said, "He's uncharacteristically quiet. Guess we shouldn't worry as long as he's knocking the piss outta the ball."

Ted heard the last part, and it made him smile. He liked Buck if for no other reason than he had the same kind of foul mouth as Ted.

In the bottom of the ninth the Cards came to the plate in a last-ditch effort to make up their late-game deficit. With two out and nobody on, the shortstop for the Cards hit a long fly ball to deep left-center field. Ted, moving to his left, ran back. In an instant he recognized he would have the best play on the ball, and then he heard Johansson's voice.

On most teams, the center fielder is the commander of the outfield because he must range the farthest, left or right, and has the better view. Ted didn't like it, but he deferred to Johansson.

The first thing he heard was, "Uur ball."

As he looked up at the towering shot and moved back and back, the crowd roared, but he could hear Johansson yell, "Lots-a ruum. Lots-a ruum."

And then—bang! Ted crashed into the wall and crumpled to the ground in a heap. Johansson fielded the ball after it careened off the wall and hit the cutoff man to hold the speedy shortstop to a triple. As Ted writhed in pain on the ground holding his right wrist, he yelled up at Johansson.

"You goddamned, reindeer eatin', syphilitic, Swedish sonuvabitch—you set me up."

"Nott mee. Eet es heerd to understoond my Eeengleesh vid de Sveedeesh akcentum."

"I understood you perfectly, ya prick."

~ ~ ~

An examination of Ted's wrist by the medical staff determined that he had just a sprain. Still, he would miss the last week of spring training—a critical time period for him to get experience batting against the Botwinders. But with luck the staff thought he would be ready to go by opening day at Fenway.

Ted's cussing was obvious, but the whole story about what happened in left-center in Louisville was kept from the press, largely due to the fact that neither player talked to the media during the week leading up to opening day. Buck Pearson was livid when he found out what happened and secretly fined Johansson. Johansson was not happy.

The team made its way back to Boston, and Ted was glad to be home. He immediately called Elizabeth to say hello to her and Johnnie.

"How ya doin' Johnnie, my boy? Doin' well in school? School's important," said Ted.

The three met at a sandwich shop on the Charles Street Wharf. Outside it was raining softly; inside Johnnie was playing vidball off in a corner, and Ted and Elizabeth got caught up. A few fans at another table were buzzing about Ted's presence but he was left alone.

"So how's the doctoring business going?" said Ted.

"Brilliant, actually; the practice is growing larger. Emily and I are very busy. I just hired Jed and Randall to take care of patients who need some ambulatory assistance and physical therapy."

"Those two'll be good for business," he said sarcastically.

"So, spring drilling was a success, yes?" she said.

"It's spring *training*, and, yes, it was okay. I have this injury but I'm all right. I'm still figuring out how to hit against the Botwinder, but I'm makin' progress."

"Would you like me to take a look at the wrist?"

"No, I'm okay," he said, but still stretched his arm across the table and let her feel the wrist a little. Momentarily, she caught herself holding his hand and pulled away.

"Well," she said, "you're in good hands. The Red Sox have more doctors than a Big Pharma junket. Will you let me know if pain persists? As your personal physician I very much would like to fully examine you soon—just to see how things are going."

"We will get to it," he said. "I know you know more about me than anyone else."

Johnnie came back to the table and they both brightened up.

Taking Johnnie in his lap, Ted smiled brightly and said, "Boy, isn't he somethin'? Look at him. You're gettin' big—and smart, too. How'd ya like that new glove I sent ya?"

"He plays with it every day," said Elizabeth.

"So, you two get the tickets I sent over? You'll be at Fenway on opening day?"

"Yeah!" said Johnnie, raising his arms.

Forty-three

After the team settled back in Boston, the Red Sox released their final roster and Ted was on it. Pearson's probable starting batting order was reported by the media. Ted looked at each report as if it were a Department of Defense briefing, commenting to himself how each player would work in the offensive and defensive scheme.

Baseball players are infamous for applying nicknames to teammates, but Ted was in a class by himself. He had a nickname—sometimes several—for each of them, whom, as a group he called "The Bald Crusaders."

The probable batting order:

Player	Nicknames	Hometown
1) **SS** – Lester Minster	"More-Or-Less," "Less-Is-More"	South Side Chicago
2) **2B** – Jesús Calingo	"Gee-sus"	El Seibo, DR
3) **LF** – Ted Williams	(Many names, in 3rd person)	Arizona
4) **CF** – Johan Johansson	"Meatball"	Ostersund, Sweden
5) **DH** – Mel Tremblay	"Trombone"	Hoboken, NJ
6) **1B** – Don Dimbrowski	"Dimmer"	Stevens Point, WI
7) **3B** – Ephram Moses	"Holy Moses"	Lancaster, PA
8) **C** – John Smith	"Smitty," "Pilgrim"	Oakland, CA
9) **RF** – Shigeaki Sakamoto	"Shitty," "Sake," "Sock-It-To-Me"	Tokyo, Japan

The Bench:

OF – José Estavo	"José-Can-You-See"	Guadalajara, Mex, (R)
RF – Ben Grossman	"Benny" or "Ben Franklin"	Saranac Lake, NY
2B – Carlos Herrero	"Carly"	Bayamo, Cuba
OF – Yoshiharu Ishikawa	"Yoshi"	Nikko, Japan
OF – Crenshaw Jackson	"Stonewall"	Birmingham, AL
1B – Mamo Kahana	"The Big Kahuna"	Hilo, Hawaii
CF – Steve Maccall	"Mac" or "Mackie" or "Stever"	Atlanta, GA (R)
OF – Alexei Novokoff	"Nova" or "Novocain"	Rostov, Russia
3B – Mike Steamer	"Mikey"	Boulder, CO
C – Tom Truesdale	"Tom-Tom" or "Wacko"	Waco, TX
SS, 2B – Tim Winneford	"Tiny Tim" or "Tiny" or "Okie"	Norman, OK (R)

A few of the players were offended at first by Ted's monikers, but most got accustomed to them. When he first met someone if Ted didn't like his name he said so, like the first time he met teammate Mamo Kahana. "Mamo?" he said. "That's a shitty name." Considering what permutations could have stuck, the 260-pound Mamo was glad that "The Big Kahuna" had won out. Many of them, if Ted liked them, he also called "Bush."

Ted completed the truncated spring training batting .326, which was disappointing to him. He knew that it didn't measure up to the 'roid ragers. His on-base percentage was only slightly higher, due to the fact that the Botwinders walked so few batters; so that didn't concern him as much. It was part of the reality in the major leagues.

On the day before opening day, Ted was declared fit to play by the Red Sox medical staff and took batting practice and tossed long balls. Pearson called Ted into his office.

"Ted, I just want ya to know, you're startin' tomorra. I got faith in ya, ol' man—or should I call ya 'The Kid?'" said Pearson.

"Whatever you like, Skip. I just want to say thanks, and tell ya you won't have to worry about me."

"That's good. Don't you worry none either. You screw up and we'll work it out, a' course."

"Of course," said Ted.

The wrist was still a little sore but manageable. Given the injury and the batting average, Ted appreciated Pearson's vote of confidence—especially batting him third.

~ ~ ~

The move back to his hotel in Boston was a welcome change. He could tie flies again, and that's exactly what he was doing the night before the big afternoon game to start the season. Once again, tying flies was therapeutic. In his former playing days, confidence, at least on the playing field, was never a problem for ol' Teddy Ballgame. Now, he was thinking about how far he had come, what an amazing situation he was in, and most of all, what an opportunity he had been given. He was determined to take full advantage of it.

He had one overarching goal: to get back to the World Series and win it this time. He thought about all the crying he had done, alone in his train compartment, after losing in the seventh game of the '46 Series, the first and only appearance he would ever make in a World Series. In hindsight, it was especially hard to think about because back then, early in his former career, he never dreamed it would be his last opportunity to suit up for the Series. He always had that hope, that knowledge that he would be back. But the Red Sox never made it again in his 19 years of playing.

For Ted Williams, a chance to redeem himself was almost an abstract concept. Not close to definition really, just a nagging notion that his was a life not complete. Most men would covet to the extreme the life that he had lived. But not Ted, not fully. He was forever the perfectionist. Never satisfied. Always restless.

And now . . . what an opportunity! No man or woman in all of human history had been given this gift. His was a second chance like no other. This was the greatest comeback of all time. He was aware of it, but he didn't want to dwell on it.

As he lay in bed that night, the quiet hum of the city in the background, before drifting off to sleep he said aloud, "I hope I play well tomorrow."

Forty-four

Opening Day in Boston dawned bright and sunny. It also dawned on Ted that one of the good side effects of global warming was that Boston could even host an Opening Day game without concern about cold weather. For so many years the Old Town Team rarely was at home at the start of the season and usually would be on the road for two weeks before coming back to Fenway.

For nearly two centuries Opening Day rituals played out across the City of Boston. Men and women would make excuses to leave the office early, kids would cut school and try to sneak into the park, weather forecasters, days ahead, would predict the temperature at game time. Excitement was in the air. After all, this was a new beginning, the raison d'être for so many fans.

And for the Red Sox, for 60 years it was the beginning of the end, for it had been that long since they had won their last World Series. But on Opening Day, all was possible. Hope was in the heart, hotdogs in the hand.

Of course, *this* Opening Day was special. A player whom many considered a baseball God would be resurrected.

The media horde was record-setting. The Red Sox had to resort to a media lottery. Reporters gathered from around the world. Photographers were even given permission to crowd onto the roof at Fenway. Prior to the game, Ted refused to give any interviews, viewing it as too much of a distraction. That only led to more intrigue and speculation as to the situation with Johansson. But mostly they were interested in "The Story."

From this point on, "The Kid" would be forever stamped "The Comeback Kid." In the history of sport there was no other comeback like this one. America always had been and always would be a nation that adores a comeback. One reporter said into his microphone: "This comeback . . . this is bigger than Washington at Trenton, Patton at Bastogne, or Tony Bennett on MTV."

Dr. Miles and Johnnie settled into their seats about 10 rows back between the Red Sox dugout and home plate. With them was a surprise addition: Marshall had flown up for the game, the Fenway ticket supplied by Mr. McBride after a discussion with Dr. Miles.

The announcer said, "Ladies and gentlemen, boys and girls, welcome to Fenway Island."

This being Opening Day, player introductions were in order. The visiting Moscow Cosmonauts were introduced first. Despite it having been 134 years since he played his last major league game, taking it all in, Ted appreciated how the uniforms looked remarkably the same. The Red Sox, in their cathedral of a ballpark, always had a sense of and a respect for history.

Because it was Opening Day, all of the Sox were introduced, not in the batting order, but alphabetically, including the bench. Ted was the exception. He was saved for last.

The crowd was on its feet and filled with nervous anticipation. Ted was nervous. When the introduction came, considering the enormity of the situation and the fact that they saved it for last, the words were understated.

"Batting third, left fielder, number nine, Ted Williams."

He was afraid his emotions would get the best of him. It was a problem—this sentimental feeling—that would not have bothered him as a young man in his former life, a predicament that comes only with age, experience, perspective and memory. His mind raced. *For chrissakes, I'm in front of fans in Fenway again.* When he turned around, the crowd, still thundering, thought he might raise his cap. But something stopped him, something inexplicable. Those old unexorcised demons? The defiant remnants of his past? Or perhaps he didn't deserve it. Not yet, anyway. He had not swung a bat in a real game. They couldn't be applauding him for being reanimated; he had nothing to do with it. Even as the raucous cheering wore on he resisted, hoping that they would somehow understand, and that he would soon earn the applause—truly *earn it*. These strange new fans, they knew only the legend.

Standing on the first base line next to his new teammates he thought about his old teammates and fixated for just a moment on Pesky's Pole in right field. Ol' "Needle Nose" and the other teammates—Dommie DiMaggio, Bobby Doer, Joe Cronin, Frank Malzone—he half expected them to be there.

As the thunderous applause and cheering continued, he sought out Elizabeth and Johnnie in the crowd. He spotted them and was at his weakest when he also spied Marshall. It was then that the announcer said something— Ted didn't know what—that caused the cheering to subside, and the teams to jog back into their respective dugouts.

By comparison, the game itself was anticlimactic. There was no visible friction between Ted and Johansson. Ted went 1 for 4. His lone hit against the Botwinder was a double to right center. He spent the better part of the game sizing up the Cosmonauts' Botwinder looking for an edge, any edge. Final score: Cosmonauts 5, Red Sox 3. Yet another inauspicious beginning for the Red Sox.

Forty-five

Over the next month, the Red Sox played less than .500 baseball, and Ted was slumping. He made some progress with the Botwinders but not nearly enough—still, the power hitting problem. The slump was producing a lot of negative headlines in the ePapers, and Pearson was already getting flak about not replacing Ted in the lineup.

One positive aspect of playing in his new body was that he was faster than his former self. Ted figured it might be worth quite a few extra points in his batting average because he could run out a few more infield "leg hits." Still, he was batting an unsatisfactory .301.

He spent extra time with Mac McCarthy to work on his swing, but it produced only an argument. McCarthy had noticed that Ted was swinging with a slight upswing and tried to break him of the habit.

When McCarthy pointed it out, Ted said, "No shit, Mac, I know I'm doing it, I always have. I do it because the mound is higher than home plate. It only makes sense."

A few days later, during batting practice McCarthy said, "Let me ask you something, Ted. When you played the last time, how high was the rubber?"

"Fifteen inches; some teams cheated and made it even higher."

"After you retired, do you remember what happened in '68?"

"Yeah, the league clamped down and standardized the height at 10 inches—boy I wished I'd played then."

"Do you know how high the mound is today, in 2093?"

"Yeah, 10 inches."

"No. It's eight inches."

"You're shitin' me," said Ted.

"No, I ain't."

"I can't believe I didn't notice or ask that question," said Ted. "I mean, I knew it was different—I never played against a 10-inch-high mound. So I thought I was adjustin' to that. A higher mound has always been a bigger advantage for the pitcher because he can achieve more leverage and more downward velocity on the ball."

"Since the advent of the Botwinders, the major leagues lowered the mound to eight inches. The Botwinders are powerful enough," said McCarthy.

"That's the missing piece I need," said Ted.

He knew from studying the Botwinders that they were all 6-foot, five-inches tall. He was 6-foot-3. Knowing exactly how high the mound is now, coupled with the exact height of the Botwinders, he would make adjustments in his swing. The predictable height of the Botwinders was key in his way of thinking.

He also came to the conclusion that, although they were machines, each Botwinder was slightly different than the others. Not that much different, to be sure. But enough, if you were Ted Williams, to notice some variation. For example, some came over the top just a little bit more, and others delivered with a slight sidearm motion. It wasn't that much, because they were all designed according to the same specs. But with his sharp eye, Ted could see the slight differences and use them to his advantage.

It began to work. Over the next month he raised his batting average to nearly .330. The fans were happier. Ted was happier. And Pearson was happier. The pressure was off somewhat about his decision to keep Ted in the lineup. More important, the Red Sox started to win more games. They were still five games out of the division lead behind the Yankees, but they were playing better, and it was only the beginning of June. Plenty of time to catch up—and increase the batting average—in a season that was 200 games long.

~ ~ ~

The Red Sox left on the Asian swing of a road trip that would take them to Singapore, Hong Kong, Taipei and then Sydney, but first they were in Tokyo to play the Giants. Ted had been to Tokyo in the past, but now it seemed more garish than ever. Most countries were like that, he thought, pleasant enough in rural areas, but overcrowded in the cities. In Japan, the comparison worked to the extreme. Always a compact island nation, with the impact of climate change and flooding, its problems, especially urban crowding, were severe.

In his former playing days Ted never socialized much with the team outside the ballpark. Now he made a conscious decision to do more. He agreed to join Sakamoto, Johansson, Calingo, and Smitty for dinner. It was obvious the invitation did not come from Johansson.

They walked among the overwhelming neon lights of Tokyo to find a restaurant. There were so many tourists, the group of foreign ballplayers—five with hairless heads plus Ted—did not stand out, which seemed a bit odd to Ted. *Good name for a rock band,* he thought—*Ted and the Hairless Heads.* He stared into the faces of so many Japanese as they walked on the crowded streets and bumped into him and his teammates.

He wondered what their stories were. He kept his thoughts to himself. He remembered how "the Japs" were reviled in WWII, how he had prepared himself to fight against "the yellow bastards." He finished the war flying Corsairs as a flight trainer—and a damn good one. The closest he got to the Pacific theatre in World War II was San Francisco. He would get his combat experience later in Korea.

But now, as he thought about the Japanese, he marveled at what a staunch ally to the U.S. the nation had become—and how anachronistic, even racist, were his old thoughts and prejudices. What made it easier to like the Japanese was their absolute commitment to and total love of the game of baseball.

The teammates were walking through the Kabukicho District, not far from the Shinjuku Train Station. Kabukicho had always been known as Tokyo's red light district. It also happened to be where some of the best restaurants were located. A native of Tokyo, Sakamoto led the way toward dinner.

As they rambled through narrow streets with bright signs everywhere, they were assaulted by an onslaught of Japanese "Hostess Girls." Ted paid little interest, but his teammates were amused.

"Hey, Sake," yelled Ted, "where the hell are you takin' us?"

Dinner would be in a small, family-run restaurant that the guys would never have wandered into were it not for Sakamoto. Ted looked at the menu and scoffed. From what he could understand by looking around the restaurant, sushi was the predominant item on the menu.

"What the matter?" said Sake.

"No offense, Sake, I like fish, but goddamned *raw* fish is what I use for bait," said Ted.

After much finger pointing and the raising of his voice, Ted thought he communicated to the waiter that he would eat anything with lots of noodles. The rest of the party ordered sushi. Sakamoto made sure the waiter understood what each of his teammates wanted and also ordered a few sashimi dishes for the table. The all drank sake, including Ted. He hesitated because during the season he always believed he shouldn't drink, but he would moderate his consumption, and it would be part of the new, more sociable, Ted.

When the first of the dishes arrived, the sashimi, Sakamoto raised his glass and with a forceful nod said, "meshiagare!" to his teammates. Ted was impressed by the artful presentation of the sashimi, though he wouldn't taste the stuff. The potent rice wine was having an early effect on the group, especially Ted. Always interested in fish, even if he wouldn't eat it, Ted said, "Hey, Sock-It-To-Me, what is sashimi anyway?"

Sakamoto explained in broken English.

"Sashimi is very fresh, thinly sliced, raw fish. Japanese delicacy. Loosely translated, it means 'pierced fish,'" he said. "After being caught, only on hand line, the fish is quickly stabbed in brain to produce instant death. The fish is quickly placed on ice. It enhances flavor because lactic acids not allowed to build up in fish flesh as would happen if fish die slowly. It keeps fish fresher."

After hearing the detailed explanation, Ted the fisherman had a new-found respect for the right fielder.

"Well, Sake," he said, "any man that knows a lot about fish can't be all bad."

He asked a few more questions about the hand lines and was convinced that Sakamoto knew what he was talking about. He also wished he could see it in action.

After dinner, the six rice-wine enthusiasts cavorted off into the temptations of the Kabukicho. The nearest hostess bar was too much to resist for the majority of the group, and Ted went along for the ride. Walking in, each teammate was greeted by a young Japanese hostess. There was a common theme: they all wore tight sequined dresses with plunging necklines. None spoke English. They didn't have to.

Four of their teammates walked off into the large, dimly lit room with the sequined dolls, but Smitty and Ted, shaking off their hostesses, headed for the bar. Each ordered a Kirin beer. The other four teammates had not gone far. Through the shadows Ted and Smitty could see them on couches in various stages of seduction.

"What goes on here?" said Ted to Smitty.

"Well, the girls work for tips, pour drinks, sit on the laps of guys, whisper in their ears, tell them what they want to hear, that sort of thing."

"So, they're pros?" said Ted.

"Not necessarily. They can arrange dates with guys later, but here its just come-ons, flattering, and massive costs for buying them drinks." He punctuated the word "dates" with the universal two-fingered quotation marks.

The nearest of the teammates was Johansson. He was sitting on a couch with his back to Ted and Smitty. The girl with Johansson was straddling his lap. As she bounced up and down and hugged him, her face rested on his shoulder and she was looking at Ted and Smitty at the bar.

Ted reached for a bowl that was sitting on the bar. He grabbed two small limes and held them out for her to see in one hand and moved his hand up and down. With his other hand he then pointed at the back of Johansson.

She raised her head out of curiosity as Ted brought his thumb and index finger together in another universal sign, meaning tiny. She may not have spoken English but she knew immediately that Ted was referring to Johansson's tiny balls. She giggled and turned her attention back to Johansson. Smitty nearly fell off his bar stool laughing.

At the bar they ordered a couple more beers. Ted thought the whole scene was ridiculous. Why go through this exercise? It reminded him of peering in through the glass of a restaurant when he was a hungry kid.

Smitty went off to the men's room. With sex on his mind, Ted's thoughts wandered off to Amanda. The alcohol fueled his lugubrious thoughts. *What is she doing now? Is she seeing anyone?*

Smitty came back and Ted said, "Let's leave."

When the two teammates hit the sidewalk, flashes pierced the air. Ted pushed through the photographer scrum and put his hands in front of several cameras. It was all he could do to not haul off and slug some of them. He and Smitty hailed a cab and headed for their hotel.

Ted Williams, the hostess bar patron, left the scene in disgust.

Forty-six

The next day, around the world, ePapers printed Ted's picture, and gossip websites ran a video of the "Kabukicho Carousing." Ted threw the eReader he was reading into his locker and said, "Fuckin' photographers." In the clubhouse he seemed to have earned new respect from his teammates; the incident provided a platform for significant razzing.

It helped that the Red Sox, and Ted in particular, were absolutely on fire. Through June and half of July his average increased to about .340. In the peculiar way of baseball, although the Botwinders were winning the majority of the battles, they seemed helpless. Ted was giddy with excitement.

Against the Sydney Sharks he hit three home runs and a triple. Batting behind him in the cleanup spot, Johansson was not pleased. From his perspective, when Ted homered, he took away most of the runs batted in that were rightfully his.

After the triple in Sydney, Johansson homered. Ted waited for him at the plate, gave him the iron fist high five that was popular among the teammates, and said, "Hey, Tiny Testicles, nice shot."

Johansson grumbled something unintelligible.

The Boston ePapers noted that not since the tandem of Ortiz and Ramirez had the Red Sox seen such a one-two punch in the 3-4 spot. By the time they hit the All-Star break, the Red Sox were tied for the division lead with the Yankees.

~ ~ ~

Because of his slow start, Ted did not make the All-Star team, but he came close. No matter, he thought, he would value the few days of free time. Back home, he immediately called Elizabeth and Johnnie and made arrangements to pick Johnnie up to go fishing for blues.

Ted arrived very early the next morning at their condo. Elizabeth opened the door yawning and in her bathrobe. Johnnie Jumped up to hug Ted and Ted gave Johnnie another bat.

"That's one of my own," said Ted. "Someday that might be worth somethin', son."

"I think it might be already," said Elizabeth. "What time is it, anyway?"

"It's already 5 a.m." said Ted. "C'mon, boy, we're burnin' daylight."

"Okay, Duke," said a yawning Elizabeth. "I'll get Johnnie ready and I have a surprise for you."

"What's that?" he said.

"I'm coming too."

"I never have women on my boat," he said.

"Well, you will today."

"Do you know how to fish?"

"No, but you can teach me; Johnnie didn't know how either until you taught him."

"Geezus, you know there's no bathroom out there, it's a Boston Whaler."

"You mean you didn't buy a trawler yet?" she said.

"I assume you mean an outrigger," he said. "Actually, when I go out on a serious trip, I'll hire a guide with his own boat, like I used to do. So, what about the lack of a head?"

"I'll manage," she said, guessing he meant the bathroom.

She disappeared, keeping Ted waiting for about 10 minutes before she and Johnnie reappeared ready to go. She wore an outfit that looked like it was fresh from a catalog, sort of cross between L.L.Bean and Talbots, highlighted by a hat of unknown origin, at least to Ted.

"That's a silly hat," said Ted.

"No, it's a *Tilley* hat. Do I not look fashionable?"

"You're fashionable, all right. I guarantee the audience of fish will think you look downright adorable," he said.

A short time later they were out off the Boston Harbor Islands—those that remained after the sea rise, that is—mostly islands that had been enhanced by landfill but had reverted to an aboriginal state. Ted was maneuvering the boat near a rip where he could see bait fish jumping, undoubtedly to escape a school of blues. A flock of gulls overhead was another telltale sign.

Ted was using a saltwater fly rod and alternately casting with a standard rod for Elizabeth. He knew she couldn't learn to fly fish in one morning. She had what looked to her like a plastic banana on the end of her line.

They caught many fish, Elizabeth squealing when hooking each one, and then straining to reel in the heavy fighters. Some of them weighed upwards of 15 pounds. Johnnie was good enough to fish on his own with his fly rod. Ted and Johnnie—and now Elizabeth—were catch-and-release devotees. Elizabeth was not fazed by the propensity of blues that had strained against the hook to bleed-out once in the boat.

"Sorry about the splattering of your fashionable pants," said Ted.

"No problem," she said. "I remind you that, as a doctor, I am accustomed to blood. Though, coupled with the fish smell, the effect, I must admit, is acute."

"Johnnie doesn't mind," said Ted, "do ya, son? Long as we're catchin' 'em."

Johnnie nodded his head.

During a break in the action, Elizabeth said, "So, you've been making headlines—in lots of ways."

"Yeah, well, things are not always what they seem, Lizzy."

"You mean the hitting or the, ah, extracurricular activity?" she said.

Lowering his voice, he said, "I mean, don't believe the headlines about the off-the-field stuff."

"Regardless, it seems to not have affected you on the pitch."

"Field—we call it a field. It's baseball, not a cricket match. Say, you really oughta watch more baseball."

"They're not unrelated, I should think," she said. "You know, there are many similarities between the two sports, a wooden bat and a ball, for instance. Of course, some would say that since cricket is hundreds of years older, baseball is derivative of cricket, or a game we used to play in the UK called rounders."

"You can't compare cricket to baseball, for crissakes," he said. "They use a flat bat. How prissy is that? And then there are those white outfits."

"As opposed to what, red stockings with stirrups or jerseys with pinstripes?"

"You've got a point there. I guess this conversation has turned into a bit of a sticky wicket," he said with a smile.

"Now that is astute, Mr. Williams. So, other than a disdain for cricket, how are you feeling?"

"I'm feeling great."

"Given your limited time off, will you come in to see me tomorrow so that I can examine you?"

"If I must."

"If I've learned one thing about you, it is that you don't respond well to 'must.' Why don't we just say you are invited to come in?"

"So be it," said Ted.

Forty-seven

Early the next morning Ted had an appointment with the folks over at the Jimmy Fund in the Dana-Farber Cancer Institute. It seemed the Jimmy Fund had been the Red Sox charity forever. He was glad to know it still was. Ted was one of the founding players to dedicate time, energy and financial resources to support kids and families dealing with cancer. In fact, his involvement with the charity had begun in the late 1940s, before it became the official charity of the Boston Red Sox.

His frequent hospital visits with kids and adult Red Sox fans were legendary, even though he shunned the spotlight and fanfare during the visits, preferring to spend quiet time with the kids. In many special events during his first life, he raised millions of dollars for the Jimmy Fund.

On the way over, he relived many happy memories of Jimmy Fund visits and fundraisers, coupled with sadness for the patients he knew who were lost. *God*, he thought, *this disease, this scourge, is still around. Medical science could do this with me, but this disease is still here. I don't get it.*

He was made very welcome. It was, indeed, a homecoming. The Jimmy Fund doctors and executives had granted his wish and no media were present.

The welcoming group of about six people, was split evenly between doctors and executives, and was led by Dr. Aakar Desai.

After introductions, the group sat in a windowless conference room with screens or writing boards on all four walls. Dr. Desai was dressed in a white lab coat and stood at the head of the rectangular table with Ted, the guest of honor, to his right.

Dr. Desai gave Ted an overview of their good work and their challenges complete with a graphic presentation on the main screen behind the head of the table.

"We have made quite a lot of progress, but there are still stubborn cancers that we have not cured. Over the last 90 years, Ted, successes were made with antitumor or monoclonal antibodies and anti-angiogenesis therapies. But there are so many more cancers that are not tumor- or target-specific cancers, deadly diseases like Leukemia and many Lymphomas that still persist."

"I'm surprised," said Ted. "I thought by now there would have been a lot more cures."

"There have been. We have made great strides, but some cancers have proven to be tougher than others, like the blood cancers. Multiple myeloma has been particularly difficult."

Ted nodded in deep thought. He thought about his own son's death from Leukemia as an adult after Ted passed on. His mind wandered further. He regretted not spending enough time with John Henry and his girls when they were young.

When the presentation was complete, Ted's face brightened and with a burst of enthusiasm he said, "Well, when can I visit the kids?"

~ ~ ~

As Ted made the rounds from room to room on the kids' floors, word spread. He made time for everyone. Kids whom doctors thought were in the depths of illness got out of their beds and began to follow him around. He handed out signed baseballs and posed for pictures. The pied piper of pediatric patients was beaming. The staff looked on in absolute amazement.

"If we could bottle this," said one doctor, "we'd cure these kids in a heartbeat."

The hugs, kisses, photos and tender moments went on for hours, and Ted loved every moment of it. Ted Williams, the greatest hitter who ever lived; Ted the medical miracle; Ted the businessman; Ted the outdoorsman; Ted the Marine; Ted in all his incarnations, The Kid himself, was a man in full when surrounded by children.

Forty-eight

Later that afternoon Ted was in an examination room in the medical offices of Dr. Elizabeth Miles, halfway up the hill on fashionable Mt. Vernon Street on Beacon Hill. Ted was dressed for the occasion, wearing a lovely hospital gown, predictably open in the back.

"Why do these johnnies—is that what you call them?—always look like they've been washed 400 times?" he said.

"Because they have," she said.

As Dr. Miles scanned him with two hand-held medical screening devices, Ted sat up and she listened to his heart with a stethoscope.

"All the medical-device advances in the world, Lizzy, and you docs still use that thing?" he said.

"There are other ways to listen to your heart, but this is the fastest, and still very reliable," she said.

After listening to what Ted called his "ticker," she then asked him a litany of questions.

"So, any muscle aches? Headaches? Bowel movements okay? Are you sleeping okay? I know your eyes are fine. Anything at all to report?"

"Yeah," he said, "I feel faint. In a moment I'll need mouth-to-mouth."

"That is the oldest line in the book."

"Yeah, well, I'm an old-fashioned guy."

"You are, aren't you?" she said.

She shook off the pleasant thought and returned to her clinical self.

"I would like to take a blood sample."

After extracting blood, she said, "I'll give you my final report in a few days when we have the results from the blood sample, but you look just fine."

"I could have told you that," he said.

"Yes, I know—we've had this discussion before—I would like . . . let me rephrase . . . I need to monitor your progress."

"Well, I'm hittin' around .340."

"That is not the progress to which I refer, although that physical achievement is a good sign—actually, it is quite a surprise."

"You mean, you never thought something like this could happen?" he said.

"Quite right. My initial hope was that you would merely have a decent quality of life, that you would be fully ambulant, that you would possess memory of your former life. That you would also have neuromuscular or brain-muscle memory and be able to transfer that to your new body . . . well, your actual results are more than I could have asked for."

"What is muscle memory?" he said.

"In the strictest sense, muscles have no memory. They respond to direction from the brain, and they develop a physiological response to repetition. In your case, you have been able to transfer real memories in the brain to your completely new muscle mass. It is quite astonishing."

"You're not braggin', are ya?"

"No, quite the contrary. In my considered medical opinion, and in the tradition of hundreds of years of medical progress and innovation, I would have to say—we got lucky."

"Nothin' wrong with lucky, though I've always said it's never luck that makes the difference, it's preparation. Are we through?"

"Not quite," she said. "Get dressed and come into my office; we will finish up in there."

He dressed and proceeded down the hall and into her small office. It was standard fare for a doctor—a single file cabinet, stacked papers, medical degrees hanging on an exposed brick wall. He sat in the consultation chair next to her diminutive metal desk with a faux wood surface.

"So, may I remove myself from your clutches?" he said.

"I want to ask you a few more questions. I know things are going well now, but if your performance started to wane on the field, would you be tempted to take the performance-enhancing cocktail?"

"C'mon, Lizzy, you know me better than that—absolutely not. I can't stand even the idea of it."

"Yes, and I've heard you say it before, but I also know that you are a fierce competitor. I just don't want you to be tempted. In your case, I think it would be quite a disaster."

"Don't worry about it," he said. "It ain't gonna happen."

"Good," she said. "How are you holding up to everything—not physically, but emotionally?"

"Geezus, Lizzy, stop the psychological horseshit."

"You may think it is . . . it is, well—horseshit, but it is important to know the answers to these questions to completely monitor your wellbeing," she said.

"That's just it; I don't need nobody monitorin' my wellbeing. I'm playin' baseball again and hittin' .340—that's my wellbeing. Look, I appreciate your wantin' to look after me, but I'm fine."

"But what about emotional attachments? Are you making new connections—with teammates, friends, anyone? I am guessing you miss Amanda."

"That's it. I'm outta here."

Forty-nine

For the rest of July and halfway through August the Red Sox remained in a heated pennant race with the Yankees, alternating half-game or one-game leads in the standings. Ted not only continued to bat around .340 but also had a positive influence on the other players, especially the younger guys. At first Buck Pearson was annoyed with Ted's constant yammering with the guys about the strike zone and waiting for good pitches, but some of it was rubbing off on his teammates.

As a team, they were leading the league in pitches per plate appearance (3.98), first pitches taken (78 percent) and chase percentage, that is, pitches out of the strike zone. They chased only 18 percent of pitches out of the zone. The major league average was 21 percent. Pearson monitored a boatload of sabermetric data and all of it showed the team improving.

Perhaps more important, the renewed discipline at the plate was causing a recalibration by the Botwinders they faced. To the extent it was possible for opposing machines to secondguess themselves, even ones with artificial intelligence, the Red Sox were making it happen. Opposing teams were also reprogramming their Botwinders, a move fully acceptable under major league rules. Some of the downloads came only prior to playing against the Sox. The recalibration, Ted surmised correctly, would only make hitting tougher for him and his teammates.

~ ~ ~

Ted was offered endorsement deals like he never had seen before. Most he rejected, but others he snapped up. There were Ted Williams' video games in the works, a special Ted Williams custom Cadillac FCV. And the crowning achievement: The Hasbro toy company created a Ted Williams action figure featuring Ted squaring off against an action-figure Botwinder with Yankee pinstripes. The set was an instant bestseller. Ted loved it; "a good likeness," he said, giving a set to Johnnie.

At the start of each game Fenway was filled to the gills. Over the course of many years the Red Sox had "built up" the ballpark's capacity, it was a paltry 50,000 compared to other major league teams who built new parks and were pushing capacity to 100,000.

What was most impressive was the worldwide media attention. The game had long before expanded to many continents, but now, with Ted on the team, the media interest from global non-sports reporters had skyrocketed. His hitting success was impressive and that was certainly well covered, but there was also a pervasive interest in his personal life. Photographers were once again stalking him full time.

Perhaps the most disturbing part of all of the coverage was speculation as to the God question. He refused all interview requests except those that took place in the clubhouse and answered only questions about baseball. When the questions veered off, he would say, "Next question."

But the God questions and speculation persisted. Why would he not talk about it, they wondered? PR consultants were interviewed: "He should realize that not talking about it only leads to more speculation, assumption and worry." When Ted didn't answer, indeed, the media made up its own answers: "If he's not talking, that must mean that there is no God; he's afraid to tell the world."

There was one "rabloid"—a popular portmanteau word for rabid tabloid—that even suggested since he was so profane, using God's name in vane and in peculiarly creative, blasphemous ways, it was proof positive that there was no God. None of it made sense. "He was alone in the world," they wrote, "not a believer, not an agnostic, not an atheist, but a 'knower.'"

Ted just wanted to play baseball.

And that was fine with the Boston fans. It had been 60 years since the team won a World Series and now, midway through August there was no swoon, no nosedive into the great abyss that had characterized so many seasons, no agony in the heat. Instead, there was approbation, love, excitement. All of it directed at Ted Williams.

Fifty

During the last two weeks in August and into mid September, the ePapers and broadcasts in Boston and throughout the world were dominated with the news of a new American military conflict. In Boston people were consumed only with the thought of the Red Sox proceeding to the postseason, and having a chance to win it all. The team was two games in front.

As Ted read the ePapers in his suite at the Dongkou, he said aloud, "I can't believe this."

The headlines were jarring: U.S. Again at War in Afghanistan. Satellites Gone. Military on its Heels.

In the penultimate phase of his epic return to baseball, in the heat of a transcendent pennant race, Ted Williams received a phone call. He was incredulous when the operator in his hotel said it was General Francis P. Case, commandant of the U.S. Marine Corps.

Thinking that it might be a hoax caller, he had the operator take a number and then called back. It appeared he had reached the Pentagon.

The voice on the other end of the phone said, "Semper fi, Captain Williams. This is General Case."

"No offense, *general*," said Ted, "but how do I know you are who you say you are?" He pronounced the word "general" long and hard.

"Well, let me read to you the elements of your service record:

1941:	Classified 3-A, mother dependent on Williams.
1942:	Following U.S. entry into WWII, classification changed to 1-A.
1942:	Williams appeals to draft board. Board agrees status should not have changed. Williams makes public statement: once he increases mother's trust fund, he intends to enlist. Note to file: press and baseball fans upset with his actions.
May 22, 1942:	Enlists in the U.S. Navy. Joins V-5 Naval Aviator Program. Note to file: Did not receive or refuses easy assignment to play baseball for Navy. Doctors report astonishing 20/10 vision.
Oct. 1942:	Reports to Preliminary Ground School at Amherst College, Massachusetts. No college experience. Receives six months of instruction in math, navigation and flight dynamics. Achieves 3.85 grade point average out of possible 4.0.
May 1943:	Reports to Preflight School at Athens, Georgia.
Sept. 1943:	Primary training at NAS Bunker Hill, Indiana.
January 1944:	Intermediate training at Pensacola, Fla. Note to file: Set records in aerial gunnery.
May 2, 1944:	Williams receives his wings and commission in the U.S. Marine Corps.
June 1944:	Attends gunnery training at Jacksonville, Fla. Note to file: set gunnery records.
Aug. 1944:	Returns to Pensacola. Serves as instructor at Bronson Field.
June 1945:	Reports to Jacksonville, Fla. for Corsair Operational Training.
Aug. 1945	Reports to Hawaii. Awaits orders as a replacement pilot when war ends.
Dec. 1945:	Williams returns stateside.
Jan. 28, 1946:	Discharged from the U.S. Marine Corps.

Note to File: Williams resumes extremely successful baseball career.

May 2, 1952:   After eight years, recalled from inactive reserves to active
                 duty for Korean War, 33 years old, married with one child.
                 Note to file: Williams may have resented being recalled along
                 with other WWII vets.

June 1952:   Reports to Cherry Point, NC. Trains in F9F jets.

Feb. 4, 1953:   Joins VMF-311 in Korea.

Feb. 17, 1953   After taking ground fire, survives crash landing.

July 28, 1953:   Relieved from active duty. Combat record: 39 combat
                 missions.

Med. History: Problematic. Chronic head colds and severe ear infections."

It took the better part of 15 minutes to read it all but Ted paid attention, intent on judging the records' accuracy.

"Need I go on and list your commendations and medals, Captain Williams?" said Commandant Case on the phone.

"No, that's pretty goddamned thorough, although not altogether accurate, especially the part about my illness," said Ted.

"Ted," said the Commandant, "I'd like to come up to Boston tomorrow and meet with you. Are you free?"

"Well, what's this about?" said Ted, becoming annoyed.

"I'd rather not say over the phone. Can you find the time to meet?"

"Well, we've got a night game tomorrow. I suppose late morning would be okay. Come here. We can use a private conference room at the hotel."

~ ~ ~

The next morning a team of Marine advance men arrived. They screened the conference room for bugs. A sniffer dog swept the room. Two Marine security guards with automatic rifles stood sentinel at the door. The weapons were not ceremonial. Ted was mildly amused at the hullabaloo but was never one to disrespect anything that the Marines did.

The general and Ted met at the door. Ted said, "Sir," and instinctively snapped to attention. For a Marine, Commandant Case was a short man. He had a prominent, crooked nose, as if he had once been a boxer. The rest, however, was standard issue: jarhead, square jaw, and all spit and polish.

In the conference room, two Marine colonels, to whom Ted was introduced, flanked the general. The door was closed, and a large screen was lowered in preparation for a briefing.

The visiting brass wore enough fruit salad on their chests to approximate a farmer's market. The commandant, four gleaming stars on each collar and shoulder, did the talking.

"Ted, the President of the United States sends her regards."

"Tell her I said hi, although it's hard for me to get used to the fact that the president is a woman."

"She's quite a woman, operates with an iron hand. As a member of the Joint Chiefs of Staff, I have been authorized to speak to you personally," said the general.

"Pardon my interruption," said Ted, "but do I call you general or commandant, sir?"

"Either is fine, and Frank is fine, too."

He continued, "Ted, you've probably been reading the headlines. The news is not good for our country right now. Things have changed dramatically since you were in service, or when you were last alive, shall we say. The radical government in Pakistan, with a small army, has invaded Afghanistan, a country that has been our ally since 9/11."

"Wait a minute," said Ted, "I've been reading about this. What I don't understand is what brought this on."

"Well, Pakistan and India, historic enemies, engaged in a nuclear war about six decades ago. Pakistan ceased being a U.S. ally years before when the government turned pro-Taliban. Millions of people died in the nuclear war and some people still suffer from radiation sickness. India recovered sufficiently, but not much was left of Pakistan. Its infrastructure, technology and culture were virtually wiped out. Since that time, a series of fledgling Pakistani governments tried to coalesce and pull the country out of severe medical and societal woes, and all failed. They were mostly radical groups or tribes intent on forcing their own agenda, largely hatred of the West.

"About 10 years ago, three of the tribes—the Bangulzai, the Zehri and the Durrani—formed a government. They no longer have nuclear power but they have become increasingly militarized, acquiring weapons from China and Russia. They even have a rudimentary air force."

"So, why did the confederation invade Afghanistan?" said Ted.

"We think for a number of reasons. Afghanistan is the ancestral homeland of the Durrani, and they may want it back. They were sort of regional royalty in the past, and want what they think is rightfully theirs. They are resentful of the Popalzai Tribe that largely make up the Afghani government and have been the democratically elected rulers of Afghanistan, allied with the U.S., for decades now. Also, the confederation wants the poppy industry."

"What do you mean?" said Ted.

"We think the Pakistanis want in on the lucrative Afghan narcotics industry, probably to buy more weapons. The decades that followed the U.S. defeat of the Taliban and al Qaeda in the region were highlighted by the economic growth of Afghanistan. Much like the impact that a growing South Korea had on the North Koreans, which you may remember, Afghanistan's success has made various Pakistani elements resentful and jealous."

"You mean they're pissed off because they're not in on the drug trade?"

"That's a succinct way to put it, Captain Williams."

"So, as an ally of Afghanistan, the U.S. is in the opium and heroin business?" said Ted.

"Well, I wouldn't say it in such black-and-white terms—it's more of a gray area," said the general. "The Afghans are in the business—there are medicinal uses you know. We support the Afghans to provide stability in the region. At first we tried to get them to change their ways, but there were few viable economic alternatives for the majority of Afghans, particularly in the southern provinces. So they reverted back to the farming of poppies. They are our allies; we have strategic interests in the region, so we have protected them."

"So what's this I hear about losing satellites—our satellites?" said Ted.

"In a preemptive strike against the U.S. military and in coordination with the invasion of Afghanistan, Pakistan has systematically taken out U.S. military satellites. When our satellites were knocked out, it became clear the Pakistanis possessed a good deal more of advanced technology than our intelligence predicted. They used ground-based lasers, probably acquired from the Chinese. Every time we move another satellite into position, they take it out. Our countermeasures onboard the satellites have been ineffective, probably, we believe, because someone, not necessarily the Pakistanis, used an electronic Trojan horse."

"So they're in cahoots with someone else?" said Ted.

"Yes. We think that is the case. Unbeknownst to us, the Trojan horse was built into the satellites—a secret, hardware-based back door with a kill switch. They disabled the countermeasures built into the satellites allowing the ASAT—antisatellite weapons—the ground-based lasers, to take them out. It was, indeed, asymmetrical warfare. We haven't been as surprised by an event like this since our hypersonic Aurora spy plane was shot down. How the hell it happened we're not sure—probably because we outsourced much of the chip production. Anyway, it happened fast. We were taken completely off guard. We war-gamed for losing satellites, even had some replacement satellites, but not enough. It was the Trojan horse that we didn't anticipate. At the same time they managed to take out almost all of our satellites, the Pakistanis began their invasion of Afghanistan, overrunning our bases and then taking the poppy fields."

"So, are we going it alone?" said Ted.

"Well, the Afghan military is still viable in the north. However, after that, we may not have much help. NATO has long since dissolved so, as has been the case so often in the 21st century, we'll have to fight largely alone."

"What's the president's position on all of this?" said Ted.

"President Muller is a former naval officer. She has been meeting daily in the situation room with her cabinet, the Joint Chiefs of Staff and other senior defense advisors. After a recommendation from her military advisers, the president authorized the redeployment of the bulk of U.S. naval power to the Arabian Sea. Congress has been discussing the possibility of a new draft."

Ted was shaking his head in disgust. "Tell me, general, why were we caught so off guard?"

"After 9/11 and especially after 8/22, the geopolitical landscape changed. We no longer fight for oil. We fight against the disenfranchised. We are occasionally concerned about the Russians and a little more so about the Chinese, but together we have so many cross-border business investments that none of the big three wants to upset the applecart to a great degree. Or so the theory has gone."

"So who are the disenfranchised?" said Ted

General Case pointed to several key hot spots on a world map projected on the screen at the front of the room.

"They are the real threat worldwide, small countries, or loosely organized states or radical elements that can be accurately labeled the 'I-Ain't-Got-None-and-I-Want-Yours.' We say it as a bastardized acronym, the 'I-AG-NAI-WY.' These are entities that don't have significant foreign investments. No ability to be real economic players. They're often fragmented, amorphous. If they are a country, they have a low GDP, but may have enough resources to invest in militarization. Their purported ideologies are all over the place—religious fanaticism, for example—but basically they're pissed off because they are the Iagnaiwy. That is our enemy. It's obvious now we've had a tendency to underestimate them, even going so far as to call them the 'Iagnaweenies.'"

"I would venture to say that the problem worldwide is the economic divide," said Ted. "It is tied more than anything else to the historic lack of property ownership by the underclasses. Property ownership is the foundation for wealth creation in succeeding generations, isn't it?"

The general and the two colonels looked at each other nodding. "Yes, it is," said General Case.

"What capability did you lose when you lost the satellites?" said Ted.

"Well, it was a real kick in the ass," said the general. "There were the obvious losses like diminished communication, losing battlefield eyes in the sky, and command and control losses. But the biggest hit was to our air command. You see, we are a much different defense force—Army, Navy, Air Force, Marines, even the Coast Guard—than when you were in the service, Ted. Over time, we migrated away from standard aircraft and invested heavily in UAVs."

"What are UAVs?"

"Unmanned Aerial Vehicles," said the general. "You might remember them as drones."

"Geezus, even you guys went for the goddamned robots?"

"Well not greatly at first. It was a gradual process," said the general. "For a long time we believed that UAVs could play a role in combat operations, save some lives, and inflict heavy damage on the enemy, but they wouldn't fully replace flesh and blood pilots. That's why 40 years ago we still relied heavily on the 'Lightning II' F-35 Joint Strike Fighter. The Marine version was the F-35B— the STOVL variant—short-takeoff and vertical-landing, later the F-35H."

"You mean a hover jet?" said Ted.

"Yes. It was a strategic advantage in the Marines' primary mission—close air support and strategic air-to-ground targeting. Operationally, the aircraft was a proven success. The planes flew for decades with new upgrades before problems developed. In later versions the technology, particularly software, was shared and developed with so many foreign partners that we lost control and there were major security lapses. The software was compromised and fell into enemy hands. Surface-to-air defenses, countermeasures, even stealth technologies, were compromised. Rather than risk the same things happening again during the development of a new generation of aircraft, the U.S. moved into an almost total reliance on drones, even fighter variants. The political will to avoid combat deaths was the final straw for piloted aircraft."

"Huh," said Ted.

"Now, because we lost most of our satellites," said the general, "we have no way to control the drones, which previously we could control from anywhere in the world. We even stopped production of AWACS aircraft many years ago that had some weapons control and replaced them with drones. We have mobile command and control centers but they have to be very close to the frontlines to work—difficult to position in a combat situation—and without the satellites, the drones now have a very limited range."

"Interesting stuff, General, but what's this got to do with me? Why did you come all the way up to Boston?"

"Captain Williams, we believe we cannot develop and launch secure new satellites for the better part of a year. We're taking the old F-35s out of mothballs—they're the only things we've got—and we need pilots. We want *you* to fly again for the United States Marine Corps."

Ted stood up. "You're shittin' me," he said.

"I assure you, Captain Williams, *shittin'* you is not the goal of the U.S. Marines or the president of the United States of America. Please, sit down."

Ted complied.

"We need your help, Ted. We'll retrain you in flight school in an accelerated program and get you into the air as soon as possible."

"But why me?"

"There are, in fact, many reasons we want you to do this, not the least of which is, we need people with some aviation experience. Also, if *you* reenlist it will help us recruit other pilots, of course."

"Of course," said Ted.

"Think it over," said General Case. "Your country needs you, and it needs you now."

Fifty-one

In the game that night, Ted played poorly against the São Paulo Piranha, but the Sox won. At first he told no one about the decision he had to make. For two days in the middle of the Red Sox' home stand, when not on the field, Ted was holed up in his suite at the Hotel Dongkou.

He thought long and hard. On the one hand, he was patriotic to the extreme and his country needed him. On the other, the Red Sox needed him, too. What about all of their fans—his fans? What about his own dream of winning the World Series? He had learned in '46 that thinking another opportunity would present itself was a fool's errand. He also thought much of it was beyond his control. He wasn't a golfer controlling his own destiny. His was a team sport. He could stick around, play well, see the team's hitting blow up, and still miss or lose the Series. And what about his health? The Marines assumed he was fit to fly. Was he? And there was the issue of fighting for poppy fields.

~ ~ ~

Ted called Elizabeth, and they made arrangements to meet right away at the top of the hill on what remained of Boston Common. Flagstaff Hill was the site of the Soldiers and Sailors Monument dedicated to the lost men of Boston who died on land and sea in the Civil War. Ted and Elizabeth sat on one of the many benches surrounding the impressive Roman-Doric column of white granite with the "Genius of America" statue on its peak.

"You know," said Ted, "when this thing was dedicated, both Civil War generals McClelland and Hooker were in attendance. Ole 'Fightin' Joe' Hooker, a Massachusetts guy, has his own statue, right over there on the State House lawn. 'Course, ole Joe may be more well-known for the association with prostitutes."

"He was a rogue?" said Elizabeth.

"No, not him personally—least I don't think so. But there were so many whores following his army around during the Civil War that they became known as hookers, though the term may have preceded him. Helluva thing to be remembered for."

"Really?" said Elizabeth.

"It's a sad fact of life that most people pass by all these monuments and statues in Boston every day and have no idea of the meaning of them all. Did ya know that a statue of "Old Blood and Guts," Georgie Patton, is over on the Esplanade? Least it used to be, before the flood and the loss of the Esplanade. Wonder where they moved it? His wife and in-laws were from Boston, up on the North Shore, I think. But he was a California boy, like me. Ironic isn't it? Patton was the one who believed in reincarnation."

"Ted, I have the feeling you're having difficulty telling me something. What is it?"

"Well, Lizzy, I'm thinking about going back into the Marines."

She stared at him silently, with unblinking, wide eyes. He told her the story about the commandant's visit and got as far as the need for pilots.

She could not contain herself any longer and interrupted, "Ted, that is bullshit."

"Why, doctor, you are profane," said Ted. "I kinda like it."

"But Ted, what about the team—forget that, what about your health?" she said.

"What about my health? That's why I'm here, to ask you."

"I'm not sure. I don't know how you are going to hold up to the—what do you call them—G forces? I have to do some research."

"What is there to research?" he said. "Since I'm the first and only guy to be reanimated, I *am* the research."

"Ted, that is rubbish, and you know it. Once again, we are in uncharted territory here. I would like the opportunity to discuss this with colleagues at Harvard Medical School."

"Fine," he said. "But can they keep it confidential? No one else knows."

"Yes, I have complete confidence they will do so."

"Good, then I need an opinion by the end of the day tomorrow."

"Ted, are you sure you are not rushing into this? Will my opinion even matter?"

"Yes, but keep in mind, there are only two kinds of people that understand Marines: Marines and the enemy. Everyone else has a secondhand opinion. An Army man said that. Anyway, yes, your opinion will matter to me."

~ ~ ~

Twenty-four hours later Dr. Miles was in Ted's suite, wearing a worried look.

"So what's the verdict, doc? Or should I say 'judge'?" he said.

"Well, my colleagues reached no consensus. No one is sure how you will hold up. There is concern about your neurological functions, meaning the stress on your brain when you go through the rigors of flight, particularly repeated stresses that will come with multiple flights."

"You know, of course," said Ted, "that I will be flying close air support and bombing missions? We don't expect to see much air-to-air action."

"Yes, but there is always the possibility you would face the same kind of stress. For example, pulling away from a target, yes? Or you might hit full throttle and maximum G forces with a booger on your tail."

"It's bogey—bogey on your tail," he said. "Actually, if you know who it is that would be a bandit."

"Yes, well, the point is there will be situations, even in training, where you stress your body and your reconstructed and delicate brain to the extreme."

"And you know about the anti-G suits?" he said.

"I've learned that the state of the art is a flight suit with an anti-G suit worn over it in anti-blackout and anti-fatigue mode. Pilots call them 'high-speed chaps,' I believe. I know that air bladders automatically inflate to try to prevent, during extreme maneuvers, stagnant hypoxia that can cause the pooling of blood and other bodily fluids in the extremities and in the buttocks. I also know that the flight suit doesn't always match up to the capabilities of the aircraft you will be flying. When the pilot accelerates, particularly through a fast-banked turn, the brain is stressed as blood flows out and down to the extremities. Increasing the body-surface area compressed by the anti-G suit helps, but it's not foolproof. In addition to the blood-pooling problem, the heart and diaphragm are forced lower, inhibiting the blood pressure needed to maintain blood flow to the brain. In addition, at high Gs the pilot's field of sight narrows when blood-flow to the retinas is reduced. Last but not least, in the worst-case scenario, the pilot loses consciousness from insufficient blood flow to the brain."

"Hell, yesterday you didn't know what Gs were, today you sound like a flight surgeon," said Ted.

"One of my consultants was, indeed, a former Royal Air Force flight surgeon. Apparently, they didn't go into the all-drone mode like the U.S., though they don't have many traditional planes. Ted, let's not get distracted here. Do you want to hear my professional opinion?"

"Yes, I do."

"Well, then, here it is: The repeated exposure to this kind of stress on your particularly sensitive brain will not be a good thing. Think about all of the work that was done on your neurological system to get you to where you are today. I cannot recommend that you do this."

"Does that mean you believe that I cannot do it, that my body will fail? Are you guaranteeing that?"

"No, but that is just the point: We can't guarantee anything."

"So I might be all right?" he said.

"Well, yes. But you might just as easily experience catastrophic failure. Frankly, I can't believe the Marines are asking you to do this."

"The Marines have always asked a lot of their people. It's who we are."

"Oh, Ted, don't give me a load of that bloody gung-ho bollocks. Even you questioned getting called back into the service during your first life."

"Why, Lizzy, you're doing it again. Such profanity."

"You are a jackass," she said, and then turned on her heels, and stormed out of the suite.

"She thinks she's the first one to ever notice," he said aloud. He picked up the phone and placed a call to General Case at the Pentagon. The general quickly ended a meeting to take Ted's call.

"General," said Ted, "I'll do it, but with a couple of conditions. When this conflict ends, I get to go back to playing baseball. And I want that in writing. Also, I'm not doing this just as some kinda PR stunt. I'm gonna fly and I'm gonna really fight—not just recruit or train others. Can you guarantee that?"

"Yes, I can. I can do all of that. Welcome back to the United States Marine Corps, Captain Williams."

Fifty-two

Ted went into Buck Pearson's office at Fenway and closed the door. His teammates could see but not hear the discussion Ted and Pearson had through his office window.

"Buck, I have to take a hiatus from the team."

"A hi-whatsis?"

"A leave—a leave of absence."

"What's the matter—you sick?"

"No, nothin' like that. I'm goin' back into the Marines."

Ted told the whole story. When he was finished Pearson just slumped into his chair.

"I gottta call upstairs," said Pearson.

Soon the GM and Mr. McBride were in the small office, and Ted repeated his rationale for leaving the Red Sox. It was a hard message to sink in. The Sox were so close to winning the pennant and the postseason was just around the corner. There were questions about Ted's health, questions about the timing.

"Could you wait until the season's over?" said McBride.

"No, I'm afraid not," said Ted. "The Marines need me to start training right away."

"Well, I understand," said McBride, more sympathetic than the others.

Ted made a group announcement to his teammates in the clubhouse. They were sort of numb, at first just nodding. As he cleaned out his locker, one by one they came up to him, mostly the Americans, and wished him well. Johansson and a few of the non-Americans merely gave him sideways glances and did not approach. Smitty was concerned.

"Hey, are you gonna be all right, buddy?"

"I'll be fine, Smitty," said Ted.

"Well, I admire your courage. You're giving up a lot."

Ted was stuffing a valise full of toiletries and said, "You know, I never won the Series. It's always been my dream, but when the Marines are in trouble . . ."

Smitty understood because he understood what made Ted Williams, Ted Williams.

The press and the fans were another matter. After Ted took and passed the Marine physical, the story leaked out and it set off a firestorm in Boston. The headlines, columnists and editorials were split down the middle. Some were ready to crucify him for leaving the team during the best season in years; others hailed him as a hero. If you were a typical Red Sox fan, it was one more reason to believe the fate of this team was to go on losing.

~ ~ ~

The next day Ted dialed Dr. Miles and gave her the news, which she already knew.

"So, you're going from laser-neck to leatherneck," she said, thinking it probably was not an appropriate remark from the physician who performed his surgery, but it would be okay with Ted.

"That's right," he said. "Hey, do you mind if I come over to get Johnnie and take him out for a while?"

"No, that would be fine."

Ted picked Johnnie up and they went tooling around Boston on Ted's tandem Jet Ski. After an hour and a half they pulled into a dock in Cambridge and ate fried clams, chicken and French fries at a seafood shack called McGinty's.

They talked about Johnnie's new school year, about Jet Ski racing, about the weather, about baseball and, finally, about the Marines.

"So, I guess you heard I'm goin' into the Marines again?" said Ted.

"Yeah," said Johnnie, "some of my friends are mad at you for leaving the Red Sox."

"Are you angry?"

"I won't be if the Red Sox win anyway."

"You're probably not alone in that," said Ted.

"Why are you joining the Marines?" said Johnnie.

"Well, you may not understand this now—hell, there are a lot of adults that never understand it. But there are times in life when you have to sacrifice—give up personal stuff for the good of others."

"Isn't winning the World Series good for others?"

"It might be. But it surely won't be as important as what I'm doing now, going into the Marines to fight for our country."

"Is killing people important?" said Johnnie.

"That's an awful big question from a little guy. But I'll answer it. Killing is okay only when it's done to protect your country, when your country is in real danger. There are a lot of threats to our country right now; that's why we're at war."

"There seems like there's always been a lot of wars. I can't keep track of 'em all."

"Yeah, it does seem like that," said Ted. "Well, I don't know what they'll be teaching you in school about this stuff, but I'll tell you that sometimes war is a necessary thing. I believe anyone or anything worth living for, is worth dying for."

"Is this war a necessary thing?"

"I do believe it is, son—we were attacked. I know that throughout our history, it always hasn't been clear if war was a necessary thing. I think it's the right thing for me to do now, though. If we fight now, maybe you won't have to when you come of age."

"Can I go with you?" said Johnnie.

Ted smiled. "No, you've got to stay here and take care of your mom. She needs you to go to school and be here for her."

"Will you be careful?" said Johnnie.

"I will, Johnnie; don't you worry about me."

They hugged.

Across the waterway, the last rays of the sun hit the golden dome of the Massachusetts State House, reflecting brilliantly into the blue and gold dusk.

Fifty-three

The Marines got their wish. In fact, all of the services benefited, as enlistments jumped from the publicity surrounding Ted joining the service. Ted was no sooner off to flight training when the Hasbro toy company announced it was introducing a new G.I. Joe toy, a Marine pilot in Ted's image, flying an F-35.

G.I. Joe Ted Williams was an instant hit.

The Splendid Splinter was off to Marine Corps Air Station Yuma for accelerated flight training. He got off the plane and said, "For crissakes, look at this goddamned place, sand and heat—that's all it is."

Yuma was a flat basin covering about 750 square miles of southwestern Arizona with the Gila and Laguna Mountains to the north and west, and the Mexican border to the south. Various branches of the military in one form or another had used the air station and the nearby proving grounds since the late 1920s. In 1959 the air station was taken over by the Marines who had used it continuously ever since.

In the early part of the current century there was talk of shutting the base down due to surrounding population growth. But global warming changed all that. The Gila River was now seasonally dry. As with much of the southwest, declining water resources in Yuma created a population exodus. It was enough to make the area attractive once again to the Corps, which still could collect enough water from the nearby Colorado River for the use of the base and its personnel. The extreme heat was another issue. The Marines had to just suck it up.

The class of new recruits numbered about 200, most of them airline pilots. All of them had already completed truncated versions of Basic School and Preflight Training, which Ted didn't need as a former Marine pilot. They all received commissions but not all, by a long shot, would survive the remaining accelerated training. The Marines knew that nearly 50 percent would wash out.

Barracks were assigned, gear distributed and schedules posted on the bulletin board. By appearance, from Ted's perspective, the uniforms hadn't changed much, but he was told that every piece of clothing was bullet resistant and laser reflective. He was also issued an iMaster. He didn't want to wear it, but realized that recording all of his lessons could help him with his training.

He met his barracks mates, and they all knew who he was. He shook hands and was polite with everyone but didn't go out of his way to be overly friendly. Just the way he was.

After morning chow on the first day of instruction, the Marine pilots were divided into two groups and assigned to classrooms. At the front of the room Ted entered, on a chalkboard were written the words, F-35 Transition Training, Day One. Ted took a seat in the middle of the room and immediately saw that half the group was made up of women. He stood up.

"Geezus," he said, "these women are gonna be pilots? In combat?"

One of the women tugged at his sleeve and said, "Have a seat, Neanderthal. We're already pilots."

The colonel at the head of the class introduced himself as Lt. Colonel John Rudolph. He was bald, about 6-foot-2, and had a prominent scar on his left cheek. His shoulders were unusually large and square, as if he might once have been a competitive swimmer.

"For the next six months, ideally less," he said, "you will be engaged in the most intense training schedule of your lives. You have joined the Marine

Corps from all over the nation. You have been recruited because you have some pilot experience. That's good. But it's no guarantee that you are going to make the cut. We expect you to act, behave and perform like officers of the United States Marines. Accelerated program, national emergency, or not, you will live up to the high standards of the Corps or you will be out on your ass."

Ted looked around the room. The colonel had everyone's rapt attention.

"While you are in the first phase of transition training, your aircraft are being made ready," said the colonel. "We had a mothballed fleet of about 600 F-35Hs—the Marine version of the Joint Strike Fighter. Because we can't fix 'em fast enough, we'll lose half as we cannibalize 'em for parts. The remaining planes will be fitted with the most advanced avionics we can muster, but I've got to be honest with you, especially in the first phases of training, some of it will be primitive. Just like we don't have satellites to control drones, we won't have 'em to help control avionics or weapons systems either. You may find yourself flying from the seat of your pants."

"You mean skirts," said Ted.

From the rear of the room someone hit him in the back of the head with a notebook. The room fell silent.

"That's enough, Captain Williams," said Colonel Rudolph. "See me after this class."

What am I, a goddamned eight-year-old? Ted thought.

The initial briefing lasted more than four hours. As the room emptied Ted went up front and said to Colonel Rudolph, "You wanted to see me, Sir?"

"Yes, Captain Williams, I do. Let me ask you point blank, do you have a problem serving with women?"

"Well, sir, I'm sure not used to the idea of doing it in combat."

"You better get used to it. Or you're out. If I hear any more comments from you like the one I heard today, you will spend the rest of this war mopping floors for the very same pilots you so jokingly mocked. Do I make myself clear?"

"Yes sir," said Ted.

"Look, Ted, I know about your situation," said the colonel. "There are a lot of things that you're going to have to get used to. One thing you may have going for you is enthusiasm: what the other pilots consider 'primitive' technology may be advanced for you. But I want you to be just as enthusiastic as far as women are concerned. They're here to stay. They've been in the air for a long time, serving the Marines proudly with a lot of combat experience—both years ago when we had real planes, and lately flying drones."

Ted nodded and said, "Yes sir."

"Look at it this way," said the colonel, "you were once an advocate for black ballplayers when most other people wouldn't give them a chance. Now I'm telling you to give the women a chance. They will surprise you. Frankly, we need you all. It doesn't matter who you are as long as you are a good pilot."

"Well, colonel, I'll give it a try," said Ted.

After moving out of earshot of the colonel, he said to no one but himself, "This is gonna be a goddamned, pansy-ass, girly girl air corps. I can't believe it."

~ ~ ~

The next four weeks were spent alternating classroom instruction with physical training. Pre-dawn and early hours were spent running and doing conditioning drills. Daylight hours were spent in the classroom. The training included courses in avionics, power plant, weapons systems, fuel systems, emergency procedures and tactical operations.

In a machine the pilots dubbed "The Beast," they would need to master the rigors of G forces. The Beast was a centrifuge trainer that spun around and around at speeds that produced forces up to 9 Gs. Many of the pilots, even those with civil aviation experience, couldn't hack it and didn't make the cut, thanks to The Beast. They had to master two difficult physical tasks to survive such G forces. One, called the Anti-G Straining Maneuver, or AGSM, required full contraction of the major muscles in the legs and stomach to prevent blood from pooling in the lower extremities. The second was a breathing technique known as the HICK Maneuver which, done properly, closed off the respiratory system to force more blood to the brain.

The goal was to minimize the effects of GLOC—G-induced Loss of Consciousness—and an even more dangerous condition called ALOC—Almost Loss of Consciousness—highlighted not by blacking out but by longer-duration confusion and disorientation during flight.

For Ted it was the most difficult part of his training. The flight surgeons were concerned. Ted's recovery from The Beast was particularly severe. Most of the pilots had some residual dizziness after riding, but Ted's lasted longer.

After one particularly difficult ride, he sat on a bench with his head between his knees and was approached by a flight surgeon.

"Ted, are you all right?"

"Yeah," he said wincing.

"Lie on this bench. I want to examine you."

The doctor ran a scanner over him and looked at the readings.

"Cardio looks fine. Please sit up."

Ted rose slowly.

"How many fingers?" the doc said to Ted.

He answered correctly.

"Follow my finger left and right," said the doctor, waving his index finger in front of Ted's face.

"What are you experiencing right now?"

"Just a little dizzy is all," said Ted.

"Any headache?"

"No," said Ted.

"All right. You let me know if you start to feel worse."

The continual testing to gain an understanding of Ted's tolerances would have appalled Dr. Miles. At risk was the delicate work of the team of specialists who had brought him back to life and repaired the brain damage from his previous life with all of their nanotechnologies and specialized tissue-regeneration techniques.

Despite the challenges, Ted made it through the difficult phase.

~ ~ ~

The pilot training continued to include physical exercise, classroom instruction and new forms of machine-based simulation. Most of it, Ted thought, was dedicated toward making the pilots puke.

In the evenings, when there were precious few moments of downtime, Ted used his iMaster to recap the day's important lessons but couldn't help but use it as well to follow the progress of the Sox. Things were not going well for the Old Towne Team in pursuit of the pennant.

While sitting on his bunk and projecting the story on the wall, Ted was approached by two of his fellow pilots.

"Hi, Ted," said Jerry Stetson.

"Whatya doin'?" said Cindy Washington.

Jeremiah "Jerry" Stetson was a former drone pilot and commercial airline veteran from Reno, Nevada. He was a thin man with an unhealthy pallor and dark circles under his eyes, but he'd proven to be as tough as a Ponderosa Pine. Lucinda "Cindy" Washington was another commercial airline pilot, from Amarillo, Texas. A short African-American woman with straight hair that she wore in a bun, Cindy was unusually charming with her Texas drawl. She was the woman who had called Ted a Neanderthal during their indoctrination.

Ted had recently resolved to try and be more social with his fellow pilots.

"What are you two airline hostesses doing around my bunk?" he said.

"Just wondering how the Sox are doin'," said Cindy as she and Jerry sat on an adjacent bunk.

"Not too well, unfortunately," said Ted, leaning back and folding his hands behind his head as he lay on his own bunk. "I'm trying not to think about it."

"Sure," said Cindy. "So, ya'll think they're gonna let us get our hands on a real jet any time soon?"

"I hope so," said Ted. "This is becoming a real pain in the ass."

"Did you do anything like this, ah, the first time you learned to fly jets?" said Jerry.

"No, we didn't have sophisticated training machines in the 1950s. I already knew how to fly, so after basic instruction about jet propulsion, we took to the air. There were really no other jets to train on because our's were the first."

"That ain't too dissimilar from the situation we're in right now," said Cindy.

"'Ain't too dissimilar?'" said Ted. "You know, I like you, Texas. You got a way with words."

The three shared a laugh.

"Well, y'all are makin' progress then," said Cindy. "I thought ya hated women pilots, Ted."

"Hate's a strong word. Let's just say I'm skeptical."

"Well, Mr. Skeptical, I'm still here—not washed out like a lot of the men. And there are plenty of others like me."

"No. You just might be one of a kind," said Ted.

Fifty-four

The next morning Colonel Rudolph was once again at the head of the class. Ted, Cindy and Jerry chose to sit together in the front row.

"Understanding the F-35's advanced systems is a challenge," said the colonel. "Radar systems are complicated, including air-to-air and air-to-ground modes. The ground modes include high-resolution mapping and multiple ground moving-target detection. Combat ID and how to track targets on the ground will be a major focal point in the days ahead. Understanding the missile and laser warning system and navigation during night operations will be particularly onerous for you wannabe fighter jockeys. Add to that the skill mix for electronic warfare and ultra-high bandwidth communications, and another bunch of you are gonna bounce out of the program."

Ted leaned over to Cindy and whispered, "Nice of him to be so encouraging."

~ ~ ~

As the days rolled on there were more centrifuge and altitude chamber rides. The pilots learned brevity code. The physical training expanded to include ejection seat/egress training and parachute landing and falls, and then water survival training.

The remaining recruits who didn't wash out were introduced to the F-35H flight simulator.

Ted, Cindy and Jerry were in the front of a large group of pilots facing Colonel Rudolph in building 204. Rudolph stood in front of a machine that from the outside looked like a large box on hydraulic stilts.

"The flight sim is the most critical part of your training," said the colonel. "Because the Marines have so few jets, you will not be able to train in what decades ago would have been considered adequate flight trainers—real jets for student pilots. Instead, you pilots will do all of your preflight work in the flight simulator and then graduate to the real thing—the very aircraft that you will take into combat. It is critical that all of you understand the capabilities of the F-35H."

"Now you're talking," said Ted, loud enough for his two friends to hear.

"The Marine version of the F-35 Joint Strike Fighter (JSF), or Lightning II, began life as the F-35B in about 2015," explained the colonel. "Made by Lockheed Martin, it was conceived as the ideal close air support weapon because of its short takeoff and vertical landing capabilities. Basically, it traded long-range fuel capacity for vertical take off and landing. A lift fan located directly behind the pilot and a vectoring jet engine cruise nozzle in the tail, constitute the vertical flight propulsion system. In earlier versions of the F-35 Marine JSF, these extra systems not only replaced fuel volume but guns had to be carried in a ventral pod. Later versions eliminated the need for the separate pod. For nearly 50 years the F-35 in all of its variants was the aviation workhorse of every branch of the military. The U.S. Air Force became more of a space-based branch of the U. S. military, utilizing space-to-ground killer satellites, which—along with the advent of the drones—hastened its demise. But now, as you know, the plane is being resurrected."

"Resurrected. Just like you," Cindy whispered to Ted.

~ ~ ~

A few days later Cindy was the bearer of bad news one morning in the officers' mess. Ted and Jerry were sitting at a long table among many rows of tables when Cindy approached.

"Have you seen the ePaper?" Cindy asked Ted.

She handed it to him. "Red Sox Eliminated," read the headline. The eReader went on to say the Bosox had been knocked out in the final game of the championship series against the Cuban Missiles, one win away from making it to the World Series. Ted was too frustrated to read any further.

"Yet again," he mumbled.

"Sorry, Ted," said Cindy. "Hey, at least the Sox finished ahead of the Yankees, right?"

"I don't care about the fuckin' Yankees."

"Does this mean they will blame you?" said Jerry.

"I couldn't care less who they blame," said Ted. "They always have to blame somebody; might as well be me."

"Will you give any of your teammates a call?" asked Cindy.

Ted was forking something into his mouth that could only be described as meat and potato mush.

"I'll probably talk to a couple of 'em," he said. "They don't need to hear from me just now."

"Well, maybe they will *want* to hear from you," said Cindy.

"Maybe, maybe you're right," said Ted unconvincingly.

Fifty-five

The media back in Boston did blame Ted. Many articles were written under the banner of "What if?"—what if he had stayed? On the national level, ESPN was particularly harsh. It all had an eerie familiarity to it.

He didn't dwell on it. In fact, Smitty and Calingo had reached out to him to tell him it was largely their fault. Both had slumped in the playoffs; they reminded him that no one man can be responsible for winning and losing in a team sport. He was happy to hear from them.

In the arid Arizona desert the flight training intensified. Colonel Rudolph himself was taking an active role in the pilot training. Early one morning after physical training he addressed the pilots.

"Marines," he said, "you have been doing well—those of you who are left. I salute you and your accomplishments thus far. However, I have to tell you that we are going to have to pick up the pace. Things are not going well in Afghanistan. Without air support, our Marines on the ground are suffering losses. We are moving into a new phase. It is more complicated—has been made more complicated—by the fact that we are underequipped. As our armament manufacturers race to produce weapons for your planes, we don't know which will be ready on time. We do know we will not have GPS-guided systems because we will not have satellites. That eliminates a lot of weapons from our arsenal. Your weapons bay will include a 25 mm cannon with 220 rounds and an assortment of air-to-ground missiles capable of supporting Marines on terra firma. Maybe some air-to-air strikers as well. We do not know yet how those missiles will be guided. One of the complicating factors is the fact that the F-35 was built to be piloted using helmet-mounted displays— HMD—and, well, we do not have them yet. The few that we do have are more than 50 years old and are, understandably, not working properly. So, a lot of new technology is being rushed to completion. Flying either way, with or without the highest technology, I have supreme confidence you will honor and add to the proud tradition of the U.S. Marine Corps. That'll be all."

"Attention on deck," someone yelled, and they all stood as the colonel left.

~ ~ ~

Ted was enjoying it all. There was something about the Marines that was like no other experience for him. Maybe it was the esprit de corps, maybe the discipline, perhaps the prestige. *I am at home. There is nothing else like this.*

Were he not in a 130-degree desert, it would have been perfect.

Study focused intensely on the aircraft. It featured stealth technology that would not be much use against Pakistan's modern air defenses. The pilots spent a lot of time learning the aircraft's integrated avionics and sensors. All of it was intended to improve the pilot's situational awareness and facilitate defensive maneuvers and effective weapons delivery.

The most innovative design element for Ted was the voice-recognition system in the cockpit. He had seen HMI (human-machine interaction) at home in Boston with his compuTV, and he didn't like it.

"Who's gonna be flyin' this thing," he said to one instructor, "me or him?"

"Don't worry," said the instructor outside the flight sim, "You can override it—most of the time."

Ted struggled to keep up, and his instructors knew it. Still, he persevered. *Goddamn,* he thought, *I never had to learn this kinda shit when I moved up to jets in Korea.*

The Marine Corps would give him no special dispensation, not when safety and lives were at stake. He had to qualify like everyone else.

To keep up, Ted spent extra hours studying when everyone else took off for rare R&R. He needed the extra time. His instructors took notice. They knew he was working hard to pass the regular exams on time. He didn't want to wash out.

~ ~ ~

Ted had little time to focus on anything else, but called Johnnie and Elizabeth, wondering why his phone still worked. *Civilian satellite,* he guessed.

"Ted, is it really you?" said Johnnie.

"Hey, Johnnie Boy, how's my little slugger doin'?"

"Good. I've been working on my swing just like you told me."

"That's great, Johnnie. How ya doing in school?"

"Okay I guess. Ted, did ya hear about the Red Sox?"

"Yeah, it was disappointing. I wish I coulda been there."

"It's not your fault, Ted. Besides, you'll get 'em next year."

"That's right. That's a good attitude, son. I just want to . . . I just want to say that I miss you, Johnnie."

"Yeah. I miss you too, Ted."

"Well, don't dwell on it," said Ted, knowing full well that the advice was for him more than Johnnie. "You just keep on doin' a good job in school."

"I will."

"Say, is your mom there?"

Johnnie handed the phone to Elizabeth.

"Hello, Ted. How are you?" she said.

"Gee, it's great to hear your voice, Lizzy."

"It's great to hear you too, Ted, even the Lizzy part," she said sincerely.

"Well, I just want you two to know that I'm doing fine. The training is tough but I'm hanging in there."

"How are you holding up, Ted? Have the stresses been great on your body?"

He resisted the temptation to snap at her.

"Actually, I'm doing okay. The G-forces training was difficult, but I came through all right. Don't you worry about me."

"Well, we all miss you here. Cecelia is giving me a signal to say hi, and Emily has been asking about you. Have you talked to Marshall?"

"No, but I'm planning to call him," said Ted.

"Well, I've talked to him a couple of times, and he's wondering how you are."

Changing the subject she said, "Ted, please call me if there is anything you need to talk about, yes?"

"I will. I will, Lizzy. Tell Johnnie when I get back to Boston I'm gonna take him fishing, though I don't know when that will be."

"I will, Ted."

"Well, bye for now," he said.

"Bye," she said.

He hung up the phone and was quiet, his mind filled with thoughts of home, his eyes set in a thousand-yard stare.

Back in Boston, Elizabeth had the same look on her face.

Fifty-six

On a Saturday night after a particularly grueling week, Ted met up with his buddy at a local watering hole called Spanky's. Marshall had traveled to Yuma from Phoenix to catch up with the Thumper. They gave each other a high handshake and a hug and then sat at the bar surrounded by an assortment of patrons engaged in honky-tonk endeavors.

A bartender—a 20-something blonde wearing jeans and her shirttails tied high around her waist—approached and said, "Hey, fellas, what'll ya have?"

"You Spanky?" said Ted.

"No, I'm Hanky and over there is my sister Panky."

Ted and Marsh looked down the bar at another toothsome blonde bartender.

"Nothing like a sister act," said Ted.

He and Marsh ordered bottles of Corona. No one in the large room paid any attention to Ted.

"So, how ya hittin' 'em, pardner?" said Marsh. "Ya look good."

"About as well as could be expected," said Ted. "It's harder than I thought it would be, but I'll be all right."

"What's the hardest part?" said Marsh.

"Well, the work and studying is tough enough, but they have us on such an accelerated schedule . . . well, it's a goddamned pain in the ass. Not only that, but we haven't seen a real plane yet. The simulators are amazin', though."

Hanky brought over a bowl of peanuts in the shell and two more beers.

"What's new with you, buddy?" said Ted.

"Oh, same old shit—just working."

"Yeah, how is the medical supply business going these days?" said Ted.

"Well, sales to CryoCorp are up. The scuttlebutt I hear is that intakes are up, and Bernard Cromwell is putting a lot of pressure on the staff to produce another success story like you. There's a little conflict between the staff about whether or not they are ready. Elizabeth's departure was a big setback."

"Yeah, well, don't tell her that—it'll go to her head," said Ted. "What else you been doin'? Any fishin'?"

"No, but I've been playin' a little golf now and then."

"Ya any good?" said Ted.

"No," said Marsh. "The irony is, in baseball I could hardly hit a curveball. Now every golf shot I hit is a curve."

Ted nearly spit out his Corona laughing. He clinked bottles with Marsh.

"Well, keep on workin' at it."

Ted looked around the barroom and for the first time noticed that it was about evenly split between Marines and townies, and getting louder. His eye caught two familiar faces. He motioned to Jerry and Cindy to come over to the bar from the pool table they were surrounding with other Marines.

"Jerry and Cindy, this here is my good friend Marsh. Marsh, meet my fellow planeless pilots, Jerry and Cindy."

They shook hands. Marsh held Cindy's hand for just a second longer than was customary. It was clear to Ted and Jerry that a spark had ignited.

"Shut down your afterburners for a moment there, Marsh," said Ted, "and order these two a couple a beers."

The pilots were very interested in Ted's friendship with Marsh. Marshall filled in all of the details over more beers. He then asked Cindy to dance to a slow country tune the DJ was playing.

"I think there are some fireworks goin' on there," said Jerry.

"Yeah, it's older than time itself," said Ted. "Boy biologist and medical supply salesman meets girl fighter pilot. Romantic, ain't it?"

Marsh and Cindy returned to the bar. The group ordered and drank more beers. Marsh took to calling his personal military detachment "the three amigos." The well-oiled Marines-plus-one were having a good time when a drunken townie began hitting on Cindy. She tried to spurn his advances to no avail.

"Hey, sport," said Ted, "why don't you leave the gal alone."

The townie said, "You Marines are all alike. You think your shit don't stink."

He then turned his back on the three men, wedging himself between them and Cindy at the bar and tried to whisper something in her ear. Ted tapped the intruder on the shoulder, and anyone could see what would happen next. Only, it didn't. Instead of the townie seeing a right cross coming his way from Marshall or Ted, Cindy hit him on the chin with an uppercut so hard his head snapped back like a crash-test dummy. He sprawled across the top of the bar. Other townies saw what happened and jumped into the fray. Ted got his chance at a right cross on somebody else, and the fight was on.

The room erupted. About three-dozen Marines took on an equal number of townies in a brawl that looked like Louis vs. Schmeling writ large, chairs and glass breaking everywhere. Marsh tried to defend Cindy's honor by going after the original perpetrator, but, thanks to her, he was still out cold on top of the bar. Ted and Jerry set up an Alamo defense in front of the bar and were successfully taking on all challengers.

Across the room the DJ tried to protect his computer. He then put on a record of "The Battle Hymn of the Republic." A Marine flew into the ancient turntable, and the needle careened across the record in a high-fidelity screech.

Marsh grabbed Cindy and motioned for Ted and Jerry to come along.

"C'mon," he said, "before y'all end up in the brig."

Outside they got into Jerry's car, Ted in the front, Marsh and Cindy in the back. As they drove away, Marsh and Cindy were soon consoling each other and Ted was now singing "The Battle Hymn of the Republic" at full volume.

"My eyes have seen the glory of the coming of the Lord . . ."

Soon he realized there was another hymn, much more appropriate, and he sang, "From the halls of Montezuma, To the shores of Tripoli, We fight our country's battles, In the air, on land, and sea . . ."

At Marsh's request, Jerry drove to the train station. Having avoided jail with his three amigos, Marsh said his goodbyes, kissed Cindy one more time and caught the 12:10 out of Yuma.

For the Marine aviators it was zero-dark-thirty.

Fifty-seven

After three months of compressed instruction, the pilots were finally introduced to their aircraft. In a huge hangar Ted and the others walked around several of the new/old F-35s they would be flying. As he stared at one plane, a tingling sensation coursed through Ted's body, like the feeling of waiting for the first pitch of a ballgame.

He could not believe that UAVs had replaced this magnificent multi-role aircraft. Although it had the "F" fighter designation, the F-35 was really a versatile fighter-bomber—more important, given the Marines' mission.

His mind shot back to his old F-9 jet in Korea. What primitive beasts, he thought, compared to this plane. This was chock-full of offensive and defensive weapons, and with vertical takeoff and landing, or a short takeoff with a heavy payload, it hardly needed a runway. How could you not love this bird?

The pilots were allowed to climb into the stationary, single-seat F-35s. It was a testament to the flight sim that it felt very familiar to them—right down to the close confines.

For Ted it was a warm fuzzy. "The HOTAS is kick-ass." Every control function was mounted on either side of the stick (right hand) or the throttle quadrant (left hand) to complete the Hands on Throttle and Stick. On the downside, Ted was 6-4 and it was tight.

"It's gonna feel a little cramped with my speed jeans and chaps on," he said.

After climbing down, Ted noticed for the first time a circular mechanism about a foot in diameter below and slightly forward of the cockpit on the bottom of the airplane. He had not seen it before.

"What's that pod?" he said to a flight instructor.

"It's not a pod, it's a retractable turret," the instructor said, "a laser turret."

"A laser? Geezus," said Ted.

"We know you weren't expecting this and haven't trained for it yet, but it's gonna be a major arrow in your quiver, Cap'n Williams. Our weapons people came through big time."

Though not as tall as Ted, Major Rivers was another Marine right out of central casting. He herded the large group of pilots over to a cluster of chairs in neat rows. The F-35s served as a backdrop as he addressed the group.

"I am happy to tell you jet jockeys our weapons people have transferred the latest laser technology from our arsenal of UAVs to the F-35s. Also, your flight helmets with HMD will be here next week."

A roar of approval went up.

"Don't get your fangs out yet," said Rivers. "You haven't trained for either of these FMs. Tomorrow's ride, and for many hops to come, we're just focusing on familiarization so you don't goon up. You'll use the new helmet-mounted display and ginup with lasers in the sim before you use 'em in the F-35."

Ted leaned over to another pilot and whispered, "What are FMs?"

"Fucking magic," said the pilot, "Fucking magic technology."

~ ~ ~

The next day dawned sunny and hot as usual, and the pilots were hot to fly their new planes. Ted donned his flight suit and chaps and was driven out to the runway where he did a preflight walk-around of his F-35 with Major Rivers.

"You know, I didn't notice it yesterday, but it's smaller than I thought it would be," said Ted.

"Yeah, but it packs a punch," said Rivers.

After the preflight check, Ted and Rivers saluted. Ted put on his conventional helmet and climbed up into the cockpit. Inside, he connected his umbilical cord.

Looking out the windscreen of the Lockheed Martin jet, he liked the fact that the aircraft had tremendous over-the-nose visibility. He powered up the mighty GE/Rolls-Royce single engine. He remembered Colonel Rudolph saying that the engine, lift fan and stabilizing roll ducts beneath the F-35H's wings combined to produce 40,000 pounds of lifting force during vertical take off.

The cockpit was a marvel to Ted, highlighted by the Rockwell Collins' advanced tactical display and Northrup Grumman's radar and integrated communications and navigation systems. He completed his cockpit checklist and saluted a ground controller in front of the aircraft. The controller gave him two thumbs up and high-tailed it away from the jet in anticipation of the big burn and air blast about to take place. The tower also gave Ted the green light.

Ted took a deep breath.

He initiated the vertical takeoff sequence. On the top of the fuselage the lift fan doors opened and the fan powered up. Simultaneously, the swiveling rear engine exhaust nozzle vectored downward in preparation for vertical takeoff and then began to burn. The automatic process both unnerved and amazed Ted, though he had gone through it in the flight sim.

The lift fan generated a column of cool air that provided nearly 20,000 pounds of lift, extracting power from the engine.

With increasing thrust, in a few moments Ted and his aircraft lifted straight up vertically and seemed to shake momentarily as the landing gear was relieved of its weightload. The aircraft hovered a few feet above the ground. Ted's mind wandered to an old poem that he remembered by a WWII pilot named Magee:

Oh, I have slipped the surly bonds of earth,
And danced the skies on laughter-silvered wings . . .

Quickly returning to situational awareness, still hovering, he initiated forward propulsion, and the rear engine nozzle slowly vectored from 90 degrees downward, upward toward horizontal. With a tremendous amount of thrust the F-35 moved forward. Ted retracted the landing gear, the lift fan doors closed slowly and then, faster than a speeding line drive, the F-35 tore across the desert sky.

"Wow," he said. The sensation of moving at high speed and controlling your own aircraft was like nothing else. It was as exhilarating as hitting a home run: Total freedom, master of gravity, of time and space.

. . . I've chased the shouting wind along, and flung
My eager craft through footless halls of air . . .

He climbed upward and leveled out at 20,000 feet. He pushed the throttle hard and leveled out again at 30,000. At nearly Mach 1 he performed a series of left and right half-rolls and then full, 360-degree rolls. He was amazed at the agility of the aircraft and its sturdiness. To his relief, he too had no ill effects.

Returning to 20,000 feet he lifted and lowered the nose to varying degrees of attack and tested the aircraft through high-speed turns. Both he and the F-35 passed with flying colors.

After 90 minutes he was instructed to return to base. He lowered the landing gear and landed conventionally on Yuma's long runway.

Taxiing to a stop he powered down. As the F-35's canopy opened from the rear, Ted shook his head and smiled.

Major Rivers approached as Ted climbed down.

"Well, how'd you like it?" said Rivers.

"I'll tell ya, I am never at a loss for words, but I am speechless," said Ted.

. . . I've trod the high untrespassed sanctity of space . . .
. . . put out my hand, and touched the face of God.

Fifty-eight

T he weeks ahead focused on formations, weapons switchology and air combat maneuvering. Central to all of it was learning how to use the new helmet-mounted display and the onboard laser.

The classroom instruction was becoming tedious but Major Rivers had the group's attention when he focused on the lasers.

"Most of you know that since the early part of the century, the U.S. military had been integrating high-energy laser technology into its arsenal of weapons. The F-35 uses electricity generated through the plane's engines to power a solid-state laser that releases intense radiation. The laser system on the aircraft is designed to work in tandem with the warplane's conventional weapons. Although it can be used effectively in air-to-air combat to burn up an adversary's critical flight controls, it has minimal effects on hardened structures and armored vehicles in air-to-ground combat. It is most effective in antipersonnel scenarios, or where precision, speed, number of engagements and limited collateral damage are more important than pure destructive power."

Ted interrupted. "Major, if our enemy is sophisticated enough to knock out our satellites with its own lasers, how effective will its lasers be against our airplanes?"

"Well, the good news," said Rivers, "is that our intelligence people tell us he doesn't have many aircraft. But he has some—old battleaxe Russian MiGs and a handful of rust-bucket Chinese Dragons. You shouldn't have much trouble with 'em; we don't believe they have sufficient numbers with onboard lasers. But I'm not gonna sugarcoat it. There is a concern about ground-based laser weapons. Before our satellites were taken out, we thought we had adequate defenses. They were equipped, as are your planes, with a laser countermeasure system. In the F-35 the sensor is located in the nose and the countermeasures are in the same laser turret as your offensive weapon. In theory and in practice, when a hostile laser is aimed at our asset, the laser countermeasure responds in a millisecond by illuminating a high power laser spot near the target, deceiving the attacker to lock onto the new spot and not the satellite or the aircraft."

"So what went wrong with the satellites?" someone asked.

"Two things, we think," said Rivers. "First, the enemy had installed a Trojan horse to turn off the countermeasures. Second, just for good measure, he hit each target with multiple ground-based lasers simultaneously to overwhelm the countermeasures if they were not already shut down. Unfortunately, excluding the kill switch controlled by the enemy, your aircraft carries the same vulnerability. It is vulnerable from attack if the enemy can muster up multiple ground-based illumination."

The pilots were silent, deep in thought.

After a long pause, Rivers continued, "The countermeasures are automated. You don't have to do a thing."

Jerry leaned over to Ted and said quietly, "Great, just another NOFUS."

"What the hell is No Fuss?" said Ted.

"No Operator Fucked-Up Situation."

Fifty-nine

During the last month of training the pilots focused on close air support, air interdiction, armed reconnaissance, midair refueling and air combat maneuvering.

The ACM involved both defensive and offensive strategies and electronic kills against designated "enemy" aircraft. It reminded Jerry of the video games of his youth, but now it was for real and at hundreds of miles an hour.

High above the Arizona/California desert, a large group of friendlies and enemies were engaged in a tense ACM exercise the pilots called a real sweatex. Ted was flying with Jerry as his wingman. They already had several electronic kills when they jumped two other F-35s in high velocity ACM.

The two surprised pilots, flustered and on the defensive after Ted and Jerry jumped them, made a garbled radio call, and then disaster struck. They turned into each other.

Ted's eyes opened as wide as a camera lens. He could not believe what he was seeing. The two planes disintegrated. Debris cascaded downward. Neither of the doomed pilots had a chance to eject, and both were lost.

Ted and Jerry, in their separate planes, watched helplessly from above.

The brass ordered all training flights to stand down for three days until every pilot had a chance to review with their instructors what went wrong. Ted's first reaction was anger, directed at whom he did not know. He withdrew into silence. The two dead pilots, McCallister and Whitney, were well liked and talented. Their loss was a big blow to their fellow pilots.

In a classroom filled with somber faces and pilots staring down at the ground, Colonel Rudolph addressed the group.

"I know you're all pretty down right now. But I encourage all of you to not let the deaths of McCallister and Whitney happen without some good coming out of it. Our preliminary investigation has concluded that this incident was no one's fault but McCallister's and Whitney's. I know it sounds callous right now, but let their tactical error serve as a lesson for all of you pilots. Maintaining situational awareness is the first lesson you were taught. Given the need for urgency, a longer stand down is just not in the cards. You'll return to the air tomorrow. That is all."

~ ~ ~

The next day the group took to the air and tried not to think of Colonel Rudolph as a heartless bastard. A week later, on Live Day, their moods finally shifted. The pilots would use live weapons for the first time, and they took to the air with great enthusiasm.

Ted was assigned flight leader status, and Cindy was his wingman. In total, the group included six planes. For two hours they successfully took out a series of ground based targets with lasers and conventional weapons.

Cindy made a particularly good run and took out a dummy group of ground personnel with her laser.

"Hot damn, good work. You fried those figurines, Cinderella," said Ted on his radio.

Later in the same hop, Ted nailed a flying drone with his laser that—because of the lack of satellite operations—was controlled by radio and reduced to circling in a low loop over the Arizona desert.

"Like shootin' a duck in a barrel," he said on his radio. It wasn't much of a challenge. But when it dawned on him that he was using a laser from his fighter he shook his helmet and said, "Holy shit."

~ ~ ~

Ted excelled. His reflexes were brilliant, his eyesight amazing. His mind and body were working to perfection, with no stresses.

I am becoming one with this machine, he said to himself during a great flight in which he made two kills, one at a particularly difficult angle of attack. The brass took notice.

Standing in the top of the control tower and alternating between using his binoculars and viewing the radar screen, Colonel Rudolph said, "Wait 'til ol' Teddy sees what we have in store next."

Sixty

After mastering live weapons, the pilots graduated from Accelerated Aviation Training in a hastily arranged ceremony and received the Naval Aviators' Wings of Gold, becoming official Marine Corps aviators or, as one ground crew wag so aptly put it, "150-day wonders." In fact, the task that the ground crews and armament people accomplished, starting with planes that were pulled off the junk heap, was just as impressive.

The pilots were assigned to squadrons. Ted, Jerry and Cindy were destined to go into war together. Their newly created squadron would be Marine Fighter Attack Squadron 282, or VMFA-282, assigned to Marine Aircraft Group-12, 2nd Marine Aircraft Wing. After brief deliberation, the squadron chose its nickname, the "Grand Slammers"—a not-so-subtle reference to its most famous pilot.

Ted hated it, mostly because he didn't want to be singled out and he hadn't proven himself yet. He finally came around to the idea just a little when his fellow drivers pointed out that he had proven himself in both WWII and Korea. A new patch was designed. At the top was a profile of an F-35H and underneath a massive wooden bat hitting not a baseball but the planet earth. "Anytime, Anywhere" became the group's motto. Lt. Colonel Rudolph was designated as the Slammers' commanding officer and took control of the squadron's 16 pilots and planes.

In a Slammers-only room in the officers' club, over numerous shots and beers, the pilots determined they liked the fact that their new name would have a double meaning.

"It's a 'double intender,'" offered up one of the flying bubbas in an alcohol-fueled malapropism.

With Colonel Rudolph in attendance and imbibing as well, it was time to get down to some serious business: the choosing of the call signs. In the impromptu kangaroo court, one pilot was given the task of writing down for posterity the names by which the pilots would forever be known to each other in the air and on the ground, even in social situations.

Acknowledging rank and privilege, the colonel was put up for voting first. That was the only concession to rank. By tradition, neither he nor any other pilot had a say in what name would be chosen for them. Call signs could be related to how a person looked or how he or she acted; to an incident that fellow pilots witnessed; or to something obvious that went with the pilot's name.

Though he had been in the Corps for a long time, Colonel Rudolph had never been given a call sign. There was no need with drone jockeys. Voting procedures were only slightly better than a Florida election, highlighted by verbal suggestions and shouts of "That's it, that's it." The colonel breathed a half-sigh of relief and laughed when the group announced the decision. He would be known as Lt. Colonel John "Red-Nose" Rudolph.

Jerry's appellation, after more drinking, was another obvious decision: Lt. Jeremiah "Big Hat" Stetson. Remembering Cindy's impressive performance inside Spanky's Bar, the group gave her the moniker of Lt. Lucinda "Uppercut" Washington.

Ted's chosen name caused a great roar when it was debated and when it was announced. Harking back to his first day of flight school, someone remembered his comment about women pilots and Cindy's characterization of him as a Neanderthal. Ted Williams, the man with so many nicknames he couldn't keep track of them all, became known to his squadron as Captain Ted "Caveman" Williams.

Ted laughed. Considering that many of the other names were real pissers—names like "Crabs," "Big Ears" and "Pig Nose"—he could live with "Caveman."

The colonel came over to shake Ted's hand and buy him a drink. "Caveman," said Colonel Rudolph, "you've come a long way. I'm gonna be countin' on you in the weeks ahead."

Sixty-one

The Grand Slammers were given new orders. They were to fly to Newport, Rhode Island for three weeks of training in ship-based landings. As he lifted off, Ted gave a salute to no one in particular except the hot Sonoran desert for which he hardly had an affinity. "Alpha Mike Foxtrot," he said, meaning "adios motherfucker."

The Slammers' F-35 pilots took off from Yuma with a flight plan that included midcontinent, midair refueling and then landing at Newport, not onboard ship but on an airstrip and tarmac recently redesigned to accommodate STOVL aircraft. For Ted, going to Newport, if only for a short time, meant he would try to catch up with everyone in Boston, only 75 miles away.

Excluding the Naval War College and various research facilities, for years Newport's naval capacity had been diminished to the point that hardly any ships were based there. That changed after the global warming crisis. As waters began to rise, the U.S. Atlantic Fleet moved many of its Norfolk-based ships. Newport was identified as the ideal location for the brunt of the Atlantic Navy's force of amphibious assault ships (AAS). Unlike Norfolk and even nearby Cape Cod, much of Newport was situated on high, rocky cliffs that absorbed the brunt of rising sea levels. Moreover, Narragansett Bay was the second deepest harbor in the U.S. and it no longer froze in winter.

After the Navy, like the other services, began to rely on drones, supercarriers were hardly needed any longer, with the exception of a couple that launched very large UAVs. Instead, the navy invested heavily in a fleet of Hormuz-class AASs, or "Big Deck Amphibs," deployed to support Marine forces attacking by amphibious assault. The ships were tasked to support invasions with a significant air wing consisting of drones, helos and tilt-rotor aircraft. Over the years the AASs expanded their size and role to include maintaining strike aircraft, again mostly drones. But now that lack of satellites rendered the drones largely ineffective, the ships were being outfitted once again with STOVL aircraft, as they had been in the first half of the century.

In Newport, Ted received the first of a few surprises that would come his way. Colonel Rudolph promoted him to major, doing the honors himself.

"Are you doing this for publicity purposes?" said Ted.

"Ted, I remind you," said the colonel, "you've had prior service and not only have you completed the requirements to fly again but you've demonstrated significant leadership in the process."

Major Williams and his squadron mates did not have a chance to celebrate. The new training started immediately, leaving little time for enjoying the many attractions of Newport. It was nearly February and 60 to 65 degrees each day. In some places, there was an upside to global warming. Ted heard on the news the Sox were preparing for spring training.

After receiving three days of classroom instruction and spending two days touring an AAS on the pier, the pilots conducted field mirror landing practice on land, simulating AAS landings, and then were tasked with landing on the deck of an offshore AAS. The next four days consisted of practicing fully loaded short takeoffs, vertical takeoffs and landings, all from the deck of a pitching AAS. Mostly, signaling and communication were what needed to be practiced and learned. Once again, all of the training happened at breakneck speed.

~ ~ ~

The Corps released news of Ted's having completed flight training and his promotion but did not disclose his location. They asked Ted if he would do an interview. Having worked out the right to reject such a request before he rejoined the Marines, he said no. But the media pressure on the public information officers was unrelenting. A brigadier general in charge of Public Affairs visited Ted to try and persuade him.

A compromise was reached. Ted agreed to meet with one reporter and photographer of his choosing who would shoot stills and digital video simultaneously to keep the broadcast media happy. His location would be kept secret for security reasons, and the reporter and photographer would share the interview and photos with other media. Ted chose the young reporter he first met in spring training a year before. Jack Paul from Boston eNews had impressed Ted with his homework and knowledge of Ted's hitting philosophy. Public Affairs called Paul and laid out the ground rules. He quickly agreed and showed up in Newport to interview Ted.

Ted had made a good choice. The only uncomfortable parts of the interview were questions about whether or not he had any guilt for leaving the Sox at the end of last season's pennant race and whether it made sense to go to war. Ted handled it with aplomb. The same answer applied to both questions.

"It's a matter of duty, honor and the country's national emergency," said Ted. "I heard a speech the other night by the president, and she said—I'm still gettin' use to the thought of a female president—somethin' that rang true to me. 'The nobility in being an American is what drives us all to sacrifice, even when that calling might be the extreme sacrifice.' Those are meaningful words to me."

What Ted didn't say and the reporter did not ask about was that Ted no longer feared death, something that Colonel Rudolph wondered about but couldn't ask Ted. He didn't want Caveman taking any unnecessary chances with other peoples' lives.

Ted told the reporter, "You know, what I didn't fully realize in my first life was that individual accomplishment will always be secondary to teamwork. I always said the Marines were the best team I ever played on. I know more than ever that talent and skill will help you achieve individual goals, but winning a World Series or being victorious in war takes teamwork."

Paul also asked him about his call sign and how he came to be called Caveman.

"I don't know. Maybe because of my big bat," said Ted.

~ ~ ~

The story appeared the next day all over the country with a dateline of "Somewhere in North America."

That same day, a Friday, Elizabeth took Johnnie out of school for the day and they traveled to Newport to meet Ted who had a rare afternoon free.

Ted showed off his uniform with the new cluster of gold oak leaves on the collar. They met on Newport's First Beach along Green End Avenue. Newport was not immune to rising sea levels; this beach, much smaller than the original First Beach, was about a mile up Aquidneck Island from its first location.

Johnnie went running ahead and into Ted's arms. After a big hug Ted threw him up toward the sky and caught him again to Johnnie's delight.

Ted turned to Elizabeth, and they hugged. The intensity of her hug surprised him.

"Hello, *Caveman*, she said with a wry smile and moist eyes.

After a few questions for Ted about flying, Johnnie ran ahead to chase seagulls and look for shells as Ted and Elizabeth walked closely behind. The sandy beach, not always easy to find in New England, was crisscrossed with red seaweed.

"So, how's the kid doing in school?" said Ted.

"Just great, but he misses you," she said.

"Yeah, I miss the little bugger, too," said Ted.

"And you, you're doing all right?"

What she really meant was, was his health okay, but this was a softer way to ask a question she knew would rile him.

"Yeah, I'm doing fine. A little tired is all. But we all are tired with this fast-paced training."

"How long will you be in Newport?"

"Well, I'm not supposed to tell you this, but we'll be flyin' out in about 10 days."

"Are you heading into the war zone?"

"Again, that falls under the category of somethin' we're not supposed to talk about, but between you and me, you could assume that."

"Are you ready?"

"Well, we all would have been more comfortable with additional training, but we knew goin' in that this emergency would require extraordinary measures. That's us, extraordinary pilots."

"He said humbly," she said teasingly.

"Well, in the Marines, confidence doesn't hurt. I imagine it's the same in the doctoring business," he said.

"Yes, that is true." She took advantage of the opening: "Speaking of doctoring, may I ask how you are feeling?"

"You know, I'd be a millionaire if I had a nickel for every time we had this discussion."

"Ted, you *are* a millionaire."

"Yeah, well . . ."

A full retort eluded him. Johnnie had stopped up ahead and was examining the empty shell of a horseshoe crab. Elizabeth and Ted stopped walking as well when she said, "Have you been checked out by the flight surgeon?"

"Yes, and I'm doing fine," he said, purposely leaving out his excessive dizziness after riding in the centrifuge.

"Can we change the subject, Lizzy?" he said nicely.

She nodded. After a pause, Elizabeth said, "You know Ted I never received a full answer from you. Can I ask you why you felt compelled to rejoin the Marines? Especially since it could mean giving up your dream of winning the World Series."

Maybe it was the fatigue he was feeling, or maybe it was the knowledge that he was about to fly off into war, but he opened up in a way that she had not expected as they continued their walk on the beach.

"Well," he said, "I take very seriously the motto 'Once a Marine, always a Marine.' But it's more than that. In my first life, I resisted going into the big war at first because I needed to support my mother. But I was also young and innocent, and going off to war was a sort of romantic notion. When I didn't see combat in WWII, I was kinda disappointed. When they called me up again for Korea, I was pissed at first—having served already and being at the height of my baseball career and all—though I didn't let on. But part of me thought I wasn't truly tested."

At the risk of stumbling on the beach, Elizabeth looked intensely into his eyes.

"Korea changed all that. Boy, was I tested," he said. "War is an unfaithful mistress. I got my plane shot up several times and nearly got killed in a crash landing. I guess I killed a lot of people on the ground in air-to-ground combat. It's only as an old man that you gain some perspective on all of that. I sure did. You recognize that wars are fought by the youngest of men for a reason. You're not old enough to question much of the whole shit-awful mess—and there's a lot of it that is in fact horseshit."

"That's another thing," she said. "You have spoken out forcefully against the drugs that the baseball players are taking, yet you're voluntarily going off to war to support a country that produces drugs."

"Yeah, I've thought about that. But our country, our assets, not just Afghanistan, was attacked. The way I see it, I'm helping my country, my Marines, more than I'm helping Afghanistan."

She let his insights roll around in her thoughts for a moment. Ted broke the silence.

"I know what you're thinkin'," he said. "I still haven't convinced you. You're still wondering why, with the benefit of a lifetime's worth of experience, the insight that comes with old age, and being given the chance at a new life, why am I doing this again?"

"Quite right," she said.

"A large part of it is the commitment to the Marines, but more than that, it's who I am. When people said I couldn't do somethin', well that was all the motivation I needed. I may have a new body now but I'm the same old me in every other way. A big part of it, too, is remembering what it was like back in Korea. I was gettin' shot at, and, you know, I was sick all the time from the cold weather, but I was never more alive. I know guys have said that before, about gettin' shot at. But it's true. There's something about the male makeup I guess that drives a man to be tested under extreme circumstances and some of us—I wouldn't say enjoy it—but are validated by it. Most of all, I really do love my country; it's worth fightin' for and somebody's got to do it."

She didn't question his need for validation. But she did say, "You are not doing this because I thought you could not handle it?"

"No. I just look at it as a challenge—the ultimate challenge for me."

She was astounded by his candor. She thought, *this is a man who can talk about hitting and baseball and fishing and flying and similar subjects all day long, but I've never seen him get so introspective—or not fly off the handle when I asked him to do so.*

She also thought it was an awful rationale for going to war but kept silent and said simply, "Thanks for sharing that with me."

She wanted to ask if killing would be made easier knowing there is an afterlife for the victims, or would all the killing disqualify him from that afterlife, but she knew he would not answer. Mostly, she feared losing him. She wanted to hug him and tell him please don't go, but she knew that, too, would do no good. It was all so complicated, these unanswered questions and the emotion she was feeling.

Johnnie was now playing with a stick up ahead. Ted yelled, "Hey, kiddo, howsabout we run up to the carousel and go for a few spins?"

They hopped on horses on the old merry-go-round and had a race to the imaginary finish line with smiles and laughter, chased by dark thoughts and the realization, at least among the adults, that this could be the very last time they see each other.

Sixty-two

The next night was a special evening for the Navy and Marine Corps personnel stationed in Newport. It was the night of the annual Navy Ball, a fundraiser for local charities. The grand party would take place at Rosecliff, one of many Newport mansions, great alabaster and marble dinosaurs, remnants of the Gilded Age strung out all along Bellevue Avenue. Nearly two centuries after it was created, "The Avenue" was still a fashionable address, one that was also popular among tourists during daylight hours.

Perched above a cliff with a great lawn reclining toward the sea, Rosecliff never ceased to charm. The Newport summer "cottage" that would host the Navy Ball was built in 1902 and modeled after the Grand Trianon of Versailles with magnificent Ionic columns and elegant arched windows. Its focal point was Newport's largest ballroom. In the rear of the mansion French doors opened onto a broad terrace, and then the wide lawn adorned with a huge circular fountain stretched to glorious sea views.

Entering the all-white terra cotta mansion were Navy and Marine Corps brass dressed in full military formal wear or mess dress. Evening gowns were the norm for women who were non-military guests, though there were plenty of female military personnel displaying their own formal regalia. The squadron officers of VMFA-282 would be well represented. Fast-working Jerry somehow found a local date. Cindy would have preferred to be accompanied by Marshall but in his absence was happy to be escorted by Ted. "Just as friends," he said when he asked her to accompany him.

Caveman cut an interesting figure. Major Williams wore the Marine's formal blue short-waist evening coat with strip collar and, underneath, a white shirt highlighted by a scarlet cummerbund. His finely pressed trousers matched the blue of the evening coat and featured a full-length red stripe inside a gold stripe.

Lt. Washington was uniformly elegant with similar attire including the red cummerbund, but with a stripeless, full-length blue skirt to match her own short-waist evening coat with a flat red collar. Both of the couple's evening coats featured large ornamental cuffs with fine red and gold embroidery, highlighted by the wearing of white gloves.

That is where the similarities ended, for on Ted's chest were enough medals and ribbons to approximate the decorations of Napoleon. These were another surprise from Colonel Rudolph; he re-presented them all to Ted. This night they were in miniature for the formal occasion but still very impressive. There was a DOD Air Medal; a Korean Service Medal; a Navy Unit Commendation; a Republic of Korea Presidential Unit Citation; a UN Medal; an American Campaign Medal; a WWII Victory Medal; an Asiatic Pacific Campaign Medal; and a National Defense Service Medal. Because it was technically not a military honor, a Presidential Medal of Freedom suspended from a blue ribbon was left behind. Ted received it from the president himself, the first George Bush. All of the medals were somehow reconstituted by Colonel Rudolph.

"My God, Caveman," said Uppercut, "you are blindin' me with all that hardware."

For a guy who never liked to wear a tie, he wore this kind of ornamentation proudly.

As the evening progressed the guests enjoyed dancing to the music of a large orchestra. Ted, never one to engage in much dancing, took the opportunity to wander through the mansion when Cindy excused herself to go to the ladies' room. He visited the billiard room and checked out the salon. Wandering around he exchanged pleasantries with those who came up to greet him.

In the back of the mansion's entry vestibule and to the right he stood in the stair hall at the foot of the arched central opening of the grand staircase that reached up to the second floor. It was a heart-shaped cavity that spread floor to ceiling, accommodating marble stairs with a red carpet. One flight up, the stairs divided at a central landing and returned upward in matched curving flights to the upper floor.

Ted leaned on the end of the railing, his back to the staircase as he continued people-watching. The fine architectural detail and dramatic upward sweep of the staircase were lost on him.

But someone was observing *him*. On the upper left staircase a striking woman in a long evening gown had stopped at the first angle in which she could see him standing at the base of the railing at the bottom of the Y-shaped stairs.

It was Amanda.

She wore a vintage 1940s, black, sequined tulle ball gown. The long straps spread from her delicate shoulders to a plunging v-neck that highlighted her décolletage. An elegant single strand of pearls complimented her luminescent smile. Cascading downward and cinching at the waist, the gown descended graciously to end with an inverted-V hemline just above the floor. The effect allowed flawlessly matched black platform high heels, completing the 1940s look with bows in the front, to peek out for a teasing view. This was a woman comfortable in her own shoes—even if the style was 150 years old. She made it timeless.

She moved down to the last step before the central landing above him. He was still oblivious. That is, until she called out to him.

"Hey there, Lobster Man."

He immediately recognized the voice. His head swiveled and he looked up.

"Amanda," was all he could say.

As she made her way gracefully down the dramatic staircase, he was transfixed at the vision before him.

She, too, was more than enamored with the dashing figure in front of *her*. It was obviously more than the man-in-uniform thing, though that didn't hurt. The two were former lovers. She flushed, hoping he wouldn't notice.

She seemed to Ted not to walk but to glide down the staircase, rather like his hover jet, but with no noise and bathed in sweet perfume. He shook off the silly thought.

At the bottom she reached out to him with extended hand. He kissed it and then pulled her close in a not-entirely-appropriate embrace, as if they were dancing, their faces but an inch apart. One might have called it a tango embrace. The expression on his face was not dreamy as much as it was cocky and playful.

Recognizing that they were neither alone nor dancing, he released her, yet still held one of her hands. She was taken aback by the dramatic greeting, but hardly perturbed.

Now, standing a respectful distance apart, he said, "How are you?"

"I am just divine," she said.

"Yes, you are," he said. "Yes, you are."

"What are you doing here?" she said. "I've read about you, but I had no idea you were in Newport."

"Yeah, well, we are completing our last phase of training here."

"And you're flying and you look great," she said.

"And you, you are a sight for sore eyes."

He felt a sexual rush, probably enhanced by the champagne he had been drinking earlier, made more intense by the memory of their highly sexed past.

Cindy appeared by his side.

"Hi, Caveman," she said.

At first he didn't utter a word. After looking back and forth at the two women, finally he said, "Amanda, this is uppercu . . . , ah, Cindy. Cindy, this is Amanda."

"Nice to meet you," said Amanda, and then Amanda turned to Ted and said, "Caveman?"

Cindy interrupted before he could answer. "And nice to meet you," she said to Amanda.

"Amanda and I are old friends," said Ted to Cindy.

"I can see that by the way you're holding hands," she said.

He let go of Amanda's hand.

Just then, off to his portside, Ted heard a voice and saw a figure move into their small circle.

"Hello, Darling, who are your friends?" said the man to Amanda.

Ted thought it odd that the man would use such anachronistic language and immediately drew the impression there was something effete about him. He also observed that the uniform the man was wearing was that of a naval officer in dinner dress blue jacket, a Lt. Commander, his equal in rank.

"William," said Amanda. "This is my old friend Ted and this is Cindy. Ted and Cindy, please meet William Stuyvesant."

Stuyvesant offered his hand, first to Cindy and then to Ted, who shook his hand with a rather numb look on his own face.

Stuyvesant said, "Gosh, I know you, you're Ted Williams. How are you, old boy?"

Ted thought to himself, *who talks like this, especially an American?*

"I am jolly good," said Ted.

Stuyvesant didn't appear to pick up on the sarcasm.

"Such a pleasure to meet you," said Stuyvesant.

He then turned to Amanda and said, "Darling, may I have this dance?"

She looked at Ted and Cindy and said, "Will we see you in the ballroom?"

"No, I don't think you will. We've got a big day tomorrow," said Ted.

"Well, then, nice to see you," said Amanda. She frowned as she was torn away.

"Good luck overseas or wherever you're headed," she hastily added.

Ted watched with a stern, narrow-eyed look as Amanda and her Lt. Commander walked away toward the ballroom hand in hand. She looked back at Ted and silently mouthed the words "call me."

Cindy looked at Ted as he continued to stare off toward the ballroom.

"I'm guessing there's more to this story than meets the eye," she said to Ted as he continued his silent stare.

"There is," he said, "but you know what, I am over her. Yes, I am."

He looked Cindy square in the face and, with a bit of relief in his voice, repeated the assertion.

"I am over her."

He turned and, with one arm, proceeded to guide Cindy toward the door.

"Let's go, Uppercut," he said. "We've got a war to fight."

Sixty-three

For the Grand Slammers who attended, the Navy Ball was the last of the pleasures of Newport that they would enjoy. After another week and a half of training they were indeed off to war.

As the squadron braced for deployment, Ted marveled at the training they had received but also took stock of what they did not get a chance to do in the accelerated program. He didn't miss the rifle qualification or cold-weather mountain warfare training that he experienced in his first life. But he did wonder about the all-too-brief amount of survival training for downed pilots. As pilots are wont to do, he simply said to himself, *Hey, I'm not gonna get shot down anyway*. But his inner old man knew it could turn out differently.

Now, as the pilots took off one by one from Newport in their F-35s, training was over. They said goodbye to family and friends and headed into a fate as yet unknown, leaving behind a country for which some would, as Lincoln once said, give the last full measure of devotion.

They rallied off the coast of Newport and flew in formation led by Flight Leader Major Ted "Caveman" Williams. Their ship, the *USS Pappy Boyington*, affectionately known by its crew as "the Big Pappy," had left Newport two days earlier. The AAS was now in the middle of the Atlantic headed for the Arabian Sea. The Big Pappy was at the spearhead of a Marine Expeditionary Unit or MEU that included more than two-dozen naval vessels.

The Slammers landed on the Big Pappy without incident. Over the next three weeks, the pilots on this float would fly numerous training sorties and practice a lot of night takeoffs and landings. It became routine. The men, including the pilots and the ground-element Marines, were itching to get into battle.

~ ~ ~

In a cramped room, a Marine colonel named Mance briefed the pilots about the enemy's strengths and weaknesses.

"Over the last few months the Pakistanis have held firm their initial gains in Afghanistan," said Colonel Mance. "Initially, they overran three major U.S. bases and commandeered the drones that were based there that were once launched from the airstrips. That much didn't matter because without the satellites the UAVs aren't much use. But the air bases are important. The goal is to take them back and push the Pakistanis back into their own country."

Colonel Mance paused and looked over the room filled with stone-faced pilots and then continued.

"In the effort to achieve our goal your STOVL and other aircraft will be very useful. The Marines on the ground are carving out makeshift LZs near their forward bases for tilt-rotors and F-35s. All of the aircraft are needed to support our troop movements at the front lines."

A hand shot up from the back of the room.

"Yes," said the colonel.

One of the pilots said, "Pardon the interruption, sir, but can you tell us how good is our intel about the strength of the Pakistanis?"

"Well, I'll speak plainly 'cause there are no spooks in the room. The CIA is still under fire for not foreseeing the initial invasion and not anticipating the enemy's use of high-tech laser weapons. Military analysts, pundits and the media have been unrelenting in their criticism, as you see every day on your iMasters. However, unequivocally, I have the utmost confidence in our Marine intelligence and that's what we're using as we head into the op. Also, we know where the enemy is and how big he is because we're in his face every day."

Ted liked the sound of that and nodded. There was no lack of confidence in the U.S. Marine Corps.

~ ~ ~

As the MEU steamed toward the Arabian Sea, insertion plans were made ready for the Marines on the taskforce that would reinforce the Leathernecks already on the ground in southern Afghanistan. Pakistani gains formed a wide crescent or bulge into Afghanistan from the east. In the north the U.S. Army had its hands full fighting the Pakistanis in the deep snow and steep terrain of the Pamir and Hindu Kush mountain ranges. To the south where the Pakistanis made most of their gains, the terrain was more manageable but hardly hospitable. Frequent sandstorms wreaked havoc on men and military machines and the flatter terrain left the Marines more exposed along the front.

Insertion into Afghanistan was a real bear. With major airbases in enemy hands and only hastily prepared airstrips, large troop transport missions were not yet a viable option. Most Marines had to enter the war zone through the Arabian Sea near the entrance to the Persian Gulf. To the northeast of the Gulf, Iran was unfriendly and wouldn't permit flyovers that began in Iraq, a U.S. ally. Flying over Iran presented a risk that it would enter the war against the U.S., a risk the Pentagon did not want to take. Even taking a circuitous route farther north over the former Soviet republics the military called the "Stans" was not an option. They too were unfriendly. The only option left was the shortest route from the Arabian Sea, a straight-as-the-crow-flies approach to Afghanistan directly over Pakistan. The tilt-rotors that had tried it previously were getting hammered. But now, with jets providing cover, it was hoped that the Marines could tip the balance of power.

The tilt-rotor pilots, and now the fighter jocks, quickly dubbed the Pakistani route "The Gauntlet." It was a perilous mission. The Gauntlet was filled with enemy defenses that included shoulder-fired, heat-seeking missiles, conventional anti-aircraft and laser batteries, and assorted small arms fire. Moreover, intelligence reported that the Pakistanis were setting up more sophisticated surface-to-air missile batteries. They would not be very effective against low-flying tilt-rotors but, in addition to the lasers, would be a serious threat for American jets. The Pakistanis were obviously not very interested in having American aircraft of any kind fly through their airspace.

The first mission for the newly baptized Grand Slammers would not be a milk run. The goal: move dozens of personnel-laden tilt-rotors over enemy Pakistan and into landlocked Afghanistan.

~ ~ ~

In the Big Pappy's ready room the pilots were briefed on their first mission, this time by Colonel Rudolph. Ted, Cindy and Jerry sat in the front row. Colonel Rudolph said, "From the A-rab Sea your mission will take you due north over enemy Pakistan, hugging Pakistan's western border with Iran. Running The Gauntlet means 500 kilometers of balls-to-the-wall flying before reaching the border of Afghanistan. The first 300 miles is mostly flat terrain before the border, and then another 100 miles before entering the fight on the right flank of the east-facing MEU already slugging it out on the ground in Afghanistan.

"To try and avoid surface-to-air contact, the rotary-wing aircraft will fly very low and as fast as possible. Even though they can fly twice as fast as helos, the flat terrain will still expose the Ospreys, making it more difficult to duck and cover if needed. On the positive side, the flat terrain means that many of the enemy mobile missile and laser batteries will also be exposed, perhaps working to the benefit of you F-35s drivers flying cover.

"The plan is to take half the squadron's 16 jets and fly ahead of the planned flight path of the tilt-rotors to draw enemy fire. I'll lead the eight F-35s in the decoy sortie," said Colonel Rudolph. "We are tasked with trying to take out as many of the ground batteries as possible, paving the way for the flight of the rotary-wing aircraft. The Ospreys then will receive cover from the remaining eight F-35s. After running The Gauntlet, all of you Slammers, provided you have enough fuel, will escort the tilt-rotors the rest of the way into Afghanistan."

Colonel Rudolph walked to the center of the front row and looked down at Ted.

"Major Williams, you will be the flight leader for the second group of F-35s, taking off one hour later than my first group of eight. Uppercut, you'll be flying as his dash 2," he said to Cindy.

The irony was not lost on Ted. In his first mission, a woman would be his wingman. He shunted any doubts he had about Cindy.

"I have evolved," said Ted to Cindy. "I have complete confidence in you, Uppercut."

~ ~ ~

The first wave of the Slammers and the tilt-rotors lifted off on schedule. An hour later, before lifting off, the pilots of the second wave were notified by command that the first group was receiving heavy fire from enemy batteries, but they had managed to take out several on the ground. No air resistance was reported.

With that intel, the second group of F-35s lifted off from the AAS. The tilt-rotors soon followed as the remaining eight Grand Slammers circled overhead and then all proceeded to leave the Arabian Sea and move over Pakistan.

Arriving at their initial point and escorting the flight below, Ted radioed Uppercut.

"Caveman 2, com check."

"Affirmative, Caveman," she replied.

"POS," said Ted.

"I'm at your four," replied his dash 2.

"Caveman 2, confirm visual on the chicks?" he said.

"Affirmative, the babies are in the cradle, right two, one mile low."

On that confident note the focus changed.

On every F-35, radar-warning receivers briefly went off with flashing cockpit lights and audible signals and then—nothing. The radar on the F-35s was being jammed. Not half a second later, three ground-based laser batteries quickly triangulated and took out a low-flying tilt-rotor. It careened into the ground with a sickening explosion.

The sight, and the thought of all of those dead Marines, infuriated Ted.

"Caveman 2, launch HARMs!" he shouted through his radio.

Simultaneously, he and Uppercut launched high-speed anti-radiation missiles at the ground-based batteries their HARM targeting systems had identified.

The lasers were quickly silenced. Someone else in the rear of the formation yelled over the radio, "Bogeys, left ten, two miles high."

So much for air superiority, thought Ted.

With their radarscopes still jammed, from a distance, no one could yet identify the silhouettes of the attacking jets, but their closing speed and flight path indicated they were unfriendly. Four jets were closing in fast on the Grand Slammers.

On the radio Ted said, "Caveman 2, bandits, tally, engage!"

He zeroed in on the closing aircraft through his helmet-mounted display. As if attacking planes weren't enough, bright flashes and black bursts began to fill the sky. Surface-to-air batteries were hitting the F-35s.

Someone yelled that another tilt-rotor had been hit. More bandits flew into view.

"Those Pakistani sons of bitches," Ted said aloud. "Our first mission and we're in an all-out furball."

He quickly flipped the red safety over a missile switch and prepared to launch an antique Sidewinder at the closing enemy jets.

Before he had a chance to launch, Uppercut, now riding on his six, shouted, "Caveman, break left!"

Ted quickly jammed his stick left and initiated a bat-turn that pushed the limits of his G-suit and training. In a classic rope-a-dope maneuver, enemy planes were now attacking from the right flank of the F-35s as they engaged forward. One had swung in behind Ted's plane but was quickly spotted by his wingman.

As the Dragon with Pakistani markings pursued Ted in the hard left turn, Uppercut bore in on the enemy plane. The turn moved the bandit directly across her field of fire and she got off a quick burst with her 25 mm cannon. Tracers flashed through the sky as she scored hits on the tail and the trailing edge of its wings.

The Dragon, just a moment ago in a superior position and in hot pursuit of Ted, burst into flame, rolled over, and turned into the ground.

"Good, shootin', Tex," said Ted. "There's a big smokin' hole down there!"

And then, a deadly blow.

As Uppercut followed Ted's pursuer, she heard a late warning signal but never saw the bandit moving to her six from above. Her cockpit was shattered with gunfire. The F-35 turned and plummeted straight down.

Ted yelled, "Caveman 2, eject, eject, eject!"

It never happened.

"Uppercut, Uppercut . . . ," said Ted, with his voice trailing off.

His wingman was gone. And on their first mission, no less.

Ted had to gather all of his wits to prevent him from hyperventilating. He was sickened. He was dizzy. Most of all he was angry. He had to shake it all off to maintain his situational awareness.

His radio cackled, a somber voice said, "Caveman 1, Caveman 3, we got your six."

"Roger Big Hat," said Ted. "Let's fry those fucking Urdu-babbling bastards."

So much for brevity code.

Both groups of Dragons were coming around again for another pass at the F-35s. One of the Marines got off an air-to-air missile that took out a Dragon.

Ted was being pursued by what he thought was a Dragon, but someone radioed that it looked like a MiG. He knew from his training that the old MiGs the Pakistanis mustered up could not match the turning speed of his equally ancient but faster F-35. It was a tactical advantage he would try to exploit.

He firewalled the throttle and began a banking turn. The MiG took the bait. The slower plane pursued Ted even though it could not keep up. Sure enough, by the time the F-35 nearly completed a circle, Ted had moved up on the enemy plane's tail. The hunter became the hunted.

Closing in on the MiG, Caveman padlocked on the enemy plane with his helmet-mounted display. With the plane in his sights and a nod of his head he let loose his air-to-air laser. The MiG seemed to shutter and then it lost all control. Ted saw no evidence that it had used any countermeasures. The pilot ejected and the plane vectored into the ground.

"Eat dirt, you fuckin' scum," shouted Ted in the direction of the parachute.

High above Pakistan, full-blown aerial combat was raging. The Marines lost another plane, this time by an air-to-air missile. But the Americans scored three more victories of their own.

As the jets maneuvered in a massive display of aerial combat that filled about 150 square miles of sky, the first wave of the Grand Slammers joined the fight—or at least they tried. Seeing that they were terribly outnumbered, the remaining Dragons and MiGs turned tail and fled.

The rest of the flight was uneventful. There was some concern that the F-35s had used up so much fuel dogfighting they would have to turn back or call for some midair go juice, but they had just enough fuel to finish escorting the tilt-rotors all the way into Afghanistan. After the remaining tilt-rotors had safely landed, the F-35s topped off in midair and then landed at their fire-support base.

~ ~ ~

The Slammers landed in-country at two forward fire support bases known as
ZULU Seven and TANGO Four in southern Afghanistan. With no airstrips,
the STOVL capability came in handy. ZULU Seven, where Ted landed, was in
the Helmand Province, near a place called Yasinza'i Kalay.

After he shut down his engine and climbed down from his aircraft, Ted
threw his helmet into the ground. Angry and emotional are two words that
don't begin to describe the state he was in. The other pilots and ground
personnel gave him a wide berth.

He was escorted to a bunker, a sandbagged hole in the ground that
functioned as a mess. He was given a cup of coffee that he didn't touch. He sat
on a bench facing away from a table. With his elbows on his knees and fire in
his eyes he ran his fingers through his hair with both hands. "Shit," was all he
was heard to say. He said it over and over again with various inflections and
volume.

Colonel Rudolph came in and tried to console him.

"Caveman, you did a hell of a job up there."

"Yeah, a hell of a job losing my wingman," said Ted.

"Search and Rescue recovered her body," said Rudolph, "and some of the
others. It looks like this enemy we're fightin' is gonna be tougher than we
thought. You've got to remember, we're fightin' with one arm tied behind
our back—without the most advanced technology. I'm especially beaded up
by the radar jamming. We're just gonna have to suck it up."

"Colonel, Uppercut saved my ass, but I couldn't do nothin' to save her."

Rudolph just nodded.

"Geezus, I'm thinkin' about her parents and my buddy Marshall—the
two were emailing each other every day," said Ted.

"You're going to have to write to them after they are officially notified.
They'll appreciate hearing from you directly."

"Yeah, that'll be a fine conversation—'Sorry, I let the goddamned kabob and curry munchers bounce her without getting off a shot myself.'"

"The way I hear it, you were in no position to help."

"And what about this mission, colonel? We took a pounding, all those dead Marines on the tilt-rotors . . ."

"No one's more sick about that than me," said Rudolph. "I know you're up on the governor and, in hindsight, maybe we should not have split up our force of F-35s. But, again, we're trying to do everything we once did with multiple tactical aircraft and systems—AWACS, inertial navigation, combat tracking, it's all bent. Remember, your HARMs were effective only because the SAM sites were emitting. Previously, we coulda locked on with GPS."

"That shit don't bother me," said Ted. "I flew in Korea without none of it—or barely none of it."

"Exactly," said Rudolph. "And that's why you're this squadron's most valuable asset."

"That's horseshit! My life's no more important than any one of these pilots. We've had this conversation, colonel. I want to make sure there are no special protective orders surroundin' me."

"There aren't, Ted. I mean that you are in a good position to rise above the tactical disadvantage we have."

"Hell," said Ted, "the Pakistanis are flying at the same level with the so-called rust-buckets they scrounged up. So, we're not that disadvantaged. We're just not *advantaged*—where we used to be."

"Good point," said Rudolph. "We're going to do a mission debriefing next door in half an hour. I expect you to be there. In the meantime, somebody will come by and show you to your rack. Mind the sandbags. It's my understandin' this place gets hit with frequent mortar attacks."

"What's it called again?" asked Ted.

"Yasinza'i Kalay," said Rudolph.

Sixty-four

Before Ted would email Cindy's parents or Marshall, he emailed Smitty back in Boston, trying to put off the arduous writing about Cindy's death, and he wanted to confirm that the Marines had first visited her parents' home. In the email to Smitty, he lied and told Smitty that all was well. He wasn't sure how the military could transmit email without satellites. He also wasn't sure that what he was writing would get by the military censors, but he told Smitty they were in a place called "Yas something or other."

"I've decided, I'm going to call it Yaz," he wrote, "like the guy who replaced me in left after I retired from the Sox."

His email rambled on: "It's interesting how so many left fielders for the Sox ended up in the Hall: me, Yastrzemski, Rice, Ramirez, Stonnington, Ono . . ."

The writing to Cindy's parents and to Marshall was tortuous and personal, but he got through it. The hardest part was waiting for a reply. Cindy's parents were gracious on the surface. Marshall was another story. His reply was monosyllabic and barely readable. A short time later, Ted emailed Elizabeth, told her what happened, and asked if she could look after Marshall somehow. Ted asked how Johnnie was doing and she answered just fine.

Ted was so focused on others that he neglected his own needs. He tried to ignore the dizziness he was feeling, pushing aside any thought that it might have everything to do with his medical condition and the aerial combat. *Nothing more than what I went through in The Beast*, he reasoned.

~ ~ ~

In a series of briefings over the next couple of days, Ted and his fellow F-35 jocks got the skinny on the Corps' precarious position on the front lines in Afghanistan. The F-35s would be a welcome addition to the growing arsenal of offensive weapons the MEU would need to push back the Pakistanis.

Before the F-35s could begin a series of planned missions, they would need to travel back to the AAS for rearming. The Big Pappy was now cruising through the Gulf where it could be better protected and resupplied through Iraq. Jerry was reassigned as Ted's wingman at Ted's request.

Flying at high altitude, the trip to the deck had no enemy contact. The return trip, as well. Now fully armed, the F-35s landed back at the fire-support base. The next day's hop would be a recon mission over enemy lines for Caveman and Big Hat alone.

The enemy was spread out along a front line that was hundreds of miles long. That was part of the problem. The Pakistanis had proven to be a highly mobile force. They would amass in one area and overnight move to a greater concentration somewhere else, sometimes disappearing altogether. That's why recon flights were deemed a high priority.

This day, Ted and Jerry would fly along the enemy's lines, record troop locations with their onboard cameras, and take out any targets of opportunity if they presented themselves. Almost immediately the two-plane sortie hit pay dirt. A long line of personnel carriers was spotted barreling along a dirt road that looked like it might be used to resupply enemy troops at the front.

Ted vectored in first while Jerry flew cover overhead. Caveman hit three of the personnel carriers with laser-guided missiles and marveled at how the weapons sighted their targets through the instrumentation right onboard the missiles. Korea was never like this. The vehicles may have been mine-resistant and ambush-protected, but they were no match for aerial missiles.

The radar warning receivers spiked onboard both planes indicating they were briefly painted, but their electronic countermeasures were used to quickly jam it. *At least some form of radar occasionally works*, thought Ted.

Ted pushed his F-35 higher and radioed Jerry.

"Caveman 2 you are cleared hot."

Big Hat executed a snap for the deck and then released a massive payload of cluster bombs. He took out any surviving personnel from the already flaming vehicles and many others who had exited untouched vehicles but were now running on foot out of fear that they would be torched. Their fears were confirmed.

Two planes, a few passes, and dozens were dead on the ground.

With Cindy in his mind, Ted said quietly to himself, "Die, you bastards."

Caveman and his dash 2 made one more pass over enemy lines to complete their recon mission and Ted radioed, "Big Hat, break for home plate."

As they headed for home, Ted wondered why they did not encounter any enemy aircraft. *Maybe they're more interested in defending their homeland than their troops on the line*, he thought.

Sixty-five

Ted, Jerry and other squadron mates, including new replacements, were settling into their lives at the fire support base. Aside from the occasional mortar attack, Yaz-land was becoming routine. Each pilot flew every other day, sometimes on consecutive days. Compared to the Gyrenes fighting it out on the ground, they had it easy. Still, this was a marked difference to Ted's experience in Korea when he flew out of established airbases. The emergency situation and the STOVL capability of his aircraft made all the difference. "Geezus, we're so close we can piss and hit the front lines," he said.

ZULU seven, also known as Fire Support Base Freedom, was a typical Marine FSB. The place was fortified with a series of bunkers and consisted mainly of temporary structures in desert camouflage, sandbags and concertina wire. *Temporary* was the operative word; it would be moved when the units it supported pressed forward. Personnel included an infantry battalion, medics, communications people and a platoon of engineers. Functionally, it included a landing zone for the STOVL and tilt-rotor aircraft, a tactical operations center, an aid station and a communications bunker. There were also two dozen pieces of light artillery and a fleet of armored personnel carriers.

On a Sunday morning—at least Ted thought it was Sunday, but it's hard to remember when each day's routine blends into the next—the Grand

Slammers were briefed. A Marine Force Recon group was discovered by the enemy, outnumbered, and pinned down behind enemy lines. They needed help immediately. Ted and Jerry scrambled.

Roaring east, the two F-35s soon were circling overhead with coordinates provided by a JTAC on the ground. The Force Recon platoon below the planes was pinned down in a ditch with just a few large rocks for cover. They were in a nasty firefight, taking hits off their combat exoskeletons, and desperately needed close air support.

With bullets flying all around his position, the forward air controller shouted into his radio, "Mother Goose this is Prince Valiant. Do you read?"

"Go ahead, Valiant," said Ted.

"We've got multiple targets close in. Engage!"

Exposing himself to do so, the FAC painted the target areas with a laser. Ted scored multiple direct hits with his laser-guided missiles.

Ted radioed, "Valiant, you still with us?"

"Affirmative," came the reply. "Thanks Mother. Good job. We'll take it from here."

Caveman and Big Hat were heading for home when their RWRs were illuminated. *At least the goddamned radar is working,* thought Ted. Quickly they each launched HARMS against two SAM sights and breathed a sign of relief.

The respite didn't last long.

Ted's cockpit and his helmet lit up like a Christmas tree. A SAM was tracking right for him.

Jerry saw it and radioed, "Caveman, release countermeasures!"

Not bothering to reply, Ted initiated his ECM. It didn't work. The missile was still heading right for him.

Next he released conventional chaff. It, too, did no good.

Inside the cockpit his heart was pumping fast and his head pounding. The missile was closing in fast on his six. Big Hat was in no position to help.

With his jet screaming over the desert and a missile boring in, Caveman throttled up and headed for the deck. It was a tremendous dive. Perspiration filled his helmet, and heavy breathing, his mask. He leveled off and jammed his stick right. He was initiating an evasive Split S maneuver to try and outrun the missile.

He knew that "outrunning" was an erroneous term. It was impossible to out-accelerate a surface-to-air missile, but with the right moves and a little luck you could evade one.

After the dive he came out in a different direction. Probably pushing 7 Gs. The force on his body was tremendous, but he stayed conscious.

The missile, tracking him now at very close range, used a lot of its energy to try and keep up with the evasive maneuver.

Ted shouted, "Hot damn!" as he realized the missile had exhausted its fuel and was now falling off his position.

Jerry radioed, "Way to run, rabbit."

"Home plate," replied Ted.

On the way back he suffered from intense dizziness, but he kept it to himself. He was in worse shape than this before, he thought. He was thinking clearly. He was going to be all right.

Ted noticed that his nose was bleeding. He was at a low enough altitude to take off his mask and then remove the nasal pulse oximeter probe, and try and stanch the bleeding.

He managed to land and climbed down from his aircraft. His knees buckled momentarily, and then he righted himself.

Jerry saw it and asked, "Are you all right?"

"Of course I'm all right, you goddamned mother hen piece of shit. Get out of my face."

On the walk back to his bunker, Ted felt wetness in his ear. He reached up touched it, looked at his fingers, and realized that he was bleeding out of his right ear.

Sixty-six

After the harrowing mission, the flight surgeon paid a visit to Ted while he was lying in his rack. The bleeding had stopped but not the dizziness. Seeing him, Ted sat up immediately, not wanting to promote any thought that he wasn't feeling well.

"Heard you had a rough hop," said the doc.

"Nothing more than routine," said Ted.

"How ya feelin'?" said the doc.

"I'm all right," said Ted. If the doc weren't his equal in rank he would have lashed out at him.

"I heard you stumbled when you hit the ground. You feelin' dizzy at all?"

"No. Just nerves, I guess," said Ted. "I'd appreciate it if you would keep that to yourself."

"Sure, it's perfectly understandable, Ted. Mind if I examine you?"

Ted gave no answer. The doc gave him the "How-Many-Fingers?" test and then asked him to follow his finger with his eyes. He then listened to his heart.

Ted didn't let on about the problem with his nose or his ear.

"You'll let me know if you're feeling worse or seeing any other symptoms?" said the doc.

"I will," said Ted.

~ ~ ~

After an hour of resting Ted felt okay enough to venture out and headed to the mess bunker. He was not so much hungry as he was hoping to find Jerry. He carried a book. Jerry was sitting and drinking coffee with two other Marine pilots who quickly got up and left when they saw Ted approaching.

He was never good at apologies. All he mostly did was find a way to demonstrate some form of kindness after an infraction, which, if you knew him well, was his way of saying I'm sorry.

He sat down and said to Jerry, "I thought you might like to read this."

He shoved the book across the table. It was a history of the Marines' battle in Tripoli.

"Thanks, Ted," said Jerry.

Jerry harbored no ill feelings. He was tempted to ask Ted how he was feeling, but he knew better than to ask that question now. It would have been strange to avoid a discussion about their mission, so he said, "That was a close call, eh? But you've been in close calls before."

"Yes, I have," said Ted."

"You know, you've never told me the story about how you crash-landed in Korea."

"Not much to tell, really," said Ted. "I was flying a low-level, antipersonnel mission in my F-9 and took small arms fire. On the way back my cockpit turned all to shit. Lights flashing everywhere. Hardly any avionics left—we didn't have much then, anyway. No hydraulics. Losing power. I'm mostly gliding. I thought about ejecting, but only briefly. I was concerned that with my size, after blowing the canopy and flying out, I would take out my knees. It was a little tighter than the birds we're flyin' today. So someone flew shotgun next to me and guided me in. 'Course, I had no landing gear, no brakes. Slid over a mile on the belly. Sparks flyin'. Damn near hit an emergency truck as I careened off the runway. Man, you shoulda seen how fast I got outta there. Plane blew up in flames. I was angry as hell and threw my helmet to the ground, but I hardly had a scratch. I was lucky. Later on I looked at the shell of the plane and couldn't believe how close I came to buying it. Next day, another mission."

"Speakin' of which, I hear we're flyin' again tomorrow," said Jerry.

"Yeah," said Ted. "You and I are whatcha call a hot commodity. Until they no longer need us, that is."

"Yeah, I heard that rumor, too," said Jerry. "That they're gonna be able to launch new satellites soon. You know what that means."

"Yes, I do. The shit-for-brains procurement guys in what we used to call the military industrial complex will bring the goddamned NOFUS drones back," said Ted.

"We'll go from hot commodity to obsolete," said Jerry.

"Speak for yourself, Big Hat, speak for yourself," said Ted.

After downing several cups of coffee, Ted made his way back to his rack. The dizziness had abated somewhat, but was replaced now with a headache that seemed to be an issue only when he was standing or sitting—not encouraging for a pilot. He resolved to keep it to himself.

Lying there alone in the bunker his head was filled with thoughts of his predicament. He had health problems in Korea but nothing like this. *What a fucked up mess this is.* Not just the health issues, but going off to war and all that it involved. It was as if his life was a novel, a baseball novel, and in the middle of it an entirely different book broke out. *But that's exactly what going off to war is.* All else is suspended, and if you were unlucky and got killed, gone forever. It was exactly like that in his first life. He wasn't killed, but his was a life interrupted. And here he was, doing it again. Putting at risk everything he held dear. *Geezus, I never had thoughts like this in my first life; I must be getting soft.* He couldn't help but think of home, baseball, his teammates, fishing, little Johnnie, losing Uppercut. Most of all, he realized he missed Lizzy. Combat and close calls—not to mention a second life—made him appreciate all that is important.

Sixty-seven

The next month was the continuation of routine—that is, if flying nearly every day and getting shot at can become routine. Ted's dizziness abated; there was no bleeding; he had no flights that pulled excessive Gs.

In quiet moments their Afghan allies taught the Marines the game of Kabaddi, a team sport that was sort of a cross between rugby and wrestling. Each team had seven players. The game was played on a court about the size of a volleyball court divided into halves. The teams took turns sending a "raider" to the other side of the court where he tried to touch the players on the other team and then run back to half court before they tackled him. The raider had to hold his breath the whole time and, to prove it, keep shouting or chanting the word Kabaddi over and over again.

Though he thought it was strange at first, Ted excelled at it, his athleticism coming to the fore.

There was no baseball playing; securing the large amount of space for it around the firebase was out of the question. Ted couldn't even remember the last time he'd held a baseball. Someone had given him a bat, however, which he frequently picked up, practiced his stance, and swung away against an imaginary Botwinder.

Off the Kabaddi field the Grand Slammers and the Marines they supported were making a difference. The enemy was showing signs of weakness and had been pulling back along many points on the front lines. There was even a rumor that the firebase would be moved forward.

Ted and Jerry had honed and finely tuned their ability to fly together. They had now flown roughly 15 missions, not counting the hops back to the AAS to rearm and for maintenance and repair. It was an exhausting schedule, but they realized the sooner they completed their objective the sooner they could go home.

Their biggest surprise, to the bewilderment of the entire squadron, was the enemy's lack of aerial response. After the furball over Pakistan when they entered the theater, they expected a lot more air resistance, but it was sporadic. Perhaps intel was right; the enemy could scrounge up only a few planes. For Ted, the thought made the loss of Cindy all the more hard to take—the idea that her death was more of a fluke. He would forever remember how she sacrificed her life to save his.

~ ~ ~

At their next pre-flight briefing, Colonel Rudolph had used the words "milk run," a sure sign to the Slammers that the mission was to be anything but. Intel had come across what it thought were an enemy HQ and a nearby fuel dump, and half the squadron was being tasked to take them out. Ted was designated the flight leader of the eight planes. Jerry would once again fly as his wingman. Six planes would attack in the air-to-ground mission while two flew cover overhead.

After Ted climbed into his cockpit he put on the dark, elongated helmet the pilots called "the Ant Head" and plugged in its umbilical, the critical connection for helmet-mounted display and control of the aircraft, particularly weapons. Next he clipped to the inner walls of his nose the nasal pulse oximeter probe. Anything called a "probe" the pilots were bound to hate, and this was no exception.

The "nose picker," as the pilots had dubbed it, was designed to monitor the pilot's physical responses to excessive Gs, that is, anything over 7.5 Gs. If pre-GLOC were occurring, the monitor would pick up the decline in blood flow to the brain and initiate an alarm. If the pilot did not respond to the alarm, the system would engage the autopilot, take control, and decrease the speed of the aircraft and the G load on the pilot. It was yet another redefinition of the term "fly-by-wire."

To the pilots it wasn't FM. It was just fucked.

No one wanted anyone—or any *thing*—flying their aircraft. Each time he flew Ted connected the probe according to orders but did it with extreme disdain, as he did this day. Finally, adjusting his mic and oxygen mask under the elongated black helmet, he completed the entomological ensemble.

Darth Vader meets Atom Ant.

Truthfully, the HMD wasn't all bad. Anywhere the pilots could turn their heads, they could target enemy aircraft. This meant they could literally swivel their heads greater than 90 degrees, get a bandit in their sights through the helmet, and fire a missile at a target *behind* the plane. The electro-optical missiles would fire forward but then pivot and home in on the target even if the pilot discontinued visual contact. Not bad for a squadron whose primary task was air-to-ground missions. "Fire and forget" was easier said than done, however, if a bandit was boring in on you.

The flight to the two targets was once again short. There was some conventional flak but SAM batteries didn't paint them. Again, no enemy planes. One by one the Slammers hit the targets.

A huge black cloud emerged over the burning fuel dump when Ted radioed his wingman.

"Caveman 2, Caveman 1. Alpha check."

"Caveman 2. Angels 15. Home plate is in L-O-S.

Big Hat may have had a line of sight for home, but what he didn't see was a group of bogeys that, due to jamming, malfunction or both, did not pop on the Slammers' radarscopes.

Ted radioed first. "Caveman 1. Gorilla contact."

One of the squadron mates, who in his excitement did not ID himself, responded. "Tally, right two, two miles, low!"

Ted thought to himself, *Shit, they're already on us. What'd they do, just take off?*

He responded with a directive for the squadron, "S-Eight, bandits, engage!"

Almost simultaneously, all of the F-35s jettisoned any remaining outboard air-to-ground ordinance hanging on their pylons for better speed and flight characteristics.

Jerry radioed his flight leader, "Caveman 1, tally, press!"

Knowing Jerry had his six, Ted and the rest of the squadron, winged over and firewalled their throttles to engage the enemy. There appeared to be an equal number—at least eight—of enemy planes barreling right into the Slammers. A Mexican standoff it wasn't.

Attacking the enemy from above under normal circumstances would have been an advantageous firing position. The short distance, angle of attack and closing speed were so severe, however, that none of the F-35s could fire a laser or missile shot. Some of the Slammers did a quarter-roll and passed the enemy canopy-to-canopy, all at close to the speed of sound. The best that the F-35s could do was get off a few canon rounds to little effect.

It was clear they were engaging Pakistanis driving Dragons. As the F-35s roared past, they split into two groups to come around.

The dogfight was on.

Ted zeroed in on a Dragon that had split off from his group, perhaps beginning to attempt a flanking maneuver. Without a wingman, the Dragon pilot made a deadly mistake. In hot pursuit with Big Hat behind him, Caveman got a line on the enemy Dragon. Realizing he was within the gun sights of an F-35, the Dragon starting jinking left and right. It was a fruitless endeavor. Ted let go a missile that was up the Dragon's tailpipe in a fraction of a second. In fact, Caveman and Big Hat had little room to maneuver out of the way of the midair debris.

Caveman and his wingman were silent as they rejoined the dogfight that was playing out among their squadron. The sky was filled with intricate patterns of contrails traversed by all manner of deadly armament in a full-blown furball. Their radios were filled with shouted directives from their fellow pilots.

Just then, a Dragon flashed across Ted's field of view from right to left. He hit his stick hard and vectored in to rejoin the hunt. As he did, his radio caught his attention.

"Caveman 1, break left!"

Ted followed his wingman's order and Jerry shouted again. "Your seven o'clock. One mile."

Ted looked to his left and then further behind. He saw another Dragon padlocked on him.

Using his helmet-mounted display and voice-firing capability to their full potential, Ted, having swiveled his head to the rear and sighting the enemy on his helmet, yelled, "Fire fire, one one."

An electro-optical missile launched from his outermost left pylon. At the same moment, Jerry fired on the Dragon. Ted's missile did nearly a complete U-turn in front of him and accelerated as it streaked toward the Dragon. The Pakistani found himself with not one but two gift-wrapped packages from Uncle Sam boring in on him in a deadly pincer. He didn't have a chance. A big pile of debris cartwheeled toward the deck.

Half in elation, half in relief, Ted keyed his mic and said, "FM my boy, FM!"

The fucking magic didn't last long.

Seemingly out of nowhere, Big Hat was hit with cannon fire. The high-caliber rounds ripped across his fuselage and tore through the gas tank in his left wing. Warning lights and alarms filled his cockpit. Then, a catastrophic failure: His left wing tip blew off.

What remained of his plane rolled over in a fiery mess. Ted turned to see his wingman going in.

"Holy shit," he said.

Before he could key his mic, Ted saw Jerry eject. *At least he had the ability and wherewithal to eject,* Ted thought. *Maybe he'll be all right. So much for the pea-brain, long distance, fire-and-forget freaks who predicted dogfights would never happen again.*

Ted called for Search and Rescue in the hope that they would soon pick up Jerry. Caveman had to clear his head and maintain SA. Jets were still screaming across the sky all around him. The Slammers were both predators and prey.

Underneath his mask Ted was grinding his teeth and pursing his lips. In an effort to gain tactical advantage he pushed his throttle to the limits and roared upward. From high above the furball he hoped to see better, support his fellow pilots, and take advantage of more targets of opportunity. He didn't reach his goal before he spotted a Dragon right on his tail.

Without a wingman, he was at a disadvantage. Tracers sped by his canopy. Immediately his instincts told him to initiate a J-turn. He'd learned the Herbst Maneuver for the first time at Yuma. It was only possible with post-stall technology, something he never experienced in his former piloting days.

Ted initiated the maneuver at greater than Mach 1. Pointing upward, he decelerated rapidly. Now pointing virtually straight up, he exceeded standard aerodynamic limits and needed thrust vectoring to maintain control and not stall. Quickly he coned and, at the apex, headed downward in a new direction and accelerated to high speed.

The once-pursuing Dragon had no chance to keep up. The Pakistani had turned tail. Ted caught sight of him as he tried to bug out. Closing fast, Ted let loose a heat-seeking missile. Quickly, there was a massive explosion.

"The goddamned Dragon is breathing fire, all right," he said.

And then, another problem. Ted's RWR indicated a SAM was heading right for him. "It's close, goddamn it," he said.

In the middle of the dogfight he had missed the signal. He released countermeasures to no avail. The missile was still boring in.

He would have to try a repeat of the split-S that saved him once before. This time, though, he was much higher, the missile was closer, and he needed to get to the deck faster.

Flying at about 20,000 feet, he reached up into his oxygen mask and ripped out the nasal pulse oximeter probe.

"No fuckin' autopilot is gonna fly my plane," he said.

He knew he needed all the speed he could muster with a missile closing in on him at nearly Mach 3.

"Here we go again."

Roaring toward the deck, he blocked out the other planes engaging in a torrid dogfight all over the desert sky. His plane accelerated downward. He began to feel the crushing force on his chest and lap. The G suit was doing its job, but all of his wits, skill and determination, he knew, would be needed to defeat this threat and stay conscious.

As he screamed toward the ground, dead ahead he could see colorful Afghan poppy fields rising up to greet him. Strangely, his mind wandered; he thought of how beautiful they were—gorgeous reds, pinks and whites, like a painting. *How could desert irrigation produce such beauty?*

He shook his head. The SAM was now *very* close. In his cockpit the warning signals were louder and more intense. He was aware that he was sweating profusely.

As his field of vision narrowed, he initiated the turn that would either save him or cost his life. The pressure was unbearable. He remembered to engage proper breathing technique and to use the Hick Maneuver. *Maneuver this, maneuver that; too many goddamn maneuvers to remember in the U.S. Maneuver Corps.*

He was pulling greater than 8 Gs, the upper limit for any pilot and hardly what his airplane was rated for. The pressure seemed to ease. Consciousness was illusory.

And then, blackness.

Sixty-eight

When Ted woke up, all was quiet and peaceful. He was floating above the poppy fields. He looked up to see nylon. As the flowers beckoned, he realized he was drooling. In a few seconds he hit the ground with great force, hardly prepared for the jolt.

Lying among the flowers and pods, he tried to untangle himself from the lines of his chute and the harness. He became aware that he was bleeding again through his nose and his right ear. He stumbled trying to get up and then realized he should probably keep down.

About 500 yards away he could see the smoking wreck of his F-35. Beyond that, about a half-mile away, he could see the enemy leading Jerry off at gunpoint.

What the hell happened? he thought. And then it hit him: An onboard sensor had automatically ejected him when close to the ground, it determined he had no chance to make the maneuver he was attempting, and the plane was at the proper angle to survive ejection. NOFUS had saved his life.

Surviving now was another matter.

He was on one knee in the middle of a wide-open poppy field. He put pressure on both his nose and a finger in his ear to stanch the bleeding, but it didn't seem to be working. Blood covered his shoulder and his chest. He knew it was only a matter of time before the enemy would be upon him, attracted by both his falling parachute and the smoking plane—or what was left of it.

He did a 360, scanning the horizon. Off to the west where he'd seen Jerry he thought he saw figures moving toward him. He gathered up his chute with the thought of burying it somewhere but realized he didn't have the time. Still holding onto the chute, he pulled out his service pistol and tried to run, stumbling, in the opposite direction from which the enemy was coming. He was still bleeding about the head.

The endless poppy fields were disorienting. Which way should he run? Where to go? *How am I going to hide?*

After several minutes of panicked running he came up to an irrigation ditch. He followed the flooded ditch for a hundred yards where it turned into a culvert that ran under a dirt road. He jumped into the muddy water and ducked into the corrugated steel pipe, hoping to be able to hide there. Crouching down, he was in the water up to his neck. He submerged the parachute with one hand and his feet and held the pistol above water with the other hand.

He could now hear voices. He hoped they didn't see him enter the culvert. The voices and the shouting grew louder. He didn't know if the language was Urdu, Brahui, Balochi or any of the other languages or dialects he was told the enemy spoke. He was determined to not let himself be taken prisoner. The propaganda value for the enemy would be too great for him to bear. His grip tightened on the pistol, and he checked the clip.

As he swung his head left and right listening for the voices, he saw that the entrance to each side of the culvert was covered in reeds growing out of the water. Or maybe they were cattails without the brown cylindrical ends that as a kid he used to call "punks." He rushed to the reeds and broke off a few of the cylindrical plants. He blew through one and confirmed they were hollow. He would try a trick he remembered from what he thought was an old Indian movie he saw as a kid.

It was now clear from the rising volume of the voices that they were headed right for his location. At the last possible moment he ducked under the muddy water face up with the tubular reeds in his mouth sticking up out of the water near the rest of the plants. He struggled to control his breath and remain as quiet as possible as he breathed through his improvised straws. He knew his naval-issue amphibious pistol would be useful above or below the water, but he would be outnumbered.

Pakistanis converged on both sides and looked into the culvert. In his submerged state, Ted heard the muffled words that he could not understand even if he had not been underwater.

After what seemed like an hour but was only a few moments, the voices went away. He sat up out of the muddy water. The old Indian trick had worked. *Ted Williams—last of the Mohicans.*

Now, what to do?

He fished his emergency-locator transponder out of his flight suit. It was soaked and appeared not to be working. To dry it out, he put it up on a muddy ledge near the top of the pipe. He knew he was at risk of developing hypothermia if he spent a long time half-submerged in the drainage pipe but recognized that it was just too dangerous to get out, at least until dark. One good side effect of being submerged in the cold water: It seemed to stop his bleeding. The risk of infection was another story.

His plan was to wait it out in the water until dark and then take his chances and search for his fellow pilot.

Jerry, where the hell are you?

Sixty-nine

After dark Ted crawled out of the culvert and immediately began to shiver. The good news was that the transponder now appeared to be working. He knew that a search and rescue team would not attempt a rescue until morning.

The nighttime desert air was brutally cold. He thought he might be better off staying in the ditch even if he were half-submerged; the water was warmer than the night air. Near dawn, he would search for Jerry and hope that Search and Rescue would pick them up together soon after sunrise.

It was a long night. He shivered in the cold water. He threw up several times. He fought off the impulse to sleep, fearing that hypothermia would do him in. As the night sky began to faintly brighten, he grabbed the transponder from the ledge and shoved it back into his flight suit. He checked the clip on his pistol but could barely summon up the agility to move his fingers. As he waded out of the culvert, his entire body was wracked with shivering. His muscles ached. He was wet, exhausted and still dizzy.

"I've got to get Jerry," he half-shivered and whispered aloud.

He moved in the direction he had seen them take his wingman the day before. Jerry could be anywhere by now, Ted realized, but maybe luck would be with him.

In the distance he could see a series of three freestanding houses each with its own courtyard surrounded by rectangular walls. All of the courtyard walls had entrances but no gates. Through the entrance to the one on the far right he could see light coming from the interior building and, as he got closer, he saw the entrance was guarded by a man wearing what looked like pajamas and a towel on his head. The man held a rifle.

That's got to be it.

Holding his pistol in his right hand, Ted crouched down and then crawled on his belly through a poppy field. When he thought he was about 100 yards away from the building with the light and the guard, he raised his head just high enough to get a better view of his target. The man at the courtyard entrance appeared to be dozing; he was leaning with his back on the wall and his hands on the rifle which would have fallen out of his hands were it not supported by a strap slung over his shoulder.

Of greater concern was a similarly dressed and armed sentry that Ted spotted doing clockwise loops around the perimeter of the limestone wall. The man moved briskly. Ted counted how many seconds it took him to complete each circle around the exterior wall. The light from the interior of the courtyard and the house highlighted the kicking up of dust each time he passed in front of the entrance. He didn't seem to acknowledge the other lethargic guard when he passed.

Ted's shivering abated now as his adrenaline began to flow. A frontal assault would not be a good idea, so he moved to his right flank, still on his belly. Moving forward now, when he emerged from the poppy field he hit dust and, due to his dampness, he became covered in dirt from face to foot. Camo was never so easy, though in his mind's eye he envisioned he looked like a breaded veal cutlet. He chuckled silently and threw off the silly thought.

He was concerned about the gathering dawn but had to risk being spotted. About 50 feet from the right wall of the compound he waited and then sprinted for the wall and hid in the shadows. All the while counting in his head, he timed his attack perfectly. As the sentry rounded the back right corner of the perimeter wall, Ted was ready. He hit the sentry with a two-handed, sledgehammer blow with the butt of his pistol. The Pakistani went down face first.

"That's what happens when you go to war in your jammies," said Ted.

Moving quickly, he stuffed the pistol inside his flight suit, peeled the pajama-top and towel off the sentry and put them on, took the rifle, and then continued on the sentry's path around the building. He turned around the right front corner of the wall and walked toward the stationary guard. Sure enough, the guard was looking in Ted's direction.

The guard, still half-asleep, only gave him a passing glance. Despite the dirty face, the pajama getup worked. Ted crossed in front of the courtyard entrance, tapped the guard on the shoulder and put a bullet under his chin. He was relieved his pistol worked, not to mention its built-in silencer.

Goodnight, Sleeping Beauty, he thought, but did not say it aloud.

He took the guard's rifle and propped it up on the wall just outside the courtyard entrance and moved inside. Holding the other rifle he crept along the right courtyard wall leading to the house. There were no windows, which was good and bad.

The wall met the house and he followed the mud-brick exterior to an open door. He maintained his crouch. He could hear voices and what sounded like slaps and punches. He did not recognize the language but could tell the men were angry. He guessed there were three, maybe four voices.

The voices grew louder and he could discern one speaking in broken English.

"You don't talk to us? You think, alive, you will leave here, American?"

Ted heard another punch and winced.

It was not exactly dynamic-entry protocol but he would be outnumbered and he wanted a look before he breached the door. He leaned in and quickly pulled his head back.

A single lantern hung from the ceiling. Jerry was seated under the lamp with his hands tied behind his back. His face was a bloody, pulpy mess, and his chin was resting on his chest. There were four men in the room. They were all standing and facing Jerry with the exception of the English-speaker; he was sitting next to Jerry and pointing a handgun to his head. The three pajama-clad comrades were smoking, their rifles resting against the back and side walls of the small room.

This might be the break I need.

The English-speaker raised his voice again.

"So, American fly-man, who you think will save you, John Wayne?"

Ted leapt through the doorway. He kept the muzzle of his semi-automatic rifle still and scanned left and right before turning his attention to the interrogator. Ted got off two shots that blew the English-speaker backward before the interrogator could get off a shot with his handgun.

The three remaining pajama-men scrambled for their rifles. Ted took out two of them before they could turn and fire. The third grabbed his automatic rifle, wheeled, and fired in Ted's direction. Bullets whizzed by Ted's head, barely missing him. Maintaining muzzle control for Jerry's sake, Ted fired at the assailant, hitting him in the center core, knocking him against the wall and down.

Ted looked at Jerry and nodded. Jerry didn't say a word as Ted went over and kicked the English-speaker to be able to stare him in the face.

"Life is tough, but it's tougher if you're stupid," said Ted. "John Wayne, *Sands of Iwo Jima.*"

He unbound Jerry and said, "C'mon, buddy, we're gettin' out."

Ted pulled off the pajama top and towel and helped Jerry to his feet. He tried to move him, and then realized that Jerry had a bad leg wound. Ted held his rifle in one hand and tucked the other around Jerry.

They scrambled across the courtyard and lunged out the door. As Ted expected, the shooting had awakened personnel in the other two buildings. He raised his rifle and took out two approaching from the right. He grabbed the rifle he had previously propped up against the wall and gave it to Jerry.

"Fire at will you leatherneck jet jockey," said Ted.

They made their way arm-in-arm, limping, and firing to their left and right flanks, as the enemy scrambled out and chased them into the poppy fields.

They heard the unmistakable sound of a tilt-rotor.

"Semper fi!" yelled Ted. "The Marines. No one left behind!"

Onboard the tilt-rotor, the pilot announced what everyone knew already: "We're comin' into a hot L-Z."

The landing zone was about 150 yards from Ted and Jerry in the middle of the poppy field. They ran, still arm-in-arm, wheeling around and firing at the enemy running behind.

In the tilt-rotor, a machine gunner opened up to provide covering fire but was limited by fear of hitting Ted and Jerry.

The dense poppies and their seedpods were an impediment, lapping at their brown boots, threatening to trip them up. But still they ran.

At about 100 yards Ted and Jerry thought they heard shouting above the roar of the rotor blades. Instinctively, they dropped their rifles to be able to move faster. Two Marines jumped into the field to meet them. The Pakistanis were still pursuing, probably 10 of them.

Ted and Jerry stumbled forward and leapt for their comrades in arms who led them back to the tilt-rotor. As they jumped onto the ship, automatic weapons fire was pinging off the fuselage. One of the Marine rescuers, still on the ground, was hit in the shoulder. A SAR crewman with a helmet and mic helped the two rescuers and Ted and Jerry into the ship and swirled his index finger in the air. The two massive rotors increased their speed and the ship lifted off the ground with a tremendous roar. Now the onboard machine gunner was free to shoot and was unobstructed. He took out most of the remaining combatants. The tilt-rotor took off like a helicopter but flew out as an airplane.

Safe in the confines of the aircraft, Ted said, "Hello, boys. Oo-rah!"

Seventy

On the way back, Ted learned that the engagement 24 hours ago resulted in all eight enemy planes down. In addition to Ted and Jerry, The Slammers lost another plane that was hit with a laser and crashed. The pilot didn't make it out. The Slammers hit the enemy with a kill ratio of 8 to 3, but didn't exactly hit a grand slam.

After landing back at the firebase, Jerry was stabilized in the medical bunker in preparation for being evacuated for better care. Ted walked in and approached the litter he was lying on. Jerry was bandaged around the leg and about the head. Ted hadn't cleaned up yet.

"You look like a veal cutlet," said Jerry.

"Funny, I thought the same thing. And a little while ago you looked like *raw* meat," said Ted.

"Yeah. Thanks for saving me, Caveman."

"Wasn't nothin' you wouldn'a done for me."

While they talked and Ted sat at the edge of the litter, the flight surgeon and two corpsmen began to attend to Ted. They ran a scanner over him but missed most of his injuries because the water, and then the dust, had obscured the blood on his flight suit.

Pointing at Jerry, he said, "He's the one who needs your attention, goddamn it."

He turned his attention back to Jerry.

"Well, we made it, buddy. Your job now is to get some rest."

"Yeah, I thought I was gonna be Pakistani fertilizer for a while there, but everythin' came out all right, thanks to you. You hurtin'?" said Jerry.

"Just a little banged up is all," said Ted. "And cold. Fuckin' cold."

"Well here's a little nugget that'll warm you up. Word is we're goin' home soon," said Jerry.

"The drones? They're coming back?"

"Yep. I just heard," said Jerry. "The engineers are gonna complete an airstrip not far from here and they'll be shipping in the NOFUS bastards within a couple of weeks."

"What about the satellites to control them?" said Ted.

"I guess they solved that problem, too," said Jerry. "It's official. You and I are a couple of pterodactyls in speed jeans."

Colonel Rudolph appeared in the bunker.

"Hello, men," said the colonel. "How ya doin', Big Hat?"

"I'm gonna be fine, colonel," said Jerry.

Two Marines came in and began to lift Jerry up, taking extra care with the IV on his arm.

"I guess this is your evac," said Ted.

Jerry reached up to shake Ted's hand.

"I'll see you stateside. I'm coming to a Sox game," said Jerry.

"You bet," said Ted.

Despite being indoors, both Ted and Colonel Rudolph saluted Big Hat as the men carried him away.

The colonel turned toward Ted.

"Caveman, I'd like to talk to you; I understand you had quite a thrill ride not to mention a picnic on the ground," said the colonel.

"Yeah, it was great if you like poppy seed," said Ted. "Personally, I never want to see another godforsaken poppy again."

"The docs tell me you're a little banged up."

"I'm all right, colonel. I've got my legs and arms. That's more than I can say about the squadron mates I lost."

"Don't you think for one minute that you didn't do all that you could have done to save those people," said the colonel.

"More times than I did, they saved me."

"I don't believe that's entirely true, but that's the way it works in combat. And look what you did to save Big Hat. You flew brilliantly Ted—in the fine tradition of the United States Marine Corps."

"Flew?" said Ted, "as in past tense? Is it true, colonel? Is the rumor true about the drones coming back? Are we on the goddamned junk heap?"

"Well, I wouldn't put it that way, Ted. But, yes, it's true about the drones. The government has been able to launch new satellites—with proper defensive capabilities, I assume—that will make the UAVs operable once again."

"So no more pilots?"

"Well, not exactly. A few will be rotated back stateside for retraining as UAV handlers. Should be an easy transition."

"Yeah, if you like flyin' combat in a trailer 10,000 miles from the battlefield and going home each night to a nagging wife and kids."

"In your case, it doesn't matter," said the colonel. "You've been banged up enough. You're going stateside, and you'll be discharged like a lot of the other reserve pilots. That was our promise to you. You've more than fulfilled your commitment to the Corps. We've nearly won this war, thanks to men like you. Major Williams, a grateful nation thanks you."

Ted was silent. Only 20 missions, but it seemed like 20 years. He was going home.

Seventy-one

For the next three weeks Ted was dizzy, and this time the medical staff took notice. The spells would come and go. He would be fine one moment and feel nauseated the next.

Back on the amphibious assault ship before being flown home, he was awarded the Distinguished Flying Cross from a Marine Major General. Ted thought he didn't deserve it.

"Given your heroics on the ground, there could be another award in your future," said the general. Ted was respectful but looked mildly annoyed.

He extracted a promise from the Marines: He did not want his discharge or his award announced right away—to avoid any publicity or hullabaloo before he was settled back into his old life. He would give the Corps the signal to announce it. Only Ted Williams could make—and get—so many demands from the Marine Corps.

~ ~ ~

He arrived stateside in North Carolina and immediately hopped on another transport to Washington, D.C. After landing he hailed a cab and headed to Arlington.

At the cemetery he paid the cab driver, walked silently and unrecognized through the massive gates and visitors center, and stood motionless to survey the landscape, row after row of headstones for so many heroes.

He stopped a raking maintenance worker to ask directions, and the worker pointed. Ted walked for about 10 minutes before he found the still-fresh sod over the grave and the new headstone.

In the early morning sunshine the maintenance worker viewed him from a distance through the trees. The groundskeeper had witnessed this scene too many times before: a solitary figure in uniform staring down at the grave of a lost comrade.

Major Williams tried in vain to blink back tears. At the foot of Cindy's grave he crouched down. He wanted to speak but words were failing him. Still blinking, he repeatedly opened his mouth and then bit his lower lip; unable to say a word until, finally, the words came.

"I'm sorry."

The tears were now pouring down his face as he stared at the grave of his wingman.

"You saved my life, but I couldn't save yours, Uppercut. You were a damn good Marine—and a hell of a woman," he said aloud.

He smiled at the thought of how wrong he had been about women pilots.

With his bare hands he peeled up a small patch of the loose sod, removed his Distinguished Flying Cross, and buried it with his wingman.

He stood up, straightened his backbone and said, "Until we meet again. Semper fi, Uppercut."

What followed was the most heartfelt salute of his life.

Off through the trees the maintenance worker rested his hands atop the rake handle. Witnessing the scene at a respectful distance, he nodded in somber recognition.

Seventy-two

Elizabeth, Johnnie and Cecelia were going about their normal morning routine in Boston when there was a knock on the door.

"That's odd," said Elizabeth, "the doorman didn't announce anyone."

She opened the door, and there was Ted—unannounced and unrestrained.

"My God," she said.

They hugged.

"Johnnie, Cecelia, come here," she shouted, still clutching Ted.

Johnnie and Cecelia rushed to the door and all engaged in a hug that lasted for several minutes. Finally, Cecelia broke off from the formation and promised to return with coffee.

In the living room, Ted said to Johnnie, "Boy, you're getting big!" Turning to Elizabeth he said, "Just look at him. Isn't he something?"

Ted, dressed in civvies, reached into his pocket and said to Johnnie, "I've got something for you," and handed Johnnie the wings from his uniform.

"Wow, can I keep them?" said Johnnie.

"You sure can," said Ted. "Hey, Johnnie, how's Little League going?"

"It's really good. I'm batting .350."

"Well, there you go," said Ted. "I knew you had it in ya. 'Course, I find it hard to understand why they keep track of those stats at your age anyway."

"They don't," said Elizabeth, "Johnnie does it on his own."

"Is that right? Gosh, that's great," said Ted. "That's my boy, Johnnie, a good hitter and smart, too."

Cecelia brought in the coffee and what looked like a homemade strudel. Ted inhaled the coffee.

"Ted, I can't believe you're here!" said Elizabeth. "So why didn't you tell us you were coming? Is everything all right? Are you home for good?"

"That's a lot of questions, Lizzy."

"I'm sorry," she said. "It's just that it's so unexpected. But we're *so* glad you're home!"

"Well, I'm here to stay," he said. "I'm being discharged."

He told them about the drones coming back, how pilots were not as in-demand any longer, about the advances the Marines were making.

"So, was it rough over there?" said Elizabeth.

"It was fine. I did my job, and now I'm home," he said.

"And are you feeling okay?"

"Just great."

Over coffee and pastry, now sitting at the kitchen table, Elizabeth, Johnnie and Cecelia did more for Ted's state of mind than any shrink could do in a hundred sessions. There were smiles, laughter, taunts and teases. The stuff of home.

Eventually, talk came around to the Red Sox. They filled Ted in. It was mid May and the Sox were floundering in third place.

"Maybe they could use another bat," said Ted.

As Johnnie yelled, "Yesss!" and jumped up and down, Elizabeth gave Ted a half smile, raising her eyebrows in something less than approval.

~ ~ ~

After Ted settled into his old suite at the Dongkou, he called the Red Sox and set up a meeting, telling them it was strictly confidential. Arriving at Fenway early the next morning he was surprised to see all of the senior execs there, from the owner on down. Even Buck Pearson was there to meet him in the reception area of the executive offices.

Mr. McBride was the first to reach out to him. He shook Ted's hand and then pulled him in for the man hug with the backslap.

"Welcome home, Ted," he said.

After handshakes and backslaps all around, the group moved into the conference room and sat down, Ted at the place of honor at the head of the table. After several minutes of small talk, he recounted the coming home story—minus the ill health. The elephant in the room was the question of whether or not he wanted to play baseball again and, from his perspective, whether or not they would have him.

Feeling the awkwardness, he decided he would simply blurt it out.

"Mr. McBride, Buck, all of you folks, you have been very good to me. I know I left you in the lurch by bugging out for the Marines last year, but if you have it in ya, I was wonderin' if you would give me another chance to play ball."

"Why Ted," said McBride, "you can't possibly think that—"

"I know I'm asking for a lot," said Ted.

". . . that we would let you out of your contract," said Mr. McBride

McBride laughed loudly. "Of course you can come back!"

"We already discussed it," said Pearson. "Providin' you pass the physical, we'll send you down to Pawtucket for a while for a tune-up stint. See how you do against the Triple-A opposition."

Ted decided he would take his chances with the physical.

"Besides," said Mr. McBride, "how could we kick a war hero off the team?"

He lifted an eReader up from the table. On the front page of the Boston eNews was a photo of Ted entering the Dongkou. The headline read, "War Hero Returns Home."

"So much for keeping this quiet," said Ted.

~ ~ ~

The next day Ted showed up at Fenway for a physical. The medical staff gave him an exam that lasted two hours. Then they sent him over to Mass. General for more tests. Near the end of the day he was exhausted from treadmills, stationary bikes, monitors, and all manner of prodding and probing, but no worse for wear. Most important, they didn't seem to spot anything wrong with him, and they did not have access to his Marine records. He flat out did not tell the truth about the physical problems that he encountered while flying. The Red Sox sent a boat over to Mass. General to pick him up and deliver him back to Fenway. Someone came down with word that Buck Pearson wanted to see him.

Pearson met him at the door of his office.

"Heard you did well," said Pearson.

"Yeah, that exam gave new meaning to the word prodding," said Ted.

"Follow me," said Pearson.

They turned the corner and were in the clubhouse. Most of the guys were there in the late afternoon in various stages of dress before the night game. They didn't see Buck and Ted walk in. Music was blasting from an iBox. In the training room through the window, Ted could see the trainers handing out doses of the steroid-HGH-Anaradium-406 cocktail. Cartons of pills with the names RoidRealm and Getgo filled the shelves and drew Ted's attention.

Buck yelled out, "Boys, we have a visitor."

Someone turned off the music, and all looked up in silence. And then they exploded. The mass of manhood moved toward Ted in a wave. There were many high-fives, back slaps, and good-to-see-ya yelps. Johan Johansson was the only exception; he remained seated in front of his locker.

As the raucous celebration continued, Ted answered questions about being home for good, about his intent to play again. Finally, he cleared his throat and raised his palms to speak to the whole room.

"Thanks for the warm welcome, fellas. Truthfully, I didn't know how you would react. It's great to be back. I never thought I would say this, but it's good to see you bunch of big bald-headed bastards!"

More laughter and cheers.

Pearson signaled Ted to come back to his office. Once inside, the manager closed the door.

"Ted, now that it looks like you passed your physical, I've got to ask ya, are you plannin' on takin' the cocktail?"

"Skip, you know my feelings about that. I ain't gonna take those shots or pills or any others."

"Granted, you were good without 'em," said the manager, "but I was thinkin' again about what would be your potential if you did take 'em."

"Buck, it ain't gonna happen."

"Well, we're gonna need you to hit and hit big, of course."

"Of course," said Ted.

"I don't know how ya do it without the cocktail. In my playin' days, I couldn't hit anything over 110 without the giddyup."

Borrowing a phrase from his piloting days, Ted said, "Well, maybe it's just fucking magic, Buck."

"Maybe. All right, we'll see how it goes. Talk to Mickey down the hall and he'll give you all of the details about your assignment to Pawtucket. Take it seriously. Without spring training and coming in missing a third of the season, you're gonna need some work down there. Welcome back, Ted."

"Thanks, Buck. I appreciate it."

Seventy-three

In Ted's way of thinking, the assignment to Pawtucket, although a bit of a slap in the face for a proven major leaguer, would not be all bad. He didn't plan to be there long. Plus, it was less than an hour from Boston. He could continue to live at the Dongkou and go down there every day.

Although he wasn't there long during his first career, he was familiar with life in the minor leagues. It didn't take him much time at all to blow through the Pacific Coast League and then off to Minnesota before being called up to the show by the Red Sox as a 20-year-old kid in 1939.

Before he left for Pawtucket, the Red Sox wanted to have a press conference featuring Ted's return but he pushed back, telling management he would rather low-key it, and they acquiesced. Instead, the Marines called and Ted gave them permission to release a photo of him receiving the DFC medal. The headline also mentioned his return to the Sox. He made it clear through the Red Sox PR people that he would speak to the press only after games and only about his baseball play.

When he arrived in Pawtucket, he sat down with the PawSox journeyman manager Joe Connelly. The manager was an ex-shortstop with Popeye arms and ears that jutted out from his baseball cap at a noticeable angle.

Ted saw that Connelly's McCoy Stadium office was bigger than Buck Pearson's, probably owing to Fenway's ancient confines.

"Tell me about the Botwinders in this league," said Ted.

"The Botwinders are the same here as in the majors," said Connelly. "They can pitch from either the left or right mechanical arm but by rule can't switch in the middle of one at bat; can't switch any more than one time in an inning; and only four times in a nine-inning game. In addition, each opposing team has the ability to bring in just one Botwinder reliever."

"I always wondered why it's called a goddamned reliever," said Ted. "It's just a spare, ain't it?"

"Just tradition, I guess," said Connelly. "The reality is the reliever is rarely used; replacement becomes necessary only when there is some sort of mechanical malfunction or a failure in artificial intelligence."

"I've known a lot of pitchers with artificial intelligence," said Ted.

~ ~ ~

Ted began to spend many hours in the batting cage taking pitches from a Botwinder. When he wasn't batting, Connelly had him on a cardiovascular regimen that included lots of stretching and wind sprints. They clocked his 90-foot, home-to-first sprint at 4.2 seconds and were glad to see he didn't appear to lose much of a step. He was a bit winded with extra-base runs, but that would improve in short order the trainers theorized. For his part, Ted was itching to get into his first game, but that would have to wait.

He had little time to socialize but did take several phone calls from Elizabeth and enjoyed the time on the phone with Johnnie. Dr. Miles wanted to examine him again, but he refused. He simply told her he was in good hands with the Red Sox medical people. What he didn't say was that never again would he let her examine him out of concern that she might see what the Red Sox had not; he was not in perfect health. The dizziness had mostly disappeared but he was bothered by frequent headaches, the knowledge of which he kept to himself. Most important, his famous vision seemed to be fine.

After a week of training, Connelly put him into his first game. The Toledo Mud Hens were in town. The PawSox were in first place and Connelly wanted the team to win, but he knew that his primary job for the moment was to whip Ted into shape.

Connelly had Ted starting in left and batting seventh in the order, in Ted's mind a rather ignominious slot, but he kept his mouth shut. The stadium was full, the press box overflowing.

McCoy stadium was a fine old minor league ballpark, though not nearly as old as Fenway. Its capacity was about 12,000. It was a low-slung, fan-friendly edifice featuring a quarter-circle seating bowl behind home plate, and a grassy knoll replacing bleachers out beyond the center field fence where fans could sit, picnic and hope for a home run ball.

Ted got his first at-bat in the second inning with one out and nobody on, no score. When his name was announced, the crowd gave him a great ovation. He stepped into the batter's box. *Man, it's great to be back.* Staring at the mechanical menace before him quickly tempered the momentary joy. Hitting had always been serious business, but against a machine it took on even greater import. It was an affront to fail.

He struck out on four pitches, having connected only once by fouling off a 98-mile-an-hour changeup. Walking back to the dugout he threw his helmet inside, almost hitting the skipper who gave Ted a look of disapproval. Ted sat on the bench cussing. The game ended with the PawSox losing 5-0 and Ted going 0 for 5.

The next week was different. His focus was sharper. His reflexes seemed to improve. He was hitting, and his mood had elevated.

Ted was not just hitting but destroying the ball. The media took notice. So did the big league club. Still floundering, they were under pressure to bring him up. In a week Ted hit five homers and had 14 RBI with Pawtucket. Although the headaches continued, they were not debilitating and he kept them to himself.

What was most convincing for the Red Sox brass was the reality that the minor leaguers faced the same pitching. As Connelly had said to Ted, the Botwinders in Pawtucket, Toledo and every other minor league city threw the same as the robot-hurlers in Boston, New York and Chicago, winding, screeching and dealing at 122 miles per hour.

The call-up came quickly. Ted had spent barely two weeks in Pawtucket before he was shipping up to Boston.

~ ~ ~

Trying to stop the bleeding in his inconsistent club, Buck Pearson inserted Ted into the Red Sox lineup immediately. The skipper told Johansson that he was moving him to center again to put Ted in left. It did not go over well.

Arriving in Boston late that day, Ted had no time for batting practice. In the clubhouse at Fenway the boys welcomed him back. He tried to make peace with Johansson, finding him in front of his locker.

"Look, Meatball, I hope you understand. I didn't ask for this," said Ted.

"Fook off," said Johansson.

"Well, I'm glad there are no hard feelings."

At game time he walked through the tunnel and into the dugout. At the top of the dugout steps he paused. *The green, green grass of home,* he thought.

As if he could read Ted's mind, Johansson ran past him and said the same thing in Swedish, "En sång en gång för längese'n."

For Ted, the sights, sounds—even the *smell* of Fenway, were transcendent. *Who said you can never go home again?*

When he was announced before his first at-bat, Ted was greeted with thunderous applause. He did not disappoint.

Though there were no homers, he went 3 for 5 in the game with one assist from left field, an off-the-wall shot that he quickly corralled and with a laser throw nailed the hitter trying to stretch a Fenway single into a double. The Sox beat the Spanish Armada 6 to 0, with neither fire ships nor severe storms necessary to shut out the boys from Barcelona.

Seventy-four

The infusion of Ted into the lineup helped the Sox immediately. Ted's playing in left and Johansson's shift to center knocked out a rookie center fielder who wasn't playing well anyway. With Ted in the three hole and the righty Johansson batting cleanup, the team took off.

After a few weeks the Sox moved up to second place in the division, still four games behind their rivals, the Yankees. The tension between Ted and Johansson did not seem to lessen despite the winning. When Ted would strike out, which he did less and less, walking past him on his way to the plate, Johansson got in the habit of saying, "Nice whiff, tennis boy." In his heavily accented English it sounded like, "Nize woff, ten-nese boy." Already frustrated from striking out, on more than one occasion Ted yelled back, "I'm not from Tennessee, you stupid bastard."

Every few days the PR staff would ask Ted if he would do more than a post-game interview. He finally relented; winning had made it more palatable. Several worldwide news organizations were after him to do a sit-down, on-camera interview for compuTV. He didn't know any of the out-of-town broadcast media so he relied on a recommendation from the PR staff.

The reporter was a non-sports guy, which was probably the first mistake. He was British. His name was Nigel Wilkerson, and his style seemed abrasive to Ted—more tabloid TV than anything approximating journalism. Ted wanted to talk about baseball, and Wilkerson seemed interested only in everything else. There were uncomfortable questions about how Ted was getting along with Johansson; about his reanimation—which he thought he had moved beyond; about not taking the cocktail; and questions about his love life or the lack of it. And then there was the God question.

Ted sat there with a furrowed brow and gave monosyllabic answers. Whereupon Wilkerson, leaning into Ted, camera rolling, said, "Now, Ted, I want to ask you a difficult question, and I want a truthful answer. Is it true that in Afghanistan you were personally responsible for losing two of your wingmen?"

In one fluid motion, Ted rose out of his chair, surged forward and, quick as lighting, hit the reporter in the jaw. For a moment Wilkerson maintained his balance as he and his chair skidded across the room. But then his momentum carried him off the chair and he proceeded to do a face plant on the floor, narrowly missing a brick sidewall. Ted's blow was a punch worthy of Uppercut.

"This interview is over," said The Thumper.

He yanked off his mic and trudged down the hall into the freedom of Fenway, the camera following every inch of the dramatic walk-off interview.

That evening, the interview or, more accurately, the punch, was broadcast all over the world. The media ran with headlines including "Fisticuffs at Fenway," and "Big hit by Williams."

Ted showed no remorse. Wilkerson threatened to sue but realized it was the greatest bit of exposure he might get in his entire career. The Sox brass were not amused. Buck Pearson called Ted into his office and read him the riot act. What Ted didn't tell Pearson was that he hurt his hand when he hit Wilkerson's jaw. It reminded Ted of a much more serious injury he sustained while engaging in an altercation with a glass water cooler in his first career. Thankfully, Wilkerson merely had a glass jaw—which now was wired shut.

Ted had pain while batting and throwing for the next few days, but he kept it quiet and then proceeded to get back into his groove after a brief pain-induced slump. The media continued to cover every angle of "The Punch," which had the undesirable effect of focusing more attention on issues other than baseball, and the God question was at the forefront.

Unbeknownst to Ted, a few religious fanatics began to picket each game at Fenway, marching on the docks outside the metal detectors and gates and holding placards that said things like, "He Knows There Is a God," and "His Silence Is Blasphemy," and "Speak, Ted Williams."

After Ted was told of the protests, he responded by knocking the crap out of the baseball. Off the field he kept his thoughts and his fists to himself. Other than the religious fanatics, no one complained. The Sox were winning ballgames.

~ ~ ~

It was mid July, and the Red Sox were now just two games out of first place. Ted's biological baseball clock told him that it was time for the All-Star Game, but his clock was off. Despite the fact that he was batting around .350—on par with the best in the league—he didn't think about making the All-Star team because his season had started late.

When the team was not on the road, he took pleasure in visiting the Jimmy Fund kids at the Dana-Farber. *Nothing like seeing kids struggling with cancer to put baseball in perspective.* He played a game; they engaged in a life-and-death struggle. Always, the kids were delighted to see him. Though it was sad to see some kids losing their struggle, he drew strength from them.

On weekend mornings before heading to the ballpark, Ted spent time fishing with Johnnie at nearby hot spots or teaching him how to tie flies. "Take a water taxi over to the Donkey," he would say to Johnnie. Elizabeth or Cecelia would drop Johnnie off, and Ted and the boy spent many hours tying flies and talking about fishing and baseball.

Johnnie continued to accompany Ted to Fenway, standing behind the batting cage and never failing to be awestruck at the strength and power of the major leaguers as they sent balls over the Green Monster in left and into the Lansdowne Canal.

At the plate, Ted yammered away: He cited his book and made many other observations about the science of hitting. As everyone knew, he could go on for hours about hitting. It was Ted Williams in situ.

Johnnie didn't care, he just liked following the trajectory of the shots, especially Ted's attempts at hitting the famous red seat, 502 feet away, which marked his 1946 home run. These impromptu instructional sessions with Ted at the plate also had the effect of attracting teammates and many bald-headed bruisers from the opposing team to the batting cage. They all wanted to hear and see lessons from the professor of power hitting. "Living legend" was never a more appropriate label.

With two lifetimes' worth of experience and observation, he was now adding to his retinue, pontificating on the mastery of the Botwinder.

"He's not much different than the dumbass pitchers I used to face," he declared yet again in between BP whacks against the robot. "Even machines have habits. The trick is finding them."

He went on about the necessity of hitting with a slight upperswing given the height of the mound. He made note of the tendency of all of the Botwinders to finish with a pitch that tails slightly or "pops." There was something predictable about their mechanical delivery that in some ways made them easier to hit, he postulated. Of course, easy is a relative term when you consider that a certain amount of predictability is combined with speed greater than 120 miles per hour.

When you're batting .350, your team is winning, and you've come back from the dead, people listen to what you have to say.

Privately, when he was alone with Smitty in the clubhouse and they were talking about Botwinders, Ted had something else to say. They were sitting on a bench in front of their lockers, towels around their waists.

"You know, you guys don't know what you've been missing. Batting against the Botwinders has taken a lot of the fun out of the game. Yeah, I know it's a challenge to hit a 120-mile-an-hour fastball. But you gonad-gone bastards don't realize how much the game has changed. Geezus, even bunting: If it can get to the ball, there are no fielding errors with the Botwinder. I never liked pitchers—shit-for-brains they were. But now, with machines throwing, there are no wild pitches, no balks, no sidewinders, no submariners. No variation—or very little."

"Well, that's not entirely true," said Smitty. "The Botwinders throw every kind of pitch with fingers that have the dexterity of humans and an arm with the power of a machine. And, don't forget, it locks in with facial recognition and its artificial intelligence remembers every at bat against you— it doesn't forget. And it can be programmed to do stuff it doesn't remember."

"Yeah, but it's not the same. In the end it's just a heavy metal arsenal. All you can do is rage against the machine," said Ted. "And another thing. You see them throw no-hitters now and nobody cares—'cept the batters."

"Yeah, it's a little embarrassing when it happens to so many bulked-up guys," said Smitty.

"You watch me. I'm gonna beat the shit out of those good-for-nothin', circuit-brained, recycled tin cans," said Ted.

Seventy-five

The man entered Fenway like any other spectator. He was thin and dressed in blue jeans, a red T-shirt, and a dark blue Red Sox cap. He made his way through the main concourse and stood in line to order a hotdog and a beer.

It was a beautiful, sunny Saturday afternoon at America's most beloved ballpark, albeit, at nearly 115 degrees, hot as hell. The crowd was filled with anticipation; the anticipation that comes from your team closing in on first place. On a day as glorious as this, despite the history of the Red Sox, there were few concerns about defeat and, certainly, no thoughts of murder.

After he finished eating, the man took the long walk out to the center field stands. Just as he had done in his practice run, he put on his sunglasses and emerged in section 36. He sat at the end of a long row of seats.

To his right and across the aisle were sections 35 and 34. To most fans, this was simply known as the center field tarp area. During day games, the two small sections comprising a total of 416 seats were covered with a black tarp, darker than the ubiquitous "fence green" paint throughout the rest of the ballpark. In most other ballparks it was black as well, or maybe dark blue or green.

Baseball aficionados knew the area as the "batter's eye," the space in major league ballparks that is intended to give hitters the opportunity to see the white ball heading toward them after it leaves the Botwinder's arm. During night games it was not necessary and tickets were sold in the two sections. That's why night games at Fenway always had higher attendance. Exactly 416 higher.

Finishing his beer, the man looked at the tarp as nonchalantly as possible. The Red Sox took the field and, like the other assembled 50,000 Fenway fans, he stood and cheered. The area around him was filled with families with young kids. They would not deter him from his mission.

Looking down at the field he checked the Red Sox' positions. Smitty was catching, Dimbrowski was at first, Calingo at second, Moses at third, Minster at short. Most important, Williams was in left field. Directly in front of the man was Johansson in center field. Sakamoto was replaced in right by a rookie named Grossman.

The man would let the game progress so that he could assess whether or not he would have opposition. Thinking he would look all the more casual, he kept score with his own scorecard, not realizing that hardly anyone used a scorecard anymore.

By the fourth inning, the Red Sox were beating the Yankees 2-0, and three times he had written "F7" when Ted had caught fly balls for an out in left. How appropriate he thought, *F for final. Final 7.*

At the top of the fifth, Ted completed throwing tosses to Johansson during warmups and threw the ball to fans in the left field stands. The Red Sox Botwinder began to deal, and the fielders settled in, their complete attention on home plate. The crowd, too, settled down.

In section 36 the rhythm of the game was about to change. Rising to his feet, the man glanced over his right shoulder to see that the aisle going upward was clear. Moving to his right he crouched down and extended an arm under the tarp. His face showed signs of strain and panic as his arm moved frantically left and right under the tarp, searching.

He was spotted by security. Radios cackled to life as a security staffer, previously sitting unrecognized somewhere above, began to descend toward the man. Still searching, the assassin was in full panic now. He would make one last desperate attempt to find the weapon left by an accomplice. He moved down one row of seats.

The security staffer was closing in. Mumbling incoherently, the assassin reached frantically under the tarp. Now the crowd was aware that some kind of scene was developing. One guy yelled, "Sit down. What are ya some kinda lunatic?"

When the man emerged with a rifle, the wisecrack was confirmed. Not six feet away, the unarmed security staffer slowed. The crowd in center, shocked by what they were seeing, fell silent, and then a woman screamed. The panicked assassin, seeing that the security guy was again closing in, made a bolt down the aisle for the center field wall. He shouted, "He won't live to tell us there's no God."

He had hoped to stand there and take his shot. At the top of the 17-foot-high wall the assassin hesitated for only a second. Holding the rifle in both hands, he made a Wilkes-Boothian leap *before* a shot was fired.

Jumping onto center stage, after the long drop he landed in a heap. His hat fell off, and the rifle came out of one hand as he hit the warning track. Never was it meant to convey a warning such as this.

The crowd began to shout. Johansson turned and spotted the gunman on the ground. The assassin, staring toward left field, tried to stand up but fell down, his bowed lower right leg having been broken in the landing.

Johansson didn't hesitate; he began to run toward him.

Pulling up to one knee and raising his rifle toward left field, the assassin began to scream, "He needs to die. God lives! He dies . . ."

Ted was oblivious in left, still staring toward home plate. His only thought at hearing a ruckus: There was another fight breaking out somewhere between Sox and Yankees fans.

The crowd throughout the ballpark registered what was happening and rose as one. Screams were heard everywhere, and then, in what seemed like an inverted wave, everyone began to duck.

Johansson came on. Running with a full head of steam, he jettisoned his glove and leapt feet-first. He had made many slides to second or home plate but none like this—fully airborne. The others only *seemed* like life-or-death situations.

Ted finally turned toward center. Johansson made contact with the gunman at high speed and with great effect. A split second after he hit the assassin with the full force of his body and legs, the rifle rang out. The shot echoed and reverberated all around Fenway, as if it had been broadcast over the PA system.

Ted, for all of his fantastic eyesight and ability to see a fastball heading his way at 120-plus miles an hour, could not see the bullet just missing and whizzing by his head. It struck the steel corrugated garage door on the left field side wall, the hollow-point projectile blowing a hole the size of a golf ball in the door.

After Johansson hit him, the gunman lost his grip on the rifle, and it flew away. Acting with agility no one knew he had, after the kick-down, Johansson subdued the gunmen by kneeling on his lower back and pinning his hands behind him. It was only then that he looked over to left and saw Ted running toward him. He was all right.

After security poured out of the center field garage and grabbed the gunmen, the enormity of what had just happened hit Johansson. The adrenaline draining out of him, he fell to his side and lay on his back.

The crowd now looked on in stunned silence. When Ted reached Johansson he stood over him and said, "Are you okay, Meatball?"

Johansson nodded and said, "Oond uur oo-kay, Freak-oon-stein?"

Ted smiled, put out his hand to lift him up, and said, "Yeah, I'm fine. Thanks, buddy."

Fenway erupted in cheers.

Seventy-six

Watching at home, Elizabeth and Johnnie were momentarily panicked. The TV camera had panned away just as the gunman aimed at Ted. After the rifle shot was heard, briefly there was dead air before the announcers came back and explained what had happened, indicating that no one was hurt. Red Sox management postponed the rest of the game, and the crowd left in an orderly fashion.

In the clubhouse Ted's phone rang. Elizabeth and Johnnie wanted to be sure he was okay.

"I'm fine," he said. "Geezus, who the hell does that guy think he is? He coulda taken out some poor fan . . . Yeah, I'll come over in a little while."

~ ~ ~

Ted was greeted with big hugs and very few words.

"Aw, c'mon now. Geezus, don't make a scene," he said.

"How about a drink, shall we give it a go?" said Elizabeth.

They sat in the living room. Johnnie drank lemonade and the two adults whiskey.

"I was never that much of a whiskey drinker, but this sure tastes good," said Ted.

"Nothing like a good belt to calm the nerves," said Elizabeth.

After a few more snootfuls, she had to ask, "Ted, do you know what the shooting was about?"

"Well, Johansson told me, and the cops, that the crazy bastard was some kind of religious freak, spouting off somethin' about Ted Williams and God."

"I see. Does it make you want to speak about what you know?" she said

"Hell, no. Why should I? It'll just create more trouble."

"Maybe you should just tell people what you know," she said. "It's what most want to hear, I should think."

"One thing I've learned in this life—and the other—you can't please everyone."

"Good point," she said.

"So I'm not aiming to please anyone."

"Well, that's encouraging," she said.

"You know what I mean," he said.

Johnnie was now playing a video game. The adults had more drinks. The tension was easing.

"Are you sure it is the right thing to do, not to say anything, about an afterlife, I mean?" she said.

"I look at it this way," said Ted, hushing his voice so Johnnie couldn't hear. "If I tell people all that I know about the existence of God and Heaven and life after death, the messiah thing could happen and I will be chased forever. If I don't tell them anything, people are gonna assume what they want. But most people, I think, are gonna leave me alone because they won't be sure. With the exception of some of the goddamned freaks."

She was feeling the effects of the alcohol.

"Well, it certainly gives new meaning to 'goddamned,'" she said.

He didn't know whether to laugh, nor did she. They just smiled.

"Did you know in Scotland," she said, "they don't call their national drink scotch they call it whisky? Only Americans call it scotch."

"Yeah, everybody knows that," said Ted. "Whaddya think, I was born yesterday?"

"Ah, but did you know they spell it differently?" she said. "Over there they spell whisky without an 'e.' The Scots are a strange lot."

Ted thought he detected the slightest slur in her spelling lesson, and he liked it. He leaned into her. The honey aroma of her hair complemented the whiskey perfectly.

"So what do they call American whiskey?" he asked.

"That's a good question," she said. "It's not like their own—more distilling, I think. So they probably just call it bourbon, rye or American whiskey."

He decided with Johnnie in the room it was better to break whatever spell he was falling into.

"Speaking of the UK," he said, "we're about to play in London. How would you and Johnnie like to meet me there? I'll be there right before the All-Star break, and during the break I'll have a few free days to spend with you."

He turned toward Johnnie. "How about it Johnnie, do you want your mom to show us her home country?"

Johnnie mumbled what was thought to be an affirmative reply. He was a little too engrossed in his hand-held video game.

"Well, don't get too excited about a tour from me, fellows," said Elizabeth. "It's been a long time since I lived there."

"It's settled then," said Ted. "We're off to England next week."

~ ~ ~

If the shooting incident rattled Ted, he didn't show it. The next day he went 3 for 5 and continued the upward march of his batting average. More important, the Sox swept the Yankees, including finishing the interrupted game, and were now in sole possession of first place. Foremost in Ted's mind, was the fact that he was feeling well.

In London, the Sox completed their three-game series with the London Seafarers, the visitors taking two out of three. The All-Star game was being played in London, but since he was not in it, Ted had no interest in attending. He could use the time off. Since he left Afghanistan, he had had hardly a day's rest. Elizabeth thought it would be good to get away from thoughts about the shooting.

So the three Bostonians took in the historic sights of London. Johnnie wore his Red Sox hat proudly. Ted, on the other hand, had no desire to be recognized. He wore his aviator sunglasses, even in cloudy London Towne.

They attended a cricket match, visited the Churchill Museum and Cabinet War Rooms, and even took a literary tour. In the West End they attended a performance of *Romeo and Juliet*. Ted was bored with the Shakespeare, but held Johnnie's arm with his left hand and loved it when in their theatre seats he put his other arm around Lizzy and she smiled.

But soft, what light through yonder window breaks? It is the east, and Elizabeth is the sun.

Seventy-seven

After the All-Star break, the Bosox were at home for a series against Cleveland, and Ted hit five home runs. His teammates marveled over how his concentration seemed better than ever and his fielding was superb.

Johansson ribbed him. It was the range of left *and* right motion that can only come from a tennis player, he said, or something approximating that, in his inimitable accent. Ted responded by telling him, "Keep poppin' those pills, Meatball. You've got muscles for brains." He no longer minded the jabs from Johansson. When someone saves your life, you can forgive a lot.

At Fenway, security was tightened for anyone entering the park even though the assassin's accomplice had been rooted out and arrested. He was an usher, also a religious fanatic.

Ted and Johansson, hitting in the 3 and 4 spots, were labeled the dynamic duo. They were simply knocking the ball all over the park. Ted benefited immensely from the fact that Johansson was batting around .355. In fact they were neck and neck in batting average. Botwinders threw Ted strikes, not wanting to put him on and then face the prospect of Johansson knocking him in.

The Sox were five games in front at the beginning of September with six weeks to go. Ted's hot hand at the plate had a lot to do with it. The excitement in the stands at Fenway was palpable. The bond between the teammates grew stronger than ever. If Ted and Johansson could get along—everyone could get along. Of course, winning makes everything easier.

Buck Pearson took note of the new détente that existed between Williams and Johansson. The two superpowers were extremely cooperative on the field—a necessity when playing in front of the Green Monster. Red Sox fans, often considered the smartest in baseball, had known for a long time that the "The Wall" was so tricky only the most strategic players in center and left could coordinate and pull off a unified defense against it.

The looming 37-foot-high Monster had its own special brand of hell for left and center fielders who didn't communicate well. Ted and Johansson reminded each other of defensive measures at the start of each game based on the tendencies of the opposition. Ted pointed out those batters that he would try to shade toward the line requiring Johansson to potentially cover more ground. They also had a system, based on the trajectory of a ball hit between them, that spelled out who would attack the wall and try to snare a line drive in the air and who would cover the carom if he missed. Rogers and Astaire with gloves on.

For all of his success on the field, Ted was still the recipient of personal attacks in the media. The empathy he'd received from the press after the assassination attempt eroded quickly. The flames were fueled by his steadfast refusal to do interviews. The media were frustrated because he would not talk about the assassination attempt and the God question. It was apparent the press was trying to make it into a cause célèbre. The media even gave him hell for not attending the All-Star game and being spotted at a cricket match instead with Elizabeth and Johnnie. Focusing on the God question, one ignorant columnist made an effort to point out the irony of going to a cricket match at a place called *Lord's* Cricket Grounds.

They also heard he took the literary tour. Ted wouldn't talk about it, so they went to his teammates, trying to stir up controversy. The teammates tried to defend him. Dimmer was on the receiving end of one of the inquiries.

"Ted? Takin' a literary tour?" he said. "He thinks *The Catcher in the Rye* was Carlton Fisk drinkin' a lot of Seagram's."

Someone from the Red Sox PR staff nearly got his head chewed off by Ted when a question from the press was relayed to him. "Was he concerned about his personal safety?"

"Get the fuck out of here, you idiot," he yelled at the staffer. "Ya think I'm gonna answer that question?"

If they weren't outright hostile, after 60 years of letdowns the media were pessimistic, waiting for another big swoon from the Sox.

One writer took to predicting that Ted would begin to fail as Botwinders around the league became more accustomed to pitching against him, their databases filling with information with every at-bat, their formidable AI used against him each time he came up to the plate. After all, the columnist reasoned, Ted had not played two complete seasons; it was bound to get more difficult.

Then there was the issue of his not taking the cocktail. "How could he keep this up?" The other cleat, inevitably, would drop.

For Ted, it was all too familiar. There were so many newspapers in Boston during his first career, each battling it out for readers; they took many a shot at him. Late in his first life, toward the end of the 20th century, he said that Red Sox players had it easy with only two newspapers in town. But now, late in the 21st, technology had wrought every kind of new media—ePapers, holographers, compuTV reporters, sports bloggers and the like—it was a lot like the days of old, with everyone competing for some little piece of information, a new angle, much of it negative. Some of it was made up.

The fans were still with him, however—except for the remaining religious picketers.

~ ~ ~

In the clubhouse, Ted finished weighing his bats, and then went over to see Smitty in the workout room. Ted jumped on a stationary bike and both were now pedaling and staring up at another absurd sports report on the compuTV.

"Hey, Pilgrim, how do you put up with all of the negative stuff from the press?" said Ted.

"Ted, I never asked you this before," said Smitty, "but why do you call me Pilgrim?"

"Because of John Smith, you know, the Pilgrim from Plymouth."

Smitty laughed, not telling Ted that he was confusing him with Captain John Smith at the Jamestown settlement. He knew that Ted never liked to be told he was wrong about anything.

"Well, you know," said Smitty, "I try to not let the reporters bother me. Don't get me wrong. I'm human. I just look at it as part of the game, a game within the game. They're just poor bastards trying to make a living like you and me."

"Yeah, but I don't make my living by being a sunovabitch that makes up shit about other people."

"Well, you gotta admit most of them don't either. There are a few good ones around."

"Too few," said Ted.

"Well, just keep hitting around .350 and that'll make it easier."

Smitty got off his bike to go to the trainer's room and take his regimen of 'roids. Ted, picking up the pace, continued pedaling on his own.

As he pedaled faster, he felt something peculiar. He looked up at the compuTV and his eyes began to blur. He slowed the pedaling, but it did not help. He climbed off the stationary bike and made his way to his locker, hoping that no one would see him staggering.

It had been weeks since he felt like this. He thought he had worked through it.

What is happening?

He sat in front of his locker for a long time, wiping his head and neck with a towel, until he felt well enough to shower and go home. He knew this was not ordinary vertigo.

Seventy-eight

The next several weeks were hell. On a road trip to Detroit, Cleveland and Baltimore, the dizziness grew worse. It wasn't that it affected his balance, not visibly anyway, so much as his vision. He tried to disguise his discomfort.

What he couldn't disguise were the results at the plate. It all turned around so quickly. He was slumping and slumping precipitously. He didn't just strikeout, he struck out badly, swinging at bad pitches—and worse, looking at the ball.

The reporters said "told you so." The Botwinders were catching up with him . . . he would not take the cocktail . . . it was all inevitable. "The new Ted Williams is a flash in the pan."

After one particularly bad Williams' strikeout, Calingo, the Sox second baseman, said in the dugout, "Un guapo look like an ol' man ou' there."

By the first week in October, Ted's batting average had dropped to .277, his on-base percentage plummeted as well. At Fenway the boo-birds came out. The crowds were upset not only with Ted: His decline mirrored that of the entire ball club. The Sox were now barely holding on to a one-game lead with less than two weeks to go before the playoffs started in mid October. And the Yankees, right behind them in second place, were coming into town.

Ted thought about telling the medical staff or Dr. Miles about what was ailing him, but he thought it would only get him benched. At this point he wasn't sure that he wouldn't get benched anyway. He girded himself to fight through this thing. The human body was complex enough, but in his case, given all of the neurological work, the repairs, the reconnections, it was just too complicated.

At the beginning of the Yankees series he was taking BP and barely connecting. When he did hit, he had only warning track power. Buck Pearson was watching near the dugout and called him over after batting practice.

"Ted," he said, "let's go to my office."

They walked through the tunnel. When they reached the office, Pearson closed the door.

"Geezus, the door's closing," said Ted, "this can't be good. What? You're benchin' me, Buck?"

"No I ain't benchin' you, Ted—least not yet anyway. I took ya in here to talk about some other stuff. You feelin' awright?"

"Yeah, I'm fine Buck."

"If I was to guess, I'd say the Botwinders are catching up to ya, or you're not seeing the ball well. You seein' okay?"

"Yeah Buck, I'm just slumping is all—goddamn it Buck, you know me. I'll come out of it."

"Well, I wanta give ya the benefit of the doubt, but we're in a critical situation here, as I think you know," said Pearson.

"I understand," said Ted.

"Listen, Ted, I'm gonna tell you somethin' and I want you to seriously consider it. You're having a tough time at the plate. Whether it's the Botwinders figurin' you out or some sort of medical problem—the docs say you're okay—I'm not sure. But I've talked to them. We don't see no harm in you taking the cocktail."

"Buck, I ain't—"

"Let me finish. Ted, I told you when you came onboard that I was always gonna be straight with ya. Well, now I'm givin' it to ya straight. You need to take the cocktail. You've seen what it can do. It might even cure what's been ailin' ya—if it's a medical issue, not psychological. The stuff is that good. Plus, it can benefit ya right away—24 hours later. It improves not only your strength but also your eyesight. I've seen it a hundred times. All it takes is an injection—your hair drops out overnight, but that's nothin'. Then a week later ya start takin' the pills. Why not take somethin' that is gonna help ya? Think of the team, Ted, think of the fans. Do it for them."

They were both standing, Pearson staring directly into Ted's face, the peaks on their baseball caps almost touching. Ted's eyes glassed over and his face flushed. His lips were taut.

"I ain't gonna do it, Buck. I won't do it. Those guys out there in the clubhouse, it may be okay for them. That's the decision they made, but I gotta go my own way. I don't believe in it, never will."

He took a deep breath and moderated his tone just a bit.

"Understand somethin', Buck; it's not the health risk I'm concerned about. Hell, you're talking to a guy who has proven you can come back from the dead. It's the principle of the thing. I don't believe in enhancin' my performance by any unnatural means—even if I'm playin' against an unnatural machine. I don't care how good the chips-for-brains, black-eyed, heavy metal piece of junk on the mound is. I am *not* gonna take the cocktail."

The irony in what he just said about his wholly unnatural self did not dawn on him. He paused and looked away from Pearson and returned to look at him again sternly.

"Don't you see, Buck? It's about me and who I am. I have to do this on my own terms. If that's not good enough for you, if I'm not playin' good enough and you gotta bench me, well then, fuck it. But I won't take the cocktail. No goddamned way!"

Pearson looked at Ted from head to toe and saw that he was shaking and his face and neck were as red as the seams on a baseball. There was a short silence, and Pearson shrugged.

"Awright," he said. "Try to settle down and get ready to play. You're still in the lineup. You're not the only one around here who ain't hittin'."

Seventy-nine

The weekend series with the Yanks was a disaster. The Sox lost all three games and fell into second place in the division. Ted went 2 for 14 at the plate and had two errors in the field. The dizziness and the poor eyesight were not going away. His manager saw him squinting and closing his eyes hard at the plate and asked him again if he was seeing okay. The medical staff looked into his eyes. He kept denying that anything was wrong.

"I'm just slumping," he said again and again, pushing them away. "Get out of my face."

Dr. Miles was worried about him as well. Even watching him on compuTV she could see there was something more to his problem at the plate than just a slump. She called him and asked if she could examine him. He refused; before he hung up the phone on her, she was able to get him to agree to meet.

~ ~ ~

They met for breakfast at a Greek café on the Newbury Canal not far from Amanda's boutique. Elizabeth ordered a western omelet with feta cheese and Earl Grey tea. Ted said he wasn't hungry and ordered only coffee. He looked annoyed.

Not wanting to dive right into his health problems she attempted to make small talk.

"I passed by Amanda's place on the way over. Do you ever wonder how she's doing?"

"Last I saw she was doing just fine."

He told Elizabeth about the chance encounter in Newport before he went off to war.

"Yes, she told me about her paramour a while back. Does it bother you?" said Elizabeth.

"Hell no," he said sincerely.

"Well, I'm happy for her; she hasn't had the best of luck with men."

"Was that a shot at me, Lizzy?" said Ted

"No, no, no. You Ted, are too thick skinned for me to take a shot at with any hope of having an impact. Anyway, 'take a shot' . . . Poor choice of words, don't you think?"

He nodded, suppressing a smile.

Ted changed his mind about eating and ordered two eggs over easy with whole-wheat toast.

"Good to see you're eating healthily," said Elizabeth.

"Yeah, well, you know how it is; gotta keep up the strength," said Ted.

"*Are* you healthy, Ted? Is there anything bothering you, healthwise?" she said.

He took a sip from his coffee, picked up a napkin, wiped his mouth, and stood up.

"I can't stand this. Leave me the fuck alone," he said, and knocked over a chair on his way out of the restaurant.

Eighty

Marshall called. Jerry called. Everyone was worried about him. The news was filled with stories about the war ending in Afghanistan. The Pakistanis had been pushed back. The next story was about Ted's slump. Only in Boston would a sports story nearly overshadow a major international event.

The press was hounding Ted to no end. Reporters took to regatta-ing outside of the Dongkou in their small boats, waiting for him to emerge. When he did, they shouted at him about taking the cocktail, about the God question, about his health.

At the ballpark his teammates were supportive. They gave him encouragement, patted him on the back, and did all of the things that teammates are supposed to do. Moses gave him an Amish prayer book. "Just what I need, prayers from Moses," said Ted. Sakamoto gave him a mini Buddha to place in his locker. "If you bring over incense, Sake, I'm kicking you in the ass," Ted told him. "It's turnin' into a goddamned shrine around here."

Still he slumped.

After one particularly bad strikeout with a checked swing he headed to the dugout and threw his helmet yet again. His teammates gave him a wide berth. He sat at the end of the bench with only the mute Red Sox Botwinder next to him. When the Botwinder swiveled its head a full 45 degrees to look at him, Ted said, "What the fuck are you lookin' at?" The Botwinder looked away.

For a while, the fortunes of his teammates mirrored his own. Then a ray of light: the team was coming on. In the last game of the season the Sox needed a win to clinch. Facing a tough Las Vegas Vipers team, Ted struck out four times. Despite his golden sombrero, including a whiff in the bottom of the ninth, the Sox still had a chance to win. In the next at-bat, Johansson, in dramatic fashion, hit a two-run, walk-off smash over the triangle in center field to end the game. The Sox were headed for the playoffs, finishing one game ahead of the Yankees.

The celebration that followed momentarily took the pressure off Ted. The playoffs would start in three days, and the fans, media and the Red Sox were relishing the moment.

~ ~ ~

With an insatiable need to fill airtime and cyberspace, it didn't take long for the media to suggest that Pearson bench Ted for the playoffs or that Ted take the giddyup. The first such story appeared the morning of the first game of the best-of-five Division Series between the Sox and the Tokyo Giants.

Before the start of the game, Pearson took Ted aside and said, "Ted, I just want you to know, I'm sticking with ya. Go out there and just be yerself. Relax. Focus on seeing the ball. If ya want any help, you'll just let me know, of course?"

"Of course," said Ted.

Wink, wink, nod, nod.

Despite the not-so-subtle suggestion to take the cocktail, Ted appreciated the support from Pearson. Still, he wondered how long it would last. Pearson and the entire front office were under tremendous pressure to make a move, to bench Ted. There were meetings between Pearson and GM Mike

Leonard—and Mr. McBride, the owner. They left it up to Pearson, who had to field all of the questions about it from the media.

Ted was steadfast in his refusal to admit that there was anything wrong with his health. The dizziness continued to come and go, but often it came at the most inopportune moments. He secretly went to visit an optometrist who couldn't help him. The doctor didn't know what to do. One day his vision was okay, the next he was seeing completely differently.

In the first game at Fenway Ted went one for five, his only hit a dying quail that dropped into short left-center. He wondered if it was his imagination, but the opposing Botwinders seemed to be making a mockery of him. He had to tell himself they don't have or show emotion. The Sox won the game on a show of offensive force by the rest of his teammates.

The calls for the benching continued in the press. Game two in the division series was no help. Ted made an abysmal throwing error after fielding a rather easy slow roller heading toward the left field corner. A double turned into a triple. At the plate he didn't get any hits. To make matters worse, when he did get on through a rare walk, he was caught napping at first. His teammates couldn't pickup the slack, and the Sox lost by six runs.

The Sox were off to Tokyo for games three and four. Before they boarded their rocket plane, Pearson took Ted aside and told him the bad news. He was benching him—for a rookie no less.

"Ted, right now, there's just too much at stake," said Pearson.

"You gotta do what you gotta do, Buck," Ted responded.

The rookie, Jimmy Sloacom, would play in center and bat at the bottom of the order. Johansson slid back to left and continued to bat cleanup. Mel Tremblay, the DH, moved up from the five hole to fill Ted's former slot batting third. The Sox won the first game in Tokyo by a 2-1 score but missed a chance to end the five game series in Japan by being on the losing end of the same score the next night. The rookie played well.

As the team headed home for the fifth game and rubber match, the press was pleased with Pearson's decision to sit Ted. The rookie was playing well, and good-looking rookies, by nature, always carry the hopes and dreams of greatness—although it rarely turns out that way.

A benched Ted Williams was not a happy Ted Williams. In the clubhouse and in the dugout Ted was miserable. He wanted to be supportive of his teammates, but the bald crusaders heard nary a word from him. He took BP, he sat, he sulked.

In the final game of the series with Tokyo, Sloacom turned out to be the hero in front of the hometown fans. In the eighth inning, on a squeeze play, he bunted home the winning run, breaking a four-four tie. Pearson looked like a genius.

Ted celebrated the victory and the series win halfheartedly with his teammates. He was on the bench, but with the Sox winning and staying alive, maybe, just maybe, he thought, there was a chance for him to get into a game again.

Eighty-one

Next up: the championship series. The Fenway faithful were trying hard not to get too excited. After all, the team had shown before—remember last year?—that it could lose in innumerable, stunning ways, and it had done so for 60 years. But fans they were, and hopeful they were, their passions fueled by 24-hour-a-day sports news.

Ted was less than hopeful. He was downright despondent, and second-guessing. *How could I come this far and be so unlucky*, he thought. *Why did I make the goddamned decision to play, anyway? It wasn't enough that I came back to a second life; I had to try and play again. So what, I never won a World Series? I never won one from the bench either.*

Grudgingly, Ted had to admit that Sloacom was playing well. "He's a tough little bastard," he said to Smitty, "all spit and vinegar. Reminds me of me when I first came up. But I could hit with power right away. This kid's got some work to do."

The dizziness persisted for Ted. So, too, the loneliness. He could not bear the thought of risking everything by telling anyone about the extent of his ailment. If he just let things be, maybe he would get better. Or maybe it didn't matter at all because he wasn't going to get another chance anyway.

The Sox were facing off against the Stockholm Vikings for the league championship. Swedish media descended on Fenway like the marauding hordes. Fans turned up wearing Viking helmets, their faux swords seized by security at the entrance gates. Johansson, a native son, was besieged with interview requests. The Sox held a press conference with Johansson as the centerpiece. He had to spend a significant amount of time dissuading the Swedish press of the notion that he was the victor over Ted, winning his old position back. He was polite, telling the media that he and Ted were teammates and that there were no longer any hard feelings. It was all true. But Ted did not make himself available, which led to speculation that there were indeed hard feelings.

Privately, he thanked Johansson for the kind words and then called into question the Swedish peoples' grasp on history. "Geezus, the Swedes were Vikings too?"

Perhaps it was the attention from the homeland, perhaps it was the fact that this was the championship series, either way, Johansson was outstanding. The "Swingin' Swede," as he was labeled, batted over .400 for the series. The Sox were on a roll. They took the first two games at Fenway by wide margins. In Stockholm, the Sox lost game three by one run, despite the fact that Sloacom hit a grand slam. So much for not hitting with power.

Ted still sat on the bench. His hope to play was somewhat buoyed by a conversation he had with Pearson in which the skipper said under the right set of circumstances he might use Ted as a pinch hitter. "Stay ready," he told Ted. But it didn't happen.

The Sox took games four and five in Stockholm negating the need to come back to play at Fenway and depriving the Fenway faithful of a home victory in the championship series. In the Sox locker room, champagne flowed freely. Even Ted got into the action. Across the Atlantic, the city of Boston erupted in celebration with a big, spontaneous party in Copley Square. The Sox had won the pennant. The Sox were going to the World Series.

~ ~ ~

Ted's excitement, of course, was for his teammates. Arriving back in Boston it quickly wore off as the reality of the situation sunk in. *My teammates won the championship series without me.*

In three days the November Classic would begin in Boston against the St. Louis Cardinals. The Cardinals were the same team Ted played against in the 1946 World Series. He didn't think much about the coincidence, the irony or his chance at redemption. He just wanted to play.

In the '46 Series, the only one he ever played in, he played hurt—but he still played. Fans and writers didn't know it, but right before the series he had injured his elbow in a tune-up exhibition game while the Sox waited for St. Louis to win its pennant.

In that World Series Ted batted only .200, hitting nothing but singles. One of them was a bunt to the empty left side of the field away from the shift. The press criticized him for that, the irony being that he had been regularly criticized for *not* hitting to the opposite field against the shift. To make matters worse, he popped up late in the seventh game to end the inning with Dom DiMaggio in scoring position. The Sox needed a hit to break a tie. St. Louis then scored in the next inning on a controversial play involving Johnnie Pesky, and the Red Sox lost 4 to 3 giving St. Louis the series. Ted later said it was the most hurtful thing in his baseball life. He always thought he'd have another shot at being in the World Series but it never happened—until now.

He received calls from his friends. All provided words of encouragement, and Ted provided tickets. Marshall was particularly encouraging on the phone.

"Ted," he said, "I have a feeling you are gonna get your chance. Don't get angry, don't get sad, just get ready. I'll be rootin' for ya."

Marsh tried to get him to talk about his health, but Ted wouldn't go there. Ted wondered if Lizzy had put him up to it.

For Ted, sitting on the bench was insulting. He wasn't accustomed to it. In his first career he had slumps and even injuries, but he played if he wasn't in a cast. When he felt he couldn't play well enough, he retired.

He was in no mood to go through the World Series sitting on the pine, but then again he had hope. He just wanted a chance. It had been three and a half years since he was brought back to life. He had worked hard to gain complete physical and intellectual capacities, discovered he could play baseball again, adapted to the Botwinders, had been diverted by the war, came back, and now this.

The morning of the first game of the series he arrived at Elizabeth's door to hand-deliver tickets. Johnnie gave him a big hug. Ted was overly pleasant with Elizabeth; acting as though the last time he saw her it hadn't ended acrimoniously. He was grateful that she did not bring up his condition. Perhaps she had become fatalistic at this point, he thought, or, more accurately, she knew that it wouldn't do any good to upset him at this crucial time.

It was Johnnie that did most of the talking, and Ted found the little guy's enthusiasm infectious.

"So what's it like playing in a World Series?" said Johnnie.

"Well, it's the most exciting thing in the world," said Ted. "There's a lot of pressure, but it's a privilege to play. The secret is enjoying every moment of it 'cause you never know if you're gonna get back."

"So you're going to enjoy it, aren't you, Ted?" said Johnnie.

He couldn't bring himself to tell Johnnie no, or to whine about not playing. Unknowingly, Johnnie had put things in a better perspective for the Splinter in winter.

"I sure am, you little squirt, and I'm gonna look for you in the stands during every game."

Eighty-two

Fenway at the start of a World Series could only be described as pulsating. Boston had always been a baseball town. Even when the championship droughts occurred and the Sox were losing, it was still a baseball town. The other professional sports teams in town drew fan interest, but it seemed the town lived or died with the fortunes of their Sox. That's why the city fought so hard to save the ancient ball yard even in the face of flooding. (Only at Fenway could droughts and flooding occur at the same time.) The flooding would have been a good excuse to finally build new digs. But tradition and memories die hard in Boston.

On the night of the first game of the series Ted still had Johnnie's enthusiasm in his head and was trying to make the most of it. The other side of his brain told him, *how the hell can I make the most of it from the bench?*

The Sox would have the home field advantage in the series, especially important if it went to seven games. Before the first game began, Ted took batting practice and still had trouble seeing the ball.

He noted that his teammates looked loose, a good sign. When they went out onto the field there was a lot of extra pomp and circumstance. Veterans of the Afghan War were honored on the field, and then the PA guy introduced Ted to join the group. He was not pleased when his name was announced. No one had told him about it in advance. The crowd gave him a loud, stirring, standing ovation that turned out to be quite emotional when he spotted Jerry on the field among a bunch of other Marines. At that moment a flight of four F-35s flew overhead, and the pilots on the ground looked up reflectively. Both Jerry and Ted were thinking about Cindy.

The full rosters of both teams were introduced, excluding the Botwinders, and they lined up along the base paths. Then a pop star named Chrysanthemum sang the national anthem in an irritatingly long rendition with lots of extra vocal flourishes. When the muscle-bound players on both teams removed their caps, the lights glared off their heads, except for one hirsute splinter of a guy with number 9 on his back.

Finally, they got around to playing baseball in front of 50,000 rabid fans and three billion people worldwide watching on compuTV, each batter jumping off the screen and appearing in hologram form in every home, workplace and barroom receiving a signal throughout the world. Ted went to the bench while his teammates took to the field. With his extra-padded catcher's mitt, Smitty finished warming up the Botwinder and the game was on.

The Redbirds jumped out to an early lead with a flurry of small-ball hitting and base stealing. The Red Sox bats were still. By the seventh inning the Cards held a 3 to 0 lead when Johansson cracked a solo home run that sailed into the Monster seats to get Boston on the board. With the score at 3 to 1 in the bottom of the 9th the Sox mounted a rally. They had players on first and second with one out and the bottom of the order coming up. Ted wondered if Pearson might pinch hit him, but his hopes were dashed when he sent up the regular order. Moses struck out, and then with two outs Smitty singled to load 'em up. The game ended when Sakamoto whiffed on a full count. Fenway was stunned.

In the second game of the series St. Louis was on the receiving end of a blowout. The Sox jumped out to an early lead and never relinquished it. It was 6 to 0 in the eighth inning with the bases loaded when Pearson sent Ted in as a pinch hitter to test the waters. Ted was ecstatic to get this shot.

Surprised at his own excitement, as the pitches came in he looked extremely uncomfortable at the plate and struck out swinging at a bad pitch. There was grumbling from greedy fans in the stands. The crowd didn't like leaving so many ducks on the pond, but their Red Sox had a big lead and, a half-inning later, the Sox had the win. The teams would travel to St. Louis all tied at one game apiece.

Eighty-three

D r. Miles and Johnnie traveled to St. Louis and were hoping to grab snatches of time with Ted. He surprised them by knocking on their hotel door.

"Hello!" said Elizabeth after looking through the peephole and opening the door. Johnnie came rushing over.

"Ted, as always, you have an uncanny ability to get into any building. How did you know what room we were in?" said Elizabeth.

"A guy from Boston was manning the front desk," said Ted.

"Yes, I see. Well, rank and being a professional ballplayer have their privileges. How are you?"

"I've been better. I came over to give you your tickets. You'll be a few rows behind our dugout. Marsh and Jerry will be there, too."

Ted moved into the room and sat on one of the beds, Elizabeth and Johnnie on the other.

She decided that during the World Series was not the time to query him about his health.

"Are you and your teammates confident about doing well in St. Louis?"

"Well, they are a tough team all right. But we've got a good bunch of guys in the clubhouse. We're gonna leave everything out on the field and see what happens."

Ted realized his response sounded like the clichés his teammates give reporters every day and he shook his head in disdain.

"Anyway, I'm just hoping to get in again; I'm mad as hell not to be playing."

His gaze narrowed, and short breaths indicated he might release another tirade. Reaching deep within himself he scaled back his anger, recognizing that all of the speeches he gave Johnnie over the last three years about good sportsmanship would have been for naught if he demonstrated a tantrum in front of the boy.

"Johnnie, ain't the World Series the fun?" said Ted.

"It's waaay fun," said Johnnie, "'specially missing school to be here."

"Yes, well, you are going to have to do some catching up when you get back," said his mom.

"Ted, there is something else I have to tell you," added Elizabeth. "Should the Series go to six games—"

"Oh, it'll go to six games," said Ted.

"Yes, well, *when* the Series goes to the sixth game in Boston, I will have to miss it. I'm giving a speech at a medical conference in Los Angeles that was scheduled months ago. But Johnnie will be there. I'll have Cecelia take him."

Ted was disappointed but didn't show it.

"As long as Johnnie is there, I'll be happy."

Ted reached across the bed, and he and Johnnie exchanged the fist slam with raised arms.

"Hammer 'n' nail," they said in unison.

~ ~ ~

St. Louis had a baseball tradition that was nearly as storied as the Red Sox'. Its fan base was as knowledgeable as the Fenway faithful, but not quite as ribald. Midwestern politeness notwithstanding, there was one fan who broke the mold, shouting obscenities at Ted in warmups before the third game even started. Ted, already on edge, shouted back and almost went into the stands to go after him.

Ted watched from the bench the entire contest. The Sox scored an incredible four runs in the bottom of the ninth to surge ahead and beat St. Louis 4 to 3. The crowd was less than enthusiastic about their Cardinals team giving up such a big lead and choking in the ninth.

Entering game four with a 2 to 1 series lead, the Sox were riding high with confidence, particularly after coming back to win in such a dramatic way in the last game. The prospects for Ted playing looked dimmer, however; the rookie was playing great defense and at the plate he was an instrumental part of the comeback in the last game.

Sitting on the bench again Ted was making a lot of faces in extremis. He also had a lot of time to think. During his first career, the rest of the world was accustomed to chuckling at the Americans who played baseball only in their own country but called their championship the *World* Series. Now it truly was a world game, with both teams having beaten the world's best to get here.

His thoughts turned back to his personal situation and a scowl returned. The best he could hope for was perhaps another pinch-hitting role.

It didn't look likely.

The St. Louis Botwinders were pitching the Sox tough. Even though they hadn't seen much of the Bosox in interleague play during the regular season, they seemed to know the Sox batters very well. Part of it was the preparation or how well the pitching staff had prepared their Botwinders with data, downloading information before the Series. The Red Sox did the same with their machines, but, in this game, the Redbirds seemed to have an advantage. Or maybe it was just that the Sox did not hit well as a team.

With Ted sitting on the bench the Red Sox lost the fourth game 4 to 1 and hardly hit at all. Pearson still refused to bat Ted.

~ ~ ~

With the series tied at two games apiece, Ted took batting practice before the fifth game in St. Louis. He did not look good at all. It was as if he was an opera singer about to sing for the first time on the world's greatest stage and he had lost his voice. It was a cruel turn of events. Of course, it was made more cruel and stunning by his extraordinary journey.

Pearson witnessed it all and remained silent. The silence just cemented the thought in Ted's mind that he was not likely to play again in the World Series.

The Sox suffered a debilitating loss in game five, losing 11 to 2. Sloacom, the rookie, was the only bright spot at the plate. The Sox were heading back to Boston facing elimination and needing to win both games to win the Series.

Eighty-four

Back home in Boston and in his apartment, Ted seemed to be moving as if in a daze. He could not have been lower. Friends called, figuring that he needed to be cheered up—Jerry, Marsh, Danny—but he just took the messages from the desk and didn't return any of the calls.

He looked at himself in his bathroom mirror. He was tired and drawn, squinting his eyes frequently. Not just any squint, but long, hard facial reconfigurations that bespoke of pain and fatigue.

The next day Ted showed up early at the ballpark but for the longest time just sat in front of his locker staring into space. The clubhouse boys asked him if he was okay, and he shooed them away. When his fellow players began to file in, he dressed quickly and went out to the field before the cage was even set up for BP.

Like a big cat in a cage at the zoo, he paced back and forth on the warning track from one foul pole to the other. Pacing. Pacing. He kept at it until batting practice began.

He took BP but it was a perfunctory, pathetic affair. Afterward, reporters and photographers tried to get his attention, but he ignored them. As Ted moved toward the dugout to go in and put on his game uniform, it was Johnnie who snapped him out of the funk.

"Hey, Ted, how's it going?" said Johnnie.

Ted brightened. Johnnie was with Cecelia. Elizabeth, he knew, was in LA to give her speech.

"Hey, how's my Johnnie boy?" said Ted.

They were standing at the wall just to the right of the Red Sox dugout.

"Hello, Mr. Ted," said Cecelia. "How are you?"

"As good as can be under the circumstances," he said. "We're losin' and I'm not playin'."

"Well, maybe this will be your day," she said. "Never give up. Isn't that what you always say to Johnnie?"

"Yes, it is," he said.

With Johnnie present he was trying to stay upbeat.

Cecelia answered her ringing phone.

"Yes, yes, hello," she said. We're fine, and you? . . . Oh, no! Are you okay? . . . Ah, huh . . . Yes, I will tell them later . . . We are at the park. . . Okay, we'll call back after the game. Bye."

"Who was that?" said Ted.

"Well, well . . . I am not supposed to tell you, but that was Dr. Miles. She was calling from her hospital bed," said Cecelia.

"What's the matter?" said Ted.

"Well, she sounded a little groggy. She said she was in a car accident and just got out of emergency surgery on her arm. She is okay, other than feeling a little lonely. She didn't want me to tell you until later, Mr. Ted, so as not to bother you during the game."

"What hospital? What hospital is she in?" said Ted.

"Cedars-Sinai."

Before she could say another word, Ted was off and running into the dugout and through the tunnel. He caught Buck Pearson in his office.

"Buck, I'm leavin'. I gotta go."

"Whatddya mean you're leavin'?"

"I gotta take care of some personal business. It's personal."

"Ted, what's goin' on? This is the fuckin' World Series we're playin' here."

"Oh, for crissakes, Buck. You ain't playin' me anyway. No one's gonna miss me. I gotta go. It's important, goddamn it."

"Well, tell me what's up," said Pearson.

"It's personal, Buck."

"Well, what the hell am I gonna tell management, and the press?"

"Tell 'em I'm not feeling well. Leave it vague."

"Yeah, that'll work," Pearson said sarcastically.

Ted turned and was gone, leaving Pearson shaking his head in disbelief.

Eighty-five

At the players' exit Ted hailed a water taxi, rode to the ferry building, jumped on a high-speed ferry and headed to the airport. People recognized him and were shocked—he still had on his baseball underjersey, warmup pants and cleats. It took him an hour and a half to get to Worcester where he chartered a rocket plane to take him to LA.

Although the flight lasted less than an hour, it seemed like an eternity. His head was filled with thoughts of Lizzy. Not once did he think about baseball or the World Series.

He arrived at the hospital near dusk. Rushing to the info desk he shouted, "What room is Elizabeth Miles in?"

"She's in 521 but—" The receptionist had to shout the rest as Ted ran away click-clacking toward the elevator in his cleats.

"Visiting hours are almost over, sir."

On the fifth floor he went flying down the hall and found room 521. Elizabeth was alone in the room. She appeared to be asleep. The World Series was on the compuTV to his right, but he totally ignored it, not noticing that the teams were in extra innings.

His eyes were fixed on Elizabeth. She was propped up in the bed. She had a cast around her left arm held up with a sling. Other than that she appeared to be fine. *She looks angelic.*

He sat on the edge of the bed. The force of his sitting awakened her. He smiled when she opened her eyes and looked at him.

"Oh my God," she said. "What are you doing here?"

"Better question, what are *you* doing here?" he said.

She reached up to give him a hug, but only could manage it with one arm.

"I had a little mishap," she said. "Look at me, I'm such a mess."

"You never looked more beautiful," he said. "Does your arm or anything else hurt?"

"No. Why are you here?" she said

"I heard you were lonely and . . . and I love you," he said. "You and your sorry little hospital-bound tuchis."

"I see. I didn't know you were a tuchis man," she said with bright eyes.

"Just *your* tuchis."

But what if my tuchis never recovereth?"

"Physical therapy—with me. Failure is not an option. I've got the tuchis touch."

"I'll look forward to it—the tuchis therapy," she said.

She glanced at the compuTV.

"Wait a minute. Aren't you playing in the World Series?"

"I was. Actually, I wasn't. Anyway, I came as soon as I heard about you. Good thing, too, 'cause you may need some help with the speech."

"I don't care about the speech anymore. You . . . you came here for me, and left the Series?"

"Like I said, I heard you were lonely—and in a little trouble."

She held his face with her good hand and looked deep into his soul.

They kissed, gently, passionately.

Resting her forehead on his, she said softly and sincerely, "I love you."

She sighed and said it again, as if it were a revelation. "I love you."

To Ted the words were magic. Intoxicating. Liberating. A sound that reverberated to his core. He had experienced two lifetimes of emotions, but this was something new. Something altogether different. Not of this earth.

Tears came. He looked into her eyes, and she was crying as well.

"I want to spend the rest of my life with you," he said.

"And I, with you," she said. "I resisted it for so long."

"What about the doctor/patient thing?" he said.

"I think we can get over it. Besides, you haven't been my patient for quite some time."

"Can we still do it once in a while?" he said.

"What do you mean?"

He climbed into bed to lie beside her.

"I mean I want to be your patient right now. My heart and body ache for you . . . If your immobile arm and little British tuchis are up to it."

"More than you know," she said.

They kissed, more passionately this time.

The door burst open, and a nurse came in and tapped him on the shoulder and told him that visitors' hours were over. He turned and the nurse recognized him.

"You're Ted Williams. Aren't you supposed to be—?"

He interrupted her with an index finger to his lips and said, "Shhhh."

"I'm a huge Sawx fan," she said, "originally from Braintree."

"Well, aren't I lucky to find the only Sox fan in LA," he said. "Is there any way you could make an exception and let me stay?"

"Don't you worry; I'm on top of it," she said, and closed the door as she left the room.

Ted and Elizabeth turned their attention back to each other, still lying in the hospital bed.

"I can't believe you're here. How did you leave?" she said.

"None of that matters," he said.

"But Ted . . . the World Series. I know how hard you worked to get there."

"It's not important," he said, leaving out all of the information about his failing health. He was sincere when he said none of it mattered now. *Lizzy is okay, and we're finally together.*

She hugged him again with her one good arm.

"Aren't you at all curious about what's happened with the game?" she said.

"Yeah, well, I guess I am."

"Let's turn up the sound on the compuTV and find out," she said.

It was the bottom of the 13th inning and the score was tied at five. Johansson was at bat with two outs and nobody on. The Card's Botwinder had run the count to 2 and 2 and then hurled an inside curveball to Johansson. Rather than bail out, the big Swede hung in there and whipped his bat around with a huge upperswing that caught the ball moving over the inside corner of the plate. Ted and everybody else watching knew immediately that it was going out. The ball arced over the center field wall and landed in the stands about three rows up.

Ted jumped up. Elizabeth, forgetting herself, tried to clap. Red Sox nation would see a seventh game.

"I told him to swing up," said Ted.

Elizabeth witnessed the delight on his face, and then her own face turned serious.

"Ted," she said, "you've got to go back."

"No, I'm gonna stay here with you."

"But there's a seventh game, and I'm okay."

"Well, I'd rather be with you," he said.

"Look at me," she said sternly. "I am . . . amazed . . . thrilled, that you came here for me. But winning the World Series I know is your dream. We'll have our whole lives together. Stay with me here tonight, and then we'll both go back to Boston in the morning. If you won't do it for yourself, do it for me."

He nodded.

"I'll do it for you."

Eighty-six

During the night they made love twice. The nurse from Braintree provided security.

"My God, I've never felt this before," said Elizabeth while in the throes of delirious passion.

Ted for his part was in some kind of dreamy, romantic love zone, filled with stamina. It was a passion he had never experienced. He couldn't vocalize a thing, only staring intently into Lizzy's eyes with a look she had never seen before.

In the middle of the night Elizabeth had to stop him from a third go-round, fearing he would have no strength left to play baseball the next day.

~ ~ ~

In the morning he was awakened when the nurse came into the room.

"You still here?" he whispered to her.

"Just another long shift," said the nurse.

Elizabeth was still sleeping. Sitting up on the edge of the bed in his undershorts he said to the nurse, "Can you do me a favor and bring a pair of scissors and a razor?"

The nurse lifted her index finger indicating one minute and left the room. As promised, in short order she reappeared with the goods. Her shift was ending, and she said her goodbyes.

He slipped into the bathroom. Fifteen minutes later the operation was complete. He was completely bald. He was shocked to see himself in the mirror. Even in old age during his former life he had always had a full head of hair.

As he looked in the mirror he thought about all the ways he had pushed the limits and not exactly been kind to this body—the baseball training, the flight rigors, the stress of many kinds. All of it on a fragile, reconstructed framework of restored and re-created tissue, muscle mass, nerves, and brain cells.

"Teddy Ballgame, what have you got yourself into?" he said aloud into the mirror.

He showered and put on the same clothes he wore the day before. When he emerged from the bathroom Elizabeth was awake. She let out a gasp when she saw him.

"What have you done?" she said.

"How do I look?" he said.

"Actually, you look sexy in a minimalist sort of way."

"Just a little deception is all," he said.

"So, you didn't take—?"

"No, absolutely not," he said.

She nodded and smiled.

"Are you well enough to leave?" said Ted.

"You bet your ass I am," she said.

"Oh, the profanity again," he said. "You'll have to try that when we're in bed again next time."

"Never mind," she said.

He helped her get dressed. She needed assistance with her blouse, the arm in the cast and the sling.

They didn't bother to tell anyone they were leaving. Once again with his cleats on, he went click-clacking down the hall, this time holding Elizabeth's hand.

~ ~ ~

At the airport he chartered another rocket plane to take them back to Massachusetts and bought a fedora to cover his head.

"I must say, this is a look," said Elizabeth. "Fedora, aviators, underjersey and baseball pants, with cleats. Stylish, head to toe."

They flew back to Worcester and then jumped on the high-speed ferry from Hopkinton to Boston. Incognito to the best of his ability, in the back of the boat he borrowed an eReader and read the papers. In addition to the story about last night's game there was considerable electricity devoted to his mysterious disappearance. Pearson was quoted four different ways telling the press that Ted had left for personal reasons.

Given the time change, they arrived at Fenway in midafternoon and gave each other a quick kiss goodbye. Most of the team was in the clubhouse already, even though the game was hours away. Fedora-man breezed by them and headed right to Pearson's office. Pearson was putting the finishing touches on the night's lineup and didn't notice Ted at the door.

"I'm back," said Ted.

Pearson looked up and at the same moment Ted removed the hat.

"Huh, look at you," said Pearson. "So, ya took the giddyup. How ya feelin'?"

"I feel good, Skip—strong."

"Well, awright, then. Get yerself out there and let's see how ya do in BP."

In the clubhouse when they recognized him, Ted's teammates greeted him with backslaps. As he changed, he realized this batting practice would be his crucible. Despite the fact that nothing had changed, he had to do well to have any chance at playing.

He took an inordinate amount of time to warm up—jogging, stretching, and swinging two bats, as was his habit. There were press on the field who approached him, wanting to know where he was the night before. A few noticed the lack of hair underneath his cap in the back, and wanted to talk about it. He rebuffed them with a polite request: "Please, leave me alone."

When he took off his hat to put a batting helmet on, the baldness was confirmed. Pictures were snapped. Pens wrote furiously on pads. He had come around, they wrote. As he stepped up to the plate, crowds gathered behind the cage and at the top of each dugout's steps. Buck Pearson and batting coach Mac McCarthy were paying the most attention.

The Botwinder throwing BP literally couldn't care less about to whom it was pitching. The BP Botwinders did not possess the facial recognition software and memory used by their heavy metal brethren in games to strike out batters. They were programmed to mix it up.

Ted was tense. He was not, by far, at 100 percent, but he tried to combat it all—the tenseness, the attention, the pressure to perform—with pleasant thoughts about Lizzy. He was still ebullient after the night they spent together. *Just treat this like any other BP,* he told himself.

He hit the off-speed stuff *and* the bullet pitches. At one point he began to get dizzy, and he stepped out of the box to rub his bat. Stepping back in, he continued to hit well, even knocking a couple over the right field fence.

In the dugout Pearson nodded his approval. Ted's charade, at least for now, had worked. It wasn't enough to get him into the starting lineup—it couldn't be, given his recent performance and how well the rookie was playing, but maybe it would get him a chance later in the game.

During Ted's batting practice Johnnie and Elizabeth had entered the ballpark and moved toward the lower stands near the dugout. After BP, Ted spotted them and came over and gave Johnnie a high fist.

"Hammer 'n' nail" they said once again.

Marsh and Jerry appeared. Each gave Ted a big handshake and told him to give 'em hell. Emily and young Billy were next, and then came Danny, the gondolier, and Jed and Randall, to wish him well.

Ted took off his batting helmet.

Johnnie looked at Ted in disbelief and then said, "Ted, did you take the stuff?"

Several reporters and photographers saw the interaction and scurried over to get pictures.

"I thought you said you would never do it," said Johnnie.

His mother put her good arm around him and said, "Shhh, Johnnie."

Ted moved his eyes left and right and then refocused on Johnnie. Not wanting to give up the charade he said simply, "Your mother will fill you in, Johnnie."

The rest of his friends looked on with no comment. Ted turned on his heels and headed for the dugout. Randall broke the awkward silence as Ted walked away.

"Good luck, Bro."

Eighty-seven

It had been 60 years. Red Sox fans were hungry for a World Series victory. As the crowd filed into Fenway for the decisive game, everyone wondered, *would 2095 be the year? Just one more win, that's all we need.*

Pearson's starting lineup looked much as it had since the day he replaced Ted.

1   SS – Lester Minster

2   2B – Jesús Calingo

3   DH – Mel Tremblay

4   LF – Johan Johansson

5   1B – Don Dimbrowski

6   3B – Ephram Moses

7   RF – Shigeaki Sakamoto

8   C – John Smith

9   CF – Jimmy Sloacom (R)

No team had fans with a greater sense of history. Thus, many were drawn to the story of Theodore Samuel Williams. "Is he here?" many asked, "or is he still missing in action?"

The fans who saw him in BP wondered if he would get into the game. Sloacom was playing well and, of course, the most important thing was winning. But what if the miraculous medical man were to play? *Would he let us down?*

When the introductions were made—they introduced the entire team, not only the starters—Ted received an enormous ovation, and it surprised him. He proceeded to the bench.

It was a pleasant November evening—60 degrees at game time. When the Red Sox took the field there was enough electricity in the air to power the giant light towers that illuminated the ancient ballpark. Fifty thousand fans hollered and applauded in a thunderous show of pent-up energy as the Red Sox Botwinder wound up and delivered the first pitch.

The first two Cardinals fanned. The third hit a single up the middle. The cleanup hitter hit a high fly ball to Johansson in left. The rookie in center, Sloacom, had enough time to jog over toward him just in case, but Johansson made the catch to end the first half of the first inning. In the bottom of the first Tremblay hit a solo home run and the Sox jumped out to an early lead.

The slim 1 to 0 lead came to an abrupt halt in the top of the fifth inning. With two outs, the St. Louis shortstop hit a single. He then stole second on a bad throw from Smitty behind the plate. The next three batters all hit doubles before the inning ended with St. Louis ahead 3 to 1.

In the bottom of the seventh, Johansson hit a home run with no one on to make the score 3 to 2, the Cards still on top. The fans erupted in cheers, but it was a nervous celebration. The game was tight, and their team was still on the short end.

Time was running out for Ted as well. He sat nervously on the bench, hardly talking to his teammates.

In the top of the eighth the Sox Botwinder registered a strikeout. The next batter, the Redbirds catcher, hit a liner to deep left-center. Both

Johansson and Sloacom broke for the ball. Their closing speed immediately caused concern. At the edge of the warning track, Johansson raised his glove hand. Sloacom did the same. As ball, left fielder and center fielder converged, there seemed to be a pause and then a train wreck. Sloacom didn't have a chance. The big Swede outweighed him by nearly 100 pounds.

Hats and gloves—and the ball—went sprawling. Johansson had enough presence of mind and physical ability to get up, pick up the ball after it careened off the wall, and throw into Minster at second. The Sox had gotten a break. In his study of the impending collision in left-center, the St. Louis catcher had rounded first but missed the bag. Realizing his mistake he scrambled back and then took off for second again. Halfway to second he turned back, realizing he wasn't going to make it. Despite the collision, incredibly, only a single resulted.

The carnage in the outfield was severe. Johansson stood over Sloacom, who was writhing on the ground and holding his left knee. The medical staff rushed to his assistance. The injury was bad, but the rookie refused to be carried off. With the help of the medical staff under each arm, he hopped off the field on one leg.

Pearson needed a replacement. Surveying the bench he turned to Ted and said, "Williams, you're in."

"Where?" said Ted.

"In center."

"Okay, Buck."

Ted grabbed his glove and ran to the outfield like he was being chased. Johansson walked over to greet him.

"What happened, Meatball?" said Ted. "I thought I saw you call it."

"Ya, unlike you, his Sveedish—not so goot."

The Sox Botwinder was able to get the next batter to hit a ground ball to short. Minster threw to Calingo who threw to the outstretched Dimbrowski for the 6-4-3 double play.

The crowd was in a fever pitch. Still down by a run, the sweet spot of the Boston lineup was now coming to the plate in the bottom of the eighth—Calingo, Tremblay and Johansson, batting second, third, and fourth, the Cards still up 3 to 2.

Calingo tried to bunt his way on. Hit too hard, the ball bounded between the pitcher and third base and the Card's Botwinder fielded it with his huge metal legs shaking the ground. It then planted and threw with its rocket arm, nailing Calingo at first—not even close.

Tremblay was still hot. He singled to right. With one out Johansson then knocked a single up the middle. Now, with men on first and second, Dimbrowski stepped up to the plate. The crowd was not only on the edge of their seats but on the edge of madness. Dimmer needed only a base hit to tie the score.

In the Red Sox dugout Ted simultaneously urged his teammates on and had his eye on the batting order, assessing his chances of getting an at-bat in this inning or the next. At the plate Dimbrowski hit a hard one-hopper to the left of the third baseman who fielded it cleanly. The Cards threw around the horn to complete the double play and end the inning. The score remained St. Louis 3, Boston 2. Ted was grinding his teeth in anticipation.

In the top of the ninth with the score still 3 to 2, St. Louis, threatened early. The first batter hit a line shot up the Green Monster. Johansson leapt and just missed it. The ball clanged off the scoreboard. Coming over from center field to back him up was Ted, who fielded the carom with precision and threw into second holding the runner to a long single. The two outfielders nodded in silent recognition of another well-played Fenway duet.

Now the Sox needed to hold the runner. The Red Sox Botwinder proceeded to strike out two. The Botwinder then got the next batter to ground to short, and the Sox nailed the runner in a force at second. The Sox were out of the jam but still trailing by one going into the bottom of the ninth inning.

Eighty-eight

Moses, Sakamoto and Smitty were due up. If any of them got on, barring a double play, Ted might get his chance. In the Red Sox dugout, Pearson was silently second-guessing himself. Ted was an unknown quantity. When he put him in the game an inning before, he had hoped that it would not come to Ted getting the crucial at-bat. It still might not. On the other hand, thought the manager, Ted looked good in BP and in the field, and he had taken the giddyup.

To everyone's absolute horror, Moses swung at the first pitch and grounded out to the first baseman. Sakamoto hit a hard liner on a rope but right at the right fielder. Two outs in a matter of moments. Smitty was coming to the plate. St. Louis was one out away from winning it all.

In the on-deck circle, Ted yelled at Smitty what every Little Leaguer hears from the moment he picks up the bat: "Just make contact."

Under the circumstances, it was good advice. Smitty was not a particularly good long-ball hitter, so the chances for a game-tying crank were remote.

He fouled off several balls. After about 10 pitches, Ted, watching from the on-deck circle, said to himself, *This is a good at-bat*. With each foul ball emotions ran high throughout the crowd. Some could not bear to watch and covered their eyes. The count was at 3 and 2 seemingly forever, one strike away from ending it all.

In the midst of an interminable at-bat, Smitty got around on a curveball and pulled it into the left field corner for a double. The crowd was delirious. The Bosox were still alive.

In the Red Sox dugout, as Ted approached the plate, batting coach Mac McCarthy turned to Pearson and said, "Howsabout it, Buck, ya gonna pinch hit 'im?"

Baseball, particularly in this modern incarnation, was a game of averages, probabilities and statistical analysis. A good manager used it all. In a decision that ignored all of the sabermetrics and had career-ending implications, Buck Pearson said, "Nope. I'm goin' on a hunch and leavin' him in."

Pearson added, "Besides, if we score just one run, who am I gonna put in center that's reliable in extra innings?"

"Buck," said McCarthy, "there might not *be* extra innings."

Pearson didn't respond.

Ted looked over his shoulder just in case but did not see anyone recalling him. He had too many flashbacks to count.

The Cards called timeout, and the pitching coach and most of the infield approached the mound while Ted took practice swings near the batter's box. On the mound, they handed the Botwinder a new glove; he would move to the left hand to pitch Ted lefty on lefty. The move, not unexpected, was perfectly legal under the rules of major league Baseball. The pitching coach also inserted a disc of unknown content into the Botwinder. Again, it was perfectly legal under the rules. The crowd didn't like all of the activity, or the delay, and issued a round of loud boos.

Ted didn't like it either. For all of his experience, for all of the tough situations he had played in, he was feeling the pressure. The crowd had been standing continually for some time. Now, perhaps to relieve their own anxiety they raised the decibel level up several notches. It was deafening, even for Fenway.

When he stepped into the batter's box, Ted barely heard the ump say, "All right, let's play."

On second base, Smitty took a decent lead. Pitching from the stretch, the big Cardinal Botwinder reared back. Grinding, screeching and clamoring like some hyper piece of heavy construction machinery, the Botwinder threw a 122-mile-per-hour fastball over the outside corner for a called strike. The pitch was a blur to Ted—not a good sign.

Perhaps it was the pressure situation, perhaps it was Murphy's Law, but whatever the cause, intense dizziness was setting in again. He stepped out of the batter's box.

The entire Sox dugout, the press, for that matter—the whole stadium, could see that something was wrong. Ted shook his head, took a practice cut, and blinked hard. The ump asked if he was all right, and Ted said yes.

"Then let's play," said the ump.

In the right flap of Ted's batting helmet it felt moist. He knew immediately what it was. He hoped no one noticed when drops of blood dripped down and hit his right shoulder. He raised his shoulder upward in an attempt to smear the blood or mix it with sweat, which was now coming off him profusely.

The next pitch was one that he decided to take, and he got lucky. The Botwinder threw a two-seam fastball off the outside of the plate hoping he would chase. It was called a ball and the crowd exhaled.

Ted stepped out of the batter's box. In the Sox dugout McCarthy turned to Pearson and said, "All the Botwinder has to do is throw him strikes. He's hurtin', Buck. What are ya gonna do?"

"Nothin'. The machine can't *tell* he's hurt."

Pearson was right. For all of its advanced technology—the facial recognition, the artificial intelligence, its strength and power—the Botwinder was just facing Ted Williams like it was any other game.

Or was it?

Ted stepped back into the box straining to see the Botwinder, never mind the ball. His legs were shaky. It felt as though his knees might buckle. The Botwinder dealt a fastball over the outside of the plate. Ted hacked at it feebly and fell to the ground in a pathetic heap.

Strike two.

Pearson immediately ran to home plate. Ted had managed to right himself.

Back in the dugout, McCarthy was called over to the side where an overflow of photographers, holographers and reporters were viewing the game in the photographers' well. Jack Paul, one of the few reporter/photographers Ted respected, and the man who interviewed him in Newport almost a year ago, leaned over and told McCarthy something under his breath. McCarthy immediately made a beeline for Ted and Pearson.

McCarthy heard Ted say to Pearson, "I can do it, Buck," then McCarthy pulled them further away from the ump and the Cards' catcher.

"They slipped him a disc-ey," said McCarthy.

"Slipped who a what?" said Ted.

"The Botwinder," said McCarthy. "They gave him a disc with all of your previous at-bats from your first career. It's got everything."

Ted and Pearson said "Huh" simultaneously.

The ump then interrupted. "Can he go on?" he said sympathetically.

Ted nodded and turned to Pearson.

"It's okay, Buck. I know what I gotta do."

Pearson put his hand on Ted's shoulder and gave him an encouraging nod before he and McCarthy headed back to the dugout. The count was now 1 and 2. One strike and it was over.

Ted stepped into the batter's box and took a couple of awkward swings to stay loose while the Botwinder prepared to deal. Ted planted his feet, paying particular attention to the back foot. Nervously, he tapped on the handle of his bat. The crowd did not make it easy. The noise was counterproductive. The Botwinder couldn't notice it, only Ted.

As he stared at the Botwinder, Ted was racking his brain. *It's got everything. What will it pitch to me? What is it thinking about? Is the goddamned thing really thinking?*

On second, Smitty took another lead. As the Botwinder pulled up into the stretch, the thought hit Ted. *I know what it's gonna throw!*

He clenched his bat tightly and said, "C'mon you titanium southclaw sonovabitch. I got your number."

The arm of the Botwinder came over the top like any other pitch. But when the ball left its artificial fingers the angle was vastly different. The trajectory of the pitch was almost straight up.

With few exceptions, the intelligent Boston fans saw it for what it was. Since they were already standing, they could do nothing but raise their arms. As they did so, in what seemed like perfect unity—half gasp, half shout—the crowd bellowed, "the Eephus!" and then grew silent.

Just like in '46 during the All-Star game with Ted at the plate, the ball seemed to hang forever in the air. That was exactly what the floater was supposed to do—moving probably no more than 50 to 60 miles an hour.

Despite the fact that blood continued to drip on his shoulder, that he had all the pressure in the world on those same shoulders, the adrenaline took over. As the ball reached its apex and began its long decent, he waited. And waited. It was like watching a replay in slow motion, but this was in real time.

It was reported later that he seemed to lunge or skip at the ball. The swing was anything but in slow motion. He cocked his front knee backward and then released it forward with the velocity of a bowstring. He adjusted his swing and hit the ball with the greatest upperswing of his baseball lives.

When the bat connected, dust blew off the ball. The crack of the bat seemed louder than any that anyone ever remembered. The ball exploded off the wood and arced high into the night sky. It was headed in the direction of the Green Monster—the opposite field.

At the plate, there was monumental recoil. Ted stood and watched the ball soar into the moonless night. For a moment, it appeared like it might hit the GETGO sign beyond the Kenmore Marine Station and shatter it into so many neon pieces.

It flew. And flew.

When it came down, it had cleared all of the Monster seats and splashed into the Lansdowne Canal. Boaters scurried. Some dove into the water to get it.

He had done it.

Inside the ancient ball yard—pandemonium. No one noticed Ted struggling on weak legs to run around the bases. With all of the fans on the field, he barely made it to home. After he touched home plate, his teammates and the fans lifted him aloft.

When he came back down, Elizabeth, Johnnie, and the entire Williams' entourage were now on the field. Fans, media and friends vied to congratulate him in one giant celebration. Ted bear-hugged Johnnie.

Elizabeth approached and said, "You did, it! Well done! Ted, are you all right?"

"Of course, I'm all right. We just won the Series," he yelled back.

He raised his helmet in acknowledgment to the crowd.

"Ted, are you tipping your cap?" shouted Elizabeth.

"I sure am, Lizzy. I sure am!"

Hundreds of adoring fans now surrounded him.

"And you hit to the opposite field," she said.

"That's right. That's right," he said.

Looking at Marsh and Johnnie, he pointed at his head.

"This head—it's the result of a razor. I never took the cocktail."

As people tried in vain to lift him up again, he added, "And I've got big balls."

"You sure do," shouted Marsh. "You sure do."

Marsh, Jerry, Randall, Jed, Danny the gondolier, Bev the mailwoman, and half of the bellhops, bartenders, maids and taxi drivers in Boston he had befriended, appeared and slapped Ted on the back.

Ted hugged Johnnie again. The crowd surged. Everyone wanted a piece of him.

At first, hardly anyone, except those immediately around him, noticed. He had collapsed.

Nearby, the celebration came to an abrupt halt.

Eighty-nine

Ted was hospitalized. Dr. Miles supervised a battery of tests over a period of a week. She and a dedicated team of physicians could not determine what was wrong with him. They knew only one thing for sure. Vital signs and bodily functions were deteriorating; he was dying.

Elizabeth came into his hospital room to give him the news. He was lying motionless but awake, with an IV in his arm.

"Well, you look like hell," he said.

She sat on the edge of the bed. "Ted, I don't know . . . I don't know how to say this . . ."

"I know," he said softly. "You don't have to tell me."

For a dying man with half his face in a palsied slump, he was remarkably lucid and verbalizing well.

"I see," she said. Her clinical side gave way to her emotional self. She began to weep and hugged him. After a few moments of crying she sat up again.

"I am so sorry," she said, "so sorry I did this to you."

"Hey, Lizzy, don't you fret over me," he said.

Her head shot up in a moment of euphoria. "Ted, we don't know exactly what's wrong with you now, but we might in the future. Do you want to go through cryopreservation again? Number nine, do you want nine lives?"

He grabbed for and held her hand.

"No," he said sternly.

There was a long pause.

"There's something important that I've got to tell you," he added. "I owe it to you to tell you more about what happens next."

"You mean after death?" she said.

"Yes. It's a wonderful thing, Lizzy."

"It is?"

"Well, look at me. Do I look panicked about going back? The only thing I'll miss is you and Johnnie."

With his good hand he reached up and gently held the side of her face.

"You know, in my first life I wasn't a very religious person. But I knew there musta been a higher power; he saved Teddy Ballgame's ass a couple of times, especially in Korea. When I passed, I was transported to a place I never knew existed. Well, it doesn't really exist, but then again it does."

"What are you saying?" she said.

"Heaven is a hell of a place."

She laughed and wiped away more tears.

"Well, I assumed so. . . from our previous conversations. But are you not just telling me more now to make me feel better?" she said

"I'm telling you the truth. I've always told you the truth . . . well, maybe not about my health, but I didn't want you to worry."

"Yes, I gather you've known about your declining health for quite some time."

"I'm sorry. I didn't want to concern you, and I had to do my own thing."

She decided it was a moot point to dwell any longer on his health.

"Ted, why didn't you tell more people? About God, I mean."

"Well, I told you—maybe not real good. Like I said, I didn't want people looking at or treating me like some kind of messiah. And look where that got me—almost assassinated. I just figured I was damned if I did, and damned if I didn't. I just wanted to live a normal life."

The utter absurdity of that notion was not lost on either of them.

"Tell me more about it," she said, "about Heaven."

"Well, it's not all angels and fluffy clouds and that kinda horseshit. The best way to describe it is . . . joy, all-knowing joy, inner peace and fulfillment. All is forgiven, and all is well. It was an epiphany."

"And what about loved ones who have passed?"

"They are all there, friends and family, and all is sublime. My mom has plenty of time for me. Even my son, John Henry, has a job."

"I have never heard you use words like epiphany and sublime before. Tell me something, in Heaven, they put up with your swearing as well?"

"Well, I had to tone it down a bit."

"And I tore you away from it all. On one hand I feel better knowing what you're going back to, and then on the other . . . Just as we became . . . My God, I am going to miss you."

She leaned down to hug him again, soaking him with tears.

"I know. I know," he said. "But this is the natural way, and we will be together again."

She moved from resting her head on his shoulder, and they kissed gently.

"Yes. Yes, we will," she said softly.

"Tell me something. Have I led a good life?" he said.

She raised herself again, surprised by the question.

"Oh, Ted—yes you have."

She began to tear up again.

"Johnnie. I think of Johnnie. You've been brilliant with him . . . And the good friends you've made."

"Yeah, Marsh called. He's coming in to see me tomorrow. And Jerry, too."

"You see, Ted?"

"I tried to do a better job," he said, "with everyone. I was often a pain in the ass in my first life. It was all based on insecurity, you know. But once you've been to where I've been, once you know what's ahead of you, what's there to be insecure about? That helped me a lot in this life, though I had a few setbacks. Old habits die hard, I guess. Still, I hope I did better. How many people get a second chance to live another life with that kinda knowledge?"

She nodded and said, "Well done, you."

He gave a half smile.

"Can I ask you another question?" she said. "What does God think of what I did—bringing you back? Some people called it playing God."

"Well, it wasn't like I was sittin' on his right knee, for crissakes, so I don't have every answer. But I think it boils down to the free will thing. He gave it to us. Sometimes mankind has done well; sometimes we screwed it up. The only hope I guess is that we learn from the mistakes. Generally, that does occur. Everyone learned the hard way about global warming, and now it seems to be getting better. Now I wish baseball would get the message about the 'roid and robot mess."

"Maybe they will now," she said.

"I don't know. It could be too far gone."

"Let me ask you another question," said Elizabeth. "In the future, if other people come back, how do you believe they will live their lives?"

"Will the next defrosted piece of meat do much better?" said Ted. "Maybe he'll be able to reinvent himself more than I did. What would I have done if I didn't try or couldn't play baseball the second time around? Maybe I'd still be driving a water taxi to survive. That woulda made me miserable. What's predictable, I think, is that many people who come back are gonna repeat themselves. For better or worse, it's got to be human nature. I played baseball, went fly fishin' and flew jets again because it was the familiar, and I had the physical ability."

They didn't say anything for a long while. He stared off somewhere in the distance and then his head turned back to meet her eyes.

"I thought it was about doing those things again, 'specially winning the series," he said. "Turns out, it was all about relationships. In my first life I learned about batting; in the second I learned from my mistakes. Even after repeating too many."

She nodded.

"Maybe other people will be less interested in coming back," said Ted.

"What do you mean?"

He strained to reach over and pick up a diary and handed it to her.

"Cecelia bought this for me a while ago. I've written it all down—the God stuff—everything. I want you to have it printed after I'm gone. It'll pay for Johnnie's college education. When people find out about the afterlife, it may put a cramp in ol' Bernie's cryonics business."

They both chuckled.

"Lizzy, it's been a great ride. I consider myself lucky; I got two trips around the bases to take care of some unfinished business."

They were still holding hands, she still sitting on the side of the bed.

"You know," she said, "when you're gone, there will be no one in my life who will be so brutally honest with me. I can't tell you how much I'm going to miss that."

He nodded and squeezed her hand more tightly.

Neither spoke for a while. And then he said, "Ain't it just a kick in the head? I finally figured out what love means between a man and woman, and now I won't be around to fully experience it. I'm sorry I'm doing this to *you*."

She leaned down to hug him again, her teardrops once again wetting his hospital gown.

She sat back up.

"Johnnie is outside. He doesn't know about you yet, but I know he would like to see you."

"Well, bring him in," said Ted. "I'll tell him."

She sighed.

"You know, he still has a little way to go but you made him into a man, Ted."

He looked deep into her eyes and shook his head.

"No, he made *me* into a man."

Ninety

Elizabeth returned to Ted's hospital bed with Johnnie and said, "I'll leave you two fellows alone."

"Johnnie, come up here," said Ted.

"Your face looks funny," said Johnnie.

"Well, yours ain't no trip to the candy store either," said Ted.

Ted looked at him more seriously now.

"Son, I am dying."

"Yeah, I was wondering about that," said Johnnie. "Are you afraid?"

"No, son, I am not. I'm afraid I'm gonna miss you, though."

"I'm gonna miss you, too," said Johnnie, his eyes welling with tears. His mouth contorted in an effort not to cry.

"Don't cry for me, son—well, cry if you want to. They say it's good for you, especially boys—frees up the emotional side, I guess. Anyway, there are a few things I need to talk to you about. The reason you don't have to cry is, I'm going to a happy place. And, after you've had a long and happy life, I will see you there again someday."

"Can't you just let Mom bring you back?"

"Well, son, your mom is a miracle worker. But there is more to it than that. I'm going to Heaven—there *is* such a place."

"Will you see my dad there?"

"I'll be sure to look him up. He knows you love him and that you miss him. Understand this: We are there for eternity, so in the whole scheme of things, you and I, and you and your dad, will be together again in the blink of an eye. There are lots of people who love each other there and everyone gets along— even former lovers.

"But in the meantime, you've got some living to do. Remember to always take care of your mom. She'll be your mom forever. In her later years she'll need you as much as you need her now."

Johnnie nodded.

"I've never been one to philosophize," said Ted, "but do you remember that time we went fishin' up in Maine? Do you remember that blueberry patch that we stumbled on? Well, think of this son. Life is like a wild blueberry patch: the berries are free, but you still gotta pick 'em. Only then do you discover which are sweet and which are sour. Do you understand what I'm saying to you, Johnnie?"

"You want me to eat all my fruits and vegetables."

"Well, no . . . I mean, yes, that's true. Let me just say this. I want you to work hard and have fun, too. Reach out to people. Lend a helping hand. Take time out to appreciate the simple things in life. Seek out your own passions, things that you like, and go for it—whatever they may be—and you'll be happy. Even at your age, I see in you an amazing intellect. I see creativity, a zest for learning and knowledge. I don't know if you will be a first-rate academic, but don't worry about it. Some of the most creative, successful people in the history of the world were no great shakes in the classroom. Just do the best you can, graduate, and above all else—absorb. Learn throughout life—it will make life worth living. Curiosity, that's the key."

Johnnie was staring intently into Ted's eyes.

"You're a little young, Johnnie, but I'm gonna talk to you about women," said Ted. "I'm probably not the one to be giving advice in this area, but this is the only chance we'll get. Maybe this part you shouldn't discuss with your mother. You see, women are complicated."

Johnnie had a blank look on his face.

"You can learn all you need to know about a woman by watching how she observes herself in a mirror," said Ted.

"And if that ain't enough, never marry a woman until you've seen her drunk—but don't drink yourself until you come of age, and then not so much."

Ted took a deep breath.

"Always remember son, as you wander through life, I will be with you. When you swing at that ball, hit or miss, I will be there, cheering you on. When you wear that silly looking graduation cap, I will be there. When you stand at the front of the church with someone you love, I'll be right behind you. When the sun shines, the rain pours, and the wind blows, I will be with you."

Johnnie curled up in the hospital bed with Ted. They both were crying; Ted smiled from ear to ear until he drifted off to sleep.

~ ~ ~

An hour later, Dr. Miles headed back toward Ted's room holding a cup of coffee. From a distance she could see that Johnnie was seated outside the room, crying softly. She leaned against a wall in the hallway, temporarily unable to approach him.

A colleague in a white coat stopped and said, "Is everything okay, Elizabeth?"

"Yes," she said, a far-off expression on her face, "and please, please call me Lizzy."

~ ~ ~

Inside Ted's room, he had fallen fast asleep, not just any sleep, but a slumber so deep as to plumb the depths of two lifetime's worth of memories, good memories: playing pepper with Johnnie Pesky, Bobby Doerr and Dom DiMaggio . . . fishing in the dappled sunlight of the Florida Keys . . .

comparing bats on the dugout steps with the Yank's Joe DiMaggio . . . the home run in the '41 All-Star Game . . . visiting kids in the hospital . . . beating down the Botwinder to finally win the Series . . . hooking a salmon with Marsh . . . drinking with his fellow pilots . . . his tribute at the 1999 All-Star Game in Fenway . . . making love with Lizzy, the love of his two lives . . . and playing catch with Johnnie. All of it blended into a magnificent montage, somehow ethereal and tangible at the same time, drifting from one vision to the next. It was life-affirming, joyous and serene.

Ninety-one

A week later, with Lizzy, Johnnie and Marsh at his bedside, The Kid died. The funeral included the Marines and full military honors. This time, they buried him in a real grave. The cremains from his original body were buried with him.

Across the Back Bay and up the Charles River estuary, just outside of Boston, the mortal remains of Ted Williams would spend eternity on a hill in Mount Auburn Cemetery, not far from the grave of his old buddy, sportscaster Curt Gowdy.

Many adoring fans visited Ted's grave. Lizzy and Johnnie provided a simple gravestone; on the top were a couple of crossed bats. X marked the spot. The epitaph was divine:

Theodore Samuel Williams
US Marine
The Greatest Hitter
Who Ever Lived
1918 – 2002 . . . 2092 – 2095

At Fenway his number was retired again. During home games, Johnnie, wearing a number nine jersey, sits in the only red seat in the deep right field stands, never missing a game.

The folks from the Louisville Slugger company shipped up a small ash tree that Lizzy and Johnnie planted behind Ted's gravestone. In no time at all it grew into a mighty ash with giant leaves and incongruous spindly limbs reaching toward the sky.

On certain summer evenings on that hill at Mount Auburn, in the distance you can see the glow of the lights at Fenway. When the wind is just right and blowing up the Charles, if you listen carefully, you can almost hear the crack of the bat. And then, enduring and eternal, forever rising, the great roar of the crowd.